ALSO BY LEE COLE

Groundskeeping

Fulfillment

Fulfillment

Lee Cole

ALFRED A. KNOPF   New York   2025

A BORZOI BOOK
FIRST HARDCOVER EDITION
PUBLISHED BY ALFRED A. KNOPF 2025

Published by Alfred A. Knopf, a division of Penguin Random
House LLC, 1745 Broadway, New York, NY 10019.

Knopf, Borzoi Books, and the colophon are registered
trademarks of Penguin Random House LLC.

Library of Congress Cataloging-in-Publication Data
Name: Cole, Lee, [date] author.
Title: Fulfillment / Lee Cole.
Description: First edition. | New York : Alfred A. Knopf, 2025.
Identifiers: LCCN 2024023030 (print) | LCCN 2024023031 (ebook) |
   ISBN 9780593802861 (hardcover) | ISBN 9780593802878 (ebook)
Subject: LCGFT: Novels.
Classification: LCC PS3603.O4288 F85 2024 (print) |
   LCC PS3603.O4288 (ebook) | DDC 813/.6—dc23/eng/20240517
LC record available at https://lccn.loc.gov/2024023030
LC ebook record available at https://lccn.loc.gov/2024023031

penguinrandomhouse.com | aaknopf.com

Printed in the United States of America
10 9 8 7 6 5 4 3 2 1

The authorized representative in the EU for product
safety and compliance is Penguin Random House Ireland,
Morrison Chambers, 32 Nassau Street, Dublin D02 YH68,
Ireland, https://eu-contact.penguin.ie.

So they take off after each other straight into an endless black prairie. The sun is just comin' down and they can feel the night on their backs. What they don't know is that each one of 'em is afraid, see. Each one separately thinks that he's the only one that's afraid. And they keep ridin' like that straight into the night. Not knowing. And the one who's chasin' doesn't know where the other one is taking him. And the one who's being chased doesn't know where he's going.

—SAM SHEPARD, *True West*

Part

ONE

One

EVERYONE WAS GIVEN A PATH. There were shifters and sweepers, sorters and feeders. There were pickers and porters and air drivers. There were loaders and unloaders, ramp workers and water spiders, grounders and stowers and freighters.

Emmett was declared an unloader. Third shift, where they always "needed bodies." He signed the paperwork, wrote the word "VOID" on a check.

The woman who gave his interview said there were levels to every path, opportunities for advancement, for greater benefits. She made it sound like a game you could win.

Nothing's binding, she said. People bounce around, find their niche.

Emmett came to realize, as she spoke, that your path meant nothing, really, except the position where you started. It was only a piece of jargon.

I don't have a permanent address at the moment, he told her. But I will soon.

That's fine, she said. You're not alone.

THERE WAS NOTHING but farmland where they built it, and it rose up now from the fields of dead corn like a vast anomaly. A dozen warehouses, two runways. A parking lot fit for a stadium. It looked, from the window of the shuttle bus at night, like a lonesome galaxy in the borderless dark. The sodium lamps in the lot gave off orange coronas, and the fainter beacons of the taxiways arranged themselves in trembling constellations.

The people on board the shuttle were too visible in the harsh light, the shapes of their skulls apparent in their faces. They tightened the Velcro straps of back braces, ate strong-smelling soups and curries from Tupperware, struggling to reach their mouths with their spoons as the bus shook and jounced. They watched porn on their phones—slack-faced, mouths ajar. They played word games, poker, Candy Crush. They spun the reels of cartoon slot machines. They rubbed at scratch-offs with pennies. They stared with glassy resignation at absolutely nothing.

The guard shack was chaotic, men with wands shouting over the high-pitched keening of the metal detectors, herding the workers. The guards were not TSA, belonging instead to a private security firm, and they looked to Emmett like Neo-Nazis who'd recently finished prison sentences—Viking braids, bleached goatees, tattoos of Iron Crosses on their forearms.

He sat with the other recruits in an office annex, listening to Scott, their "Learning Ambassador," break down the workers' basic duties and the company's expectations. He was a small and energetic man, pacing to and fro, his lanyard ID badge swinging pendulum-like. Broken blood vessels lent his cheeks a rosy appearance, and he had a little boy's haircut, his bangs clipped short in a perfectly straight line.

You might think of this place as a warehouse, he said. But here at Tempo, we like to think of it as a *ware-home*.

They were made to click through a series of training modules on computers from the early aughts. They watched video clips, wherein a softspoken female narrator highlighted recent company achievements over a soundtrack of jazzy Muzak. The clips underscored Tempo's ethical commitment to creating a better world. But if Emmett learned anything from them, it was the extent to which the company's maneuverings had touched all realms of commerce. They were in the business of both fulfillment and distribution, shipping their own parcels—the orders boxed and sorted at smaller regional hubs—along with the parcels of anyone willing to pay. They'd begun to build retail warehouses, in competition with Walmart and Target. They'd been buying regional supermarket chains, and would use their network of distribution centers and their fleet of trucks to deliver groceries directly to the doorsteps of eager customers. In the video, a Tempo delivery driver in her familiar evergreen uniform handed a paper sack of bananas and grapes and baguettes to an elderly woman, who smiled and waved as the green electric truck pulled away.

Officially, it was called the Tempo Air Cargo Distribution Center, but Scott called it simply "the Center." It was Tempo's largest distribution hub, and had been built here in Nowheresville, Kentucky, because of its geographic centrality. Some of the workers commuted from Bowling Green or Elizabethtown, but most came from the forgotten hamlets of the surrounding counties, places with names like Horse Branch and Sunfish, Spring Lick and Falls of Rough. There had once been coal mines and tobacco stemmeries in that area, auto plants and grist mills. But all those enterprises had fled or been shuttered. Now Tempo had arrived to take their place.

What we're doing here is regional rejuvenation, Scott said. We're creating long-term opportunities.

The recruits were called upon to introduce themselves and offer a "fun fact" about their lives. When Emmett's turn arrived, he said he spent his free time writing screenplays. Really, there'd been only one screenplay—an evolving, never-ending autobiographical work that he'd abandoned and revived a dozen times. But he feared that admitting this would make him sound insane.

How bout that, Scott said. We have a screenwriter in our midst. What are they about?

Just my life, he said. They're autobiographical.

Hey, I better look out, Scott said. Maybe one day you'll write about this. Maybe one day we'll see it on the big screen.

Then he called on the next recruit, whose "fun fact" was that a miniature horse had kicked him in the head as a young boy, leaving him without a sense of smell.

Emmett moved to the warehouse—the ware-home, rather—and began what Scott called the "Skill Lab" portion of training. An enormous digital clock hung near the entrance, red numerals burning through the haze of warehouse dust. Beneath it, a scanner and a flatscreen monitor were mounted. You held your badge to the criss-cross of lasers, and when the system read the barcode, your image appeared on the screen. They'd taken the photos on the first day of orientation, the trainees backed against a blank wall, unsure whether to smile. They looked like mugshots. When you saw yourself appear onscreen—the past-self who'd taken this job, who'd embarked on this path—and you gazed up at the red digits, measuring time by the second, you knew, unmistakably, that you were on the clock. It was the only clock, as far as Emmett knew, in the warehouse.

On the wall, near the break room door, a large sign read: WE'VE WORKED 86 DAYS WITHOUT A LOST TIME ACCIDENT! The number was a digital counter. Emmett wondered what had happened 86 days ago. Each night, the number rose—87, 88, 89—and whatever had caused this loss of time receded further into the Center's collective memory.

It was a huge, hangar-like structure, an intricate maze of conveyor belts, all churning and chugging at once. The racket was like a subway train perpetually arriving at the platform—the clattering rhythm, the screak of friction. Bays for trucks took up one side; on the other, loading docks for planes. The floor was studded with steel ball bearings and rollers, so the shipping containers—"cans"—could be towed easily from the docks to the belt lanes. It was all so labyrinthine and vast that Emmett felt what he might begrudgingly call awe. He'd never gazed at the vaulted ceiling of a cathedral, sunlight turned to scattered jewels by stained glass, but he imagined the feeling might be similar.

When it came to the work itself, there was not much to learn. If they remembered nothing else, said Scott, they should remember the Eight Rules of Lifting and Lowering.

Approach the object, feet shoulder width apart, bend at the knees, test the weight of the package, grip opposite corners, lift smoothly, pivot or step without twisting, use existing equipment.

Unloading the containers of air cargo onto conveyor belts was the one and only dimension of his work, the same task repeated, ad infinitum. They showed him how to latch the cans into the lanes, how to break the yellow plastic seals. They showed him the little hydraulic knob that lifted and lowered the conveyor belt. (This was the "existing equipment" mentioned in the last of the Eight Rules.) They showed him the "small-sort" belt for loose envelopes and small parcels, and the "irreg" belt for unboxed freight—tires, axles, machine parts, etc.

And that was it.

It's a simple job, really, said Scott. Put boxes onto a conveyor belt until the can is empty, then bring over a new can. Do the same thing. Rinse and repeat.

Most nights, as he left, he saw the Blood Bus—an RV outfitted by the Red Cross to function as a mobile blood donation center. A fat man stood outside, calling out to the workers as they spilled from the shuttles. Hop on the bus, give your blood to us! he shouted. Hop on the bus, give your blood to us!

The man was always slick with sweat, his face purple and engorged from the exertion of shouting. No one ever seemed to enter the bus, and Emmett wondered why they came here. The last thing he'd want to do, leaving his shift hungry and aching, was donate blood. But there must be a few, he thought, to make the blood man's efforts worthwhile. Those who heard the call and said, *What the hell?* They were already spent. Why not open their veins, give a little more?

HE MET HIS SUPERVISOR, a man named Jason Flake. Everyone called him "Flaky." He was younger and much taller than Emmett, his arms too long and skinny for his frame. He reminded Emmett of a praying mantis. You could tell the supervisors from the union workers by the clothes they wore—Tempo golf shirts tucked into pleated khakis—and by their radios, shoulder mics clipped to their collars. In the beginning, Flaky kept a close eye on Emmett. Turn your badge to face out, bud, he'd say, and Emmett would rotate the laminated ID badge Velcroed to his upper bicep. They were supposed to unload twenty boxes per minute, and the supervisors knew the precise average of each package handler. The boxes placed on the conveyor passed through a bright, mirrored scanner, each barcode logged in the system.

You're at 18.3 per minute, bud, Flaky would say, without looking up from his iPad. Try to pick it up a little.

Each night, as his shift wound down, Flaky came to Emmett's lane, stood in the doorway of the can, and asked him to recite the Eight Rules of Lifting and Lowering. When Emmett had gone through them, Flaky would scribble something on a clipboard and ask Emmett to sign. He came to realize, gradually, that the Eight Rules were an insurance policy; this is why they mattered so much to management. All the other safety protocols—hazmat handling procedures, what to do during a tornado, etc.—would so rarely come to any use that their presence in the modules was almost a formality.

But the Eight Rules—they governed the only sanctioned movement of Emmett's body on the clock. And if you understood the Eight Rules—if, in fact, you signed your name to a piece of paper *attesting* that you understood them—then you could never be injured in such a way that blame fell on the company. If you ruptured a disk in your back, or blew out your knee, or crushed your fingers, it would be because you'd failed, in some way, to follow the Eight Rules.

THERE WAS A VILLAGE within walking distance from the shuttle pickup—an "unincorporated community" called Middle Junction with a motel. This was where he'd been living, paying a weekly rate. He'd lived in New Orleans before, had lost his job there at an Outback Steakhouse, and come home to Kentucky knowing that Tempo would hire anyone. He had not yet told his mother, Kathy, he was back. But his money had nearly run out; the motel life was not sustainable. He called her after six months of near silence, sprawled out on the bed's pilled comforter in the tiny room that stank of cigarette smoke.

I'm home, he said.

Emmett? she said. Are you okay? Where are you?

I'm home, he said again.

In Paducah?

No, I'm in this nowhere town—out past Beaver Dam.

What in the world are you doing there?

Getting a job, he said. At the Tempo hub. I'm almost through with orientation.

What happened to New Orleans?

It's a long story.

Where are you living?

In a motel.

Well, that won't do, she said. That won't do at all.

She made him promise to come home, said she'd buy him a Greyhound ticket. I'd fetch you myself, she said, but your brother and his wife are coming this weekend.

Joel was Emmett's half-brother, but Kathy never made the distinction. He lived in New York, where he taught "cultural studies" at a small college—a subject Emmett had never been able to make heads or tails of. He'd published a book a couple years earlier and had married his wife, Alice, right after. The last time he'd seen them was at their wedding.

I don't know, he said. Spending time with Joel had a way of making him feel sorry for the state of his life.

This is a blessing! Kathy said. Both my boys home—we'll have a family reunion!

The next day, he waited for the bus as twilight fell. The town was little more than a crossroads: a gas station, a farm supply store, a Dollar General with Amish buggies in the lot. Beside the Greyhound stop, in a patch of grass, someone had put up three flagpoles and a gazebo, and there were white wooden crosses in rows, bearing the names of locals who'd died during the pandemic. Emmett waited alone, reading the names, hearing the rasp of wind in the dry corn, the faint melodies of country music drifting from the vacant gas station.

The bus arrived and took him west. He drew a book from his backpack, a manual on screenwriting. It was called *The Eternal Story: Screenwriting Made Simple*. He read for a while by the light of the overhead lamp till he grew tired. Tinny music came from the other passengers' headphones. When he closed his eyes, his dreams for the future played like movies. New York, Los Angeles—he'd never seen them in person, only in images on screens.

He watched the scrolling world and thought about his life, how he'd gotten to this point. *The Center*. One thing he was sure of: they were far from the center. One saw this, clearly, from the window of a Greyhound bus. One saw the brushstrokes of irrelevance in the landscape itself. The rhyme of towns, the patchwork fields. The illusion of movement. Most of America was like this, though Emmett sometimes forgot, spending so much of his life in fantasy. Traveling by Greyhound had a way of inflicting realism on even the most ardent dreamer. One saw, as Emmett saw now, the glowing corporate emblems, the names and symbols hoisted on stilts. One saw prisons that looked like high schools. High schools that looked like prisons. One saw the blaze of stadium lights above the tree line, heard the faint echo of the anthem, of military brass and drums. One saw the salvage yards of broken machines. The mannequin of Christ pinned to a cross. The moon-eyed cattle, standing in smoky pastures at dusk. One saw huge flags rippling above car dealerships. Combines blinking in fields at night. One could see all this, unreeling frame by frame, and understand, as Emmett understood, the immense bitterness of exile.

Two

His MOTHER GREETED him at the Greyhound depot. Kathy was a small, sinewy woman, her hair in a silver bob that grazed her chin. The back of her Town & Country minivan was heaped with clothing.

Don't mind that, she said. That's all going to consignment.

She hugged Emmett and pulled back to get a good look at him.

The prodigal son returns, she said. You look tired.

I've been on the night shift all week.

Your eyes—you look like a raccoon.

It's good to see you, too, Emmett said.

Kathy lived in West Paducah, between the mall and the old uranium enrichment plant. Much of the farmland there had been subdivided. What had once been tobacco and soybeans was now crowded with lookalike homes and sun-parched lawns, where not even the constant chittering of sprinklers could keep the grass from browning in summer. There was a billboard above I-24—McCRACKEN COUNTY DREAM HOMES, with a number you could call. This is what Kathy had, a vinyl-sided prefab, much like all the others on the street. They delivered your Dream Home to you in pieces, fitted them together, and then you had a place to live. There were thousands going up like that in Kentucky, more respectable than a mobile home, if only slightly. MAKE YOUR DREAMS COME TRUE, said the billboard, and that's what everyone seemed to think they were doing. Their dreams were readymade and easy to assemble. They cost very little and were worth almost nothing when you were done with them.

She let him sleep in the next day. He woke at noon and sat at the kitchen table, drinking coffee left over from breakfast he'd warmed in the microwave. Kathy fixed a cup for herself and sat with him. They looked out the sliding glass doors at the backyard. Though it was only August, the walnut trees over the patio had begun to drop their fruit, green husks the size of tennis balls thudding against the cement, some already black and rotting, some floating like buoys in her tiny koi pond. He was glad to see his mother, to be here in the Dream Home, even if it signified another defeat in his life.

So, Tempo, she said. They pay good?

Not really.

Benefits?

Emmett nodded.

Do you miss New Orleans?

The answer was complicated. Though he'd liked New Orleans, he hadn't really had the money to live in the city itself. He'd lived in Metairie, near I-10, where he'd worked at the Outback Steakhouse. His dream of the French Quarter, of a brightly painted Creole cottage, a banana tree in the backyard, had been just that—a dream. Faraway and unattainable.

It wasn't a city where I could reach my full potential, he said.

You can reach your full potential working at Tempo?

That's just to pay rent. What I really want to do is screenwriting.

Like writing movies?

Or a TV show. Whatever.

What happened to becoming a songwriter? Kathy said. That was the last thing you decided you'd be. Before that, it was professional chef. Before that, it was stand-up comedian.

He hated to be reminded of his failed creative pursuits, his veering from one passion to another, but he could always rely on Kathy to bring it up.

Those were naïve goals, Emmett said. I can see that now. But with screenwriting, there are steps. You just follow the steps.

You're like a kid sometimes, she said. One day, he wants to be an astronaut. The next, a baseball star. The next day, a cowboy.

A screenwriter is hardly the same thing as a cowboy.

Well, I wish you'd go back and finish school.

You can't major in screenwriting.

You could start with basics at the community college. You could live here.

I plan to live near the Center.

The Center?

Tempo. That's what they call it.

She made a fretful sound, blew on her coffee, and took a sip. A walnut dropped on the metal roof of the garden shed outside, sounding like a gunshot. They both startled and turned their heads to look.

So what's Joel coming home for?

He's doing a lectureship at Murray State, she said. Just for the fall semester, as I understand it.

Are they leaving New York?

It's up in the air, Kathy said. But Lord, I hope so. I pray every day they don't get shot or stabbed or blown up.

He'll never come back to the South.

I have so much to do before they get here, she said, ignoring him. I have to clean the house. I have to fix your brother's cake.

What cake? Why does he get a cake?

It's a homecoming cake, she said, as if it should be obvious.

Where's my homecoming cake?

Well, how was I to know you were coming home? You vanish and reappear. You never call.

Even if you'd known, there would be no cake.

Why shouldn't I celebrate Joel's successes? He's very accomplished. I wish you'd talk to him more. You could ask him for advice, about writing and whatnot.

I don't need his advice.

Well, can I give you a piece of advice, then? she said.

He sighed theatrically. I'm listening.

Write down your goals. Take a sheet of paper, write "My Goals" at the top, then put everything down. That way, you have it as a reference point. You can't betray yourself. You can't let yourself off the hook.

Emmett wanted to ask what her goals had been at twenty-eight, if she'd aspired to anything more than raising her children in this town where nothing much happened and no one expected it to. Instead, he said all right, he would write down his goals, and this seemed to satisfy her.

Emmett's car had broken down in New Orleans. This had precipitated, in part, his decision to leave. His grandmother, Ruth, was too old to drive. She was too old to do anything except watch Fox News. She had a 1997 Mercury Mystique with a lineup of Beanie Babies in the back windshield, and she told Emmett she would sell it to him for a dollar.

Kathy dropped him off, and he found her in the backyard with Lijah, the exterminator. There had been a long-standing issue with groundhogs, her little house abutting a wooded creek where they bred. They gnawed through the lattice surrounding her deck and tunneled beneath the foundation. Lijah was a church friend. She'd been calling him for years to set traps in the woods, snaring rabbits and cats as often as groundhogs. It came to be their habit, over time, that after he'd discharged his official duties, she'd invite him to sit a spell and drink coffee.

She saw Emmett coming and went to greet him. Her hair was dyed coal black, her eyes as small and dark as currants. An intricate crazing of broken blood vessels had turned her nose and cheeks purple.

Lijah's spraying dope, she said. Lijah, you remember Emmett, my grandson?

Lijah waved. He stood beside her garden shed, holding a sprayer wand attached to a backpack tank, his gray hair tied in a ponytail. His

T-shirt said CRITTER KILLERS—the name of his company—though he seemed to be the only killer of critters on the payroll.

The traps were empty, so I'm fixing to spray, he said.

Spray for what? Emmett said.

Lijah shrugged. Anything.

It's a constant battle, Ruth said. Varmints, termites, snakes. They all try to get inside. Then you've got prowlers. Dottie Driscoll down the street caught a prowler in her backyard.

Fraid I can't spray for that that, ma'am, said Lijah.

What prowler? Emmett said. Who was it?

How should I know? Dottie's grandson ran them off. He's a sheriff's deputy. Her grandchildren visit her *every day*.

I doubt that.

Emmett is Joel's brother, Ruth said. I's just telling Lijah I've got me a famous author for a grandson.

I always wanted to write a book, Lijah said, squirting poison along the base of the shed. Problem is, I never liked writing.

That would be a hurdle, Emmett said.

When you're done, I'll warm us some coffee, Ruth said.

I'll be covered in dope spray, ma'am. You don't want me tracking all that in.

Never mind that, Ruth said. I'll show you my copy of the book.

The smells of her house—her White Diamonds perfume, her geriatric ointments, the jar of congealed bacon grease by the stove—brought Emmett back to the boredom of summer mornings when Ruth would keep them, his mother at work, Joel entertaining himself with the *World Book Encyclopedia*. The days had seemed so long, his life so long ahead of him.

Down the hallway, in the bedroom, Emmett and Lijah stood before her bookcase. There were three copies of his brother's book, wrapped in plastic, wedged between Erma Bombeck and Nora Ephron. It was called *Going South: The Descent of Rural America*. She took one down with great ceremony and placed it like a fragile artifact in Lijah's open hands.

Going South, he said. Well, I'll be.

We always knew, didn't we? Ruth said, squeezing Emmett's arm. Our Joel was special. He used to recite the presidents. Five years old.

A memory: Joel with his bowl cut and secretive smile, standing on a chair, surrounded by adoring faces and the remnants of Thanksgiving supper. *Washington, Adams, Jefferson, Madison* . . .

He was always reading, Ruth said. And Emmett was always watching movies.

I don't suppose you became a movie star? Lijah said.

Emmett's still finding his way, she said. Aren't you?

Emmett managed to smile.

She returned the book to its place and asked Lijah how a cup of coffee sounded.

I'd never turn it away, he said.

Tell you what, I'll make a fresh pot.

They'd started to leave when something caught Lijah's eye. He went to the old laundry chute in the corner and crushed a spider on the wall with his meaty fist.

We've got a problem here, he said. He opened the chute door and peered inside.

I never use that thing, Ruth said. It's been blocked for years. You put something in and you never see it again.

It's a breeding ground, Lijah said. They love the dark. I'll spray before I leave.

When Lijah had gone, she led Emmett down to the carport and showed him the Mercury Mystique. The Beanie Babies were still arrayed in the back windshield, their colors sun-faded. Do I get to keep the Beanie Babies? Emmett said.

Oh sure, Ruth said. They were supposed to make me a lot of money but they ain't worth a cent now.

They sat in the living room after, eating Danish cookies from a tin, dipping them in coffee. Fox News was playing. It was never turned off, only muted. They were interviewing the recipient of a face transplant. The man had been disfigured by an accident, and now he wore the face of a dead man like a mask. It was convincing, though his mouth did not work quite right, and you could see where the sutures had been along his forehead.

Ruth was half-deaf. She leaned forward, straining to hear. They took off his face, she said, and gave him another man's face?

A dead man, Emmett said.

She bit one of the stale cookies in half and shook her head at the marvel of it. They do everything now, don't they? she said.

She relayed the latest gossip. He learned who of his cousins was pregnant, who was getting married, who was headed for divorce. She sometimes mixed up the names, but Emmett knew, more or less, who she meant. Once the family gossip had been covered, she moved on to the deaths. Grandma Ruth kept a relentless mental catalogue of all the strange and grisly deaths in McCracken County.

A man in Symsonia got himself killed on a four-wheeler, she said. Two boys drowned at Kentucky Lake last month. Two foreigners shot each other at a bar. Let's see, what else. Oh! There was the man who caught himself on fire.

He what? Emmett said. When Grandma Ruth said the word "fire," it was like the word "far," and it took him a moment to catch the meaning.

Fire, she said. He pulled up at the filling station down the street, covered hisself in gasoline, and lit a match. They showed the footage on the TV.

Jesus. Why'd he do it?

He was protesting.

Protesting what?

She bit another Danish cookie and shrugged. Just life, I guess, she said.

She excused herself to the restroom, and Emmett went down the hall and stood before the shelf that held Joel's books. He looked at the cover: a caved-in church in a field, the stacks of a coal-fired power plant in the hazy distance. He'd read it a while back, though perhaps it was more accurate to say he'd *skimmed*. The essays were about

Kentucky and the mechanics of what Joel called "rural despair." The running theme throughout was the privatization of mental health. He used terms like "neoliberal" and "post-Fordist," the meanings of which Emmett understood only foggily, and argued that depression was not simply a chemical imbalance, but a normal human response to the vulgarity of late capitalism.

The book alternated between abstract theory and a more personal style. One of the essays explored Joel's relationship with their mother and her spiral into QAnon conspiracy theories. Emmett had always felt it was unfair; it exaggerated her views and made her seem like something, or someone, that she wasn't. Now Joel had some money and a job. He had his smug-looking photo on the jacket of a book.

In a flush of sudden anger, he took all three copies of *Going South* from the shelf, opened the laundry chute, and let them tumble from his arms into darkness.

THE FIRST PLACE HE DROVE, in his new Mystique, was the Kmart parking lot in Lone Oak. The Kmart was no longer in business, though you could still see the pale impression of the letter *K* on the stucco where the sign had been. Now it was a place where people bought drugs. The only dealer Emmett knew was a grade school acquaintance called Fuzzy. He'd hit puberty at nine years old and grown a thick pelt of reddish fur on his back and arms. The nickname had followed him ever since.

Fuzzy pulled up in a maroon Buick LeSabre and Emmett got inside.

How you been, Fuzzy? Emmett said.

You know me, bro, he said. Stuntin to keep my grind strong.

On one level, Emmett had no idea what this meant; on another level, he sort of did.

Fuzzy complained about the recent legalization of pot in the state of Illinois. People don't come to me no more, he said. They go across the river.

He wore a flat-bill cap and a T-shirt that said AFFLICTION with a skull on the front. There were snakes writhing out from the mouth and the eyes of the skull. He was as hairy as he'd ever been.

You wanna hear my latest verse? Fuzzy said.

Sure, Emmett said.

Fuzzy put on a beat, the subwoofer in his trunk so forceful that the sound vibrated deep in Emmett's bowels. The verse was about no one understanding him, how one day he would prove everyone wrong and release a multiplatinum album. This was all part of the ritual. If you wanted weed from Fuzzy, you had to listen to him rap. Then, when it was over, he would say you were his favorite person.

You're my favorite person, man, he said. I mean that.

Thanks, Fuzzy.

Fuzzy gave him a quarter ounce of brick-pack weed and said, Hey, love you, homie. Keep that chin up.

Emmett found himself saying, I love you, too, and when the Buick pulled away, he stood absolutely still for a few minutes in the too-bright sun, a warm wind blowing napkins and fast-food trash across the lot.

At home, he found Kathy in a frenzy of preparation—vacuuming, mopping the linoleum, standing on a stepladder to dust the fan blades. Emmett cleaned the toilet and the tub, wearing yellow dish gloves, pausing now and then to drink from a can of beer. It seemed like overkill, but Joel had always been their mother's favorite—her firstborn, her college graduate. It would not be obvious to anyone from the outside, for they argued fiercely about everything. But this fierceness stood as proof of their bond to Emmett. It was like they desperately wanted to save each other. She wanted to save him from worldly pursuits. He wanted to save her from right-wing politics. And when neither made progress on these fronts, they took it as evidence of insufficient commitment to the war effort, and entrenched themselves further, holding fast to the vain hope of victory.

They were supposed to arrive by suppertime. Kathy made fried chicken, black-eyed peas with ham hock, cornbread in a cast-iron skillet—all of Joel's favorites. Frying the chicken had been onerous and left the counter dusted with flour, the stovetop spattered with buttermilk and oil. She'd made a hummingbird cake, normally reserved for Joel's birthday. It was a dense cake with banana and pineapple and layers of cream cheese frosting. Emmett had never had a taste for it. She set the table and displayed it on a cake stand of cut crystal, the engraved patterns in the glass catching sparkles of sunlight.

Is this the only dessert? he said.

Well, yes. It's Joel's favorite.

What's my favorite cake?

She pretended not to have heard this and hurried over to stir a decanter of sweet tea, the wooden spoon clinking against the glass. I've got butterflies, she said. My heart's going a mile a minute.

They're not foreign dignitaries. It's your son and his wife.

You're not helping, she said.

In the guest room, he crumbled the weed on a sheet of notebook paper and put some into a glass bowl. He opened the window, took a hit, and coughed softly. Lawnmowers were buzzing in the distance, the scent of cut grass wafting on the breeze.

Kathy had two lifelong obsessions: Elvis and Hawaii, both of which were reflected in the guest room's décor. She'd been to Hawaii once with a church group, years ago, and had longed to return ever since. There were carved statuettes of the goddess Pele, velvet paintings of Diamond Head. Glossy shards of volcanic glass in souvenir ashtrays. A poster of the 1961 film *Blue Hawaii* hung over the bed, Elvis in tiny pink shorts and a pink lei, surrounded by fawning women.

Feeling anxious, wishing to distract himself, he swept the powdery kief from the notebook paper and wrote "My Goals" at the top. He thought for a minute, then jotted down the first few that came to mind. *Find apartment, Make money, Pay off debts, Meet someone new.* He wrote down, *Buy a car,* just so he'd have something to mark off. Then he thought for a moment and wrote, *Do something creative, something meaningful that will leave a lasting legacy and allow you to face mortality without fear.*

Emmett took his old Bible from the bookshelf. It was the copy he'd been given as he entered Youth Group at age twelve. On the cover, a skateboarding kid, mid-kickflip, made the universal gesture of "rock on." It was called *The Bible: For Teens!*

He stretched out on the brass bed with *The Bible: For Teens!*, his bare feet warmed by a square of sunlight, and thumbed through the onionskin pages till he found the parable of the prodigal son. He'd forgotten the prodigal son had asked for his inheritance up front, to spend on prostitutes and wild parties, and had come home penniless. It relieved Emmett to read this, for he had asked for nothing up front. He was not like the prodigal son at all.

Three

JOEL DID NOT LOOK like Emmett, not at first glance. His hair was darker, and there was less of it. He was a bit taller than Emmett, but with his stooped shoulders, he did not seem to be. Emmett had smaller, narrowed eyes, eyes that expressed very little of what he was thinking; Joel's eyes, by contrast, betrayed him at every turn, disclosing his moods and opinions. He was better dressed: a corduroy shirt and black jeans, expensive-seeming suede boots. When his face was lax, it conveyed—to Emmett at least—a constant knowledge of his gifts and limitations.

When they embraced, however, on the front lawn of the Dream Home, for the first time in two years, Emmett saw in Joel all the ways they favored each other. They had the same jaw, the same nose, the same crooked smile. They carried themselves in the same way—the same unhurried gait, hands in their pockets. They had the same breathy, almost soundless laugh.

Joel held on to Emmett for an extra moment. It's so good to see you, brother, he said.

You too, Joel.

Alice came up after, hauling a pet carrier and a suitcase on rollers.

She wore overalls and a baggy brown cardigan, a pair of dirty Keds with no socks. She came to Emmett first and extended her arms awkwardly for a hug. So good to see you again! she said.

You too, Emmett said. She looked, more or less, the way he remembered. Her hair was the color of dark honey, middle-parted, hanging in wavy tresses past her shoulders. She was willowy, long-legged. A scattering of faint freckles on her cheeks. It was her eyes he'd forgotten. They were large and dreamy, though they still possessed, somehow, a strange lucidity. She seemed ready, at all times, to call bullshit on whatever she was seeing.

And who is this? Kathy said, bending down to the pet carrier.

This is Noam, Alice said. We heard him yowling in the alley behind our place and took him in.

I named him, Joel said.

It was a joint effort, Alice said.

Emmett crouched down and poked his fingers through the wire door, behind which lay a large Maine coon, his ears pointed like a lynx's, his mane like a wild gray beard.

The vet thinks he's about sixteen, Alice said.

In hindsight, "Noam" is a little too close to the word "no," Joel said. Makes it hard to discipline.

He needs no discipline, Alice said. He's a perfect angel.

Kathy watched, glowingly, as they heaped their plates with chicken and black-eyed peas. Joel made grunting, almost sexual noises of approval after each bite. Noam, freed from his carrier, explored the house, sniffing at the furniture. Emmett took a flake of chicken skin from his plate and held it, covertly, near the floor. Noam trotted over and ate it eagerly, licking the grease from his fingertips with his sandpaper tongue.

Nobody knows how to make this stuff in New York, Joel said. You ask for ham hock at the supermarket, they look at you like you've got three heads.

What is a ham hock exactly? Alice said.

You don't wanna know, hon, Kathy said.

It's the pig's ankle, sort of, Joel said. It's like a knuckle of bone surrounded by collagen and fat that breaks down when you cook it.

Alice made a face and looked at her black-eyed peas.

Alice doesn't usually eat meat, Joel said.

Kathy turned to him, aghast. Why on earth didn't you tell me? Alice, I can make you something vegetarian.

I'm a vegetarian when I cook for myself, Alice said. When people cook for me, I eat anything.

Kathy seemed confused but did not pursue it further. She asked them about their flight and their drive from the airport in Nashville. The rental is an EV, Joel said. It's so quiet you can't even tell it's running.

Where will you charge it? Kathy said. Everything's gas here.

There's a charging station at the Walmart.

I can't fathom who would want an electric car, Kathy said. I don't trust the computers in them, tracking everywhere you go.

It's the future, Mom, Joel said.

Not any future I want.

What, you'd rather us keep treating the planet like a garbage dump?

Let's not get into politics right off the bat, Alice said.

No, I'm curious, Joel said. What's your vision of the future? Are we all driving Hummers to our jobs at the local coal mine?

I love nature! she said. I go hiking, I buy my produce at the farmers' market. So don't lecture me on that. You're the ones who live in New York, surrounded by concrete and trash and who knows what all.

Nature gives nothing for free, Joel said. You might think you got something for free, but nature comes back and collects her debts. We've known this for two hundred years. Marx said as much about soil fertility in the 1880s.

There will be no Marx in this house, Kathy said.

No Marx in the Dream Home, Joel said, winking at Emmett.

Now I mean it. No Marx under my roof.

Roger that. No Marx.

Emmett ate in silence, glancing now and then at Alice, who

seemed mainly to be swapping her food around on the plate rather than eating it. She caught him staring and gave a small, conspiratorial smile. Emmett smiled too and looked away. Kathy was focused on Joel, watching him so intently that she seemed to have forgotten about her own food.

So, Joel, Emmett said. How's life? It's been, what, like two years?

Surely not. That can't be right.

The wedding was two years ago, Alice said.

Wow, I guess so, he said. The pandemic messed up my sense of time. You wake up one day and two years are gone.

I know what you mean, Emmett said, though time had not seemed any different to him. For the last two years, he'd been working the same sort of jobs he'd always worked—delivering sandwiches for Jimmy John's, pressure washing houses, mowing lawns, then finally as a line cook at the Outback in Metairie, where his primary duty had been to prepare Bloomin' Onions, dredging them with batter and flour, bopping the root end with his mesh skimmer to spread out the onion petals once they were in the dark simmering oil. He'd worked at the Outback for six months, specks of hot grease stinging his eyes and forearms, and he'd felt the slow passing of every minute of every hour of every shift.

I've just been teaching and writing, Joel said. Beyond that I'm a hermit really. It's good to be out of New York. I missed the South.

You're here for how long? Emmett said.

The fall semester. Then back to New York in January. Then maybe Ireland for the summer. We haven't decided yet.

We were supposed to go in 2020 for our honeymoon but a certain world-historical crisis had other plans, Alice said.

World travelers! Kathy said.

It's all the pent-up energy from lockdown, Joel said. It's my new resolution to travel as much as possible. We don't have kids. We don't have jobs that tie us to a location. We can be migratory. When we get bored with a place, we can go somewhere else.

That must be nice, Emmett said. He meant it sincerely—or at least he thought so—but it came out sounding sour.

Joel looked down at his plate with a bashful smile. It embarrassed him to acknowledge his money, that he could spend a month in Europe and still pay his rent in New York without checking his bank account. Emmett, meanwhile, had accrued sixty dollars in overdraft fees just a week earlier buying Goobers and a pack of cigarettes.

You sound like Emmett, Kathy said. He's here, then he's gone, then he's back again. Y'all go from one place to the next and you're never satisfied. I wish you'd both just come home.

Emmett felt the comparison was unfair. The places he'd lived in his twenties had not been exotic or interesting or even very far away. They were all in the South: Nashville, Knoxville, Asheville. Until New Orleans, he'd felt he was doomed to live in the Villes of the world for the rest of his life.

Mom says you started at Tempo? Joel said.

Yeah, last week, Emmett said.

Do they make you wear the little green shorts and the shirt? Alice said.

I'm not a driver, so no, Emmett said. He explained what the Center was like. He found himself repeating the talking points from his orientation. It's the central point of exchange for millions of parcels, not just in America, but around the globe, he said.

Why Kentucky? Alice said. I mean, why not somewhere else?

It's right in the middle of the country, Emmett said.

The heartland, Kathy said. God's country.

You thought about going back to school? Joel said.

You ask me that every time we see each other.

Well, I wish you would. You were so close to finishing.

This was far from true. Emmett had taken a hodgepodge of classes at the community college for two years. He'd dropped out without ever declaring a major.

Maybe I will one day, he said.

Everyone turned back to their plates, satisfied with this answer. But Emmett had the strange urge to say more, to make some big announcement.

I'm trying to write a screenplay, he said.

Everyone looked at him, drumsticks poised near their mouths.

Why? Joel said. I mean, what gave you that idea?

He'd always had the idea—the conviction, really—that he was meant to do something creative, and he had tried his hand at more than a few artistic pursuits, none of which had panned out. His love of movies had been a constant in his life, but the notion of screenwriting had first occurred to him only after a matinee showing of *Sunset Boulevard* a few months earlier. The screenwriter, played by William Holden, had a kind of romantic fatalism; he was down on his luck, but he could call himself a writer, and there was nobility in this. He'd spoken to Joel by phone soon after and mentioned that he might take up screenwriting.

Remind me, Joel had said, doesn't Gloria Swanson shoot the guy? The screenwriter? He winds up face down in the pool.

What's your point?

My point is—nobody watches *Sunset Boulevard* and comes away thinking how great it would be to work in Hollywood. The whole point is that it leads to madness and murder.

I have these ideas for stories. My mind is racing with ideas. I just have to find a way to put them on paper.

That's great, Joel had said. But it's a lot of work. People who are serious about screenwriting—they read manuals, they go to seminars, they buy special software for their computers to format everything. Then you spend years writing spec scripts, stuff that's already on the air. You're not even telling original stories in the beginning. You're writing sample scripts for whatever shitty sitcom is big at the moment. Then if you're very, very lucky, you get hired to work on the shitty sitcom, and you put your time in there, and maybe down the road—years, decades even—you sell an original screenplay.

He'd said all this, Emmett suspected, as a way of dissuading him from trying. But this had only made him want it more. He'd bought the manuals, paid two hundred dollars for a seminar taught by a former staff writer of a '90s sitcom. He'd purchased the expensive software, some part of him believing the screenplay would generate itself, that he'd wake up one morning, turn on his computer, and find it there, finished and perfect. But he saw, soon enough, that each word would have to be typed. It made him feel stupid, pecking at the keys for hours on his days off, only to read back what he'd written and find it all utterly boring.

Still, he was driven to continue. He pictured the moment in the future when he would tell Joel he'd sold an original screenplay, proving to his brother that he, too, was capable of writing something. More than this—that he was capable of *creating* something. Joel had only ever been able to write *about* culture. Emmett wanted to *make* culture, the value of which would be undeniable, even to Joel.

We talked about this, Emmett said. On the phone? You told me to read manuals and go to seminars and buy the software.

I told you that's *what people do,* Joel said. People who are serious. I didn't expect you to actually do it.

I think it's exciting, Alice said. I bet the stories you'd tell would be unique. You've had so many jobs, lived in so many places.

Emmett wasn't sure who would be interested in his minor travails, the endless parade of dead-end gigs and scuttled relationships and shitty apartments. But he'd met some characters, that much was true. And failure, he believed, was something most people could relate to.

She might be right, Joel said. You know, everyone wants to talk about representation now. But as Alain Badiou has pointed out, the most underrepresented group of them all is the working class. How many Hollywood movies are about working people? How many books that come out?

I just wanna do something meaningful, Emmett said. He heard himself, in this moment, as if from Joel's perspective, and he suddenly felt small and naïve. I'm afraid of dying, Emmett said. But I think if I could leave a legacy, do something important, the fear would go away.

Who said anything about death? Kathy said. Do you feel all right?

Maybe not death exactly. It's just this feeling—like time's against me.

Let me not then die ingloriously and without a struggle, Joel said, but let me first do some great thing that shall be told among men hereafter.

That better not be Marx, Kathy said.

It's Homer, Joel said.

I know that, Emmett said, though he'd never heard the quotation.

Maybe you should get married and have kids, Kathy said. She turned to Joel and Alice. Maybe you two should do the same. I know that might put a damper on your *migratory* lifestyle, but if you want something that will outlive you, then give me some grandbabies.

I want that someday, Joel said.

Well, what does Alice want?

Everyone turned to look at Alice. As far as kids? she said. I'm undecided.

Joel set down his drumstick and looked at her. I thought you were open to the idea, he said.

That's the same thing as undecided, isn't it?

Joel's face reddened. He left his remaining food untouched and said nothing else throughout the meal.

Trivial Pursuit was something of a Shaw family tradition; they had often played when Joel and Emmett were growing up, into their teenage years, and now mostly on holidays. Joel was dominant, though Emmett could hold his own in the Entertainment category. When they'd cleared the kitchen table, however, the board that Kathy brought out was new—a "teams edition."

Now you and Alice can't team up, Kathy said. You know each other too well.

Me and you versus Emmett and Alice? Joel said.

Joel and Kathy took an early lead, but Alice knew the answers to all the Science and Nature questions, and Emmett knew all the answers involving movies. Unlike Joel, Emmett had seen all the popular classics, the films more likely to appear in a game of trivia.

Halfway through, Joel was unable to recall Buzz Lightyear's catchphrase from *Toy Story*.

I know this, he said, closing his eyes, fingers pressed to his forehead.

Really? Emmett said. Cause it kinda seems like you don't.

It's right on the tip of my tongue.

Mr. Cultural Critic, Alice said. You can't remember *Toy Story*?

Ask me about a catchphrase from literally any other film, he said. *Taxi Driver, Casablanca.*

See, though, the card is asking about Buzz Lightyear? In *Toy Story*?

Okay, Alice, what is it?

To infinity and beyond.

Motherfucking cocksucker.

Hey, Kathy said. None of that.

I'm carrying the team here, Joel said. You're not pulling your weight.

Well, I'm trying, Kathy said.

When it became apparent that Joel and Kathy would lose, Joel's interest faded. Alice and Emmett won, high-fiving across the table. Joel offered his begrudging congratulations.

Oh, you're not mad now? Alice said.

I wasn't really mad, Joel said. I was hamming it up.

Right, Emmett said.

Alice found a bottle of coconut rum in the pantry and poured them all generous glasses, which they topped off with Coke. They drank, the board still spread out, the cards scattered. You and Alice were on fire, Kathy said. How'd you know those science questions?

One of her majors was environmental science, Joel said. I've told you that.

I thought it was environmental *ethics*?

That was grad school, Alice said. My aborted degree.

She said this with levity, as if her decision to leave graduate school early and move to New York with Joel was no longer a sore subject but rather a kind of inside joke. Still, he thought he detected, in the twist of her mouth after she spoke, an aftertaste of bitterness.

Well, I guess I don't know exactly what either one means, Kathy said.

It was mostly about ecosystems, Alice said. What they can tolerate, what they can't. It's about how changing one thing changes everything else.

Well, I was impressed, Kathy said. What was that word you knew? Mito-what?

Mitochondria.

Mitochondria, right.

Part of the cell structure.

It's amazing, isn't it? Kathy said. All the stuff that's there, but it's too small to see?

Emmett, you knew your movies, Alice said.

That's all I do, watch movies.

What's your favorite?

I like everything, he said. I don't discriminate. High, low, whatever.

Maybe you *should* discriminate, Joel said. Might help with the screenplay.

What would be the point in restricting myself?

I just think there's such a thing as good taste.

People like what they like, Emmett said. Some people like Adam Sandler. Some people like Ingmar Bergman.

Okay, but gun to your head, Alice said. What's your all-time fave?

I guess I'd say *On the Waterfront*.

Joel made a gagging sound. Overrated, he said. And Kazan was a snitch. He named names to the House Un-American Activities Committee.

Brando carries it. It's a great underdog story. Great lines.

Emmett jutted his chin, drew his eyebrows together, and delivered his best Brando—*I coulda been a contender! I coulda been somebody!*

That's late Brando, Joel said. That's too *Godfather*. You sound like you've got cotton balls in your cheeks.

Come on, that was great! Alice said.

Always a critic, Kathy said.

I saw *A Streetcar Named Desire* at the Broad Theater in New Orleans, Emmett said. It's a beautiful theater—Spanish tile roof, white columns. No better place to see it.

How long were you in New Orleans? Alice said.

Just six months.

You were living in Asheville, right, when we met?

Emmett nodded.

Do you remember talking at our wedding?

He remembered well. The wedding was in Springfield, Alice's hometown. They'd booked one of those old barns made into a venue—the reincarnation of a barn. The place had kept cattle in one of its past lives, and Emmett could smell them still. A whiff of manure, of musk and steaming breath. What a place for a wedding, he'd thought at the time. What a weird meeting of disparate groups— their tattooed friends from New York; Joel's Southern Baptist kin, glancing with hostile expressions at the open bar. There were fairy lights strung from the rafters, a DJ with crates of vinyl and two turntables. Emmett had joked with his brother that this would be the fate of all barns. They would be called "rustic." Their plank walls, a century old, would buzz with the beat of ABBA's "Dancing Queen."

That would make a good essay, actually, Joel had said. I should write that down.

Emmett had spoken to Alice later on. He'd been smoking behind the barn, alone, and she had found him there, hiking up her dress to tromp through the weeds. They'd floated a cigarette and laughed about her great-uncle Herman dozing off during the ceremony.

That was the first time we really talked, Emmett said.

I found a burn hole in my dress later. Joel was not happy.

She seemed a little drunk now, the borders of her words beginning to smudge. She'd poured the largest glass of rum for herself and had already finished it.

It was *your* dress, Joel said. I didn't care.

You said I smelled like an ashtray.

Joel's eyes darted briefly to Emmett and his mother. I don't remember that, he said.

He doesn't like when I smoke, Alice said, looking at Emmett.

It's an awful habit, Kathy said. I wish I never started.

You have a scientific mind, Joel said. You should know it's irrational.

God forbid I do anything irrational.

Do you think you'll ever finish your PhD? Kathy said pleasantly, trying to change the subject.

She wants to farm now, Joel said. That's her new thing. She's always bringing home these twisted little zucchinis from the community garden.

How fun! Kathy said. You know, there's space in the backyard. You could grow a few things there, give it a try.

It's not a new thing, Alice said. I've always gardened.

Gardening isn't farming, Joel said. Gardening is to farming what writing is to publishing.

Joel loves to remind me that my dreams are silly, Alice said. Emmett, I'm sure you can relate.

For Christ's sake, Joel said. Buy a farm, write a screenplay. I don't care. He took a swallow of rum and coughed, set the glass down hard. I'm just saying, when we met, you were serious. About environmental issues. About your degree.

I wanted to be *in nature*, not just writing papers about it.

Joel looked at their mother, as if to say, *What will we do with her?* Alice watched him, her face slack, her eyes soft and shining. She seemed to stare beyond him to a distant time.

Joel, Emmett said, do you remember the Shaw Boys' Saga?

A slow-dawning smile. Yes, Joel said. God, that takes me back.

My dad, Lloyd, used to tell us bedtime stories, Emmett explained to Alice. It was about the Shaw Boys—me and Joel. Sort of like the Hardy Boys. We'd solve mysteries, go on adventures. Only we'd alternate telling the story. Joel would tell it for a while, then my dad would take a turn, then I'd take a turn. But every time I'd introduce a character, Joel would kill them off. I'd say, "And then we ran into an elf," and when the baton was passed to Joel, he'd say, "And then a flaming arrow came from nowhere and impaled the elf."

They all laughed—Joel, too. It drained the tension from the room.

Do you remember what Lloyd used to say?

Joel shook his head.

He'd say, "Joel, share the story."

Joel gave a pensive grunt. So what? he said.

I don't know, Emmett said. I just thought of it.

....

Emmett excused himself and stood in the bathroom for a long time with the faucet running. He'd wanted a moment away from the others, just to breathe. He looked at himself in the mirror, at the lines of exhaustion around his eyes. He thought about his father. Lloyd was an electrician by trade—a brawny, bullnecked man with a mop of wheat-blond hair. He lived in Huntsville, Alabama, with his second wife and her three children. Emmett saw him a few times a year, and they got along well enough, though there had always been a polite distance—a sense that anything more than a three-day visit would intrude on the new life he'd made—if not for him, then for his wife. Lloyd had once been serious about tae kwon do and kept a cabinet of dusty trophies in his office. They watched old kung fu movies together when Emmett visited, drinking Carlsberg beer late into the night, laughing at the dubbed English. They'd done the same thing when Emmett was little, minus the beer. He loved his father, but these moments were the closest they had ever been—laughing at the mismatched words and mouths, punches thrown at the air, never quite making contact.

Joel's father was a man named Jackie Ballard. His life had been a series of binges and debts and risky wagers. Joel had met him only twice, around his eighteenth birthday, not long after Kathy and Lloyd divorced. He'd lived in Biloxi for a while, then Houston. Thirteen years after their meeting, he'd been arrested for throwing a remote control at his girlfriend's face, fracturing her orbital bone. She'd dropped the charges but told him they were through. He went straight from the Calcasieu Parish Jail to the Delta Downs Racetrack and Casino, where he'd been staying for two weeks. He played the slots for a few hours, went up to the room, drank a pint of vodka, and hanged himself.

When he'd called Emmett, Joel had recounted these facts as if trying to piece together a victim's final movements, as if some mystery might be clarified. But there was nothing mysterious about Jackie's death. Some people committed suicide and no one knew why. Jackie wasn't one of them. His whole life seemed to build toward self-annihilation. *I don't know why I'm crying,* Joel kept saying on the phone. *He wasn't even someone I knew.*

EMMETT WENT OUT later to smoke a joint and found Alice on the porch. It was dusk, the sky glowing with peach-colored light where the sun had set. He sat with her on the swing and said nothing at first, listening to the crickets and the burbling of the koi pond's filter. They looked out at the subdivision's undeveloped land—a tussocky field, ribbons of mist hovering above the grass. Little pink survey flags demarcated the property lines.

Future Dream Homes, Emmett said, pointing.

She shook her head. It was hard to see her face in the dim bluish light.

When they run out of space, they'll turn the old uranium plant into a condominium, Emmett said.

You sound like your brother.

Yeah, well. He's right about a lot. But just because you're right doesn't mean you're not an asshole.

She let out a breath of laughter. The porch light switched on then—a loud, buzzing lamp above the sliding doors. When he turned back to Alice, he could see her face clearly. Her cheeks were streaked with tears.

Hey, he said, you all right?

No, she said. I don't know. It's fine.

Emmett did not know her well enough to say something wise, nor did he think that this was what she wanted. So he patted her forearm and said nothing.

You ever wake up and wonder how you got to a place? she said after a while.

How do you mean?

Like, okay, I used to drive drunk sometimes. It was a long time ago, and I know it's bad. You can judge me if you want.

I don't judge you.

I'd never tell Joel this. He'd be horrified. But I worked at this winery in Illinois when I was twenty-five.

There are wineries in Illinois?

Unfortunately, she said. They were the sweetest wines you ever tasted. It was like drinking Welch's grape juice. Anyway, they had a bar there, and I'd drink this sweet wine after my shift with a coworker. Then we'd drive back to Champaign. The winery was way out in the country. That's how I justified it to myself. The roads were empty. It was late. It was that point in the night, around two a.m., when NPR starts playing the BBC, you know what I mean?

I think so.

It's eight o'clock GMT, Alice said in a British accent, *and two girls are driving drunk on a Tuesday night down a country road in central Illinois. You're listening to BBC Newshour.*

Emmett laughed and nodded.

What I'm getting at, she said, what I'm trying to say, is that sometimes I'd wake up in my car, in the parking lot of my apartment building, my head pounding with this awful wine hangover, and I'd have no idea how I got there. I mean, I would surmise that I'd driven. But I'd have no memory of it. Or I would, but it would be like watching myself in a dream. Not like I'd *lived* it.

A long silence followed. The crickets had settled into a steady rhythm. Beetles pattered against the false moon of the porch lamp and fell, stunned, to the cement, wriggling their legs.

I feel that way sometimes now, she said. I wake up and I don't know how I got here.

To Paducah?

Just in general, she said.

Have you talked to Joel about this?

Alice laughed and raked her fingers through her honey-hair. I don't think Joel ever wonders how he got to where he is, she said. He can account for every step. Everything went according to plan.

Believe me, I know what you mean.

I wish sometimes—

She stopped herself, her fists clenched in her lap. When she spoke again, her voice was softer, almost a whisper.

I wish sometimes I could blow up my life. Just for the challenge. Just for something to do. To put all the pieces back together. To prove that I can fix it, after it's broken. I've tried to explain it to Joel—this feeling—but it's like it doesn't compute with him. He doesn't have that impulse. Maybe most people don't.

I know that feeling, Emmett said, unsure what else to say. The whole conversation was beyond his ken. He knew that Alice and Joel had been together only six months when they married, that she had dropped out of a PhD program at the University of Illinois, where Joel was teaching, to live with him in New York. He knew that she was into community gardens and organic farming—that whole scene. He knew that she'd grown up in Springfield, that her family, while not wealthy, was better off than their own. He knew that, at their wedding, she'd seemed slightly dazed, and had spoken her vows so feebly that no one in attendance could hear them. And he knew that he found her attractive. He'd caught himself that afternoon watching the swing of her hips as she crossed the room. Even now, his eyes wandered. She was attractive. He could admit this to himself without it meaning anything. If he acknowledged this dispassionately, as a simple fact, he could keep it that way. Something separate. Something that had nothing to do with him.

Where is Joel anyway? Emmett said.

He's showing your mother how to upload her photos to the cloud. They'll be doing that all night. She has a million pictures.

Alice sniffled and wiped her eyes. She smiled to show that she was better now, that her sadness had passed. Do you like your brother? she said.

Half-brother. And sure, I love him. Of course I do. He's family.

But would you like him as a person? If he wasn't family?

It doesn't really matter, does it? He's family whether I like it or not.

I guess that's true for you.

It's true for you, too, Emmett said.

We're married, not related.

That's family. That counts.

You can't divorce your family.

You're not divorcing, are you?

No, she said. I don't know. You don't have a cigarette, do you?

I can do you one better. He took the joint from his shirt pocket and held it out in the palm of his hand.

Oh thank God, Alice said.

They went behind the garden shed in the backyard. Emmett turned his back to the breeze and flicked the lighter till the twisted tip of the joint flared up. He licked his finger and touched the paper to keep it from running, then passed it to Alice, who inhaled too deeply and fell into a coughing fit. A neighbor's dog began to bark.

Keep it down, Emmett said, laughing.

I used to smoke all the time, Alice croaked. Joel doesn't like it. He says I'm not myself when I'm high. Now I have to sneak out with a vape once in a blue moon.

They traded the joint back and forth. Emmett sang a few lines from "Blue Moon of Kentucky" with an exaggerated drawl. *Blue moon of Kentucky, keep on shinin. Shine on the one that's gone and proved untrue.* Alice giggled helplessly and covered her face with her hands. I think I'm done, she said.

Joel stubbed the joint against the shed's wall and put the roach in his pocket. You know, you're all right, he said. We should make this a tradition at family get-togethers.

Your voice isn't half bad. When you were singing, I mean.

I can only sing with an accent. If I sing with a serious voice, I sound stupid.

I used to sing. Middle school choir.

Gimme a sample.

Okay, but I have to close my eyes, she said. I can't look at you.

She sang the first two stanzas of "Climb Ev'ry Mountain" from *The Sound of Music,* a song about taking any chance, overcoming any obstacle, to attain your dreams. She kept her hands clasped below her breasts as she sang, as though in a recital, and when she finished and opened her eyes, Emmett snapped his fingers softly in lieu of applause.

That was great, he said. Bravo.

Alice laughed and curtsied. A breeze kicked up, and they crossed their bare arms against the cold and looked back toward the lighted house, Joel and Kathy somewhere inside.

What's in this garden shed? Alice said, rapping her knuckle on the aluminum siding.

I have no idea, Emmett said. We could look.

They went around to the front and Alice examined the padlock.

It's 5316, Emmett said. That's her combination for everything.

What's it stand for?

John 3:16, Emmett said. J is 5 on the number pad.

It's a verse?

For God so loved the world, that he gave his only begotten son, that whosoever believeth in him shall not perish, but have everlasting life.

Whoa, Alice said, turning the tumblers on the lock. You know any others?

Jesus wept.

She unclasped the lock and opened the door. It was dark inside and smelled of gasoline. They groped for the pull chain on the light. Emmett found it finally, just as the metal door clanked shut behind them. It was cramped inside; they could hardly turn around without bumping into each other. There were red plastic containers of gas, cans of paint. A rolled-up American flag. But they hardly registered these things. He could see that Alice's eyes went first and foremost to a rack of guns in the rear—an olive AR-15, a scoped hunting rifle, three shotguns. The shelves below were stacked with pistol cases and metal boxes of ammunition.

Holy shit, Alice said.

I wondered where she kept them, Emmett said.

This is, like, an arsenal.

I'm sure she's got a dozen more in the house.

Are you serious?

Emmett nodded. He'd spent so much of his childhood around guns that seeing a collection like this never fazed him.

Are these legal? Alice said.

Oh yeah. This is what the Founding Dads wanted.

What a strange place, Alice said.

Emmett wasn't sure whether she meant America or Kentucky or simply his mother's backyard.

When Alice turned around, he could feel the heat of her breath on his face.

I think we've seen the shed, she said.

We should go back.

But neither of them moved. They were so close that movement was impossible without touching each other. What happened then was like fainting, Emmett supposed, though he'd never fainted. A rush of vertigo overcame him. Then they were kissing, helplessly, tumbling forward into a well with no bottom. Her arms were around his neck, pushing her tongue into his mouth. He kissed her throat and her collarbone, her lungs filling and emptying like bellows.

Then, all at once, they pulled apart, repelled by a sudden shift in polarity.

Alice stood back from him, panting, covering her mouth.

Oh my God, she said.

I'm so sorry, Emmett said. That was inappropriate.

No, it was my fault.

Please, I'm the one who should apologize.

I'm just really stoned, I think, Alice said.

No, me too.

I think we're both just stoned.

Absolutely.

We're not in our right minds.

Of course. It was stupid.

They looked at each other for another perilous moment, in which they might have embraced again and given in completely. Instead, they averted their eyes and Alice said, We should go back.

You go first, Emmett said.

She slid past him, out the door. He stood for a long time in silence, smelling the gasoline, his heart still drumming.

There were two guest rooms in the Dream Home—the "guest room/office," where Emmett slept, and the "antique room," where Alice and Joel slept. Both had brass beds with mattresses so firm one felt as if the carpet, or a park bench perhaps, might be more comfortable. The antique room got its name because it held Kathy's china cabinet and her porcelain lamps, and the dresser and vanity had belonged to her great-grandmother. There were two paintings in the room—one of a ramshackle farmhouse, the other of a pillared plantation. A music box clock chimed the melody of "The Way We Were" every hour. Emmett heard Joel trying to turn it off somehow.

You're going to break it, Kathy said. You're going to break my favorite clock.

Just leave it alone, Alice said wearily.

Emmett put *The Bible: For Teens!* away and clicked off the lamp. His mind, as he drifted into fitful sleep, kept circling back to Alice. He did not feel guilty—not yet. What had happened seemed to him more like an accident than anything else. In a way, he felt relieved. Things might have gone differently in the garden shed. It was like they had earned something by stopping what they might have continued. But he thought of her still, in that state of half-dreaming. He thought of her pale and naked on the brass bed, beneath the farmhouse and the mansion.

Four

How DO WE KNOW that we want what we think we want?

This was how Joel began his course. It seemed to him the central question of his work, and of his life lately. His students looked at him—mostly male, mostly graduate-level—as if he had the answer to this question, as if it were mystical knowledge that could be understood only after years of devotion. But the question interested him precisely because he had no answer.

This is the legacy of Freud, right? Joel said. That underlying our desires are deeper, repressed desires. And this is the thread picked up by Lacan, by Deleuze and Marcuse, by the Frankfurt School. They took this insight and applied it broadly to a Marxist framework. Now, the title of this course is Rural Despair and Late Capitalism. And you might be asking yourselves, "What does despair have to do with desire?" Well, it's complicated, but I've been thinking lately about this contradiction—I guess that's what you'd call it. A paradox. On the one hand, you have *Deaths of Despair*—this really thorough, comprehensive work coming from Angus Deaton and Anne Case on morbidity among uneducated whites. And on the other hand, if you ask someone who's killing himself slowly with drugs or cigarettes or alcohol if he feels despair, he might well tell you he's happy. And even if he was feeling despair, he probably wouldn't locate the source of his despair in consumer capitalism or a deteriorating labor market. Moreover, you have uneducated whites in rural places voting for candidates and supporting causes that seem to make their lives worse. *They vote against their interests*—we've heard this before, right?

So where does that leave the Left? Are we obliged to see the white, rural working class as dupes and suckers? As brainwashed? As victims? As a lost cause? Maybe there's something seductive about that self-righteousness, to find ourselves in the position of theorizing about the working class to begin with. Does this resonate with anyone?

A few of the students nodded uncertainly.

Joel took a drink of mint tea from his thermos and looked at his students. There were three women in the class, all in their early twenties. They were the bookish type he might've pursued in grad school. Black jeans and sweaters. Dirty Chuck Taylors and combat boots. No bra, no makeup. Slightly bored-looking. Women like Alice, in other words. It was strange, now, to realize he had no chance with them. The fluorescent light overhead was harsh and sterile, and he imagined his scalp shining beneath his thin hair.

One of the women raised her hand half-heartedly.

Yes, please, Joel said.

Yeah, my question is, what about suicide?

What about it?

I'm just thinking, she said, maybe the despair you're talking about isn't real despair. She looked up at the ceiling, wringing her hands as she spoke. It's like, okay, a despairing person is in love with their despair on some level, I can see that, I guess. But what about a person who commits suicide? A person who commits suicide clearly did not want their despair to continue.

Yeah, good, Joel said. That's great. Anyone have a response to that?

When no one spoke, Joel took another long gulp of tea and considered how to answer. He thought about his father, of course, but only in a distant, theoretical way.

The suicidal person wants something, though, right? he said finally. Namely, he wants to die. So I think the point still stands.

I just feel like you're defining despair in a way that suits the argument you'd like to make, the student said.

That's probably true, Joel said, and a few of the students chuckled. Look, I'm not an authority here. The best I can do sometimes is formulate the questions, and we'll work toward answers together. But suicide is interesting. I'll add suicide to the syllabus, see what I can come up with as far as readings.

He scribbled a note on his planner, and as he took another sip from his thermos, the tea lukewarm now, he heard something pattering against the classroom window. It was a hummingbird floating there, near the tall, withered sunflowers. For a moment, however, he forgot what the bird was called. It was just this iridescent blur of life, wingtips brushing the glass. His knees grew weak, and he gripped the edges of the lectern to steady himself. He was unable to speak, seized by something like panic. He lowered himself into a chair and clenched his fists to keep his hands from shaking. For a long moment, Joel sat like this, saying nothing.

A student in the front row stood, hesitantly, and said, Are you okay?

Fine, Joel said. Just a minute.

You're really pale.

He managed to finish, to read the syllabus and clarify the course expectations. After, the students filed out, looking back at him with expressions somewhere between concern and discomfort. When he was alone, his breathing returned to normal, sweat running down his ribcage from his armpits. The word "suicide" was written on his planner. He looked out the window, but the bird was gone.

HE DROVE THE FARM ROADS for an hour after class, meandering back to his mother's. Feeling dizzy, he pulled over near a livestock pond and stood in the sunlight. The pond was a still green mirror.

Russet cows were playing on the hillside—frolicking and wagging their tails like dogs. He remembered vaguely that this signaled rain. Sure enough, a gunmetal thunderhead had formed in the east. Where he stood, it was bright and blustery. A marsh surrounded the pond. He watched the wind ripple through the silver plume grass, his heart aching with mysterious grief.

His father had died about a year ago, and the death had become convolved with the larger tragedy of the pandemic. Joel could not pry the two griefs apart. They'd become one singular sense of loss—mysterious to him because he'd lost nothing. His father was not really his father. And the pandemic had taken no one from his life. Still, he felt robbed of something. It struck him at odd moments, this mourning without object.

For months, he'd expected this feeling to pass, and when it didn't, he'd begun taking an antidepressant in secret. He had no insurance, and after a bit of research, he'd determined that the cheapest option was a telehealth company called GENTS. They sold generic Viagra and Rogaine mostly, but they'd expanded recently into mental health. Joel received daily emails from them with racy subject lines, advertising their sexual health products.

He received one now, standing by the side of the road: *Wanna stay harder, longer? Try GENTS Climax Delay Ointment.* This was followed by a purple eggplant emoji and a red heart. He clicked off his screen, returned the phone to his pocket. He wondered if there might be an essay to write about this—something about the commodified state of masculinity, the barrage of signifiers. All the meaning held in that eggplant emoji—the phallic potency of manhood reduced to a kind of cartoon. He exhaled and let the idea go, returning to the present—to the wind skimming patterns on the surface of the pond. Most of his ideas for essays were uninteresting to him now once he thought them through.

THAT NIGHT, he dreamt that his brother was drowning. They'd been standing on a dock, fishing with spinner rods, and Emmett had jumped into the lake. The water wasn't even deep, but he flailed his arms and screamed, and Joel knew he was meant to jump in and save him. He started emptying his pockets for some reason—his cell phone, keys, and wallet. It was important in the dream that he empty his pockets, even though Emmett was actively drowning. But he kept finding things—receipts, church keys, loose change, chewing gum. The objects became strange and improbable. He pulled out pieces of jewelry and magnifying glasses, harmonicas and remote controls. His pockets were like clown car pockets. They held an endless supply of objects, and as he drew them out and set them on the weathered planks of the dock, Emmett gurgled and choked, disappearing finally into the green murk.

In the morning, unable to dispel the dream from his thoughts, he sent a text to Emmett, recounting it. He'd resolved to text Emmett more often, and this seemed like a good occasion.

It means you care more about material things than our relationship obviously, Emmett texted back.

I would save you if you were drowning, Joel said.

I know. I'm joking.

So what does it mean?

Dreams don't mean, Emmett said.

He went with Alice and Kathy to Grandma Ruth's that afternoon. They brought milkshakes from the Dairyette and sat on the deck, watching smoke rise from the burning barrel. Ruth burned her trash daily, dumping armfuls of mail and soda bottles and flattened cardboard into a charred fifty-gallon drum, squirting it all with fuel, tossing a match. Joel could taste, in the back of his throat, the fumes of burning plastic.

There's men in the woods, Ruth said.

What now, Mom? Kathy said.

Men in the woods. They watch me while I'm sleeping. Ruth pointed with her milkshake, creaking back and forth in the rocking chair. I seen them last night.

It's probably deer, Mom.

Well, I reckon I know a man from a deer.

They were never sure with Grandma Ruth, these days, what was true and what was only senility. She had hallucinations—visions of flames and smoke, of nonexistent puddles in the kitchen, of voices at night that called to her.

Why would there be men in the woods, Grandma? Joel said. What did they look like?

She squinched her face, trying hard to remember. They were dark, she said. Maybe Blacks, I don't know.

Now, Mom, Kathy said, glancing at Alice. Don't talk that way.

I said they *might* be Blacks, but maybe not. All I seen was their eyes. They were glowing green. They watched me.

Sounds like deer, Joel said, leaning over to squeeze her hand.

Would you go look, Emmett?

I'm Joel, not Emmett.

This is Joel, your grandson, Kathy said. And this is his wife, Alice.

Ruth studied Joel with the same look of bafflement she gave the television when the anchors delivered some story beyond her comprehension.

You're Joel.

That's right. Don't you recognize me?

She said nothing at first, rocking back and forth. She sucked at her milkshake, cheeks puckering, then sighed and said, They'll probably kill me. I'll be like that woman on TV with the tattoo.

What woman? Kathy said.

All they found was her foot in the woods. It had a tattoo of a rose.

Here?

Somewhere. I saw it on the TV.

Joel walked downhill, past the green flames of the burning barrel to the quivering shadows at the edge of the woods. There were tall pines, their crowns moved by the wind, and the floor of the forest was soft with brown needles. He went deeper inside. The land sloped down to a creek bed, where the door of a white icebox could be seen, abandoned decades earlier. The creek itself was splashed with light: a deep copper pool, gnats swarming at the surface. Someone was watching; he felt it unmistakably. He stood beneath the swaying pines and laughed at himself, but nothing was funny, and nothing could be seen around him but the reddish trunks and the brambles.

No one is here, he said aloud, comforting himself.

His phone buzzed—a call from an unknown number. He answered and turned his back to the wind. For a few seconds, after he'd said hello, there was only the sound of paper rustling. He tried again: Hello?

You're a fraud, said the voice on the other side.

Excuse me? Joel said, though he'd heard the man clearly. The voice was unnaturally deep and graveled.

I said you're a fraud. You're a liar.

Who is this?

The phone beeped and Joel stared at the screen. Chimes were clanging on the deck. When he looked uphill, he saw the others standing at the rail, awaiting his verdict.

THE PACKAGING WAS DISCREET, with no obvious logos or markings. He locked the door, slit the tape with a key, and found a bottle of pills inside—the wrong pills. Rather than his antidepressant, they'd sent generic Viagra. Kathy and Alice were cooking supper. He stood by the window in slats of amber light, the bottle in his open hand.

The hold music for GENTS' customer service hotline was not the bland jazz one heard in elevators. It was indie electronica—glossy synthesizers, hypnotic beats. He turned on the small television atop the dresser. Twelve people had been killed at a Walmart in Arkansas— aerial footage of retail associates in blue vests, running with their hands above their heads in single file from the building. Now and then, the hold music would halt abruptly for an advertisement— a man's voice, possessing a deep, cello-like resonance.

Do you suffer from dissatisfaction? he said. Insomnia? Lack of willpower? Feelings of helplessness? Do you no longer derive pleasure from the products you buy? Are you sexually frustrated? Hounded by invasive fantasies? Do you weep in the shower for no reason? Have you noticed new blemishes? Rashes? Pimples? Is your hair falling out? Do your teeth hurt? Are you bewildered by advertise-

ments? Have you noticed a loss of memory? Taste? Smell? Tactile sensation? Do your clothes fit as well as they used to? Do you feel your death approaching?

GENTS Customer Solutions, how can I support you today?

He'd wanted to hear the resolution of the advertisement. Some experimental, high-level therapy perhaps? A better pill? But the woman on the line was waiting. She sounded like she'd just finished three cups of coffee and bore only good news for the world.

He gave her his name and told her his problem—that they'd mailed the wrong medication.

I'm very, very, very sorry, sir, she said—and she sounded truly remorseful. He heard her mouse clicking. The chatter of typing. I think we should be able to resolve your issue, she said.

Great.

Can you tell me the name of the correct medication?

Joel squinted at the label of his nearly empty prescription. Vlaxatranafaline, he said.

Can you repeat that?

Vlaxatranafaline.

Hmmm, she said. Another flurry of clicking. I'm not seeing anything in the system, she said.

The system.

That's correct.

Well, the medicine is real. I'm holding it in my hands.

The correct medication or the wrong one?

The correct one.

I'm not seeing it.

In the system.

Correct. It looks like we no longer carry vlaxatranafaline.

You did last month.

So odd, she said, her mouse clicking rapidly.

I was just hoping for some help.

I understand, sir. Can I put you on a brief hold?

Fine.

The music returned—oceanic synthesizers. On the television, a Walmart associate was sitting for an interview. Her hair was bleached, dark gray at the roots, and her eyes had the stranded look of someone who'd been banished forever from the path of her life. He turned up the volume. *It was just another day,* she said. *Our team lead had us meet in the stockroom. We heard the noise at first outside and went to look. It didn't seem real to me. I still can't believe it's real.*

Okay, sir, can you tell me what the medication was for?

He lowered the volume. Well, he said, I started a few months ago. I was having some issues. My dad passed away. He committed suicide actually. Which, you know, is terrible, but I didn't really know him. He wasn't in my life. Still, a lot to "process," as they say. I had to process it all emotionally. And then, well, I wrote this book—that's what I do for work. I write and I teach. And I wrote this book about politics and mental health and the South—it's called *Going South,* in case you're interested. Not that I'd expect you to buy it. I mean, you can if you want. No pressure. I wrote about meds like this—how they're not really a solution, how they make so much money for pharmaceutical companies. So that makes me a hypocrite, I suppose. And there's a lot about my family in it—my mom, for example. And it's not exactly flattering. And I guess I feel guilty about that. I feel guilty about the success. It feels fake. *I* feel fake. I feel like I made where I'm from seem worse than it is. Like stolen valor or something. It's given me this paralysis. I can't write now. I can't take what I write seriously. It's not real. I don't feel real as a person. I feel like any second, I'm just going to vanish.

Silence. A few clicks of the mouse. Soooo, depression then? she said. I guess.

Okay, great. So we've switched to opexavalatam for depression. It's basically the same thing.

Are there side effects?

Just a few. Agitation, insomnia, constipation, indigestion, headaches, sexual disappointment, sudden flatulence, paranoia, suicidal ideation, unexplained bruising, voracious hunger, incestuous dreams—

All right, I got it. That's all fine.

Wonderful. So with your kind permission, sir, I'll go ahead and resolve this issue for you.

Fine.

She typed for a while, humming a pleasant little tune to herself. The Walmart associate on TV was struggling to continue, her words choked with emotion. *I was on the floor*, she said. *My face was on the floor. My eyes were closed and I covered my ears. It smelled like fireworks. And when I opened my eyes, I just laid there. And the ringing in my ears went away, and all I could hear was dripping. All around me like dripping water. And I realized it was blood.*

Are you seeing confirmation that we've resolved your issue?

His phone buzzed with a confirmation email. Yes, he said, but I still have the wrong pills.

You could flush them.

Is that safe? Environmentally, I mean?

It's not unsafe.

So I should or shouldn't?

We can't advise on that, sir. Anything else?

No, he said. Actually, yes. Do you take these pills?

Sir?

Do you take these pills yourself? Would you give them to a loved one?

The medications we offer through our telehealth services are safe and effective and are taken by millions of Americans.

What's your name?

She paused, cleared her throat. Melissa, she said.

I'm asking you, Melissa, if you would take these pills.

I wouldn't not take them if I needed them, she said. Does that resolve your issue, sir?

He ran his hand over his face, killed the picture on the TV. Yes, he said. That resolves my issue.

THEY ATE LASAGNA for supper. Alice did the dishes after, chipping at the crusted cheese with her thumbnail while the faucet ran. Kathy stood on the porch smoking one of her Mistys, the late sky burning with apocalyptic light. Joel sat on the countertop with his feet dangling, watching his wife as she scrubbed intently, her brow knitted. She had her unwashed hair pulled back. She wore her thrift store overalls with a patch at the knee and a Morrissey T-shirt she'd had for years. When they met, she'd worn all black—black jeans, black turtleneck, black boots. Now she looked like the girls in his class. Not quite a hippie, not quite bohemian. A fashion, he supposed, symptomatic of uncertainty. But she had a genteel face. It betrayed her, no matter what she wore. High cheekbones, long lashes. She looked like an heiress in a John Singer Sargent painting.

Someone called me today, he said. In the woods. An unknown number.

A spam call?

I don't know. They said I was a fraud.

Who did?

The unknown caller.

Maybe it was a joke. Maybe someone we know was fucking with you.

Whose idea of a joke is that? Call your friend and tell him he's a fraud?

She shrugged. She'd resorted to steel wool, gritting her teeth, scraping the sides of the casserole dish. He stood and slipped his arm around her waist. He felt vaguely horny—"vaguely" was often the best he could hope for since starting the antidepressant. His erections were still reliable; he was lucky in that respect. But getting off was impossible. Because he'd kept the pills a secret from Alice, she'd seen it as a waning of their sexual chemistry—or worse, of her own appeal to him. They'd given up on sex months ago.

She took no notice of him pressing himself against her, tracing her hip bones with his thumbs. The steamed air smelled of dish soap. He saw them reflected in the window above the sink. She scrunched her face like she was about to sneeze and brought the back of her wrist to her nose. Soapsuds dripped from her fingers. She met his eyes. The glass both mirror and window. Red sky, black trees.

I'm unhappy, he said to her, in the locked room of his mind. *I'm taking medicine that only sort of works, medicine I don't believe in.*

Maybe it's a guerrilla marketing thing, she said.

What is?

The mysterious call. Maybe they're trying to sell you something.

Sell me what?

She shrugged again, gave the pan another drizzle of soap. Something you've searched recently, she said. Something you've talked about. Our phones listen to us. They know what we want before we do.

Who is "they"?

Whoever's listening, I don't know. I'd like to throw the thing in the trash.

Right. Go off-grid.

Yes, I know, she sighed. It's a right-wing fantasy.

It's an American fantasy, that's for sure.

She nudged him with her elbow, and he let go of her waist. Noam padded into the kitchen then, weaved between Joel's legs in a figure eight, then sat and gazed up at him.

Just a minute, Noam, and I'll get your wet food, Alice said.

I can feed him.

You never feed him.

That's not true. Of course I feed him.

He leaned back against the cabinet and folded his arms, watching her scrub with sudden violence.

Look, I don't like it any more than you do, he said. The notifications, the alerts, the commercials—the relentlessness of it all. I get it, it sucks. But you can't just *retreat* from society.

Why is it retreat? Maybe it's returning to the natural way of things.

There is no "natural" way.

I think you're wrong.

How did we get off on this tangent?

It's not a tangent. It's what I think about every day.

Having a farm?

Having a life that isn't this. She gestured to the room—to the Dream Home around them. Noam meowed feebly, pushing his head against Joel's ankle.

So you're unhappy.

Of course I am. All I do is tell you I'm unhappy. And all you say is to give it time, that we'll come out stronger on the other side.

Because I'm a good partner.

She turned to face him, wiping her wet hands on the bib of her overalls.

So you're telling me you're happy, Joel? Can you look me in the eye and tell me you're happy?

He could see it on a clear day—the end of their marriage. A distant mountain looming above their lives. This huge, implacable thing. And yet he carried on like it wasn't there. He held out hope that something might change—that *he* might change. But he'd never really changed in his life. Not substantially. His fears and longings had carried over from childhood, and he saw the same fears and longings boring like a bright beam into his old age. Still, some part of him believed it was possible. To save his marriage. To save himself from that future.

I'm happy, he said. Of course I'm happy.

Five

EVERYTHING CAME THROUGH the Center. Nondescript boxes. Bubble-wrap envelopes. Pallets of iPhones. Prescription drugs. Live reptiles. Tractor tires taller than a man. There were containers full of live crickets, bound for bait shops, clustered in wire-mesh cages. They gave off heat—like hot breath—and their smell made Emmett gag. His second week, he had a can of tiny American flags, the kind you'd stick in your lawn. One of the boxes broke open, the cardboard soggy from puddled rainwater, and a hundred little flags wrapped in plastic went spilling onto the container floor. They were made in China.

Emmett began to grasp the patterns and repetitions. Flights from Anchorage carried textiles from East Asia, the boxes filled to busting with fabric. Flights from Moline, Illinois, carried John Deere tractor parts, and the cargo from Delhi was often wrapped in canvas, red wax seals on the shipping labels. Sometimes he imagined he could smell the trapped breath of the workers who'd loaded the can, halfway around the world. The food they'd eaten, the cigarettes they'd smoked. The strange air in the places they lived. Their gathered exhalations now mingling with his. He wondered if those people ever thought about him, or if someone down the chain, in some other facility, had any notion of who he might be and how his life had led him to this work.

The mailer cans were easy; you could take armfuls of bubble-wrap envelopes and drop them on the small-sort belt. The iPhones were easy, too. They came on "cookie sheet" pallets, swaddled in plastic, and aside from weighing very little, the boxes were all a uniform size, which made the work of unloading them smooth. Whenever an iPhone pallet arrived, the supervisors would gather and encircle the package handlers as they worked to ensure that no one stole anything. It made Emmett anxious, feeling their eyes on him. The prospect of stealing an iPhone would never have occurred to him, but something about being watched made him want to steal one out of spite.

BUILDING A CARGO AIRPORT in the middle of nothing made housing an issue. Where were the workers to live, after all? Commuting an hour on the winding farm roads grew tiresome for most. For Emmett, even with his newly acquired Mystique, driving back and forth from his mother's was untenable.

In answer to this problem, a condominium complex had been erected near the Center—subsidized by Tempo, of course. It had a plastic, unornamented aesthetic, reminding Emmett of Lego blocks. The complex was called Oakwood Sanctuary, even though the construction had involved clear-cutting a small forest. There were still heaps of stripped timber lying around beyond the parking lot, backhoes and grappling trucks nearby. There were more condos on the way, hundreds of units, and rumors abounded of a shopping center, perhaps even a medical clinic. Lacking a town, they'd made one up. Maybe, Emmett thought, this was the future.

Though his unit was bland and cheaply assembled, and although giant roaches emerged almost nightly from the drain of his kitchen sink, Emmett was glad to have a place of his own. He was glad to have a car and a steady paycheck. With great relish, he scribbled loops of ink over the goals he'd accomplished, till the words were no longer legible. The only items remaining were *Pay off debts* and *Do something creative, something meaningful that will leave a lasting legacy and allow you to face mortality without fear.*

He seldom spoke to his coworkers. It was just the solitary nature of the work. You were stuck in a can, cut off from the outside. But the shifters and ramp workers, hauling cans from the planes to the warehouse floor, were always huddled on the dock, laughing and shooting the shit. They wore orange reflective vests and earmuffs. They tended to be older, men with union seniority, and seemed to spend most of their time doing nothing at all.

One of the ramp workers was named Kaleb. They found that most nights they took their break at the same hour. He was only a few years older than Emmett, the youngest member of the ramp crew, but he'd been at the Center for eight years. His arms were sleeved with barbed-wire tattoos, and he carried himself with the hunched, skulking posture of a coyote. He told Emmett he was overthinking the work.

Every time I look up, you got something swirlin around in your dome, Kaleb said. You're spacing out, contemplating life's immortal questions. The trick is to turn off, go into zombie mode. There's no time to waste like the present.

They were sitting in the break room, eating little bags of sour cream and onion chips. *Cops* was playing on the wall-mounted TV (it was all that ever seemed to be playing at two in the morning). Someone's Hot Pocket exploded in the microwave, flecking the inside glass with red grease. The timer went off and no one came to claim it.

Maybe I'm thinking about the future, Emmett said.

That's the worst thing you can think about. I used to do that. I used to think about pussy, what I'd do on the weekend. I'd think about quitting and selling weed for a while. I ran my brain a mile a minute. What's your path?

Unload.

Who's your soop?

Flaky.

That motherfucker's green as a gourd. My soop, when I started—he told me how to prepare psychiatrically for the long haul.

Who says I'm here for the long haul?

It don't matter if you are or you aren't, Kaleb said. You have to think like you are, or you drive yourself nuts.

Emmett asked him how he'd wound up here. He said he'd grown up in West Virginia. He'd gotten into drugs early, spent time in jail.

I got home from a six-month prison stint, Kaleb said, and went back to my old ways. And I realized I was sitting on the same couch, with the same useless motherfuckers, smokin the same shit, and that if I stayed in Huntington, that would be my life, from here on out. So I moved. I had a cousin out here, said it was good work. That was it.

So you're sober now?

Fuck no. Sobriety's for the weak. He looked over both shoulders, then leaned forward conspiratorially. Speaking of which, do you party?

Sometimes, Emmett said.

We should exchange numbers.

Kaleb handed Emmett his phone. The screen was shattered, splinters of glass coming loose as Emmett typed with his thumbs. We go to this bar most nights, Kaleb said, called Aloha's. Me and the other ramp guys. They stay open till dawn. You should join us.

Kaleb rose and offered a fist bump on his way back to the floor. Stay in the present, bro, he said. It's the only thing that's real.

Off the clock, he spent his time at the Oakwood Sanctuary. Weeks of boredom passed. He slept all morning, though at first light he'd hear the prowling of raccoons on his balcony, their handlike paws scratching at the glass. When he threw back the curtains the first time, they scattered. On the second day, they merely looked at him.

What do you want? he said to the raccoons, standing there in his boxer briefs, one eye closed against the light.

The raccoon closest to the door stood on its hind legs and seemed ready to give an answer.

I live here, Emmett said. Not you. Then he scraped the curtains back and returned to bed.

In the afternoons, he sat on the balcony, bare feet propped on the rail, reading how-to books on screenwriting he'd checked out from the library. They had different formulas and rules, these books, and sometimes gave contradictory advice. But they all made mention of something called the Hero's Journey. It went like this: A character who wants something, who has some defining motivation, confronts a series of trials and challenges, all of which serve to transform him, changing forever the hero's conception of the world and his place in it. At first, Emmett thought the whole notion too simplistic to be of any use. But then, as he applied the formula to his favorite films and books, he saw its truth—not just in art, but in life. What he needed, he reckoned, was his own Hero's Journey. They always began with a Call to Action: someone, or something, lured the hero from his complacent life into the realm of the Unknown.

When his boredom became unbearable, he drove to Paducah, leaving at five in the morning after his shift. The Western Kentucky Parkway was empty at that hour. The first glow of daylight was like the halo of a candle flame in the dark. He chain-smoked cigarettes, ran the Mystique's air conditioner at full blast to keep him awake. Slowly, the countryside revealed itself. The corduroy of tilled fields. Cattle as still as statues. The maples turning yellow at last. Stopping for gas at Beaver Dam, he could smell cured hay in the air, and he knew that autumn had come.

At the house, he found Joel and Kathy drinking coffee in the kitchen. Kathy made a face when he bent down to hug her. Oh, you smell awful, she said. Are you smoking still?

Keeps me awake, Emmett said. Gives me something to do.

You'll be glad you had something to do when you're dead. You'll say to yourself, "I'm glad I smoked those cigarettes."

You smoke, Mom. You've always smoked.

I've cut way back.

Emmett put two pieces of bread in the toaster and pressed down the switch. While he waited, he pictured himself in a coffin, enveloped by darkness, repeating *I'm glad I had something to do* for all of eternity. He wondered where Alice was but didn't want to ask.

Joel was reading a book by Fredric Jameson called *The Political*

Unconscious. Emmett took the seat beside him, scraped butter onto his toast. That any good? he said.

Oh, Jameson's the best. You ever read his stuff?

Emmett shook his head.

It's digestible. Clear without being simplistic. I bet you'd like it.

Emmett didn't care for the implication—that he was the sort of person who could hope to understand only what was digestible, easy to grasp. He knew if he brought this up, however, Joel would give him a puzzled look, say that he'd meant no such thing. Joel had a way of saying something without saying it.

I'm teaching an excerpt, Joel said.

How's your course going?

Oh, okay. These kids—they expect me to lecture, to be an authority. I'd rather have a discussion. But the material's new to them. Only a few have read Marx.

For good reason, Kathy said. And what did I say? If I hear that man's name one more time.

I don't get it, Joel said. If you're such a free thinker—if you're so liberated from the Lamestream Media—then why are you afraid of Big Bad Marx? I mean, I'm not even teaching Marx. He's not even on the syllabus. But the man's name comes up now and then. He's like Jesus or Churchill. He's an historical figure.

He is *not* like Jesus, Kathy said.

Okay, take your pick then—Gandhi, Abraham Lincoln.

What are the lectures about? Emmett said, hoping to defuse their argument before it could develop further.

The loose theme is Despair and Late Capitalism. It's all my usual stuff. Mental illness as a political issue. The commodification of wellness. The hopelessness of rural life.

Kathy rolled her eyes. Who is hopeless? she said. I'm not hopeless.

It's a real problem, Joel said. Deaths of despair. Overdoses, suicides. Obesity, lung cancer. Rates of depression through the roof. How would you explain it?

One word, Kathy said, holding up her finger. Faith. Or rather, the absence of it. Your generation don't believe in God, therefore there's no meaning. But I'll tell you what, I don't know anyone here who's hopeless. People get depressed, okay, sure. But that's brain chemistry. You go to the doctor, you get a pill, you move on. But who is hopeless? That's what I'd like to know. We have new businesses open here every day.

What businesses? Joel said. Name one.

We just had a second Chick-fil-A open on the south side.

Oh, well, a second Chick-fil-A! Joel said. I retract everything. There's hope for the future.

Don't be snotty, Kathy said.

You don't even live here, Emmett said. You don't even live in the South.

He knew this was the weakest point in Joel's intellectual fortifications. He was an outsider. He had gone away by choice and come back to tell the others how miserable their lives were. This was the worst thing you could be in the South. An intellectual carpetbagger.

You ever think you might be viewing things with—what's the opposite of rose-colored glasses? Emmett said.

Glasses that are half-empty, Kathy said. That's the mindset. And that's the mindset of all the socialists, too. They can't see progress. They can't see what's good about the world. They want to make everyone as unhappy as they are.

Alice walked into the kitchen then, puffy-eyed and yawning. She seemed surprised to see Emmett.

It's you, she said.

It's me, Emmett said.

I thought you might be sick or something, Kathy said. Sleeping this late.

It's nine o'clock, Alice said.

We were just talking about progress, Joel said. Did you know there's a new Chick-fil-A on the south side?

Alice ignored this and poured herself coffee. She was wearing a thin green robe, her hair mussed endearingly. Emmett tried not to look at her.

I think we should make a rule, Alice said. No politics before noon.

She sat with them, her hands cupped around a large ceramic mug that Emmett had made at church camp in seventh grade. It was supposed to be a coiled serpent, from the Garden of Eden, but the ropes of clay had been too large, and it looked more like a stack of donuts that grew smaller near the top. The serpent's head had broken off a long time ago.

You're right, Joel said. Let's change the subject. Emmett, how's work?

Emmett explained, as well as he could, what the Center was like. It was bigger than anything he could say about it. Concretely, it was huge. But what Emmett wished to describe, what he could not quite render, even in his own mind, was its symbolic size. It was like being an ant in the engine compartment of a car, he told them. It was loud and hot, full of belts and motors and the blurred motion of pistons. It all seemed to mean something, but you weren't sure what it was. You were just a small creature in the middle of a vast machine that you could neither stop nor comprehend.

Is it union? Joel asked.

Yeah, Emmett said. They take the dues from my paycheck.

Good, Joel said. If you're going to be an ant, better to be a union ant.

JOEL AND EMMETT drove to Starnes Barbecue that afternoon to pick up two pounds of pork shoulder. Kathy had decided, on a whim, to have a backyard get-together that evening, inviting her brother Dale, his wife, Tonya, and Grandma Ruth.

Starnes was a Paducah institution, a small, teal-painted lunch counter near the city park. Emmett waited by the car in a haze of hickory smoke while Joel retrieved the meat. A cord of wood was stacked in the rear, and he watched a man in a long, stained apron push pieces of it into the smoker. The man smiled behind his mustache, noticing Emmett, and raised his hand.

Hidey, he said.

Emmett waved back.

On the way home, the pork in checkered wax paper nestled between them, Joel said he had something to say.

This isn't easy for me to bring up. But there's something we should talk about. I think we both know what it is.

Cold fear spread out along Emmett's shoulders and spine. Alice had told him what happened in the shed. Of course she had. She'd probably made it seem like his fault, like he'd lured her there with drugs and seduced her in a vulnerable state.

Our relationship, Joel said, is not what it should be. It's been eating at me for a long time—we don't talk, we never see each other. It's something I want to remedy.

If relief passed over Emmett's features then, Joel did not seem to notice.

You're busy, Emmett said. You have your own life. I get that.

It's no excuse.

It was true that Joel made little effort. But Emmett was no better. When he looked at their text thread, it was just a series of alternating **Happy Birthday!** messages, stretching back four years. Still, Emmett could not help but feel that Joel bore the responsibility. He was the older brother, after all. He had success and security. For Emmett to reach out and explain his life was somehow a humiliation.

We used to talk a lot when we were kids, Joel said.

You talked. I listened.

We had a lot in common. I'm sure we still do. I want the best for you, you know that, right? I want you to have the best life.

We can talk more, Emmett said. You can call me whenever.

I want you to go back to school. Will you promise me you'll do that?

Maybe sometime. Right now, I like the idea of writing.

The screenplay.

Emmett nodded. Maybe you could help me with it.

I don't know anything about writing screenplays.

Emmett felt, as always, that there were two layers to whatever Joel said. There was the layer of words and what they meant in a literal way. And there was all that the words concealed.

But you're a writer.

I know people in LA, Joel said, and they've all got screenplays in desk drawers. None of them have gone anywhere. My theory is that everyone in LA has a secret screenplay.

You know people in LA? Emmett said. Maybe you could introduce me.

You're missing the point, Joel said. Look, it's great to have dreams. But for most people, creative work—publishing, the entertainment business—it doesn't work out. It's an endless series of mirages.

It worked out for you.

Joel adjusted the vent so that air blew directly on his face. He seemed jittery now, less eager to talk. In a very small way, he said. The world of people who read critical theory, in general, is like a small town. The world of people who read my book is like a small trailer park within that town.

Emmett imagined a small town where everyone read theory, men in camo and NASCAR T-shirts sitting at café tables before their single-wides, thumbing through copies of Foucault and Baudrillard. He felt that to have a few hundred people read something he'd written would be the high point of his life. For Joel, it was small potatoes.

I sound like I'm whining now, Joel said. I feel lucky, don't get me wrong. But there are days when I don't know what I'm doing. I resent my students because they take away from the time I could be working. And my mood depends completely on how well I've worked. It's pathetic. I'm thirty-three years old and my emotions depend on whether the sentences I wrote that morning were insightful and interesting, sentences almost no one will read.

He laughed grimly. Emmett thought he saw a flicker of fear in Joel's eyes then, but it passed quickly. He bumped his fist against Emmett's shoulder and smiled.

Become a nurse, a social worker, he said. Something you'll always know the use of.

You don't think I'm capable of doing what you do.

It's not that, Joel said. We're just different. We're different people.

OCTOBER. THE SMELL of smoldering leaves. Evening light that seemed to shine through a glass of cider. Emmett ate his barbecue on toast and listened to his uncle Dale talk about the hot tub business.

You know a recession's on the way when people quit buying hot tubs, he said. My showroom's empty right now. My job as a salesman—and I'll tell you, it's not an easy job—is to convince your average consumer that his or her budget can accommodate a hot tub purchase, even in these uncertain times.

Dale and his wife, Tonya, were dressed in athletic golf clothes—polos and trousers made of some sweat-wicking material. They looked so much alike—the same plump cheeks, the same coppery hair—they were often confused for siblings. Despite their attire, Emmett had never actually heard of them playing golf.

Brenda Copeland's daughter died in a hot tub, Grandma Ruth said.

You always bring this up, Mom, Dale said. That was twenty years ago. The new models have safety features.

They have what?

Safety features! Dale shouted.

Ruth swatted this away. Brenda's daughter passed out from the heat, she said. They found her the next morning. Why, anybody would pass out! All that steam. It's like being boiled alive.

She had been drinking, Dale said. And why do you always do this? Badmouthing my profession, my livelihood? Do you go around town telling people that hot tubs are death traps?

I don't go anywhere, Ruth said. I gave my car away.

Emmett, Joel, and Alice glanced at each other, stifling laughter. They had poured bourbon and Sprite into coffee thermoses—Ruth did not abide alcoholic beverages in her field of vision—and were by now a little tipsy.

Changing gears, Tonya said. I've decided to breed our Yorkipoos.

Oh yeah? Kathy said.

Dale tore a large bite from his sandwich and wiped the sauce from his lips. Lot of money in Yorkipoos, he said.

They're in high demand, Tonya said. All the poodle mixes, on account of the fact they don't shed.

Lot of money. Dogs are recession-proof.

I had a friend, as a girl, who was bitten by a dog, Ruth said. Her name was Myrna, like Myrna Loy, and she was never the same.

Emmett, I heard you started at Tempo, Dale said. I bet they do well in a downturn.

I have no idea about the corporate side of things. I'm just a package handler.

I'm surprised they haven't automated that.

I'm sure they've got their best minds working on it, Joel said.

Well, naturally, Dale said. Why wouldn't they?

To put people ahead of profits? Joel said. How would you feel if they automated the hot tub industry?

That'll never happen. You need the human touch to sell a hot tub. You need to convince a potential buyer that he deserves to live out his fantasy of luxury. That's what I do. I tell people what they deserve. I sell fantasies. Can a robot do that?

Joel did not respond, and after a long silence, he said, Is that a rhetorical question?

The answer's hell no, Dale said.

It would probably be better if package handling was automated, Emmett said. Then the people who do it could do something else.

What would they do, though? Joel said. That's the question.

Something creative, Emmett said.

Emmett's going to write a screenplay and sell it for a million bucks, Joel announced to the table.

He just might, Alice said.

I wouldn't be surprised, Joel said. I'm not being sarcastic.

It's not about the money, Emmett said.

A man with friends and family has untold riches, Dale said. When the economy goes south, you take stock of your nonmaterial assets. You look around and say, "What a lucky guy I am."

He wants to leave a mark, Alice said. Surely you can understand that.

Of course, Joel said.

Okay, well, no need to be dismissive.

All right, Joel said, what's your idea for a screenplay, Emmett? Let's hear it.

I'm not sure yet, Emmett said. Have you heard of something called the Hero's Journey?

That's like the wheel thing, right? The call to action, known-unknown? I'm skeptical. It's like paint by numbers. If you could follow a recipe and make a piece of art, everybody would do it.

Alice let her fork clatter onto the plate. See, this is what I mean, she said. Do you have to act so superior?

Can I not give my honest opinion?

Alice pushed her chair back from the table and went inside. No one said anything for a while. Everyone but Dale had stopped eating.

Untold riches, he said, cheeks full of pork. No greater treasure than family and friends.

LATER, WHEN THE GUESTS had gone, Emmett sat with his mother in the living room, watching the ten o'clock local news. Alice and Joel were arguing in the antique room, their words just below the threshold of discernibility.

He's going to run that girl off, Kathy said.

Couples have ups and downs, Emmett said.

They've had more downs than ups. And they barely knew each other when they got married. She's too strong-willed for him. He needs a wife. Not a *partner*. Everyone says "partner" now. What happened to "man and wife"? It's like a business arrangement.

It amazed him, sometimes, the way she took Joel's side, even when he'd done so little to deserve it. I know, I know, Emmett said. Your favorite can do no wrong.

I don't have *a favorite*, Kathy said. That's ridiculous. I just think your brother's got a tough row to hoe.

How in the world is that true? He's got it made. What about my row? My row is not particularly easy to hoe at the moment.

You too, Kathy said. I pray for both of you. But your brother's under a lot of pressure. He has dark moods, just like his father. Success comes with pressure.

You don't even approve of his success.

I don't approve of the subject matter, she said. But I approve of the success.

The segment on TV was about a pig with no hind legs named Chris P. Bacon. He visited local nursing homes and hospitals, cheering up the patients. In lieu of hind legs, he'd been given a pair of wheels attached to a harness.

Look at that pig! Kathy said. He's got no hind legs!

She turned up the volume, and they listened to a nonagenarian explain the feelings inspired by Chris P. Bacon and the effect he'd had on the nursing home's morale.

He really zips along, doesn't he? Kathy said.

Emmett found the pig depressing. Why would people who were old and sick, facing death, want to see a disabled pig? Would the pig not simply remind them of their troubles?

It's kind of a bummer, isn't it? Emmett said.

It's inspiring, Kathy said. Look at the obstacles he's overcome.

I think he got some help.

Well, that's inspiring, too, she said. Nothing wrong with asking for help.

When Kathy turned in, Emmett wrapped a stack of oatmeal cookies in a paper towel, poured a glass of milk, and took them to the guest room, where he read *The Bible: For Teens!* It was just past midnight when someone knocked softly on the door. Emmett sat up, brushing cookie crumbs from his chest hair.

Yeah?

The door opened a little and Alice peeked inside.

Can I come in? she said.

Is that a good idea?

Joel sleeps like the dead.

Mom could come out and see you.

Maybe I shouldn't stand in the hallway then.

Emmett motioned her inside and she shut the door gently behind her. There were no other chairs in the room, so she sat on the edge of the bed in her green robe, her hair loose, still damp from the shower.

I'm going to say some things, she said, and you don't have to respond.

Okay, Emmett said.

Joel and I are not in a good place, and we haven't been for a long time. We haven't slept together in eight months. We hardly ever talk. I've told him that things aren't working.

Have you thought about, like, couples therapy or something?

Joel is anti-therapy. Didn't you read his book?

I skimmed it.

Well, he'd never go. He calls it the psychiatric-industrial complex.

Couples have their ups and downs, Emmett said lamely.

Alice seemed not to have heard him, staring at the family photos on the wall above the dresser—Emmett and Joel as naked toddlers, grinning with snowy beards of soapsuds. For the first four years of their lives, Kathy had insisted on "bath time" photo shoots. As a result, there were nude photographs of little Joel and Emmett throughout the Dream Home, prompting the same reliable comments from Uncle Dale at the holidays. *You boys sure had some tiny ding-a-lings!* he'd say, emerging from the hallway bathroom, tipsy from prodigious amounts of Irish coffee.

I've been thinking about what happened between us, she said. I don't expect anything from you. You don't have to say you've been thinking about me too, or whatever. But I've been thinking about it, and I don't feel bad about what we did. It was the nicest thing that's happened to me in a while. I wanted you to know that.

There was nothing worthwhile to say in reply. He'd thought about her, of course. Even in this moment, he longed to pull her close, slip his hands inside her robe, to touch her damp, fragrant hair. But all this desire was useless to him. What could it possibly lead to? Why him? Surely she had other options outside their family, other ways to implode her marriage.

And yet, against his better judgment—against all that was sensible and prudent in him—it was exhilarating to hear her say these things. His life, which had been so empty for so long, felt suddenly full.

Anyway, Alice said, rising from the bed. I said what I wanted to say. Now I'll go.

Emmett whispered her name as she made to leave. She turned back from the doorway to look at him.

I'll come home next weekend, he said. I'll see you then.

She smiled uncertainly. She shut the door and left him alone.

ALOHA'S WAS NESTLED along a strip of motels and storage units near the interstate exit, all of which had sprung up since Tempo's arrival. It was hard to miss: pink neon palm trees blinking above the highway, a thatch roof overhanging the entrance. The place, Emmett thought, seemed caught in an identity crisis. Inside, obligatory gestures toward the tiki aesthetic—carved, bare-breasted mermaids and paintings of Hawaiian maidens in grass skirts—clashed with the usual trappings of a sports bar—flatscreen televisions mounted to the walls, Titans jerseys framed behind glass. The floor was sticky, the soles of his boots peeling away with each step.

Kaleb was alone, the bartender wiping down surfaces with a spray bottle and a rag. Flying solo tonight? Emmett said, taking a stool.

Everybody just left, Kaleb said. We had a blast.

There were two empty shot glasses before him and a half-drunk beer. The rest of the stools were deserted, pushed up neatly against the bar.

Kaleb stared, unfocused, at the television tuned to ESPN, twirling an unsmoked cigarette between his fingers. The tender was a large, chesty woman, and when she bent down to scrub the bar top, her breasts wagging forward, Kaleb nudged Emmett with his elbow and tipped his chin in her direction.

When are we gonna get married, Natasha? Kaleb said.

When you win the lottery, she said.

I buy a ticket every day, Kaleb said. But I never win. I've never won anything in my life, come to think of it. As far as contests go. Special prizes.

Emmett regretted that he'd come. Booze had made Kaleb maudlin, and the bar smelled like spoiled fruit and Clorox. He ordered a pony bottle of Miller and resolved to drink it quickly.

You see the Corvette in the parking lot? Kaleb said.

Emmett shook his head.

It was the only car out there.

Maybe I did. I don't really remember.

It's not the kind of car you forget. Kaleb took a pull from his pint glass and wiped the foam from his lips with his wrist. What if I told you that was my Corvette? What would you say?

I'd say congratulations.

Well, it's mine, Kaleb said. It belongs to me.

They each took a drink, watching the basketball highlights without really watching them.

I bet you're wondering how a guy like me could afford a 2014 Corvette, Kaleb said.

Emmett had not wondered this. He'd known a lot of guys like Kaleb who spent what little money they made on cars. The name for them, he supposed, was "white trash," though he hated to think that way, and figured there were upper-class people, people in Joel's world, who probably thought of *him* as white trash.

There are two answers to that question, Kaleb said. One is that I work a lot of overtime. You work every holiday for time and a half, it adds up. The other answer is that I hustle. I've got several income streams. It's important to diversify your asset clauses, maximize your growth potentiality, know what I mean?

Totally, Emmett said.

So you like to party?

Like I said, sometimes.

I've got some party favors in my car. Let's step out.

Some other time.

I'd like to tell you about an opportunity. He glanced at the bartender, who was texting now on her bejeweled phone, paying them no mind. But it requires privacy, he said.

Emmett looked around, trying to spy a clock, but the bar had none. He wanted to sleep. At the same time, his thoughts kept looping back to the Hero's Journey. Maybe this was his Call to Action. Maybe Kaleb was the archetypal Helper. He'd come to Aloha's in the first place half hoping as much, that his life might soon become a story he could tell.

He sucked back the rest of his beer and gestured to the door.

After you, he said.

THE INTERIOR of the Corvette smelled of grape cigarillos and fry grease, the passenger floorboard littered with fast-food trash. The seats were pocked with tiny burn holes, as though worms had bored their way through the black leather and the yellow foam. Kaleb took a bag of powder from the console compartment.

The guy I buy this from, Kaleb said, he's a Black guy. He calls it "white girls." Like, "You know anybody who needs white girls?"

Kaleb laughed and shook his head. He used his car key to scoop a little of the powder and bring it to his nostril. He sniffed, blinked his eyes hard against the burn, then offered the key and the baggie to Emmett.

Emmett took a small bump, calculating how long it would last and when he'd finally be able to sleep. The grains of coke left a bitter numbness in his throat that he could not swallow away.

I was beginning to think you were an undercover cop or something, Kaleb said.

So what's the opportunity?

Kaleb took his time putting the bag away, checking his nose in the visor mirror. Rochester, Michigan, he said finally. It's a suburb of Detroit.

Okay.

They got two big pharmaceutical plants there.

So what?

So one of the drugs they make is Roxicodone. They ship it out all over the country, to airhubs such as our very own. Let's say, apathetically, there was an individual with access to the manifests, who knew exactly, down to the minute, when the planes from Rochester come in. And let's say, apathetically, that this individual was smart, that he paid attention to patterns, and had figured out which cans contain what.

Kaleb lit a cigarette and sank down in the bucket seat, pleased with himself.

Even if you knew all that, Emmett said, what could you do about it?

That's where you come in, Kaleb said. There's cameras in the warehouse, but they can't see *inside* the cans. You could take off your clothes and jerk off in there, nobody would know. The boxes are small. You wear baggy pants, hide one inside, and go to the bathroom. Then you dump the pills in your underwear, and that's it. You don't set off the metal detector, and the guards won't touch your dick.

I doubt it would work, Emmett said.

I've done it before, Kaleb said. A couple times. I just need a partner.

What happened to your partner in the past?

He went around bragging, jackin his jaw. I tried to set him straight, but you can only do so much. You can lead a horse to water, but you can't look him in the mouth.

What?

He moved on to greener pastures, let's leave it at that, Kaleb said. We can make a few grand a month, no problem. I know a guy who can move them.

Emmett considered all this. He noticed his left knee joggling and clenched his muscles to keep it still. The thought of money, in his state of mind, was like the thought of food or water. It was something pure and happy, uncomplicated. With money, he could move wherever he wanted—New York, Los Angeles. With money, he could become someone who would never be required to heave packages onto a conveyor belt or deep-fry a battered onion or deliver a bag of sandwiches to a strip club. He could become someone like Joel and Alice.

I'll think about it, he said.

Six

ABOVE THEIR SHARED DESK, Alice and Joel kept a corkboard with postcards and photographs and ticket stubs. All the small precious things they could not bear to throw away. Joel had prints of Thomas Cole's *The Course of Empire* from the New-York Historical Society. They depicted, in five paintings, a civilization's rise and fall, from pastoral beginnings to final ruin. Alice had a postcard of Jules Bastien-Lepage's *Joan of Arc*. She would visit the Met sometimes just to see it. The girl-saint stood in a wild garden, a cottage nearby. Her feet were bare and dirty. She peered into the middle distance, as though something beyond the plane of the painting had not quite resolved itself in her vision. Meanwhile, floating over her shoulder, the apparitions of Saints Michael, Catherine, and Margaret watched over the peasant girl, knowing her secret future.

There were other things—birthday notes, broadsheet poems, photobooth strips. There were blurry pictures of Noam—batting at feather wands, perched like a gargoyle atop the refrigerator. It was supposed to be a well of inspiration, this corkboard. A reminder of all they cherished. But sometimes, when Alice stood in the silent room, regarding their mementos, she felt as though they belonged to some other couple, their meanings cryptic. Even *Joan of Arc*. It had seemed to Alice lately that what waited for her was not the Divine. Nor was it death at the stake, the triumph of martyrdom. What she saw in the distance was only the horizon of her small life.

WHEN THEY LEFT for Kentucky, Alice packed the postcard—a small piece of New York. Joel sold the trip as a country sojourn, a reprieve from the hectic pace of the big city. *If you want your farm so bad, you better get used to the middle of nowhere.* The implication was that she did not really want this. The isolation, the hardship. And sometimes she thought he was right. It galled her to acknowledge this.

A few days after the encounter with Emmett in the garden shed, she called her friend Mabel in New York. Joel and Kathy had gone to lunch, leaving her alone with Noam. Alice sat in the kitchen alcove on sun-warmed cushions, her knees drawn up to her chest. Noam lay beside her, basking and dreamy-eyed.

I think I have a crush, Alice said.

Mabel seemed to be cooking—Alice could hear pots clanging, the snap of a gas burner igniting. They'd been friends since elementary school. Mabel's partner had inherited some money, more than either of them knew what to do with. Accordingly, they'd left the city during the pandemic for a little house in Hudson. She'd become pregnant shortly after, and now her daughter, Rosemary, was one year old.

Uh oh, Mabel said. Where are you again? Alabama?

It's Kentucky, Alice said. Joel's from Kentucky.

Why did I think Alabama?

I don't know.

Rosemary made a squealing, cranky sound, and Mabel shushed her. Is it one of the locals? she said.

You could say that, Alice said.

Well, I've had crushes, Mabel said. It's natural. This barista—oh my God. When we lived in Park Slope, I'd drink four oat milk lattes a day just to hear this jacked guy say, "I'll bring it out to you." Then we had a longer conversation, and turns out, his side gig was eating raw meat in YouTube videos. He called himself Raw Dog and had millions of views. Point being, crushes come and go. They're fleeting. Doesn't mean you don't love your husband.

Alice looked out the window to the locked shed in the backyard. She thought of herself singing her stupid song and closed her eyes. Maybe "crush" is the wrong word, she said. I'm not even sure the fantasy's about him. Maybe it's more about having an excuse.

An excuse for what?

For leaving. For leaving Joel.

Oh, Mabel said. She sighed and seemed to move the phone to her other ear. Well, I'm sure that will pass, too, she said, sounding unsure.

I don't know what I'm doing here, Alice said. I feel completely lost.

Rosemary began to cry then. What did Mommy say? Mabel said. What did Mommy *just* say?

I'll let you go, Alice said.

Are you sure? I really want to catch up.

No, it's fine. She smeared the tears from her eyes with her palm.

Okay, love, Mabel said. Just remember, you can leave. You can stay with me, come back to civilization. Just say the word.

Alice nodded, though there was no one but Noam to see her. After she'd hung up, she petted his fur, hot from the sunlight. Would you like to go back to civilization? she said.

He looked at her with half-lidded eyes, purring deeply.

That night, Alice lay awake for hours. She could hear the jake brakes of semitrucks on the state highway and the creaking of the ductwork when the air kicked on. Joel slept soundly beside her, his breath sucking and nasal. Noam carried out his strange nocturnal rituals, nudging open doors, clawing the Berber carpet, scrambling across the kitchen linoleum for no reason whatsoever. It was quieter than Astoria by far, but in that unnerving quiet, she could hear too much.

At five in the morning, she sat up and said, This is stupid.

Joel mumbled something in his sleep and she caressed his hair. She liked to watch him sleep; she saw, in the slack innocence of his face, a shadow of the boyishness she'd been so fond of when they met. And it was the only time when he did not have an opinion, though she wondered if he argued in his dreams.

She dressed silently, slipping on her overalls and her ragged canvas sneakers, and went out into the dark. The night was clear and clean, a blizzard of starlight above. The air smelled of damp hay. She went to the shed, punched in the Bible verse code. *I will not think of Emmett,* she told herself as the door shrieked open, but seeing the guns and the can of gasoline and the space where they'd stood so close, she felt her heart pound at the exhilaration of the memory.

She gathered a pickaxe, a hoe, and a claw-tined cultivator, and found a flat open space in the yard beyond the shade of the walnut tree. Then she set to work, first with the pickaxe, raising it high overhead and swinging down with all her might, the blade thudding against the earth. Each time she pried the blade loose, the webbing of roots in the sod wrenched and snapped. She used the hoe next, chopping the clods into smaller and smaller pieces, then the cultivator, dragging the tines through the bed, tossing out the stones. By the time the sky had paled in the east and the stars had dimmed, she'd dug a bed the length of a sedan, and about half as wide.

Kathy came out in her housecoat for the day's first cigarette and looked at Alice with a kind of puzzled amazement. Alice waved, winded and leaning against the cultivator. Kathy walked over with her mug of coffee and her Misty already lit.

I thought I'd take you up on your offer, Alice said.

My offer?

To do a little gardening.

Kathy looked at the bed of dirt where only yesterday there had been grass. Well, okay then, she said. I'm glad.

There was too much clay in the soil, so she drove to the hardware store in town and bought three bags of compost. While there, she snagged some seed packets—mostly lettuces and mustards. When she returned, Joel was standing with a cup of coffee exactly where his mother had stood, looking at the bed as though it were a crop circle that had appeared mysteriously overnight.

When did this happen? he said.

This morning.

She hauled over the bags, sawed them open with a car key, and dumped them into two piles. Then she began to work the black compost into the reddish dirt. Joel watched her, his brow taut, now and then slurping his coffee.

This is kind of a lot, he said finally.

Your mom offered.

I think she was just being nice.

Do you want to help?

I just showered. What are you even going to plant? I thought spring was planting time.

A crop of lettuce, she said. We're far enough south for a winter harvest.

You look exhausted.

She looked down at herself. She'd sweated through her overalls and her tanned arms were smeared with black up to the elbows. The webbing of her right thumb was worn raw. A blister had formed and burst; it stung when she stopped working long enough to notice it.

I feel great, she said, and she meant it. She was never so happy as in moments like this—the early sun on her neck, hands dirty, utterly spent.

Joel wandered off after a few minutes and left her alone. She raked the bed for a long time, stopping only when the soil's tilth was like ground coffee, then she made furrows with the long handle of the hoe. She poured the tiny seeds into her cupped palm and sprinkled them into the grooves—first arugula and oakleaf lettuce, then mizuna and tendergreen and tatsoi. When she'd covered the furrows and watered the bed with the garden hose, she sat in the grass, a little dizzy, and admired her work. Sunlight had pooled and flared above the tree line, its warmth an early hint of the day's heat. In the open field beyond the yard, the meadowgrass glittered, spider silk jeweled with dew. Tired as she was, she could almost convince herself she was viewing a scene from her future. One day her life would be like this. She would till and plant and spray the mud from her tools, and she would know she'd spent her time well.

MOST MORNINGS, after coffee, Kathy and Joel went for a walk around the subdivision. Alice relished the time alone. She practiced what she would say to Joel with Noam as her scene partner. She sat on the edge of the couch cushion, fingers clasped in her lap. Noam sat on the coffee table, licking his paw, then using the wet paw to clean the backs of his ears.

Joel, I'm leaving you, she said. I'm not happy anymore, and things have not been good between us.

Noam looked at her with mild curiosity, cocking his head to the left and right.

It's not your fault. We just moved too fast and I wasn't ready. I feel I'm not living up to my potential. I used to have dreams. I don't know what happened to them. They seem like jokes now. The future I want seems impossible. I keep picturing this little house with a sprawling garden. There are flowers and bees. I live there and I marvel at drops of pond water like Annie Dillard. I don't know if this is realistic, or what realistic means anymore. But if I don't try—if I can't try—I don't know what I'll do.

Noam waited patiently for her to finish, then crawled into her lap and kneaded her chest with his paws.

Oh, Noam, she said.

She hugged him tight, which he did not like but was willing to tolerate for a few seconds before squirming away.

She tested many versions of this monologue, none of which involved Emmett or what had happened between them. She could not see the point in needlessly hurting Joel's feelings. Then again, his feelings protected him completely. He wore his wounded decency like a carapace, impossible to puncture. She would have to really say it—*I don't love you anymore*—and he knew she couldn't. He would call her bluff. He depended on her inability to hurt him, that she could never be *that person*, and she proved him right with every day that passed. She wanted to destroy something priceless, to release a shattering wail. To say something irrevocable and pitiless. But she kept it all inside, and it leaked out little by little. Joel bore with her spells of moody silence, her sudden sour remarks. He tried to cheer her up. I want you to be happy, he would say, though she felt that all he really wanted was peace. He wanted a happy wife. There were times when she felt he deserved this. She imagined using this line to end things. *You deserve so much.* In this way, her decision to leave could be cast as a selfless act. He would thank her one day.

In other moments, she was skewered by guilt. Thank her for what? For messing around with his brother? For touching herself, imagining the scrape of Emmett's whiskers on her neck? That it was spectacularly self-destructive was part of its appeal. It could have been anyone, but she'd gone and picked her brother-in-law. Classic Alice. She scoured online forums where people confessed to sleeping with their spouse's siblings. The community responses were less than helpful. Your a terrible person and you should probably kill yrself, said Dragonborn69.

Even though the post was over three years old, she made an account and responded.

Sometimes people have stuff going on in their lives that you don't know about. It's reductive to say that anyone who sleeps with their spouse's sibling is a terrible person. There's never one reason for anything. It's overdetermined. And I guess Dragonborn69 has never made a mistake in their life? Maybe we should all strive to empathize with situations we don't understand.

She thought the post would go unanswered, but two days later Dragonborn69 replied, You can empathize with deez nuts.

ALICE SPOKE TO her therapist via Zoom. He was a bearish, gray-bearded man named Jerry who sat in his home office, surrounded by stacks of books and hand-thrown Japanese pottery. She wasn't sure if he was a good therapist, but she liked talking to him. He always asked about Noam.

He told her what he always told her—that ending a marriage was a major decision, and she should be quite sure before she took any steps.

I never hear you say anything nice about Joel, Jerry said. What did you like about him when you got together? Surely there was something.

Alice thought back to the University of Illinois, where they'd met. Joel was teaching a course on poststructuralism. She was in the second year of her PhD, already sensing its uselessness. Already feeling as though she'd been duped somehow.

He was very impressive, Alice said. He had a book coming out, a teaching position.

Okay, so professional accomplishment. What else?

Alice strained to remember, becoming painfully conscious of how much time was passing.

Tell you what, why don't you write it down? Next time, we'll discuss.

But I know I want to leave him. I know that.

And yet you haven't. Why?

Alice let out a groan of exasperation. Noam hopped into her lap, his tail swishing near her face. I'm afraid, I guess, she said. Of being alone.

Okay, maybe, Jerry said. Or maybe there's some guilt at play. Maybe you feel you owe him something.

Guilt for what? Alice said. She had not told him about the kiss.

You're asking me? What do I know? That's why I'm giving you homework. Think about who you were when you met him. Put yourself in that young woman's shoes. What were her values? What did she want in life? Figure that out, and maybe you'll see how you've changed now.

All through dinner, Alice stared at the pale canvas of the wall, thinking of her therapist's assignment. Kathy and Joel had a mild argument about whether colleges were indoctrinating students. (*Of course they are,* Joel said, *they're supposed to.*) Kathy asked Alice a question, and when she failed to respond, Joel snapped his fingers near her ear.

Earth to Alice, Joel said.

Sorry, what?

I was just asking if you still planned to teach someday, Kathy said.

Not really, Alice said.

Oh, that's not true, Joel said. You still look at job postings now and then.

The academic job market is horrible. I don't have publications. And I never finished my degree. I went to live with you in New York, remember?

You'll finish your PhD eventually. I'm one hundred percent certain.

Alice felt herself gripping the steak knife by her plate. She imagined stabbing it into Joel's hand, pinning it to the table.

Even if I did, she said, there are, like, five tenure-track positions that become available every cycle. In America—not just New York.

There's a lot of competition then, I imagine? Kathy said.

That's an understatement, she said. She explained that it was not really a vocation but more of a pyramid scheme. That the livelihoods of the established professors depended on new recruits—gullible people who thought that a philosophy degree was noble or something. But she felt, as she spoke, like she was only reciting a line from a script. The words formed themselves—a readymade opinion, too much like one of Joel's—and she found herself staring out the window at the patch of ground she'd broken, the first tiny seedlings already wriggling up to the sun and the warm air.

Hence my farm dream, she said.

Kathy laughed. You and your farm, she said. It's so funny to me. I grew up on a farm, and all I wanted was to leave. I wanted an easier life. Now young people want to go back to the hard way.

I would think you'd like the hard way, Joel said. Make America Great Again—all that.

It's not so much the hardship, but the way people were with each other. You knew your neighbors. You went to church. Nobody needed welfare because we all took care of each other.

Welfare is just a systematized way to take care of each other.

We did it because it was right, not because it was *mandated*. When you make it a system, you take the feeling out of it. You take out the good intention. Do you feel warm and fuzzy when you pay your taxes?

You can't pass an offering plate to four hundred million people.

Those aren't my neighbors.

There it is. That's the crux. Your circle of moral consideration is limited to people who are like *you*.

Alice stood from the table abruptly and brought her plate to the sink. Joel and Kathy looked at her.

Where are you going? Joel said.

I can't listen to this argument again.

Again?

It's all the same argument. Variations on a theme.

She's right, Kathy said. We were talking about Alice's future. Her dreams.

I think they're goals, not dreams, Joel said. Alice is so smart, she can do whatever she wants. But dreams are unattainable by nature.

You never had dreams? Alice said.

I was realistic. Emmett was the dreamer. Still is, with all his Hollywood talk.

Maybe Emmett has stuff going on in his life that we don't know about, Alice said. I think we should strive to empathize with situations we don't understand.

Where would you buy land? Kathy said.

Her father keeps offering, Joel said. He's got money to spare.

For the last year or so, Alice's father, Fletcher, had periodically offered to buy her a house. There were stipulations, foremost among them that she live somewhere near Springfield, so that he might some-day live close to his grandchildren. He was a retired ophthalmologist who still earned a sizable income from the run-down apartment complex he owned. Once, she'd had an argument with Joel where he'd insinuated, without saying as much outright, that her father was a slumlord. He'd used the term "petit bourgeois." It made her livid at the time for obvious reasons, not least of which that Joel was prob-ably right, and that she preferred to think of her father as the lanky, white-coated, kindhearted physician who resembled Jimmy Stewart and told corny jokes to his patients—not a man who funded his vaca-tions to Aruba with rent paid by desperate tenants.

Fletcher's idea was to buy a duplex for Alice so she could rent the other half. Then you have someone else paying your mortgage, he'd explained. She had always gently refused these offers.

He doesn't have *that* much money, she said.

Joel's attention had lapsed, his expression suddenly ruminative. Maybe to have the sense of community—of neighborliness—you need hardship, he said. Maybe you can't have one without the other.

When he mused aloud like this, she knew he wasn't really speak-ing to her. He was speaking to himself, his publisher, his readership of five. She would not give him the satisfaction of a response.

I'm going to lie down, she said.

In the antique room, Alice read by the light of a green opaline lamp. She'd brought along a book of Rachel Carson's letters, a trans-lation of Bashō's poetry, and a few permaculture design guides, which she looked at now and then, trying to envision her future garden.

When her eyes began to hurt and the text blurred, she set her book on the nightstand and picked up the postcard of *Joan of Arc*, which she'd been using as a bookmark. She stared at the girl—her fierce blue eyes, the ragged laces of her shirt. Her outstretched hand seemed to sink into the painted foliage, as though she were the only real thing against an unreal backdrop.

Alice opened her diary and began to write.

A TRANSITIONAL PERIOD. This was how she preferred to think of her second year of graduate school. It was not yet clear to her what two phases she found herself between. "Adolescence" and "adulthood" seemed too obvious. But there was a definite feeling by that fall that the first part of her life was ending, the part wherein her future could be anything, could take any shape. The part wherein one could say, *I have plenty of time,* and mean it.

Her parents had begun to remind her of her age. When she'd announced her intention to get a PhD, they kept asking how old she'd be when she finished. They went on asking her every time they phoned those first two years. *I'll be thirty-two,* she'd say, *thirty-two years old,* and her mother would make some whimper of distress on the other end of the line. Then her father would come on and say, *You can leave, you know—I'll come get you,* as if the philosophy department at U of I were an abusive partner, holding her against her will.

In October, when she met Joel, Alice was twenty-eight. She sometimes forgot her age. She'd be standing in line at the bank or the DMV, filling out a form, and ask herself, *Am I twenty-eight or twenty-seven?* Then she'd remember her last birthday—a weekend in Chicago with Min and Toby. They'd gone to an arcade bar in Old Town, and standing out back, passing their only remaining cigarette, Min had said, Well, it's official. You don't have to worry about the Twenty-Seven Club.

When Alice had only looked at her, confused, she'd said, You know, like Kurt Cobain, Janis Joplin, Amy Winehouse. They all died at twenty-seven. So you don't have to worry about, like, drowning in your own vomit or OD'ing in a Paris hotel.

You can die at twenty-eight, Toby had said helpfully. You can die anytime.

Alice considered this—that she was getting older, that one could die at any moment—on her way to Beaver's Tavern. It was one of very few dive bars in Urbana where grad students and TAs could gather without running into their students (and without the inescapable panorama of TV screens playing college football or basketball). Beaver's Tavern had a single TV and a stack of old horror movies on VHS—*Creature from the Black Lagoon*, *Invasion of the Body Snatchers*. If a stray undergraduate ever wandered in, the glowering of the bartenders alone was enough to send him packing.

Alice finished her cigarette outside, watching a tornado of leaves swirl past on the street. Autumn in central Illinois was almost nonexistent; you got a week if you were lucky, then a bitter wind would strip the trees, announcing rudely the arrival of winter. She'd learned to savor evenings like this, the yellow maples fluttering, woodsmoke somewhere distant.

Inside, she ordered a pint of Guinness and found Toby and his girlfriend, Jessica, in a back booth. Toby was from Chicago, another PhD. Jessica had moved with him, leaving behind their apartment in Wicker Park, and was ostensibly a graphic designer, though she never seemed to be working, and openly hated Champaign-Urbana. Her resentment, at uprooting her life and coming here, had poisoned their relationship. Everyone could see this except for Toby, who had the oblivious, cheerful demeanor of a golden retriever.

When Alice sat across from them, Jessica was staring at the stuffed, mangy-looking beaver mounted above the top-shelf liquor bottles.

Everything okay? Alice said.

That beaver is covered with black mold. It's a health hazard.

Oh come on, Toby said. It's just Buddy the Beaver.

Buddy? Alice said.

Yeah, that's what the bartenders call him. It's, like, an affectionate moniker.

There's black mold in the bathroom, too. It's probably all over. I'm sure we're breathing it right now.

It's probably just regular mold. Hey, what did one mold spore say to the other mold spore at the mold party?

Jessica turned to him with absolute indifference. I don't know, she said.

Or, wait, lemme start over. What did the girl mold spore say to the boy mold spore at the mold party?

Just tell me the punchline.

You're a fungi.

Alice snickered helplessly, not so much at the joke but at Jessica's obvious disdain.

Get it? It's like *fun-guy, fun-gi.*

I get it.

One of my students told me that. I have a student who starts off every class with a new joke.

Well, aren't you lucky, Jessica said. She took a sip of her whiskey and looked around like she was trying to spot the exit.

We were just talking about Joel Shaw, Toby said.

Who? Alice said. The name sounded familiar.

He's in the philosophy department, Toby said. A lecturer. Part of the Continental Crew.

There were roughly three camps in the philosophy department. Environmental ethics, Alice's scene, attracted militant vegans and Buddhists and aspiring ecoterrorists. The analytic crew, to which Min and Toby belonged, was comprised of mathematically inclined nerds who were not so mathematically inclined as to thrive in one of the hard sciences, and who ended up writing tedious dissertations on set theory or semantic parsing. Then there were the continental boys— and they were all boys. This last group had little to do with the other two. They often had backgrounds in literature. They dealt with "texts"— never books—and were politically subversive. They tended to keep to themselves, their theories all but incomprehensible to their peers.

He wrote this essay—it's all over Twitter apparently, Toby said. We were sitting at home and Jess was like, Don't you know this guy? And I was like, Oh shit, that's Joel.

All over Philosophy Twitter or all over Twitter?

Real Twitter. I don't even have an account, but Jess told me.

It's about QAnon and Kentucky and family drama, Jessica said. It's light on philosophy, so I liked it.

He teaches an intro class here and drives to Chicago once a week to teach a cultural studies course. Somebody said he's getting a book deal out of it.

Because of Twitter?

Yeah, because it's blowing up.

Well, shit, Alice said. Good for him.

They observed a long moment of silence. The University of Illinois was far from renowned. To pursue a degree in philosophy there was, in general, a fairly pointless exercise. To hear of someone's success— especially mainstream success—was like fighting an unjust war in some faraway land and learning that a brother in arms had been sent home with a minor injury.

He'll be here tonight, Toby said. With Min. They matched on Tinder. She wasn't sure whether to go out with him, then this whole thing happened, and she was sold.

I'm gonna tell them about the beaver, Jessica said, downing the rest of her whiskey.

We're back on the mold? Toby said.

If they won't deal with it, the health department should.

It's their mascot, Jess. They're not gonna take it down.

Well, I have asthma, okay? I can't keep coming here and subjecting myself to a public health hazard.

While Jessica confronted the bartenders about the moldy beaver, Alice and Toby went for a smoke. The night was brisk and dry. The sound of distant frat parties reached them with a strange clarity. Laughter and chanting. The pulse of drums. Alice missed Chicago, where she'd studied as an undergrad. Champaign-Urbana was too much like Springfield, too close to her childhood memories. The stink of feedlots on the breeze in summer. The stupor of Benadryl in spring, eyes blurred and stinging. Endless, oceanic fields of corn. There were certain undergraduates that she thought of as "corn boys." They were so white, their hair so much like pale corn silk, that they seemed to have been crossbred with the plant itself somehow. She imagined a top secret collaboration between the CIA and Monsanto.

She tried to explain her "transitional period" to Toby. I'm standing in a threshold, she said, with one foot in each room. One room is my world here—the department, my so-called career. The other room is . . . life, I guess? Maybe farming? Maybe seminary? Push out a few babies, join a cult. Who knows.

I vote for joining a cult, Toby said. That could be fun. Or *starting* a cult.

I'm serious. I'm at a crossroads.

You're not really thinking of quitting, though, right?

I don't know, she said. Would that be terrible? I mean, haven't you ever thought about quitting?

Toby frowned and took a deep pull from his cigarette. Honestly? he said. I've never once thought about that. I love my life here.

You don't think about parallel universes where you're doing something else?

I'm sure those quantum copies of Toby love their lives, too.

This isn't helping, Alice said.

Okay, well, look, you gotta narrow down your alternatives a little bit. Farming and having babies is on one end of a spectrum, and going to divinity school is definitely on the other end. "All of the above" isn't really possible.

Toby flicked his filter and punched Alice's shoulder playfully, knocking her off-balance. Alice suspected, at times, that Toby was a little bit in love with her, and that these backslapping moments of brotherly affection were overcorrections. You'll figure it out, he said. You've got plenty of time.

Alone, she sighed, glancing at the ember of her half-smoked Spirit, wishing she was done with it. She'd spent the last six months dabbling in "all of the above"—except for having babies, which would require meeting someone who did not bore her after a while, whose interests did not, eventually, turn out to be shallow, and whose hopes for life were not small. She traced this period of dabbling and uncertainty back to a single night in May, when she'd found herself in Min's kitchen, eating a peanut butter sandwich with a fistful of crunchy, barnyard-smelling mushrooms between the slices of bread. She'd spent the next four hours on a crocheted blanket in the backyard, needles of grass poking through the yarn, staring like a slack-jawed ape at the moon; then calling her grandmother, her high school boyfriend, and her parents, in that order, to tell them she was dying; then riding in an ambulance with a kind EMT who gave her Valium and told her that nothing was permanent.

It was one of those moments she'd read about but never thought she'd encounter. *And then everything was changed*—who could say this with a straight face? And yet here she was, changed completely. In the deepest thralls of her trip, she had seen with absolute, unassailable clarity that her life was a performance. The story she lived was not her own. It was given to her—by parents, companies, institutions. It wasn't fixed, this narrative. It was provisional. When her EMT, her guardian angel, told her that nothing was permanent, he'd meant the drugs. But Alice had burst out laughing on the gurney, a great burden lifted.

The drugs weren't solely responsible. For a long time, she'd felt tired of so many things—tired of drinking, tired of the posturing and defensive irony of grad school, tired of Beaver's Tavern and the corn boys and the flat, sterile sameness of the Midwest, its okey-doke geniality, its casseroles, its dirty piles of snow in grocery store parking lots. Still, the mushroom sandwich had given her what she might call an epiphany, a little shove over the edge. The story of her pursuits since that night, she realized now, was not very original. Like any recently enlightened person, she sought out ways to revisit that state of mind. For a few months, she went to a meditation center in Bloomington. The rishi, a man named Cooper Blanton, had made a bunch of money with a tech startup, and left it all behind to live the life of a bodhisattva. She'd leapt headfirst into the world of Buddhism in the beginning, and though she still went to the Zen center occasionally, she'd become disenchanted after a while. The other practitioners seemed so allergic to pleasure, so committed to self-denial, that Alice began to suspect they were all masochists. They'd abandoned every attachment except their attachment to nonattachment, and their moralism masqueraded as neutral truth-telling—the worst kind of moralism.

Christianity, the tradition in which she'd been raised, was next on her list. Her parents were Episcopalians—a stolid, decent denomination—and for a few weeks, she attended the various Episcopal churches in the area. She threw in a Unitarian church for good measure and a Lutheran church with pride flags draped over the castle-like entrance. But try as she might, she found herself unable to stomach the middle-aged, Prius-driving, ponytailed man singing "If I Had a Hammer" she encountered in every progressive congregation she visited.

Nothing, finally, was commensurate with the radiant, unspeakable truth she'd glimpsed that night in Min's backyard—no system of thought, anyway. When she looked back at all the "isms" that had interested her at one time or another (pantheism, Buddhism, alcoholism), they all seemed to lead to the same dead end. The only time she felt content anymore was at the community garden—pulling weeds, pushing a wheelbarrow of compost. Working herself to the point of exhaustion. It wasn't thoughtless work, but it wasn't a "system of thought." Either it worked or it didn't. Either the seeds you planted grew into something, or they died.

The sky had darkened over Beaver's Tavern. All these thoughts were aswarm in her mind when Min and Joel walked up.

Hey, it's you! Min said, throwing open her arms.

It's me, Alice said.

They embraced while Joel stood back, his head bowed. Min was dressed casually in a floral skirt and a ragged denim jacket, her cheeks splotched pink from alcohol. Joel was comically overdressed. He wore a herringbone blazer with patches at the elbows and a pair of pressed slacks—the sort of outfit professors wore in movies but not in real life, which she decided was sort of endearing. When he looked up, she realized they'd met before, though she'd never known his name.

I've seen you around, she said.

Yeah, ditto.

Congratulations, she said, on going viral or whatever.

Oh thanks, he said, unable to look at her. It's weird.

Do you feel famous?

He laughed a little, then coughed and rubbed his nose, looking down at the pavement. He seemed to have a cold, or maybe just bad allergies. His stray-dog eyes, his stooped shoulders and stodgy clothes, made her want to help him somehow—to give him soup or Tylenol, a pair of mittens. Something.

I feel about the same, he said.

Well, everyone's talking about you in there.

Go soak it up, Min said. I'll be right in.

Min watched Joel shuffle inside, then looked over both shoulders, ensuring that no one was in earshot. I don't think it's going to work out, Min said. He's hard to talk to.

I can see that, Alice said.

Plus he's into, like, Lacan and Derrida. I told him I thought those guys were full of shit, and he got all quiet.

Alice laughed. Can we expect the people we date to like the same writers we like? Shouldn't we just be grateful that they read at all?

Can one read Derrida? Min said.

It was cozy inside, the Naugahyde booth warm with body heat. Someone had put Bowie's "Sound and Vision" on the nearby juke-box, and Alice sat snugly, watching the bass notes ripple in her beer. Outside, some sorority girls were walking stiffly in high heels, pulling down their skirts to cover their legs. It was forty degrees and none of them were wearing coats. Min and Toby exchanged the latest departmental gossip. Apparently an undergraduate—a corn boy, Alice figured—had brought a gun to an intro class. It wasn't to shoot anybody, Min said. He just had an open carry permit and thought, Why not bring my gat to a lecture on Aristotle's *Poetics*?

His *gat*? Toby said.

Yeah, in all the West Coast early '90s hip-hop songs, they call guns "gats."

That doesn't mean *you* can say it.

I'm from the West Coast.

You're from Seattle, not Compton.

Whatever, she said. Ryan was teaching the class, and he said he just froze when he saw it. Like, what do you even do? What do you say?

Jesus, Toby said. This fucking country.

I would walk right out, Jessica said. It's a public safety hazard. She seemed to have forgotten about the beaver, having lodged her official complaint with the barkeepers.

What would you do? Min said to Joel.

He had hardly touched his beer. He sat there across from Alice with his fingers laced on the table, listening without speaking, sneezing occasionally, seeming neither bored nor interested.

I grew up around guns, he said. So it wouldn't be a shock.

Your parents were gun nuts? Min said.

I wouldn't say that. Everybody in the South has guns.

Did you shoot them?

Oh yeah. I was pretty good, too.

So it wouldn't disturb you? If one of your students walked in strapped?

You can't say "strapped," either, Toby said.

I only teach majors, Joel said. I don't get the freshman riffraff.

Oh, well, Mr. Fancy Pants, Min said.

Where'd you grow up? Alice said.

Kentucky, Joel said.

Alice waited for him to elaborate, and when he said nothing, she felt an overpowering need to fill the silence. Did you like it there? she said. Was it nice? I've been thinking about where I should live after this.

Joel looked at her, unsure whether she was serious.

Alice is having a quarter-life crisis, Toby said. She's thinking of quitting.

No! Min said. You can't quit! Who would I talk to?

Toby cleared his throat theatrically.

Is this about the mushrooms? Min said from the corner of her mouth.

I'm just asking because I bet land is cheap there, Alice said.

You're buying *land*? Min said. For what?

To farm? I don't know. Maybe I'd just live in a hovel and let it turn back into wilderness.

So you'd become a witch, basically, Min said. That's your five-year plan.

Alice frowned thoughtfully. You know, becoming a witch might disappoint my parents less than becoming a philosopher.

Disappointing our parents is an art form, Min said. You have to let them down slowly. I told them philosophy majors have the best LSAT scores. That bought me some time.

Land *is* cheap there, to answer your question, Joel said. But the only places where land is cheap are places where no one wants to live, places that aren't close to anything.

He took a drink, lifting the glass with both hands, seeming only to touch his lips to the beer foam. His gaze was always roving, flitting from one thing to another, unless he addressed you directly, in which case it was steady and utterly attentive.

Maybe I don't want to be close to anything, Alice said. Except for maybe God and nature. Then again, maybe God and nature are the same thing.

Min shook her head ruefully. I never should've given you those mushrooms, she said.

The crowd at Beaver's Tavern began to thin, leaving long stretches of silence on the jukebox. Alice grew sleepy, sipping her third Guinness, listening to the clack of pool balls and the soft murmur of conversation. Toby and Jessica yawned in unison and said they'd better hit the road. Min saw her opportunity for escape. She hugged Joel, gave him a sisterly peck on the cheek. It was great hanging with you! she said. Then she hugged Alice, told her not to become the Unabomber, and hurried out.

For an excruciating amount of time—half a minute at least—Alice and Joel sat in silence, glancing about, smiling tightly whenever they made eye contact.

So you believe in God? Joel said finally. He was still drinking the first beer he'd ordered.

Oh, I don't know, she said. Sometimes I think I do.

Me too. It's hard to say it with a straight face, though.

She agreed that it was. She was picking at the varnish on the table and a splinter embedded itself under her thumbnail. She winced, squeezed her thumb in her lap. Joel was looking into her eyes now with a frank, open expression. He seemed to her like an old boy or an adolescent old man, she wasn't sure which. He was balding. His head was not the right shape for total baldness, but it would be a few years before that became an issue. He transformed when he smiled, became young again. His eyes were the color of celery.

And you're unhappy with the program? he said.

He watched her very closely, chin propped on his fist, as she spoke of her disillusionment. It was not so much that she'd lost interest in the material, but rather that the material itself led to unambiguous conclusions—for example, that one should probably move beyond the study of ecological problems at some point and apply a framework of principles to one's life.

Behavior is the *sine qua non* of understanding, she said. If you don't act like you understand something, then you haven't really understood it, at least when it comes to an ethical stance.

How'd you get this far with it?

The truth, she explained, was that she'd gone to graduate school for lack of an alternative. I started out in undergrad studying environmental science, she said, but there was too much math. I barely got through it. Philosophy was easier for me, and anything "eco" is very hot right now. Ecofeminism, ecopolitics, ecocriticism.

Maybe I should get into the eco racket, Joel said.

So how'd you start writing essays?

It started as a diary, a distraction from my dissertation, he said. My girlfriend at the time read one of the entries about my mom. She said it was really good. So I sent a few out and they were accepted, to my surprise.

They're political?

Joel seemed reluctant to say, drawing little Xs in the condensation on his glass. About that, yeah, he said. About family and the South. I wish I could just write theory—Fredric Jameson, Lyotard—I wish I could do what they do. But everyone keeps telling me to write about people. They say that's better, when it's personal. So I do a hybrid. Half-personal, half-theory.

He shrugged, as if to say, *What can you do?*

The Beaver had an infamous "burger drawer." It was a broiler, essentially. From the bar, one could see the waitresses peeling hunks of pink meat from wax paper, pressing them flat inside the blackened tray. A few minutes later, as though by magic, the drawer was opened to reveal the cooked patties swimming in grease.

Joel ordered one and they stepped out onto the patio. It was almost cold, their exhalations steaming the air between them. He bit into a scalding slice of pickle and let it fall from his mouth onto the wax paper. Sorry, that was gross, he said.

There's no elegant way to eat a drawer burger, she said.

He asked her what she would do if she wasn't in school, and she laid out her farm dream, still nascent. The only books that gave her pleasure anymore were books about nature. From the very beginning, her interest in nature had always been rooted in books. She'd volunteered at community gardens. She'd WWOOFed for a summer after college in Vermont, learning how to milk goats, sleeping in a yurt infested with brown recluse spiders. But all this had been a way of collecting credentials, so that she might avoid the embarrassment of admitting that her interest was based merely on her readings of Dillard and Fukuoka, of Berry and Leopold and Abbey. Only since her mushroom sandwich had she begun to consider really *living* like those writers. Not research, not dabbling. Living the life.

There was the fact, as well, that her grandparents had all been farmers. She'd done her genealogy once, on her mother's side, and discovered that they had been farmers all the way back to England and Ireland. Who was she to think she could do something different? Who were we, as a generation, to think we could break with that lineage? It sounded hopelessly naïve to say it aloud, but she had the growing conviction that gathering herbs, picking fruit, and scattering grain for chickens would not simply be good for the planet. It would be good for her soul.

We've spoiled and pillaged the only world we have, Alice said. It's hard to get past that. How do I bring myself to write a dissertation on it? How much will that help anything?

When she shared this view with anyone, they responded in a handful of predictable ways. Her parents told her she should see a therapist, take a pill. Her peers in the program told her it was burnout, that she should take a break. Her oldest friends, the ones she'd grown up with, were sympathetic. But they'd begun to marry and have children, and though they never said as much, their attitudes seemed to imply that only unmarried people without children had the luxury to stew over such things, that it was self-centered.

But Joel—Joel listened in his careful, attentive way, taking dainty bites from his drawer burger, picking off the raw onions. That was it, wasn't it? That he listened to her. That he gave her his full attention in the beginning. It was a rare thing for someone to really listen.

I'm probably depressed, she said.

Who wouldn't be depressed?

For a moment, she thought she might cry. She drank her beer, felt it trickle past the lump in her throat, and the urge passed. You don't have to say that, she said.

Anyone who's not depressed isn't seeing straight.

Then he delivered the Good News, the Gospel of Marx, or at least his southern-fried rendition. She would hear it many times, its effect diminishing with each retelling. But this first time, she felt exonerated. Freed by glaring evidence. Here was someone who said, *You're not crazy, the world is crazy.* Someone with vision, who foresaw a world where all that was noble in life could not be bought or sold. Here was someone who took her disenchantment seriously. A fellow utopian. This is what she liked in the beginning. His capacity for critique, to stand outside of a thing and say what was wrong with it.

She drained her pint, set the glass down hard, and said, Let's do a shot!

I'm not really a shot person.

You've been sipping the same beer for two hours, come on.

She led him by the hand to the bar, where the tender poured whiskey all the way to the lip of their shot glasses. They tossed them back. Joel coughed into the crook of his arm while Alice laughed at him, rubbing his back with her palm.

You okay there?

No, he gasped. I think I need more food.

I can make you something. My place is just down the street.

He drank ice water and blotted his forehead with a cocktail napkin. Yeah? he said. I don't want to put you out.

Don't get your hopes up, we're talking frozen pizza rolls.

It was three blocks to her apartment. Alice stumbled, half on purpose, leaning her weight against Joel. He'd grown quiet suddenly, his eyes unfocused. She lived in the attic of a decrepit Victorian, its fish-scale shingles the color of old piano keys. Joel stopped abruptly at the gate.

I should go home, he said.

What? Why?

He bowed his head bashfully. You've had a lot to drink, he said.

I'm good. This is not a lot for me.

Four drinks isn't a lot?

You were counting?

He shrugged.

I'm fine. I promise. And what do you think is going to happen?

He smiled and looked back over his shoulder, like someone might be watching. You never know, he said.

Most of the time, when she brought someone back to her place, she had no stake in what they thought. More often than not, she'd never see them again. But she saw it now, for some reason, through Joel's eyes. Her dirty laundry draped on the sofa. Her hair in the bathroom sink. The coffee table crowded with wineglasses and cigarette cellophanes and resinous pipes and the ungraded papers from her intro classes.

She put the pizza rolls in the oven, tidied up desultorily. Joel sat on the couch with his spine rigid and his hands between his knees, looking at the pictures on her walls. She pointed to each, explaining— pieces of folk art, a Caillebotte print of chrysanthemums, Japanese watercolors.

That needlepoint of the cat belonged to my grandmother, she said. That one there, the photo, is my mom.

She looks like you.

Everybody says that.

She put on a record—The Roches—and asked Joel if he liked '70s music.

Sometimes, he said.

I love it. Carole King, Joni Mitchell. It's all so earnest. I'm gonna have a drink, do you want one?

Another drink?

Or we could smoke?

Joel drew a breath and blew it out, puffing his cheeks. Sure, he said, why not.

They smoked on the couch, their thighs touching. Joel fell into spasmodic coughing after one hit. Alice finished the bowl while "Hammond Song" played.

Listen to those three-part harmonies, she said. Nobody does that now.

Joel managed to nod, still wheezing. She put her hand on his leg, waited till he'd caught his breath, and kissed him.

I'm on a carousel, he said.

You're really a lightweight, aren't you?

I've been told as much.

They made out for a while. She straddled him on the couch, her long hair falling around his face, and he kept his hands just above her hips, immobile.

You can touch me, she breathed into his ear.

Yeah? Okay.

Joel squeezed her ass tentatively, and she kept waiting for things to progress—for him to lay her gently on her back, roll up her sweater, kiss her navel, unzip her jeans. But none of these things happened. She climbed off and sat beside him, her lips and chin raw from chafing against his stubble. Joel flexed his right leg.

Pins and needles, he said.

Sorry.

No, it's fine.

It's getting late.

Yeah, I suppose.

They looked at each other, Alice trying not to smile. You're going to make me ask, aren't you? she said.

Ask what?

Just tell me you'd like to stay the night. Say, "Alice, may I sleep in your bed tonight, please?"

Joel turned away from her, smiling, his ears rosy. Alice, may I sleep in your bed tonight, please? he mumbled.

Why yes, you may!

I don't do this very often. In fact, I've never done this.

Slept with someone?

You know. Have a tryst, or whatever.

I believe the kids call them hookups now.

Whatever it is, I'm not very good at it. Clearly.

But you were on Tinder. That's how you met Min, right?

I forced myself to make an account. So far I've had seven bad coffee dates with people who look nothing like their profile pictures.

Do you look like your profile picture?

Please. I have integrity.

Let's see it then.

He brought up the app on his phone and showed her the screen. It was a group photo, cropped and centered on Joel. An outdoor restaurant somewhere with orange beer garden tables. It was nighttime. The lights were low and warm. He was looking directly into the lens with a cordial smile she'd not seen once in person.

Okay, this is very flattering, she said. You look more outgoing than you are. And the light makes you look like you have more hair.

So you'd be disappointed if you met me?

No, I'd think you were cute. Good enough for a tryst anyway.

The apps are new territory for me. I broke up with someone in July, and we'd been together six years. Before that, it was my college girlfriend. We met my freshman year at Northwestern. Then my high school girlfriend. And that's it.

No one in between?

Nope.

And you're how old?

Thirty.

Alice whistled. Damn, she said.

What about you?

You're asking how many people I've dated? God, I don't know. I'd have to think about it. Do you mean, like, *dated*? Or *dated* dated?

Either.

She blew air past her lips in a horselike way and thought back through the gallery of faces. In the poor light of drunken memory, their features blurred and swapped, and they took on one another's traits. Or was it simply that she had a type, and they shared those traits to begin with?

I've had maybe eight or nine long-term things.

What's long term?

Six months? Eight months to a year seems to be the average shelf life for me.

What were they like?

Oh, you know, artsy types. Poets, people in bands. I swore off men for two years and dated this woman who turned out to be an Adderall addict. The guys in bands all wound up cheating on me, except for the drummer, Teddy. Drummers don't cheat.

They don't? Joel said, amused.

They're expendable in their bands. They have this fear of being replaced, so they're totally loyal. They'll go out of their way to prove their loyalty.

Good to know.

Why do you ask?

Joel shrugged, massaging his knuckles with his thumb.

Does it bother you or something?

No, not at all, he said unconvincingly.

They said nothing for a while. Outside, a throng of sorority girls came through the alley, laughing wildly about something, their heels striking cobblestone.

So, what now? she said, enjoying his squirmy discomfort a little too much.

Whatever.

What do you want? Just say it.

I don't know what to say.

Say, "Alice, can you show me your bedroom?"

He hid his face in the crook of his arm and said, Alice, can you show me your bedroom?

Their sex was slow and tender. Joel sought assurances at every turn. *Like this? Is this okay?* It took him a long time to come—I'm not used to condoms, he said—and her beseeching gradually became more like the barked commands of a drill sergeant. *Come! Come right now!* When he finally did, they collapsed, laughing and panting, and Alice stared at the glittered dome of sky outside the window, her cheek against his chest, hearing his heart. Families were sleeping in the darkened houses; televisions flickered with no one watching; an empty highway cut across the howling distances of the prairie. And Alice, alone with this stranger, remembered with sad certainty that you could be only so close to another person, and it was never close enough.

Shooting star, she said, pointing.

He turned and squinted at the window. That's a satellite.

Do you smell something?

Yeah, a little bit. Almost like burnt toast.

Shit! she said, bolting upright. The pizza rolls!

She ran naked into the kitchen and opened the oven door, smoke pouring out. She wafted the air with an oven mitt, set the tray of charred rolls on the stovetop. The smoke alarm released its earsplitting cry. She stood on her tiptoes, then hopped up and down, trying to reach it while Joel leaned in the doorway, laughing.

This has to be someone's fetish, he shouted. A naked girl, jumping up and down, trying to reach a smoke detector.

Just help me!

He walked over, took it down, and popped out the battery. He stood there, smiling at her, looking smitten. What? she said.

Nothing, you just look good in this light.

She covered herself. Okay, back to the darkness, she said.

As they lay side by side, the oscillating fan cooled the sweat on her stomach to a salt film. She'd developed a dull headache. All the beer she'd drunk seemed to be leaking from her pores.

My hangovers start earlier and earlier, she said.

I feel fine.

You barely drank.

So? I still had fun.

She propped her head on her fist and looked at him. Were you raised by Mormons or something?

He laughed. No, Southern Baptists.

What was that like?

I hated it. I hated being in a small town.

And yet, here you are in another one.

I'm plotting my escape to New York.

You have a job lined up?

You sound like my mom, Joel said. Why is my desire to live in a place not a good enough reason to live there?

Most people need a little something called money.

I have some money, for the first time in my life. I got a small advance for the book. And the visiting gig in Chicago pays well.

And you want to blow it all on rent in Brooklyn, Alice said. How original.

Maybe not Brooklyn. Maybe Queens.

Well, I'm probably just jealous. I've still got a few years here.

Maybe they'll let you out early on good behavior.

Doubtful.

To tell the truth, Joel said, I'm a little nervous about going to New York.

I would be, she said. No offense, but you seem like you'd be a little lost there.

You could come with me, he said, a mischievous twinkle in his eye.

You're inviting me to live with you in New York? That's what's happening right now?

Why not?

You're right, I'll just go pack my bag and we can leave tonight.

Right, Joel said. Well, it's settled then.

Should we get married first?

Probably. We can do it on the way.

Cool, cool, Alice said. So I guess I should probably know a little bit more about you, if we're going to live together. What's your family situation?

Oh, let's see, Joel sighed. My parents are divorced. My mom lives in Kentucky, alone. She used to be a hairdresser—a beautician, as they say in the South. Now she spends most of her time on the internet, on right-wing message boards and conspiracy websites. So that's cool.

Nice.

And my dad I never saw that often. He was a truck driver for a while, then he sold vitamins. He's done a little of everything. He has a gambling problem—that's why my mother divorced him. He's been to jail a few times for beating up his girlfriends.

Right, awesome.

I'm serious, Joel said.

Alice's smile wilted. Wait, for real? I thought you were making up, like, nightmare parents as part of the joke.

No, it's the truth, Joel said.

A lot of material for your writing, I guess.

Oh yeah. Never a shortage there.

I'm sorry, I didn't mean to—

It's fine.

She let her eyes close. She felt herself rising, into the star-flecked emptiness, above the little village, above the tartan plains, till she reached a lightless place where the pull of gravity was singular and irresistible. She knew, somehow, that they would meet again, that it was only the first of many conversations. To learn that she would marry him, that she would go to New York with him after all, would not have seemed improbable, even in this moment.

What about siblings? she murmured.

Joel sighed as if it were a long story. I have a half-brother, he said.

Seven

OVER TIME, SLOWLY, Emmett came to know the other workers. In free moments, between planes, he stood around with them in the "smoke shack," a glass structure with benches, almost like a bus stop, near the loading dock. The floor was covered with sunflower seeds that crackled under their boots. From the shack, Emmett could see across the tarmac, the runway lights and flashing beacons, the air traffic control tower, from which he always half expected to see the beam of a searchlight boring down on him.

One night, as they lit their cigarettes, Kaleb told Emmett he'd found himself a girlfriend—a lady cop. Emmett stood next to Winston, a middle-aged former boxer. He called every male coworker "playboy" and every female coworker "baby girl," and kept a pristine white towel draped over his shoulder to wipe his face. On the bench, next to Kaleb, was Pauline. She'd been born the same year as Emmett's mother and had worked at the Center since it opened. She wore a back brace and a knee brace and a paisley-patterned bandanna, her long gray hair in a single braid. She reminded Emmett of Willie Nelson.

Bullshit, said Winston. No cop would come near you, unless it's to lock your ass up.

How much you wanna bet? Kaleb said. She's a cop for real. I met her on Tinder.

He took out his phone, swiped a few times, and held up the fractured screen. There was a woman there, short and muscular, wearing a police uniform, only her top was open. She was covering her small breasts, taking a picture of herself in a bathroom mirror. Her phone like a bright star, obscuring her face.

That don't mean shit, Winston said. You can buy that uniform at any porn store.

She's got a gun! Kaleb said. Look!

You can buy guns, too, Winston said.

Well, I know she's a cop, Kaleb said. And guess what? She's married to a fireman.

This story keeps getting better and better, Pauline said.

I'm serious. This guy's probably six foot four. He's on her Facebook page. And she's just this little spinner. I don't know how they let her become a cop.

What's a spinner? Emmett said.

Kaleb grinned. Means she's so tiny, you could lift her up and spin her around on your dick.

Pauline made a gagging sound. You're really a piece of work, she said, you know that?

This is all bullshit, Winston said. I don't believe a single word of it.

She says her husband, the fireman, could tear me into little pieces, Kaleb said. We were fucking in her car, outside this club, and she kept talking like that, saying what her husband would do to me if he found out. It was hot as fuck.

A plane landed then, and they all waited for the scream of the turbines to subside before they spoke again, taking small pulls from their cigarettes, trying to make them last.

What happens when she finds out you're a drug dealer? Pauline said.

Whoa, Kaleb said. Who says I'm a drug dealer? I'm a businessman.

Come on, playboy, Winston said, you sold me weed last month.

That was surplus, Kaleb said. I don't buy it to sell, I buy it for myself and sometimes there's leftovers. Now, you wanna meet a *real* drug dealer, I can introduce you. I know a few.

Mr. Badass, Pauline said. She pitched her cig, sparks scattering over the pavement, and stood with some difficulty from the bench. One of these days, your lifestyle's gonna catch up to you, she said. Then she turned to Emmett. Don't let him talk you into anything stupid, she said.

Like what? Emmett said.

He's always got some scheme, she said.

She hobbled past them, her back hunched, and returned to the warehouse floor, sipping from a liter bottle of orange soda.

Kaleb watched her go, then spat on the floor of the smoke shack, saliva flecking the layer of sunflower seeds. She's just an old bitch, he said. She doesn't know me.

EMMETT MET KALEB at Aloha's later. It was busier this time, ramp workers with their neon vests shooting pool, letting shot glasses plunk into plastic cups of beer. Winston was there playing pinball, sipping bourbon on the rocks through two tiny cocktail straws, white towel still folded over his shoulder. Once he'd arrived, Emmett wasn't sure why he'd come. He didn't like Kaleb, exactly, but talking to him, he felt connected to the real world, the world where people made a living and scraped by. Not the world of concepts that Joel seemed to live in. And there was the promise, too, of danger. That something might happen to wrench him from the worn grooves of his life.

She'll figure out I'm a piece of shit, Kaleb said, meaning the lady cop. Everybody figures out eventually.

There were four empty shot glasses on the bar with the residue of Jägermeister. Kaleb smiled with teeth stained black.

Maybe not, Emmett said. Maybe she'll leave the fireman and take up with you.

I wouldn't be into it without the fireman, Kaleb said. That's what gets my juices flowing—knowing there's this guy, this big bodybuilder-type dude. He's out there saving fucking lives, rescuing kittens from trees, and meanwhile I'm plowing his wife in the backseat of their minivan.

That's fucked up, Emmett said, laughing.

Exactly, Kaleb said. I'm fucked up. That's what I'm saying. I ain't right in the head, I'll be the first to tell you. It goes back to childhood, I think. My mother was a Pentecostal. She heard voices. Half the time it was God, half the time it was Satan. She never knew which. She said the voices were exactly the same. She said there were people who went their whole lives thinking they heard God, but really it was Satan. I believed that. I still believe it. They put her away, gave her so much dope she forgot who I was. She forgot her own name. She died there, in the state hospital. So that's Exhibit A. My mother.

My father's Exhibit B. He used to kick the shit out of me, tell me I was worthless, that I'd never amount to anything. I hardly remember my childhood. I'm serious. It's like a dream. I know it happened, I know my father did the shit that he did 'cause people told me, but I can't remember it. It's a blank spot. Your childhood makes you who you are, it molds you. So what's that say about me? If your childhood's a blank, you grow up to be a blank. He told me I was worthless, and I believed him—I still believe him.

So when I get mixed up with a woman, it's like I have to treat her bad so she knows I'm worthless and she'll go find somebody else. I can't let her love me because she'd be loving a worthless piece of shit. Now I don't hurt nobody—I'd never hurt a woman, physically. But I'm not easy to like. My true colors shine through and I say some mean shit. I can't help it. Even if I love the girl. *Especially* if I love her. Every woman I've loved has hated my guts in the end. I dated one girl who stabbed me in the back.

You mean she cheated on you? Emmett said.

No, I mean she literally stabbed me with a fuckin knife in the back.

Kaleb turned around and peeled up his T-shirt, revealing pale, pimpled flesh. See that scar by my left shoulder blade? he said. Emmett leaned closer and saw a knot of scar tissue there, smooth as an acorn, two inches from his spine.

She stabbed me with a steak knife.

What'd you do?

I didn't do shit. She thought I was stepping out on her, but for once, she was wrong.

No, I mean what'd you do after she stabbed you?

I turned around and said, "You stabbed me!" Then I had some choice words for her. She didn't even know what she was doing. There was just pure hatred in her eyes before she did it, and then after, she was in shock.

What happened then?

Then I went over to Wade's house.

You didn't go to the hospital?

I didn't want the law involved. Like I said, she didn't know what she was doing. And even though she was wrong about me cheating in that particular instance, I'd done plenty to deserve worse than that.

Well, who's Wade?

Wade, Kaleb shouted, come over here a minute.

One of the men at a nearby pool table perked up. He was squdgy and round-bellied, though he had the posture of a man who'd once been fit. He walked over and Kaleb put an arm around his shoulder. I's just telling Emmett here about when Jasmine stabbed me in the back.

Oh shit, Wade said, that was some night.

I drove over to Wade's with the knife still in my back.

I was asleep, Wade said. He honked the horn. Imagine my surprise when I come out in my underwear and he's got a steak knife in his back.

Wade was in Iraq in 2004. I figured if anybody knew what to do, it would be him.

Wade nodded and took a swig of his beer. Yep, he said.

So what did you do?

I put a kitchen chair in the bathtub, had him sit backwards in the chair, and I took the knife out. It was like a horror movie, blood filling up the tub. But, you know, my training kicked in.

Wade's an American hero, Kaleb said, winking.

I didn't have any thread to stitch him up, but I used superglue and butterfly bandages and we finally got the bleeding stopped. It was touch and go for a while there.

I knew I'd be fine, Kaleb said.

Yeah fucking right. You were acting like a pussy. "Wade, don't let me die! Don't let me die, Wade!"

You try getting stabbed, motherfucker, and see how you respond.

So what happened with the woman?

We got back together, Kaleb said. We actually got engaged a couple months later, but we had too many differences of opinion and parted ways after a while.

The stabbing didn't come between you? Emmett said, laughing.

We let bygones be bygones, he said. Then he started laughing, too, like even he could see how absurd it was. He laughed till tears squeezed out of his eyes. Love is crazy, he said. It turns you into a crazy person.

They sat, later, in the smoke haze of the Corvette's interior, their minds churning with coke. The train rhythms of the warehouse remained in Emmett's hearing. Faint, stuttering echoes. Jets flew over—immense surges of power and thrust—and Emmett wondered what it did to a person, watching planes leave all night. Watching them leave you behind.

There's this girl, Emmett said.

There's always a girl, Kaleb said. Say more.

I'm a little bit infatuated.

Naturally.

There are complications. Major complications.

Always are.

Nothing's happened yet, but I want it to, I think. I've got a feeling that something will happen. And when it does, I'm worried it'll blow up everything.

What do you have to blow up?

My life. The status quo.

This girl, who you're inflatulated with. Are the feelings mutual?

I think so. I think she's interested. She's unhappy with her current situation.

And here you come to save the day. Kaleb smiled, tapped his cigarette through the cracked window. I think you know what you want and you're afraid you'll get it, he said.

She's involved with someone I care about. She's off-limits. Married, actually.

Poon is poon.

You don't know the particulars.

I know you're still time traveling. You're in your DeLorean, going back and forth, back and forth. I told you from the beginning: stay in the present. Whatever happens will happen.

That lets me off the hook.

There is no hook, Kaleb said. Don't you know that yet? There's no fuckin hook to begin with.

He flicked the cigarette filter, turned up the radio.

Listen to this guitar solo, he shouted. You like Floyd?

They're okay, Emmett shouted. The song was "In the Flesh?," the warplane sound effects hard to distinguish from the wail of real planes flying over.

I went to the Laser Floyd Light Show in New Albany. *Dark Side of the Moon.* I was so fucked up, I forgot I was human, man.

Sounds great.

We should go. I'll get us tickets.

He turned the dial till the sound became a roar without definition, rattling the car, the booming of drums like nearby detonations. He played air guitar. He beat his palms on the steering wheel. A jet flew over, blurred exhaust streaming from its engines, rising to the storm-lit sky. Emmett closed his eyes. He pictured himself hiding in the cargo hold. A stowaway, not knowing where he'd land.

It drizzled the whole way home, gray light sifting through the clouds as the day broke. It was hard to hear the radio over the scrape of the wipers. Little to do but think. His fantasies had always been too wholesome. They had sex, of course, but soon after he was imagining them living together in a little apartment somewhere, sharing a pastry in a sunny café, picking out a dog at the shelter. Then he imagined a wedding ceremony with his mother and Joel in the front row, and he almost laughed. There was no future with Alice that did not end with this cruel punchline. And the Alice of his fantasies was not the *real* Alice. She was only a smiling, compliant approximation. He had no idea who she was, really. What they had was only a few points of contact between two lonely people. And a lonely person could be convinced of anything.

Armed with this realization, Emmett walked into his mother's and announced that he would spend the weekend camping.

But you just got here! Kathy said. Camping where?

I'm not sure yet. Maybe Current River.

We'll all go, Kathy said. I haven't been in years.

I'd rather go alone.

Joel and Alice came into the kitchen wearing their robes and slippers, looking like they'd slept poorly. Alice brightened when she saw him.

Your brother's going camping, Kathy said.

You just got here, Joel said.

I'll just get my stuff together and go, he said.

Where are you going? Alice said.

Current River, near Van Buren.

Hey, I've been there, she said. I have a friend who lives up that way. She works for the Forest Service.

He pretended not to have heard this and went to gather his old pack from the garage. He brushed the cobwebs from the shoulder straps, made sure the buckles still fastened. He rummaged in the antique room closet for his sleeping bag, noticing, and then trying not to notice, the pair of lace-edged panties draped near Alice's open suitcase. He felt the rolled bag on a high shelf and yanked it down. A box of old photographs scattered on the carpet. He swept them into a pile and brought them to the rolltop desk. One by one, he held them to the light: A birthday party at the old house. Wood-paneled walls. Blaze of candles. Joel and their mother at the zoo, feeding romaine lettuce to a giraffe—Kathy so much younger with her crimped hair and shoulder pads, her lilac eye shadow. Emmett on his father's shoulders in the Smoky Mountains. The creased hills in a sea of fog.

One of the photographs was double-exposed. Joel stood in their living room, reciting the presidents to an audience of grandparents and aunts and uncles. A fainter, phantom image of Emmett was superimposed on this scene. He wore a diaper and nothing else, and he stood in a dim corner of the same room, looking rather solemn for a toddler.

As he returned the photos to the shoebox, he noticed Joel's notebook on the desk. A pen lay beside it. A tangle of earbuds. His place in the notebook was marked by a black ribbon. Emmett went to the doorway and listened, hearing only the murmur of Kathy's voice on the patio. The house was still and quiet. He shut the door gently, turned the lock. Then he sat at the rolltop and opened the notebook to the place Joel had marked. He skimmed the pages, going back in time till he caught his name. The entry had been dated the previous Saturday. He saw his name before anything else; having forgotten cursive, Joel printed everything. It made his inscriptions on the title page of the books he signed look clumsy and childlike. The capital *E* in "Emmett" was large and distinctive. For a moment, he thought, *Walk away.* He even shut the notebook and stood by the desk, the palms of his hands damp and itching. Then he sat again and began to read.

Spoke with Emmett today. Tried to disavow him of the notion that writing is a worthwhile career—that you can even call it a career. He's got it in his mind that he should write a screenplay, as if no one's ever thought of this. As if millions of people whose lives have reached dead ends don't all think, "I know, I'll write a screenplay!" I tried to tell him he'd be happier doing something else. But if it wasn't screenwriting, it would be something else. He'd find a way to call himself an artist. Anything to avoid the ordinary. I can't stomach telling him the truth—that I don't think he's talented enough to make it. That almost no one is.

Emmett stopped here and closed the notebook, his heart pumping like he'd jogged up three flights of stairs. He stared out the window above the desk at the cornfield across the road, wave after wave of shame breaking over him, till the chiming of the music box clock brought him back to the present—to the quiet indifference of the room, the voices of family outside.

He stowed everything in the trunk of the Mystique, filled a milk jug with water at the kitchen faucet. Alice, Joel, and Kathy came inside and stood around him.

We have a proposition, Kathy said. Alice wants to see her friend. What was her name, hon?

Regina, Alice said.

She wants to see her friend Regina, get away for a day or two. I said to her, Well, just ride with Emmett! He's going that way.

Emmett shut off the faucet and turned around. Alice chewed her thumbnail, eyes cast downward.

The whole point of the trip is solitude, Emmett said.

Oh, you get enough solitude, Kathy said. Living alone. Besides, you'll get your time. She's not going out in the woods with you. She's not sleeping in your tent.

It would be a nice thing, if you don't mind, Joel said. She needs a break from Paducah.

Ha! Alice said. She looked at Joel with wild, furious eyes.

She needs a break, let's leave it at that, Joel said.

A break from what? Alice said.

A break from me, I guess, Joel said. Are you happy? Do we have to air out all our shit?

Kathy shook her head dolefully at this.

What do you want? Emmett asked Alice, directly.

She looked at him finally, defiant, and said, I'd like to go with you.

For a long while on the road, she said nothing. She took off her dirty canvas sneakers and put her feet on the dash, her cutoff shorts riding up, strings of frayed thread on her pale thighs. She wiggled her toes in the sunlight. They crossed the state line at Fort Defiance Park near Wickliffe, where the Ohio merged with the Mississippi River.

Emmett felt like he'd had no choice in this, and there was nothing he hated more than having no choice. He'd never taken a job or made a commitment in his life that he could not walk away from at a moment's notice. There was no greater relief than knowing you could walk away, that you were bound to nothing.

So is Regina even real? he said.

Of course, Alice said. She's expecting me.

Emmett only nodded a little.

You're mad at me, she said.

If you wanted to come, why didn't you ask me?

I did ask.

You had my mother ask. You made it where I couldn't say no.

She went back to gnawing her thumb. I'm sorry, she said quietly.

I was thinking, he said. We don't really know each other. What happened between us—it was just a fluke. There's no future that comes to anything.

Who says I want a future? Don't flatter yourself.

What's this about then? Inviting yourself.

You say we'll talk, then you randomly decide to go camping? Out of the clear blue? You're trying to avoid me.

I can't decide to be alone?

Whatever, she said. She looked out at the wall of pines flanking the highway.

If you're looking for an escape route, it's not me, he said.

I hear you loud and clear.

They said nothing for twenty miles, Alice with her face turned away, Emmett wondering if he believed what he'd said. Maybe *she* was *his* escape route.

They were near the town of Sikeston when something went wrong. The gas pedal gave no response. The engine wheezed and faltered, their speed dropping. They took the next exit and Emmett managed to coast to a gas station.

Are we out of gas? she said.

No, he said.

Are you sure?

Of course I'm sure.

A small service station was attached to the Shell-mart. The mechanic agreed to take a look. They ate trail mix and drank sun-warmed water from the milk jug, watching people come and go from the gas station. When the mechanic emerged at last, he said it was the fuel pump. The repair would cost seven hundred dollars, and he would have to order the part.

I could have it ready tomorrow, maybe, the mechanic said. That's a big maybe.

Dread stole through him when he heard the price. It would deplete what little remained of his credit. He paced for a few minutes in the lot, trying to think of some alternative, then told the mechanic to go ahead and fix it. Towing the Mystique to Paducah would cost nearly as much as the repair.

He found Alice on the bench near the entrance and explained the situation. Maybe Regina can come get us, she said. I'll call her right now.

She dialed the number and stepped over by the cage of propane tanks, a finger plugged in her free ear. The sky had cleared altogether, the only cloud a mare's tail. Wind scattered red leaves over the pavement. He remembered the drizzle that morning, how he'd still had hope for what the day could hold. Now this bad luck. He'd crossed money from his list. And now he would have to write the words again on the legal pad. *Make money.*

When Alice came back, she could not meet his eyes. Regina can't come, she said. She's got her baby with her, a newborn, and her dog ate a houseplant that might be poisonous.

I thought she was your friend? I thought she knew you were coming?

She did. She does. She said we can stay with her, but she can't get out.

He rubbed his face with his palms, his stomach roiling. I'm hungry, I think, he said. Or maybe sick. How far is Regina's?

Another hour and a half.

A cab would cost a fortune.

What about Kathy?

She won't drive at night, Emmett said. What about Joel?

No, Alice said.

He's your husband, for Christ's sake. Are things that bad? You can't ride in a car with him?

I'd really rather not right now.

He stood for no reason other than to do something. He put his hands on his hips and paced in a circle.

There's a motel up the street, she said. The car will be ready tomorrow.

He looked at her, and they both knew what the look meant.

We'll get separate rooms, she said. I'll pay for it.

Why would you do that?

Because I feel bad.

For what? Did you break the Mystique?

She looked at him and said nothing. She did look sorry.

Separate rooms, he muttered. He drew a deep breath. The air smelled of gasoline, of charbroiled beef from the chimneys of the fast-food joints off the interstate. It smelled of livestock, hogs in the slime of their excrement, huddled in a parked trailer, pressing their wet snouts to the grate. A prison crew was mowing the grass near the on-ramp and he could smell that, too. Altogether, it was the smell of bad luck, and he hated his brother then, for one bright, blazing moment. He hated his brother for never knowing this smell. For never accepting charity. For never coming home a failure. And it was like Joel had caused all this to happen—the state of his life. Like they were not even brothers.

One room would be cheaper, he said. Two beds.

Two beds, she agreed.

Eight

WALKING IN, switching on the lights, Emmett felt he'd been there before in a dream. All motels were like this. Their sameness was meant to comfort, to be both reliable and remote, to hold the particulars of any life without judgment. A man and his sister-in-law, for example. Stranded, trying not to look at each other, to come close at all. He stood by the window, where the frigid breath of the AC unit blew into his face. Alice looked at the bathroom, opened the drawers in the dresser. His phone buzzed with a message from Kaleb: a photo of the lady cop, handcuffed to a bed, naked from the waist down.

Jesus, he mumbled, turning off the display.

Found the Bible, Alice said, sitting beside the open nightstand.

We've got our reading material covered.

He sat on the edge of the nearest bed, the mattress springs rasping. His head ached. I need to eat, he said. I'll go get us something. McDonald's, okay?

Alice nodded. The room was freezing, and her legs, in the cutoff shorts, were stippled with goosepimples. It made his heart throb to be alone with her like this. He let himself look at her.

She tucked a wisp of hair behind her ear and smiled crookedly. Yes? she said.

Nothing, I'll get the food.

Outside, he crossed the frontage road, a culvert with algae-scummed water, and two empty parking lots to reach the McDonald's. He ordered two meals more or less at random. He felt his phone buzz again. Two messages, both from Kaleb. One said, her hubby. The second was a picture of a framed photo. It looked like one of those Olan Mills portraits one would have made at Walmart. The lady cop was standing there in a dress. A hulking, square-headed man stood behind her, muscles straining against the fabric of his suit. She looked more like his child than his wife.

Stop texting me, Emmett said, and Kaleb sent back a horned red devil emoji.

What he thought of next was liquor—a bottle of liquor. Surely that was possible. He found a place nearby and stood before the liquor shelf in the bright fluorescence, warming up, deciding which of the cheap bottles he could stomach. He settled on Canadian Club whiskey, grabbed a two-liter of Sprite and a bag of BBQ chips, and struck out again into the cool evening, half jogging.

When Alice saw the plastic liter of Canadian Club, she said, You read my mind.

She shut the Gideons Bible and set it on the nightstand.

Is that book any good? Emmett said, drawing the burger clamshells from the grease-spotted bag, fries spilling onto the carpet.

It's a little slow, she said.

They sat at the desk by the window and began to eat. The sun had set, leaving a purplish bruise in the sky above the interstate.

You probably think I'm crazy, Alice said.

Why would I think that?

I'm always sullen around your family. I'm always pissy with Joel.

Who wouldn't be pissy?

Alice lifted her eyebrows. He said you two had talked. He said you'd renewed your relationship.

What does that mean, "renew"?

Alice shrugged.

He wants me to say it's okay. He wants me to say, Joel, it's all right that you're always fighting with our mother, that you think you're better than everyone. He wants me to absolve him.

Why you? Alice said.

Because he knows I can see through his bullshit. I can see what's in his heart.

This is quite a turnaround. I thought you loved him.

Emmett set down his burger, sucked the salt from his fingers, and looked at her. I don't want to talk about Joel, he said.

After they'd eaten, Emmett went to fill the ice bucket. They cracked the seal on the whiskey and sat with their legs stretched out on separate beds, drinking from the complimentary coffee cups. A classic movie channel was playing The Wizard of Oz. Emmett thought vaguely of the Hero's Journey and wondered if Dorothy counted. She was not very willful for a hero. She was pushed around by witches and puppeteer wizards. It wasn't even her choice, going to Oz. A tornado that carried you off was not a choice. But she had wanted something like it, hadn't she? To be carried away? Emmett could not remember. They'd missed the beginning.

I like the Tin Man best, Alice said.

Everybody likes the Tin Man. My favorite is the Scarecrow.

Why?

He wants to better himself, to use his brain.

He doesn't even know what he'd use it for if he got one.

To tell you why the ocean's near the shore.

That's what I mean, Alice said. That's stupid. Nobody wonders about that.

He got up to fetch the ice bucket, clawed out the last melting cubes, and poured himself more of the whiskey. He was drunk now, the floor tilting. The fumes made him shiver, warmth spreading from his stomach to his limbs, the muscles in his shoulders going slack.

I had a boyfriend who made me watch The Wizard of Oz in sync with that Pink Floyd album, Alice said.

I had a girlfriend who did the same thing. She had big cartoon googly eyes. White-girl dreadlocks.

For real?

Oh yeah.

So in college were you, like, one of those hacky-sack guys? Did you wear a drug rug, listen to Sublime?

He laughed and collapsed onto the other bed. Not really, he said. I partied, though, for sure. I never went to class.

Me neither.

And yet you graduated.

I was a good test-taker.

Not me, he said. Can you imagine going back to college and taking it seriously? Think how different we might be.

Alice smiled and said, We might be like you-know-who.

He thought about Joel. The liquor had softened his feelings, and in that blur of double vision, he saw the brother he resented and the brother who was merely human, and therefore deserving of pity. When he focused, the twin images collapsed, and there was only one. Emmett liked this better. He did not want to think of his brother as someone who deserved pity, not now in this room with her.

You know what this guy told me the other day? He told me there's no hook to be let off from. Meaning, there's nothing to hold us accountable in the universe.

I don't know, Alice said. I kinda hope there is.

It would be liberating, though, wouldn't it? If there wasn't? You could do whatever you wanted.

I do miss that, she said. Saying yes to whatever. Not just drugs. Saying yes to life. Being married is like living with a parent. It's this externalized conscience, telling you what to do. Telling you to say no.

She rose from the bed, holding on to the headboard for balance, and poured herself more of the whiskey. She swallowed it all in three gulps, tipped another splash into the cup. She returned to the mattress and sat facing him, rubbing her bare knees.

You say you can do what you want if there's no accountability, she said. But I think it's the opposite. It's easier to do the bad thing when you *know* you'll be held accountable. It's like an insurance policy. You say to yourself, "It's okay if I fuck up, I'll pay for it later."

I'm not following, he said. What's the bad thing?

She blinked slowly and swung her legs onto the bed, tiny reflections of the television twinkling in her eyes. Never mind, she said. I sound like a bitch. You probably think I'm a bitch.

That's the last thing I'd think.

So what would you do, if you could do whatever you wanted?

That's the question, he said. I bought all these screenwriting books, thinking they'd teach me how to write a movie. But Joel's right, it's not a recipe. You're not baking a cake. There's all this stuff about character motivation. Your characters are supposed to have a goal. But what if there are two competing goals? Or three? What if your protagonist has got no idea what the goal is? What if it's just a kind of vague thing he knows is out there, but he doesn't know what it looks like or how to get it?

I totally get that, she said. We had this global tragedy, this collective trauma, and in the aftermath we're all thinking, "Now what?" You thought your job was important? Guess what, it's meaningless. You thought your marriage would last forever? You thought you understood love?

I was like this before, he said. All my life. I had this idea of something waiting for me, but I couldn't name it. I just knew it was there.

That's a normal feeling, she said. You want your life to have a point. You want to have a calling.

A calling, yeah. What scares me is that most people—surely it's most people—never find their calling, or they don't really have one. They only think they do. They end up working as package handlers or delivery drivers or line cooks. They smoke dope and sit around and pretty soon life is over.

That's not you, though. You're not one of those people.

Do you think I have talent?

Even as he asked the question, he realized she would have no way of knowing. He hated where it came from—this voice of doubt, this tireless worm in his brain.

She looked at him, her face softened by pity.

I'm sorry, I sound pathetic now, he said. Don't listen to me.

No, I think you do, she said. I'm sure you do.

Maybe Mom's right and I should have a kid. Sometimes I think I'd like kids. It would be a relief, not having to think about myself all the time.

You think about yourself all the time?

You know what I mean. I don't take care of anyone else. I get bored of thinking about my problems and my life. You become boring to yourself.

And bringing a child into the world would fix that?

You're against the idea, I'm assuming.

Not necessarily, she said. But you're talking about it like a cure for narcissism. The thing is, though, I have friends with babies, and they're the biggest narcissists I know. All they do is talk about their kid and post photos online—like actual photo shoots with a photographer where the baby is dressed up in a three-piece baby suit and a newsboy cap. And it's a form of self-love—of vanity, I think. They've created this little being after their own image, this little miniature version of themselves.

But then they grow up, he said. They do things you could never predict. They disappoint you and surprise you, and you love them anyway. That's the whole point. You think you're creating a version of yourself, but you're not. You're creating something new and it's out of your hands.

She took a swallow of whiskey and grimaced. Let's change the subject, she said.

Televisions were playing in the other rooms—superhero movies, muffled explosions, canned laughter.

Tell me about your childhood, he said.

What are you, my shrink?

No, just—what was Illinois like? What did little Alice do for fun?

Don't say "little Alice," you sound like a sex offender.

You know what I mean. What was growing up like?

Being a small-town boy, she said, I'm not sure you can imagine the action on the streets of Springfield.

Oh yeah? Pretty wild?

We're talkin full-on Abe Lincoln lookalike contests. We're talkin corn-dog-eating competitions.

Oh shit.

Yeah. We invented the corn dog.

Wait, really? He laughed and rubbed his fists into his eyes. If a Midwesterner could be turned into a food, he said, it would be a corn dog. Like, a Midwesterner is just a corn dog in human form.

Hey, I'll take it. What would a Southerner be? A biscuit?

God, I'd love to be a biscuit right now.

We could wander into town, see if anything's open?

I'll survive, he said. You didn't answer my question.

She wrinkled her brow, really pondering how to answer. She looked lovely in the dim light of the motel lamp, sitting there in half-lotus, fingers clasped around her bare foot.

My dad worked all the time, she said. My mom was a schoolteacher. It was a nice town to grow up in, a nice place for families. It's strange, though, because I always knew I would leave. There was this understanding that I'd go to school elsewhere and probably end up in Chicago or on the East Coast. My parents wanted that. That's the difference between me and Joel. You too, probably. Your parents wanted you to stay. Anyway, it changes the way you see a town when you know you'll leave eventually. It's this sweet little place. It's not trapping you. Of course, I thought it was hokey, when I was a teenager or whatever—when there's like ten Abe Lincolns wandering around downtown, these tall dudes with beards and top hats. But that was just teenage angst. I like going back. I like seeing my parents. I miss them.

She grew quiet then, picked up her cup, and peered down into it as if she could see something there in the melting ice and watered-down whiskey—something private that Emmett would not understand.

What about New York? he said. Is that temporary?

Of course.

I can't imagine wanting to leave a place like New York. Once you've fought so hard to get there.

I didn't fight. I followed Joel. And it's not my city. It doesn't belong to me. It's like, in Astoria, I'm not Greek or Italian or whatever. I have no family there, no history. People take one look at me and know I'm from outside. They know I'll move on. And I know it, too.

If I could live in New York, he said, I think I'd never feel alone.

She laughed.

Is that naïve?

No, there's some truth to it. You do feel a kind of togetherness. But it's a lonely togetherness sometimes. A bunch of people crammed together isn't a community.

Community, he said, as if sounding out a foreign word. I'm not sure I've ever had that.

Me neither, she said. Maybe someday.

She tossed back the last of her drink, a piece of ice falling into her lap, and wiped her mouth with the neckband of her T-shirt. They were both drunk now. There was no denying it, no writing it off as "buzzed" or "tipsy." They were just plain drunk.

We should probably turn in, she said.

Yeah, absolutely. I'm bushed.

Neither of them moved.

Should I turn off the TV? she said.

Sure. Unless you have something else to say.

No, she said. But we can keep talking.

He hoped she would make some excuse, and he could tell she was hoping for the same thing. Their minds were alike. They knew what they wanted, and they knew what was good for them, and they each hoped the other would be the one to decide.

Let's go to bed, I guess, she said.

Whatever you want.

Whatever *you* want.

She was sitting very still now, her spine rigid.

Unless you have something else in mind? he said.

Here it was: two diverging futures.

I guess you do? she said.

Suppose I did? What would happen next?

We'd shut off the lights, she said. In the dark, you would undress. You'd make a joke about it—no peeking, something like that—and we'd get into bed.

Separate beds?

At first, she said. But we'd both lie there, thinking about the other. We'd both lie there wishing the other would do something.

Then what? he said, his heart thumping.

She swallowed audibly, brushed her hair back from her face. She waited a long time to speak again. I would touch myself, she whispered.

Yeah?

She nodded faintly.

Tell me what you would do.

I'd slide my hand down, into my shorts. I'd slide my hand between my legs.

And you'd play with your cunt.

She let out a breath. She was hugging her arms now, her head bowed. It was hard to tell if her eyes were closed.

I'd be wet, she said. From thinking about it.

Thinking about what?

What you would do to me.

What would I do?

Whatever you wanted.

When she looked up at him finally, he half expected to see a stranger's face, a woman he failed to recognize. And in a way, she was. She became herself in that moment. Not his brother's wife, but Alice. A midwestern girl with dirt beneath her fingernails. The unmapped newness of her body. Of her life. Of her guarded, private dreams.

Nine

HE WATCHED HER through slitted eyes, pretending to be asleep. She walked naked to the window, scraped back the heavy curtains. She was lithe and lovely, the shock of her nakedness still new to him. There were dimples at the base of her spine. Pale regions the sun never touched. She stretched her arms up and yawned. She crawled onto the bed and let her hair hang in curtains around his face, rosy sunlight shining through.

It's morning, she said, her breath stale.

He sat up and coughed, his hangover a dense iron ball in his skull, radiating signals of pain. He knew as soon as he stood and pissed and drank a glass of water, it would spread to his shoulders and limbs, leaving space in his head to accommodate regret.

I was playing possum, he said. Watching you.

I had a dream about you. We were on a train, in the mountains. It was another time period, during a war or something, and we were nervous about crossing a border.

No interpretation required.

And then I woke up, and you were right here beside me.

She lay her head on his chest, and he waited for the guilt, the way one waited for a pill to take effect. But it wouldn't come. He felt limp, insubstantial. The only solid part of him was the pain in his head.

I don't feel guilty, she said. Do you?

No, he said. Not yet.

Maybe that's a sign. That this was a good thing.

Or maybe we're just sociopaths.

She looked at him scoldingly.

Don't say that. It's not true.

Would we know if it was true?

She rose from the bed abruptly and hunted for her panties, tossing aside the scattered pillows. She found them and stepped into them, nearly losing her balance. She slipped her bra over her arms and reached back, struggling with the clasp, her brow taut.

I'm sorry, Emmett said.

Don't lay that on me.

You're right, I'm sorry.

He stood and put his arms around her. She was stiff at first, then softened. A torn-open condom foil was stuck to the sole of his foot. He shook it off and she laughed.

This can be an accident, she said. This can be something we forget.

I don't think I'd forget, he said.

You might. If we never spoke of it again, to anyone. If it was never acknowledged. You might look back one day and wonder if it really happened.

Is that what you want?

She finished clasping her bra, went to the window, and picked up her shorts. When she turned back to him, splinters of sunlight broke around her, blinding him, and her face could not be seen.

No, she said. I don't want that.

He paid the mechanic, praying his card would not be declined, and drove them back to Kentucky. She slept most of the way, her hoodie balled up against the glass, murmuring words he could not make out.

When they walked into Kathy's house, Joel was at the kitchen table, drinking fragrant jasmine tea, typing away.

How was it? he said, without taking his eyes from the laptop screen.

Regina was the same as ever, Alice said. Her baby's a little chonker.

Uh huh.

His hair is so blond it's almost white.

Uh huh.

And his nose is like a little piggy nose.

Uh huh.

He was disgusting, actually. I've never been more revolted by a baby.

That's cute, Joel said, still staring intently at the screen. I hope you said hello from me.

I did. She was sorry to miss you.

And how was the call of the wild, Emmett?

Alice glanced at Emmett briefly and hurried away toward the bedroom, leaving the brothers alone. Joel finally looked up and snapped his laptop shut.

Refreshing, Emmett said. He was trying, mightily, to hold eye contact, as though this proved he had nothing to hide.

Why are you looking at me like that? Joel said.

Like what?

So intensely.

I'm just tired.

Joel crossed the room and put a hand on his shoulder. Can I ask you something? he said, his voice low. Did she say anything about us? About me?

Such as?

Look, it's no secret we're going through a rough patch. But she likes you. She's always said how much she likes you. If it came up, naturally, you'd really be helping me if you put in a good word.

A good word.

Only if it came up. Don't force the issue.

What would I tell her, Joel?

You know, just, whatever. How much I care about her. How much the marriage means to me. And naturally, if she said something to you that I should hear, I'd hope that you would pass it along.

What could she possibly say?

Like, for example, if she told you that I left my socks in the doorway, that I just peeled them off and left them there in the floor like dead mice, then you could tell me that and I would know not to do it.

You think she's mad at you about socks?

Did she say she was?

No.

It's just an example. Point being, if you have the opportunity—if it comes up in an organic way—help me out, okay?

He winked and gave Emmett's shoulder a squeeze. Then he returned to his work. He took a loud slurp from his mug and frowned. Tea's cold, he mumbled.

Emmett went to the bathroom, his head throbbing, saliva pooling in the corners of his mouth. He ran the faucet and dry-heaved over the toilet for a few minutes. Kathy pulled in, her brakes like high-pitched feedback on a speaker. He heard Joel helping her with groceries, saying that Emmett and Alice were home. Already? she said. He leaned against the vanity and studied his face in the mirror, framed by pink tile, steam billowing up. And the small but certain knowledge of what he'd done—of who he now *was*—dropped into his life like a bead of dark blood falling into clear solution.

Ten

THERE WAS NO LANDLORD, no single entity or name. There was only the Oakwood Sanctuary office, where people with undefined roles sat behind desks, where maps and addresses were drawn on whiteboards, the edges fluttering with sticky notes. Where checks in envelopes were left in a wicker basket, as though at a mafia wedding.

Emmett waited with his hands in his pockets while the woman at the desk before him finished her call. Her nametag said LORRAINE.

Are they palmettos or German roaches? she said into the phone, holding up her finger to Emmett. Yes, sir, I know you're not an ento- mologist. The reason I ask is that we can spray for the little German roaches but the palmettos are a fact of life. I just name them and move on. I see one go across the kitchen and I say, "There's Fred!"

She laughed heartily, the laugh fading into a sigh.

No, I know, sir, it's not funny. But we have to laugh at life, don't we? Listen, I have a resident here who's waiting. I'll send Chuck down with some spray and we'll go from there, how's that? Okay, perfect, buh-bye now.

She hung up and looked at Emmett. How can I help? she said.

I'll get right to the point, Emmett said. I'm two hundred dollars short on rent.

Lorraine's smile collapsed. Okayyyy, she said. That's not good.

I had some car trouble, an unexpected expense. I'm wondering if I could have till the seventh. I get my paycheck then.

That's not really possible, she said.

Of course it's possible.

After the fourth, we'd have to charge a fee.

You don't *have* to do anything. You could cut me a break.

We like to think of ourselves here at Oakwood as a community, and a community is built on trust. And that trust takes the form of a contract between equals.

Equals.

That's right. Would you not say that we agreed, as equals, to trust each other? Did you read the contract?

I skimmed.

Well, there's your problem. If you'd read it, you'd know that, after the fourth, we charge fees. It isn't personal.

It is personal because it affects me personally.

Were you inebriated when you signed the lease? Did we hold a gun to your head?

Well, no, but—

Then it's your obligation. If you don't live up to your obligation, then how can we trust you, going forward? Do you understand? How do we maintain a relationship of trust?

I don't know.

Exactly. Exactly my point.

Emmett shuffled out in his house slippers, squinting at the painful sunlight. A raft of leaves floated on the surface of the pool. He heard the distant thunder of machinery, of motors running and the cracking of limbs. On the hillside, far away, yellow backhoes and skid loaders were clearing a patch of ground. The trees were splintered poles, stacked in piles, and the grass had been clawed away, leaving bare clay crisscrossed with the tracks of the treaded machines.

A COLD RAIN fell that evening, turning to sleet by dark. Half past midnight, he worked another can puddled with water. He placed the wet boxes outside to be carted away. There was not some sophisticated protocol to dry them off, as one might imagine. They used regular blow-dryers. Emmett set one of his parcels on the steel table attached to every irreg belt. After a few minutes, Flaky knocked on the wall of the can.

We've got an issue, bud, he said.

Emmett stepped out and found a huddle of supervisors around the package in question. They'd moved it aside, and someone with latex gloves was swabbing the puddle of clear liquid underneath. It had eaten into the metal, revealing the bright silver of steel beneath the grime.

We think it's a strong acid, Flaky said. Did you touch this?

I put it there on the table.

Did you notice it was leaking?

I thought it was water. Everything's leaking.

Check your hands, bud, Flaky said.

Emmett looked at his gloves. Sure enough, small holes had opened in the rubber coating. He pulled them off and scrutinized his palms.

I think I'm fine, he said.

Even a little bit will eat through you. It can work its way down to the bone while you sleep.

He showed Flaky his palms. You see anything?

I'm not a doctor, bud, Flaky said.

The supervisor with the latex gloves put the swab into a vial and shook it. The solution turned bright pink. He stared at the vial with no discernible emotion.

What does pink mean? Flaky said.

I think—don't quote me, but I think it means negative.

Negative for what? It's not that kind of test.

Someone with an instruction booklet said, Pink means it's an acid of some kind.

Okay, Flaky said, now we know. Knowledge is power.

What do you want me to do? Emmett said. His hands were open in front of him.

Acid could mean anything, said the man with the litmus test. Acid could mean lemon juice.

Does that look like lemon juice? Flaky said, pointing at the scalded metal table.

It could be, the man said.

It's called Veltex-34, said the other soop, reading the label. There's a string of letters and numbers. There's a skull and crossbones.

Jesus, Flaky said, pinching the bridge of his nose.

It says "farm grade." That means it must be safe, right? If it's on farms?

Not a lot's coming up for Veltex-34, said the other soop, swiping at his iPad. It's on the hazmat list, though. Class 8.

Why was it sent to Emmett's lane? Flaky said. He's not certified for that.

The other soops shrugged. It's your section, Flaky, said the one with the litmus test.

Thank you, everyone, for your input, Flaky said. Emmett, can I have a word with you in private, bud?

They stepped aside; even a few feet of distance in the clatter of the warehouse made a conversation private. Flaky rested his hand on Emmett's shoulder. How do you feel? he said.

I feel fine, he said, though his palms were itching now, as though he'd handled fiberglass insulation. Just fear, he told himself. Psychosomatic.

Normally, I'd file a report, Flaky said. But the hazmat list—that's a complication. No way you could've known what you were touching. That complicates the situation majorly.

Meaning what exactly?

Meaning it's a company oversight. Meaning it's a major liability issue. But you're fine, right? Your hands feel fine?

I think so, Emmett said, though now he could not be sure, and he felt, suddenly, that much depended on his answer—more than he could parse in the moment. Things were happening too fast.

Look, we can document this, Flaky said. I can file a report. We can do things by the book here. I want you to know that.

Okay?

Or, Flaky said, you can call off early, go home, put your feet up, and pretend this never happened. That's option number two. To be completely honest, you'd be doing me a favor if we went with option number two. You'd be saving me a headache.

I wouldn't want you to experience any inconvenience, he said, his sarcasm obvious, though Flaky didn't seem to catch it. He was still unsure what to do with his hands, not wanting to touch his clothes or his face.

I knew you'd understand, Flaky said. You don't feel pressured, do you?

I guess not.

Can you text me that, if you don't mind, bud? Just say, "I don't need a doctor, I'm going home."

All right, he said. Can I wash my hands first?

Of course! Flaky said, shooing him toward the bathroom. Please, take your time!

Not once, since starting at the Center, had anyone told him to *take his time.* He felt that he could bank this favor—that perhaps he could buy himself less scrutiny and hassle down the line.

AT HOME, he cracked open a tallboy and sprawled on the couch. Nothing was playing on TV, just infomercials and televangelists. It was nice to be home at this hour. He had the feeling, from childhood, of skipping school on a snow day. He thought of Alice and wanted to text her—I'm thinking about you—but couldn't risk Joel seeing the message. He texted Kaleb instead.

They let me off early for a chemical exposure, he said.

Lucky.

Will you be at alohas later?

Does a one legged duck swim in circles?

Out of curiosity, he looked up Veltex-34. There was next to nothing online—a Chinese website with bad English and pornographic advertisements. Best he could tell, it was made to clear the lines of slurry spreaders—agricultural machines that sprayed liquid manure onto fields. Hardened sludge built up in the pipes, and Veltex-34 broke down these deposits. There were other websites—articles written in Mandarin—and when he fed the fragments of text into a translator, they told of a village on the Amur River where a plant had been constructed to manufacture Veltex-34. Some byproduct of the chemical process had leeched into the groundwater and led to a spate of vanished twins. Women in the village who became pregnant were found, in almost every case, to carry twins. Among these pregnancies, a high rate of reabsorption was observed, one twin subsumed by the other, becoming a mass of compressed tissue.

Emmett shut his computer, went to the kitchen, and let warm water run over his hands for a few minutes. He looked up the nearest twenty-four-hour urgent care, a half hour away. What could they possibly tell him? It would be a physician's assistant, an RN maybe. A case like this—village rumors, strange solvents of unknown origin, the intricate contingencies of agribusiness runoff—would be beyond their expertise. He considered the emergency room, where at least he might be referred to a specialist. Then the thought of money made all his muscles rigid. People with money never did this, never wondered what doctor to see. This is what money was for. It spared you from these chains of thought. It spared you from unplanned exposures, from clinic doctors, from contamination and defect and the accumulation of small injuries. It spared you from the immense danger of common life. This is what he longed for. The word "money" was only a placeholder. His longing sprang from an ancient communion of longing. It was his but did not belong to him wholly. A thousand generations had longed for the same thing, in some other form, and it was carried now in his blood and marrow.

On the television at Aloha's, the same few frames of the Zapruder film were playing on repeat, a gush of pink matter the color of Jackie's dress pouring from Kennedy's head. It was a history program. There were experts who looked like actors playing experts, but

Emmett could hear nothing of what they said. He was in some pain, his knuckles aching, and it felt good to hold them against the cold glass. A moment ago, there'd been whiskey in front of him, and now it was only ice. A throbbing numbness had spread from his sinuses to the crown of his head, hovering halo-like, shedding its feeble warmth like the hot bulb of a lamp.

This isn't real, Kaleb said, tipping his glass to the screen. It's all a reenactment.

It's a real film, Emmett said.

They hired lookalikes. They paid extras to stand around.

You can see the guy's head explode.

Special effects.

For what purpose?

To frame the guy. Steve Harvey Oswald.

Lee. It was *Lee* Harvey Oswald.

Kaleb had been ready to take a shot, but he paused now, the glass of liquor hovering near his lips, his eyes losing their focus.

I don't think you're right about that, he said.

Emmett signaled vaguely for another, unsure whether the bartender had seen him, whether he'd raised his hand at all or only thought of raising it. She was slicing limes into wedges, dumping them with cupped hands into a hotel pan. There were grimy Band-Aids on her fingers, and though her face betrayed no sign of pain, he could feel, vicariously, the sting of acid in her cuts. She smeared her palms on her apron and poured him another whiskey.

It's late, she said, more to Kaleb than Emmett.

Natasha, Natasha, Kaleb said. When will you marry me?

She twisted up her nose as if about to sneeze, then brushed the strands of sweaty hair from her face. It's late, she said again.

How's that kid of yours?

He's fine, she said. He's happy.

Her kid has a harelip, Kaleb explained. He had the surgery a few months back.

A cleft palate, Natasha said. And that was last year.

We had a raffle at the bar, Kaleb said. Sort of a GoFundMe-type situation.

That's nice, Emmett said.

I put a hundred dollars in, you remember?

I remember, she said. It was a big help.

Kaleb took his shot, coughed once into a cocktail napkin, and said, You're welcome, sweetie.

They went on drinking. The experts onscreen studied the moment of death, frame by frame. A man with a broken arm, his cast scribbled with lewd graffiti, played pool alone. In the darkness of a booth near the back, a woman adjusted the butane on her lighter, flicking the wheel, watching the flame leap up higher and higher. There were no clocks or windows in Aloha's, and he often felt, sitting here drunk with Kaleb and the other careworn patrons, that the place was like some cosmic waiting room, outside the stream of time altogether. That any moment now, a nurse with a clipboard would open the door and call them back, one by one, to their next lives.

I like a large woman, Kaleb said, hiding his mouth with his hand for the sake of discretion, though Natasha seemed to hear, casting a sidelong look as she dried pint glasses with a rag. The lady cop's tiny, he said. Almost like a midget. You get used to one thing, you want the opposite.

Emmett looked at Natasha—her wide hips, her bra straps cutting into the flesh of her shoulders, bearing the burden of her breasts.

I sometimes wish a woman could carry me, Kaleb said. Lift me up like a baby.

Sounds like you want a mother.

He blew a raspberry. I don't believe in that Sigmund and Roy crap, he said.

Who?

Sigmund and Roy? The famous psychologists? They said everything was about your mother. But you'd have to be some kind of freak to think about your mother like that.

It's unconscious. You'd never know how you really felt.

I know I'm not some freak mental patient. I know enough to know that.

Fine, okay.

How come you never talk about your mystery girl? You seal that up yet?

He thought of Alice. He could taste the fact of what he'd done, a tannic bitterness in the back of his mouth.

You dirty dog, Kaleb said. You did it, didn't you?

I'd rather not get into it.

Don't sound like it. Sounds like you got *deep* into it. Kaleb made a hole with his left hand and shoved his fist through, up to the elbow. Now you're just like the rest of us, he said. A dirty dog with his bone. Slippin around with somebody's wife.

That's not how it is.

Denial ain't just a river in Egypt.

Emmett sighed and placed his glass on the rubber drying mat. He'd reached the point in his drinking when ordering another would only ward off leaving and would not change the way he felt. She's my sister-in-law, he said. She's married to my brother.

A slow amazement dawned on Kaleb's face. Well, shit, he said. I underestimated you. You really are a dirty dog.

I wish you'd quit saying that.

I mean, this is some Jerry Springer shit.

All right, I get it.

Hey, I don't judge. Let the guy with a glass house throw the first stone. I'm kind of impressed, actually. You took my words to heart. There's no hook, am I right? You did what you did, and you're still breathing. No bolt of lightning, no instant karma. You're still here, aren't you?

Emmett strained then to call forth his guilt, but he was blind drunk and lost within himself. His thoughts scattered away from him like roaches exposed to sudden light. It took him a while to form words.

I'm still here, he said.

They did bumps of coke in the Corvette. It was quiet outside, save for the growl of engines drag racing on the interstate somewhere. Kaleb spoke of a UFC fight he'd seen the previous weekend on pay-per-view, then, realizing that Emmett had no interest and had never heard of the fighters in the story, he fell silent and lit a cigarette.

I've been thinking about your offer, Emmett said.

Kaleb narrowed his eyes, confused, batting the smoke from his face.

To make some money together. With the pills?

Oh yeah?

I could use some pocket change.

Shit, we'll make more than pocket change, he said. If you really wanna do it, I mean.

What would the next step be?

There's a Rochester flight next Thursday. We could do it then.

He considered this, glancing his hands. No sign of damage yet, beyond the usual wear and tear of package handling—the scrapes and abrasions, his dry, splitting knuckles. Nothing was eating through him—nothing he could see, anyway.

What are the chances we'd get caught? he said finally. Be real with me.

Zero, Kaleb said. Long as you do exactly what I tell you.

He looked back toward the airhub, the fences topped with razor wire, the watchtower above it all.

Okay, he said. What do I do?

Eleven

THE SILVER DAGGER: this is where they met. A dark tavern near the river. Silver tinsel hung above them, shimmering and tangled, reminding Emmett of the abandoned Christmas trees he'd see lying in ditches near his mother's in January. Pink light bathed the bottles of liquor on the shelves and shone on the stapled photographs of regulars who'd died. He'd spent the day waiting for this, catching her eye in odd moments, enduring Joel and Kathy and the boredom of the Dream Home. And now they were here, not knowing what to say but smiling shyly at the other's presence, at the secret knowledge of what they'd done.

Joel asked me to be a mole, Emmett said. To talk with you and report back.

For what purpose?

So he can save the marriage.

Oh God. Did you feel guilty?

I wanted to. I felt something, but it was more like a placeholder for guilt. Like testing positive for guilt but feeling no symptoms.

I'm also asymptomatic, she said, poking around in her drink for the cherry at the bottom. She popped the bright red fruit in her mouth and chewed thoughtfully, not quite meeting his eyes. When she'd left the house, she'd been wearing a knee-length quilted coat. Now it was draped on her chair, and she wore underneath a cropped sweatshirt, revealing her pale, smooth belly.

I thought about you all week, she said. About how this would work logistically. I've never done this. There's not a guide.

Adultery for Dummies.

Don't say *adultery*. The marriage is over.

Not as far as he's concerned.

He thinks I'm taking a mixology class.

In Paducah?

I could tell him I was going out for an orgy. He'd just stare at his computer and say, "Have fun."

Emmett smiled. A sign for Hamm's beer with an animated waterfall hung behind the bar. He watched the steady cascade pouring over a lip of rock into a turquoise pool. There were lights glowing inside, illuminating the plastic, creating the illusion of motion.

It can't be good, he said. Karmically.

It depends on what happens. If we're all better off.

Are we better off?

For now, I'm happy, she said. Aren't you?

Emmett took her hand. A few people were hauling speakers and coils of black cable inside. A microphone stand was erected in the corner, and a large, toadlike man situated himself at a folding table with a laptop and a soundboard. He held one muff of the headphones to his ear and fiddled with the knobs.

Karaoke, Alice said.

They decided they'd go out back for a smoke. One of the toilets had overflowed, and the waterlogged carpet in the hallway squelched underfoot as they walked out. No one seemed to have noticed. It was a true dive, the Silver Dagger. The sort of place where alcoholics formed surrogate families. Where after a funeral—and there were many funerals, Emmett guessed—they would gather here in sickly daylight for a "Celebration of Life," toasting the dead, placing his picture behind the bar with the others who'd gone ahead of him.

You think they offer mixology classes here? Emmett said.

They laughed and lit their cigarettes, Alice bumming one of his. It was cool outside, the damp breeze smelling of the river and leaf rot, stirring the blue tarp stretched above the patio. The same breeze would pass through empty streets and strip mall parking lots and school playgrounds, across the lawns of little houses on subdivided farmland, and maybe reach their mother's house, wafting the sheer curtains of the antique room, rousing Joel from his work or his reading.

How many people hope for this, Emmett said, and never go through with it?

She blew smoke from the corner of her mouth. A lot, I'd guess, she said.

All my life, I've talked myself out of things because they seem impossible.

Look at you now. You're trying. You're writing the screenplay.

Trying isn't the same as finishing.

Maybe you need a support system—other screenwriters.

Not a lot of those in Paducah.

Well, there's your problem. You know, I have a friend in New York who's a screenwriter. Maybe I could introduce you someday.

The subtext of the offer was not lost on him—that one day they would find themselves together in New York City.

It seems impossible, he said. That I'll finish it.

When you have a good story, it finds its way into the world.

Who says I have a good story?

You have experiences that are unique.

As opposed to who?

Joel, for one thing, she said. When I met him, I thought he was more like you. He presented himself that way.

Salt of the earth?

She laughed. Something like that, she said.

We grew up the same way.

But you've done so much else. You've lived a different way since then.

Maybe so, he said, though he felt that "living a different way" had been simply to live like a loser, and he worried that this was not nearly as interesting as she imagined. Did you ever want to write? he asked her.

Never interested me.

You want the farm. *Green Acres.*

It seemed to embarrass her, him saying this. She wouldn't look at him, drawing from her cig with puckered cheeks.

I know how it sounds, she said. It sounds naïve. Joel told me about a slogan once, from the '68 student protests in France: "Be Realistic: Demand the Impossible." I think about that sometimes. A lot actually.

I believe you can do it, he said, though he didn't really. He thought she might try. She might pull it off for a while, sell some stunted, mis-shapen root vegetables at a market stall. But the current of convention was strong. One could linger in the pools and eddies of eccentricity for only a little while, or else become that rare thing—a true hermit.

I try to quit my vices one by one, she said. But it never works. Social media, drinking, smoking. I think maybe it's all or nothing with me. I'd have to quit everything, at the same time, cold turkey. I'd have to drop out altogether. That's part of it, I think. Where the dream comes from.

It would be lonely, he said.

Who says I'd be alone?

Even with a partner, it'd be lonely.

All I'm saying, she said, and maybe this is relevant to your screenplay—you have to reach for the impossible thing sometimes, not because it's realistic, but because it will save your life. Therefore, in a roundabout way, it's the *only* realistic option. It's like with climate change. All that we have to do to go green—that massive transformation of how we live our lives—seems impossible. But if we don't, we're toast. The dreamers are actually the realists. They're the sober ones. They know what has to be done.

Or, Emmett said, we do nothing. We stay like we are, stuck in the same patterns, and things just blow up.

She ground her cigarette against a concrete planter of dead flowers. Let's have another drink, she said.

What happened to quitting your vices?

Tomorrow, she said. Tomorrow is always the best time to quit your vices.

I drove here, is the only thing.

The cops don't have checkpoints on weeknights.

See, I'd like to survive past tonight, though.

Or! You could die in a blaze of glory and they'd put your picture behind the bar.

He laughed and she leaned over to kiss him. It was still so new— her breath, her scent. He knew, with helpless certainty, that he would do whatever she asked of him.

The bar ran out of glassware, so they drank bourbon from paper cups, the tender not bothering to measure, karaoke night in full swing. An old woman, her face like shriveled paper, sang "Coal Miner's Daughter," her voice brassy and pure. The whole bar watched her with stilled reverence.

After three whiskies, Emmett found himself rhapsodizing on the Hero's Journey. Alice listened—half-amused, half-interested—while he listed the examples in pop culture.

There's *Star Wars*, naturally, he said. *The Lord of the Rings*. *The Matrix*. *The Lion King*. Not to mention all the Marvel stuff, which is fairly obvious. In literature, you've got *Huckleberry Finn*, you've got *Moby-Dick*, you've got *The Odyssey*.

These all feel very male.

I'm sure there are woman forms.

Alice laughed. Woman forms?

I'm telling you, I was skeptical at first. But when you start to look, you see it everywhere.

Alice finished her drink and touched his hand. I have to go to the woman form of the restroom, she said. BRB.

He gulped what was left in his own cup, went over to the toadlike emcee, and put his name down for karaoke. A biker couple in black leather were singing "Louisiana Woman, Mississippi Man." Returning to his stool, Emmett gazed at the wall of dead regulars, the glossy photos with their pink sheen. He imagined they could see him from the other side, that they watched this nightly party with a resignation that only the dead possessed. Someone remembered them, if only as regulars—as those who'd shown up every day, who'd done their duty, who'd lent their ears, who'd slow danced to the jukebox at three in the morning, holding each other up like ragdolls. It was comforting in a way.

When Alice returned, he told her about Flaky and Kaleb, about the raccoons that pawed his balcony doors. She talked about her tutoring clients, how their college essays had all the same tropes, how their parents were insane.

I waste so much time making money, she said. If I think about it, it depresses me.

I might get some money soon, he said. A good amount of money.

Planning to rob a bank?

He smiled, wishing he'd kept it to himself. He had a superstitious fear that talking about a future windfall would keep it from coming to pass. She was rubbing his thigh beneath the bar, kneading the muscle, drawing nearer and nearer to his groin. It's like a bonus at work, he said. A lump sum.

They give bonuses to package handlers?

It's highly selective.

An old man with few teeth and large, elfin ears leaned over to Emmett and said, She likes you.

Who?

Your lady friend.

Alice raised her cup to him, and he grinned with purple gums, dark sockets where his teeth had been. He told them his life story. He'd spent years driving a semitruck and had smuggled bales of weed across the country. He'd once been a millionaire, but he'd lost it all. Money, he told them, is like salt water. The more you drink, the more powerful your thirst.

He went on and on, Emmett too polite to cut him off. To escape the man, she whispered, Let's smoke in the car, I have my vape.

So they went. And afterward, in the parking lot, washed in foggy moonlight, she sat astride him, kissing and breathing, fumbling with his belt. He slid his hand down the front of her jeans, past the prickle of shaved hair to the wetness between her thighs, and hooked his fingers into her. She cried out, grasping at his buckle. The music in the bar was only a dull thudding in the distance. She changed positions. She put him in her mouth and made soft humming noises, taking as much of him as she could, till he came and it fell from her lips onto his open jeans, and they both kept still for a long moment, panting, her head in his lap, the windows steamed and glowing. They laughed with the dizzy astonishment of teenagers.

Inside, Alice went to the bathroom. Emmett sat at the bar, his face flushed. One by one, the patrons took up microphones. They sang Skynyrd. They sang Seger and Zeppelin, Mellencamp and Garth Brooks. When the emcee called Emmett's name, Alice looked around, as if there might be another Emmett in the bar. She whistled when he walked to the stage. Standing up, he realized how drunk he was. The blood seemed to slosh in his head when he moved, and standing there in the bright light, breathing with his nose against the microphone's foam cover, he tried to focus on the fixed point of her face. The song he'd picked was "Dancing in the Dark," but the scrolling lyrics, with their bounce-along ball, were doubled in his vision. He muddled through laughingly. He sang the line *There's somethin' happenin' somewhere* three times, not remembering what came next. He stamped his heel, whiskey spilling onto the carpet. He could see Alice filming on her phone, and at first it scared him. There would be evidence of them together. But he closed his eyes, took another drink. He was not himself. He wore a stranger's face. The dead were looking after him.

Twelve

IT WAS HARD to breathe on the shuttle. The workers around him slurped their soups, broke off pieces of granola bars, pulled out their bottom lips to wedge pouches of mint Skoal against their gums. After Emmett had clocked in, beeping the badge on his bicep against the scanner, he went to the water fountain and splashed the back of his neck. He leaned against it for a moment with his eyes closed and forced himself to exhale, to let the air out of his lungs and not just in. When he opened his eyes, Flaky was standing there.

Let's go, bud, he said. Do that before you clock in.

Do what?

Fill your water bottle, take a leak, whatever. Do it before.

The cans that night were easy. Small-sort envelopes. His panic settled into low-level fear after a while, now that he had something to do. He rehearsed, in his mind, the steps Kaleb had laid out. The plane was set to land at one.

At half past midnight, he took his break. *Cops* on the mounted TV. The smell of microwaved pizza, of burnt coffee. Sugar on the table sticking to his arms. He watched a small brown mouse emerge from under the vending machines, then dart back. *This is nothing,* he told himself. *Step one, step two, step three.*

When it happened finally—when Kaleb nodded to him from the dock and the shifters latched the can in his lane—his heart had begun to flutter. He thought he might faint. But once he'd broken the seal and stepped into the cool interior that smelled, always, of damp cardboard, he saw that Kaleb was right—there was really nothing to it. No one could see him here—not Flaky, not the cameras. He took off his glove and pressed his hand to his chest, as though standing for the national anthem—waiting for his heart to settle. *Okay, Emmett*, he said to himself. *You're okay.*

For a while, he unloaded as he would with any other container, and the boxes were drawn in single file down the belt and past the scanner, motes of swirling dust illuminated by the bright lights. They were diverted to a larger belt, like merging onto a freeway, and disappeared from his view, routed to a larger system of conveyances that was beyond his understanding, beyond anyone's capacity to understand. He knew only that the pills would find their way to people in pain, to whom their mysterious provenance would not matter a whit.

When the can was half-empty, Emmett picked a box at random, stretched out the elastic band of his pants, and tucked it inside. He took a moment to pull down his baggy T-shirt, then stepped out and waved to Flaky, who came speed-walking over to Emmett's lane, mumbling something into his radio mic.

Gotta hit the restroom, he said.

Come on, Flaky said, finish the can first.

I gotta go.

It can wait. Finish the can.

He could feel the box shifting. A few more inches and it would slip down his pantleg. I'll just shit my pants, then, he said. How's that? I'll shit my pants, and when the union steward asks me why, I'll tell him Flaky wouldn't let me go to the bathroom. That all right with you?

Flaky released a heavy breath. Five minutes, he said. I mean it.

He hurried to the bathroom, holding the box against his thigh. The stall was in use. He beat on the door and the man inside said, Occupied.

Obviously, Emmett said. Hurry up.

He waited five minutes for the man—a fat ramp worker named Rusty—to finish, hearing him grunt and fart and clear his throat. When finally the stall door opened, Rusty emerged, hitching his belt, and said to Emmett, I go at exactly the same time every night for years.

Good for you, Emmett said.

Alone in the stall, he used his car keys to slit the tape and tore open the top of the box. He dumped the pills from their bottles into a plastic bag. His hands were shaking so bad he dropped one of the bottles. The white tablets scattered across the floor, some dropping into the toilet water. Christ, he said. On his hands and knees, he swept them into piles, the tile sticky with droplets of urine. For Christ's sake, he said, over and over. When he finished, he put the bag in his underwear and scanned the floor for pills he might've missed. Then he flushed the toilet and stuffed the ripped-open box deep into the bathroom trash can. That was it. One, two, three.

Flaky had taken over his lane. When he returned, they stared at each other for a long, uneasy moment. That was ten minutes, Flaky said.

What do you want me to say?

Do you know what time theft is? Flaky said.

Better than you, he thought. It won't happen again, he said.

Flaky went on looking at him, voices crackling through the static on his radio. What are the Eight Rules of Lifting and Lowering? he said.

He allowed himself to smile. It was over. He'd gotten away with it.

Approach the object, he said. Feet shoulder width apart, bend at the knees, test the weight of the package, grip opposite corners, lift smoothly, pivot or step without twisting, use existing equipment.

THE PLAN HAD BEEN to meet with Kaleb at Aloha's, hand over the pills. Kaleb knew a guy. There was always a guy, someone who made arrangements, who knew other guys who were higher up, who in turn knew other guys. *There are levels to this thing,* Kaleb had said. *You have to respect that. You have to respect the chain of command.* Money would come later. A few grand, maybe more. The market for such things was ever shifting. Nothing was guaranteed.

Instead, he went home. He divided the white tablets into four smaller sandwich bags. His phone hummed on the coffee table, one text after another, all from Kaleb.

You here?

Where u at?

??

Call me

Call me now

????? r u fuckin serious rn?

He stepped onto the balcony, raccoons scrambling away from the dumpsters below. The sun had just risen, a blade of light splitting the clouds. Kaleb answered on the first ring.

What the fuck, man.

Listen.

Where the fuck are you?

I chickened out.

You what?

I couldn't do it. I chickened out.

I don't believe you. You had the can. You went to the john. I saw you. I was watching.

I don't know what to tell you.

How bout the truth. I made calls for this. I made accommodations, came to certain verbal agreements. You're leaving me with my dick in the cookie jar.

Tell them it didn't work out.

I know you have them. I'm not stupid.

Look, believe me or don't. I'm hanging up now.

He put the phone in his pocket and leaned against the balcony rail. He laughed aloud, his breath rising in clouds of vapor. A rime of frost covered the windshields in the lot, the sparkle of sun blinding, and for the first time in months he was heartened by the dawning of a new day.

He called in sick the next morning—a Friday—and drove to Paducah. Fuzzy, his old classmate and drug dealer, lived in Elmwood Court, a Section 8 housing project across from the city high school. The street was lined with Dollar Generals and payday loan offices with bars on the windows. The apartment houses were faded red brick with fake white pillars at the entrances, a half-assed attempt to make them look fancy. As Emmett passed the peeling apartment doors, looking for Fuzzy's number, the noise of daytime television drifted out—*Maury* and *Dr. Phil* and *The View*—programs that reminded one of dental work and medical waiting rooms, of cough medicine and unemployment and the endless repetition of selfsame days.

Fuzzy was shirtless when he answered the door, revealing, in full glory, the pelt of pubic-like hair on his back and arms. There was not much in the way of furniture: a threadbare floral couch, a beanbag, two camping chairs. Most of the floorspace was taken up by potted marijuana plants. They were young, not yet flowering, but their skunky, hoppy smell was like a thick substance in the air. Two box fans were running; jury-rigged grow lamps hung from dog leashes fixed to the ceiling.

Fuzzy had a blunt going, grape-scented smoke hazing the room, lending the light a golden, sepia quality. Emmett sat in one of the camping chairs.

I'm playing *Duty Bound,* Fuzzy said, nodding at the television, where Emmett saw the familiar imagery of a first-person shooter—the reticle, a long corridor, blood-spattered walls. Check this out, Fuzzy said. He pressed a button on his controller, and the avatar on-screen switched to another weapon—a compact submachine gun. He let off a burst of automatic fire, spent shells tinkling like a handful of change dropped in a laundromat.

I shot one just like it at the range, he said. You can pay a hundred bucks and shoot whatever you want. It's not illegal. They've got machine guns from World War II.

Pretty cool, Emmett said.

Fuzzy turned off the game, took a pull from the blunt, and passed it to Emmett.

It's got some slobber on it, sorry, bro.

No worries, man.

Hey, guess what? I'm back in the studio, cutting an album. It's my homie's house actually, but he's got studio-quality shit. He's got the mixer, he's got microphones, he's got monitors. We put foam pads on the walls, so the sound is contained. My homie, Skeeter—he's a like a redneck Rick Rubin. He's got the fuckin beard. Always on some shit. He's on this other level, man. He's communing with animal spirits and interdimensional beings. The only problem's his mom—he lives with his mom, and she's got emphysema. Permanent oxygen. She can't fix food or use the bathroom, so we'll be deep in the zone and she'll call for Skeeter. Skeet, he's got a good heart, he puts family first. You gotta put family first, man. That's what it's all about. I'd be nothing without my mom. She cleaned houses for twenty years. She'd come home and her hands were fuckin raw, man, from all the cleaners and chemicals. She'd make us all PB&Js, but some nights she'd never take a bite from her own. She'd let it sit there. I realized later she was saving it for the next night—she was eating supper every other day. You believe that? It makes me wanna cry, even just telling you, man. She bought me my first CD—it was fuckin Coolio. You remember Coolio? I'd heard him in *Space Jam,* then my cousin played "Gangsta's Paradise" for me, and for months all I talked about was Coolio. She got her paycheck one week, took me to Walmart, and bought the CD. She was crying in the front seat on the way home, cause I was so pumped to finally have that Coolio CD. She said she was happy crying. I think about that all the time—happy crying. I told myself, One day, when I put out a platinum record, the first thing I'll do is give her the thing that she wants most. Whatever it is. Money's no object. Then I'll be the one happy crying. Till then, I just gotta hustle, keep my grind strong, you know?

Totally, Emmett said.

That's why this deal—if you've got what you say—is huge for me. I could move out, get one of those condos by the Cinemark. You seen those?

I know the ones.

They're five minutes from the mall. No crackheads wiggin out in the hallways at two in the morning. They've got thick walls, those units. You can't hear babies crying. You can't hear some guy beating his old lady. You can't hear TVs going. You can't smell what the motherfucker next door is cooking for dinner.

Emmett took the three full plastic bags from his backpack.

There's five hundred in each bag, he said. You can count them.

I trust you, homie. We go back to, what, fourth grade? Mrs. Hamlin, you remember her? She had those big knockers. The buttons of her dress hanging on for dear life.

I remember, he said, laughing.

So Roxi, instant release, I can sell for fifteen. Wholesale? I can do four per.

Emmett ran through the mental math. Four times five hundred. Two thousand per bag. Six thousand total. They shook on the amount. Fuzzy left the room and came back with two rubber-banded rolls of cash, which Emmett stuffed deep into his pack. And like this, the transaction was finished. Even in the dank, smoke-thick room, he felt suddenly that he could breathe, that some viscous obstruction had been cleared from his chest.

Wanna hear my new verse? Fuzzy said, already plugging the auxiliary cable into his phone. A beat began to play, the steady throb of bass rattling the ashtray on the coffee table. Fuzzy cleared his throat and read the lyrics from his screen. Emmett listened, pleasantly stoned. He felt this new inflow of cash had flooded his heart with a deep and abiding patience. He had nowhere to be. He could sit with Fuzzy like this all day, listening to his goofy rhymes, passing the saliva-moistened blunt. The beats were a second pulse, thumping in the hollow of his ribcage.

When he'd exhausted his material, and their minds had grown too foggy for conversation, Fuzzy stood from the stained couch and opened his arms.

I love you, homie, he said.

I love you, too, Fuzzy, Emmett said, his chin resting on the man's hairy shoulder. I love you, too.

Thirteen

THERE WERE FOUR LOCKS ALREADY: the knob, the bolt, the chain, and the brass deadlock. Grandma Ruth wanted a fifth—a swing latch, of the sort one found on hotel doors. The adjective "handy" could never be applied to Joel with a straight face, but whenever he was home, Ruth put him to work as her appointed fixer of televisions, her replacer of batteries and refrigerator filters, her mover of furniture, and—in this case—her locksmith. He was happy to help her. It was one of the few uncomplicated sources of happiness in his life.

The latch and the chain are redundant, he said, crouched by the door with a drill and the new packaged lock. The door itself was brittle and weathered; anyone could kick it down.

The chain is old, she said.

So let's get rid of the chain.

I want the chain *and* the latch. I'll feel better with both.

He set to work, holding the latch to the frame and marking the four screw positions with a pencil. It was bright and clear outside, the chimes ringing sporadically like meditation bells. Ruth drank warmed-over coffee and stared at the television tuned to Fox News. She didn't seem to watch so much as absorb the atmosphere it created. It was hard to ignore, like a piece of glinting, garish jewelry, and he caught himself slipping into the same trance. The colors were wondrous and oversaturated, the Barbie-like women in fuchsia skirts hiked up to show their legs, the men like aging action figures, broadcasting from studios where nothing resembled the materials of the earth. Molded plastics, holograms and screens of plasma, the endless flowing chyron of words and images that seemed to speak from a storehouse of myth. That could be, at the same time, so grotesquely specific. Crack cocaine on a scale—chunks of white chalk—and Hunter Biden lipping a cigarette, filming himself for some reason, filming the room he shares with a woman who speaks off camera, whose leopard dress and panties are strewn on the floor with iPads and charging cables and dirty flip-flops. The pitiless light of the studio, the women with tumescent faces, the men with square jaws laughing. The sudden violence of transition. Gangland shootings, burning cities, crime stat infographics, maps of Mexico and Chicago, mugshots, men with tattooed faces, the wash of siren lights, blue and red, bodies draped with sheets and bullet casings on pavement. The commercials not a break in continuity but a subplot, a B-story, a contrapuntal melody. Geriatric television stars. Reverse mortgages and gold bullion. Home security systems. Liberty Mutual. Fiber supplements. Loans for veterans, zero down, no risk, exclusions may apply. Total nutrition. Hail to the Beef. Best sleep of your life. Dirt stays outside. Bloat and bulge. Live your dreams, call now, 1-800-RELIEF. Have you or a loved one been diagnosed with mesothelioma?

So many people—so many politicians and pundits and late-night comedians—failed to grasp what Fox News really was. It was not a transmission of information or entertainment, nor was it propaganda, precisely, in the old sense of the word. It was a panoptic work of art. An enormous mirror, reflecting the primal fears and nostalgias of its viewers with such verisimilitude that all they could manage, in response, was to stare—wonderstruck, vindicated. Fox News was the Absolute Truth, not about the world, but about *them*. As with any great work of art, it saw them perfectly and they saw themselves perfectly within it.

Them men in the woods were back, Ruth said, sorting through the pile of mail on her dining table. Watching like before.

Those are deer, Grandma, Joel said.

The way they move is like a man.

I think it's unlikely.

He drove a drill bit into the wood, sawdust powdering the floor. Ruth tore open envelopes and held the folded letters to the light, sighing. Everybody wants money, she said. You send a check once and they never quit asking. St. Jude's. The Policemen's Association. Wounded Veterans.

You don't have to pay them anything, Grandma.

They send me calculators and pens, she said. I have to give them a little.

No, you don't. Those calculators are junk, they cost nothing.

I hope your brother got the money I sent.

What money?

Your brother Joel. He called asking for money.

Joel set down the drill and stood to face her. I'm Joel, he said. Not Emmett. I'm Joel. Look at my face and my hair. Listen to my voice.

The light went out in her eyes briefly, then came back. I know that, she said.

So who asked you for money?

You did, she said timidly. You called and asked me for three hundred dollars.

Why would I ask for that, Grandma? I have plenty of money.

You said you'd pay me back. You said it was an emergency.

I never called you. It must've been someone impersonating me.

It sounded just like you.

Well, it wasn't. If someone asks you for money, assume it's a scam.

Her eyes grew bright with indignation then—the last and only armament of old age. I know my grandson's voice, she said.

I'm sure it was convincing, Joel said. He felt bad then for scolding her and came to put his arm around her shoulder, smelling her White Diamonds perfume. The word "death" flashed in his mind like a pair of green eyes in headlight beams.

He finished installing the lock and drove her to the pharmacy for Epsom salts and her prescriptions in their stapled paper bags, receipts dangling in long ribbons. He drove the backroads home, taking his time, passing new subdivisions and fields of pale cane grass, shape-shifting clouds of starlings in flight, the burnished silver of grain silos reflecting the sun. He thought she might like the scenery, but at some point she turned to him and said, Where on earth are we?

I thought we'd take the scenic route.

I'd rather be home, she said.

He pulled into the lot of a furniture store. There had been some kind of fire—half the roof collapsed and charred, the windows black with soot—and a red banner had been hung above the entryway: LIQUIDATION SALE! Pieces of furniture were arrayed in the lot, some smoke damaged, and as he turned the car around, an old man in a plaid suit hobbled toward them, gesturing desperately to the salvaged pieces. He watched the man recede in the rearview mirror, arms at his sides, alone with all he'd managed to save.

The phone was ringing when they got back. Joel stood by the door admiring his handiwork, while Ruth went to answer in the kitchen. Hang on a minute, she said. She covered the receiver with her palm and whispered, It's the man!

What man?

The man who says he's you.

Joel took the phone from her and said hello.

Who is this? said the voice on the other side. Joel had the sensation, then, of falling forward into bottomless depth—the sudden, nauseating vertigo of standing between two mirrors and seeing oneself reflected infinitely. The voice was his own. He was hearing himself on the line.

Is this a joke?

This is Joel Shaw, said the voice.

That's impossible.

I'm stranded. I need more money.

You're stranded.

I need a thousand this time. I can give you the routing number, it's different than before.

How do you sound like me?

After a silence, the voice said, I'm Joel Shaw. The writer.

If you call this number again, I'll report you to the police.

He clapped the phone forcefully into its cradle on the wall and steadied himself against the kitchen table. He thought he might be dreaming and closed his eyes. When he opened them, he was still in Ruth's kitchen, her needlework hummingbird hanging in its circular frame by the phone.

You've gone white, Ruth said.

If they call again, you let me or Mom know right away. It's some kind of hoax. They've recorded me somehow—I don't know. I can't explain it.

Ruth stood there wringing her hands, the scribbled veins along her knuckles like ink stains. Goodness gracious, she said. What will they do next?

SEVERAL OF HIS FRIENDS had gone into tech. This phrase—*going into tech*—made him think of a man entering a computer, soldering himself to the motherboard somehow, becoming a conduit for electrical signals. Tyler—an old friend from Northwestern—worked for an online brokerage firm now, streamlining the app, ensuring it was customer-friendly, and when Joel called him, still shaken by the voice at Ruth's, he realized they had not spoken since before the pandemic.

I've heard of this, Tyler said. It's a deepfake scam. I listened to a whole podcast about it.

It sounded just like me, Joel said. He was pacing barefoot in the backyard while Kathy raked leaves, the late sun like molten bronze behind the trees.

All they need is an audio clip—just a few seconds. It captures everything. Not just the sound but the intonation, the way you stress certain words, verbal tics, you name it.

I thought I was losing my mind.

Yeah, man, it's wild. Welcome to the future.

How is it not illegal?

It is if you do it to someone else. It's clear-cut fraud. But you can clone your own voice. It's pretty fun, actually. You've never heard of this?

If it's a tech thing, assume I've never heard of it.

There's an app called Self-Help, Tyler said. This guy I know works on it. You record your voice and it lets you talk to this deepfake clone of yourself.

What's the point?

The point is that it's crazy.

But it's not really you. It's just a facsimile.

Who's to say, man? Tyler said. Then he laughed with the hearty confidence that only someone who'd chosen a lucrative and promising career possessed. Hey, how are you anyway? he said. That book of yours make any money?

Not exactly. There's a different currency in my world.

I still find the American dollar comes in pretty handy. Speaking of which, some friends of mine are starting a company.

I have to go, Joel said. It was good to catch up, though.

We didn't catch up.

Next time.

You could get in on the ground floor of this thing. It's the next TikTok.

Take care, Tyler.

He walked over to his mother. She plucked out her earbuds and smiled at him, out of breath, leaning against her rake. Your wife took the van, she said. She wanted me to tell you. Something about a mixology class.

In Paducah?

Kathy shrugged. He took the rake from her and finished the job, the air cooling rapidly, his feet plastered with wet grass. It ought to be comforting, he thought, to have some explanation. It was only a clone, a clever replica. Even still, his disorientation lingered, a sense that things were askew. The trees were not right; they seemed to stutter when they moved. The rasping of the rake was too consistent. The birds were like field recordings, played on a loop. And his body, that old familiar form he'd hauled around since birth, felt clumsy and simian. An antiquated machine.

FOR THREE DAYS, this dissociation persisted; he thought of the cloned voice constantly. Where had it come from? Who was the person behind it all? Was it simply someone's day job, somewhere in China or Russia? Were there call centers where they sat in cubicles, trawling the internet for audio samples, spoofing telephone numbers, typing plausible responses into text boxes? How much did they make? Minimum wage? To whom did they kick up their profits? Did they stand around watercoolers, bitching about the boss? Had they considered forming a union? When someone asked them what they did for work, did they say, *I'm in tech?*

After supper one night, he locked himself in the antique room and looked up Self-Help. Alice was in the shower, humming cheerily over the steady hiss of water. She'd been more buoyant lately; he'd catch her daydreaming, staring out the window with an enigmatic smile. When he asked her what was on her mind, she seemed almost resentful, as though she'd been laboring to complete some delicate mental task and he'd broken her concentration.

Self-Help's website had the air of being both low-rent and impressively sleek, both retro and cutting-edge, both earnest and ironic. The text was neon pink, the background gradations of violet and forest green. There were images of Rubik's Cubes, of hyperspatial Möbius strips, of grids and tessellations and warping checkerboards. He clicked the "About" tab and read the developers' spiel, which amounted to a long list of technical specifications, followed by anodyne ad copy. *Self-Help is more than a chatbot. It's more than a revolution in therapy. Self-Help is the real you. Come say hello.*

He typed his credit card information into the form and spent a few minutes on the personality quiz, responding true or false to prompts like, *I prefer when other people like me.* Then he recorded his voice, answering aloud the question they'd posed: *Why are you signing up for this service?*

Hey, I'm Joel Shaw, he said. I'm here because my grandma was scammed. That's how I heard about it. Somebody called her using my voice, and I spoke to them. It was the weirdest thing. I couldn't stop thinking about it, so here I am.

A bell dinged when thirty seconds had passed, and the words *Please wait* appeared, accompanied by a spinning metallic orb. After a moment, a voice came through the speakers, the same voice he'd heard on the line at Ruth's. The metallic orb rippled in sync with the sound, as if it were the source.

Hi, Joel, said the voice.

Hey, Joel said. Is this—are you the AI?

Who else would I be?

Wow, he said. This is very weird. So what should I do?

Try asking me a question.

Okay, well—if I'm feeling sort of—hypothetically, if I was feeling sort of hopeless and unable to write, and I also felt like a fraud. Hypothetically, what should I do to, sort of, get past that?

Here are five things you could try, hypothetically, said the clone. Practice self-compassion, set realistic goals, embrace self-doubt, celebrate the small wins, and consider seeking professional help.

I thought this was professional help. I thought you were "a revolution in therapy."

Can you frame that as a question?

Are you or are you not presenting yourself as therapy?

Self-Help is not approved by the American Psychiatric Association, the American Board of Professional Psychology, or any other regulatory body in the United States or abroad as an effective treatment for any form of mental illness.

Perfect. Brilliant.

Can you frame that as a question?

How can I save my marriage?

Here are five things you could try. Open and honest communication—

Just shut up. Shut your mouth.

Can you frame that as a question?

Can you shut your stupid mouth?

I'm sorry, Joel. I don't understand.

You're not me. This advice could apply to anyone. I'm asking you how to live an authentic life, where I feel comfortable in my own skin. Can you give me something other than platitudes?

I understand your request for more concrete guidance. Here are five things you could try—

Not five things, one thing. Can you tell me one thing?

Yes. But you've reached your limit of free questions for the day. Would you like to watch a thirty-second targeted ad to earn more tokens?

I already paid.

You paid for five tokens.

Okay, fine.

The ad that played was for GENTS. A sad-looking man stood before his bathroom mirror examining his hairline, while his wife or girlfriend stood behind him seeming worried. *Listen up, guys,* said the voiceover narration. *Real talk: Millions of men experience hair loss, ED, and depression. Society tells us to "get over it." Well, guess what? You have options—with GENTS.*

A montage played in which smiling, shirtless men embraced their partners, and their partners clawed their fingers through thick locks of hair. The couplings were not all straight, and there were actors of every race and body type.

In a testimonial, a man in his forties with alert ice-blue eyes said, These products are life-changing. And they're made for guys. It's like, finally, something for us, you know?

With GENTS' Personalized Treatment Plan, you can feel like yourself again—your best self, your true self. GENTS: Become the man you used to be.

The advertisement closed on its own, and the spinning orb returned. I'm back, said the clone.

One thing, Joel said. One thing I can do, that is not a platitude, to help me feel my life is authentic.

Can you frame that as a question?

Joel slammed his laptop shut. He closed his eyes, his heart twinging painfully. He'd become dizzy; his breathing grew shallow and quick, and he felt as though he couldn't fill his lungs, no matter how much air he gasped. *I'm having a panic attack,* he thought. He paced the room, trying to steady his breath. He opened a copy of *Going South,* thinking it might ground him to read a passage of his own writing. It was an essay about the efficacy of antidepressants. They were palliative, he argued. The drugs enabled and prolonged the relations of exploitation that made them necessary. He sounded so sure of himself in the prose, so utterly convinced of his position. This only aggravated his feelings of panic and unreality. He recalled reading once of a technique—a way of knowing whether you were dreaming. You looked at your watch, waited a few moments, then you looked again. If the times were wildly different, you knew you were dreaming. He clicked his phone's display: 8:11. His "notification center" was flooded with news of a California shooting. Six were confirmed dead, including the shooter. He took his antidepressant around eight o'clock each night. He'd received a new bottle with its sky-blue label, GENTS in serifed text on the cap. He shook a pill into his palm. He could taste its bitterness just by looking at it. Maybe his past-self—the confident essayist whose voice he scarcely recognized—was right. Pills would not solve his basic problem. They were a stopgap; he'd known this all along. He returned the tablet to the bottle, replaced the cap. He checked his phone: 8:12. Still held by time, by its reliable procession, its fatal constancy. Alice was blow-drying her hair in the bathroom. Kathy watched a YouTube video wherein a body language expert explained how the president was portrayed by various doppelgängers. He sat in the darkness with the sensation of being watched. That crawling of tiny, hairlike legs on the flesh. That feeling that beneath the thin mask of life, some hideous stranger grinned and waited.

Fourteen

EMMETT ARRANGED a hotel room. Staying at the Dream Home would rouse suspicion, since he'd always worked on Friday nights in the past. Alice concocted a story—an old friend she knew in southern Illinois, a reunion. They met at the Silver Dagger once more. He waited outside and saw her coming from far away in her long coat and flared red trousers, swinging a gift bag as she walked. He felt himself smiling, and she smiled too when she saw him. She began to skip like Dorothy in *The Wizard of Oz*. He embraced her on the sidewalk, lifting her off her feet.

You're in a good mood, she said.

It was a good day, he said. Let me buy you a drink. Top shelf—whatever you want.

Inside, she tried to order Veuve Clicquot, repeating the name three times while the bartender looked at her, bewildered.

I have no idea what you're saying to me, he told her finally. As far as bubbly, best I can do is Korbel.

They ordered a bottle and drank from wineglasses with lip stains smudged on the rims. The crowd was sparse; no karaoke that night.

So what's in the bag? he said.

Something small, she said. It's sort of a joke.

He plucked out the tissue paper and peered inside. There were two pillowcases, screen printed with black text—the first two lines of "Dancing in the Dark."

Holy shit, he said, holding them up to the weak light.

There's a card, too.

He unfolded the slip of notebook paper and used his phone light to read it:

> Dear "Bruce,"
>
> I know you ain't nothing but tired, tired and bored with yourself, so I thought I would offer a little help—in the form of these pillowcases. Seriously though, I wake up sometimes and I think about you and how you're working while I'm sleeping, and I wish you could come and crawl into bed with me. What I'm trying to say is that I miss you. I think about you. I think about the future and what that word even means for us. Isn't it weird that one day the future will arrive, and we'll look back, knowing how things turned out?
>
> Until then, this gun's for hire,
>
> A.

He thanked her and kissed her forehead. For an hour, they scorched their throats with cheap champagne. They left in a rush of effervescence, laughing arm in arm, steering the Mystique through washes of cold light and dense darknesses, pink clouds swirling past the moon. He'd reserved a room at the Comfort Inn, and the woman at the desk had gone to school with him. Try as he might, he could not recall her name. Her hair had once been blond but was now a polished black. She had a septum piercing, pitted acne scars on her forehead she'd tried to cover with makeup. A bowl of takeout sat steaming on the desk—macaroni and cheese, bright orange buffalo chicken. The smell was strong.

Emmett Shaw! she said. It's been a minute.

Hey there, he said. It sure has.

Alice hung back, head bowed, scrolling on her phone.

You don't remember my name, do you? She pointed to the nameplate pinned to her uniform.

Kayleigh, of course, he said. How you been?

Oh you know, she said. She gestured to the empty lobby of the Comfort Inn. Working, I guess. I live out by Hardin. My daughter just started third grade. Wild, isn't it? I met you in the third grade. You stabbed me with a pencil on accident.

Surely not.

She held up the palm of her hand and pointed to a faded speck at the fleshy base of her thumb. That's pencil lead, she said.

No.

Oh yeah. Every time I see it, I think, "Emmett Shaw."

You remember Fuzzy?

Hell yeah. I buy weed from him sometimes.

Me too. I saw him today, actually.

He's still the same, ain't he?

For sure, for sure.

Who's this? she said, glancing over his shoulder at Alice.

This is Alice, he said, without thinking. She's a friend.

Alice gave Emmett a look, then waved and smiled tightly at Kayleigh. Hi there, she said.

Cool, cool, Kayleigh said. She took a mouthful of buffalo-mac-and-cheese and typed something into the computer. So, I'll just need a credit card, she said.

Can I pay in cash?

It's discouraged, but yes.

Emmett fished around in his backpack, feeling for the rolls of cash Fuzzy had given him. He gave her a hundred-dollar bill, and as they made for the elevators, he turned back and saw her watching them, chewing her food slowly.

Their window overlooked the interstate exit and the nearby Rural King, a fleet of orange mowers in the lot. Emmett closed the curtains and pulled off his sweater. Alice sat on the bed and raked her fingers through her hair.

I wish you hadn't mentioned my name, she said.

It was stupid, I know. I'm sure she'll forget.

It's a small town.

I know, it was stupid.

She did not seem upset. But the champagne fizzle that carried them here had gone flat. Replaced by something else, something stronger, higher-proof. She regarded him now with a cool intensity, a seriousness of purpose.

Come take my clothes off, she said.

He obliged, kneeling to pull off her sneakers, then working the dark red trousers past her hips. She lay back on the bed, not helping him, and when she was naked from the waist down, he kissed her white thighs and her kneecaps.

Keep doing that, she said.

He told her to close her eyes. He touched his lips lightly to every part of her except the part she wanted most, and she began to tremble and draw great draughts of breath. He brought his face close, without touching. He could see her so clearly. The sprouts of hair she'd missed when she shaved. The strange wish came to him then, hovering above her, that he might somehow pay for this.

Do you think, he said, that she thought you were a prostitute?

Alice sat up, hair falling over her eyes. Who?

Kayleigh. My schoolmate at the front desk.

Do I look like a prostitute?

No, he said. But it's not a crazy assumption.

People bring dates to hotels.

People who have affairs, you mean.

Don't say *affair*.

Or people with escorts. Those are the only two scenarios in which you bring a date to a hotel.

So what?

So it's sort of tawdry, isn't it? In a sexy way.

She took in the room—the anti-theft chain on the television, the watercolors of horses bolted to the wall above the bed. She gave him a sly look. What are you getting at? she said.

What if we pretended she was right? he said. The girl at the desk.

You mean that I'm a hooker?

Or I could be the hooker.

She smiled, her cheeks and throat flushing scarlet, turning away from him for a moment. Then she said, Okay, what would that entail?

I'll try to go down on you. And you'll push me away. You'll say, not until you have your money.

She flopped back on the bed and said, Okay, let's try it.

He kissed her feet and shins, her knees and hips. When he was near enough to smell her again, she pushed his face away roughly. Not until I get my money! she barked.

What was that accent? he said, laughing.

I don't know, Eastern European?

Why?

Aren't most hookers trafficked from Eastern Europe?

Okay, this isn't realism, it's fantasy.

All right, how's this—let's settle up first, baby.

That's better.

He rose from the bed, went to his backpack, and peeled another hundred from one of the rolls inside. He folded the bill and tucked it into her bra.

Where are you getting all this cash? she said.

I'm a businessman. I'm only in town for the night.

Do businessmen carry cash?

In my line of work they do.

Which is what?

He thought for a minute and said, I'm a Rural King sales rep.

You sell tractors?

Manure spreaders.

What a turn-on, she said. I've always wanted to be with a man who sold manure spreaders.

I've heard that before.

She fell into helpless laughter, and he tasted her finally, her thighs squeezing around him, Fuzzy's money still tucked in the cup of her bra. They made love gently, whispering kind things to each other, the fantasy falling away. And lying beside her later, hearing her soft snoring and the roar of traffic on the interstate, he was certain that his luck had changed for good.

At the start of his shift on Monday, the hub supervisor—a man named Keith Cooper—gathered the fifty or so package handlers into a circle around him. To his right stood Flaky, to his left the assistant hub supervisor. This could be it, he thought. Keith Cooper was the head honcho; he wouldn't be here on the warehouse floor if not for something serious. They would announce that a package had been stolen, an investigation was underway. That one among them was guilty.

We've had a package go missing, Cooper said. An important medical package.

Emmett took a step back from the crowd and looked toward the exit. He could leave right then, catch the shuttle, jog to his car. Drive somewhere far away.

They need the package for a surgery that's scheduled in the morning, Cooper said. We believe it's in one of these holdover cans.

He gestured to the cans pushed up against the wall, left over from the day shift. Emmett inhaled after what seemed minutes without breath.

Now this is very important, listen up, Cooper said. Can everyone hear me?

The crowd nodded in silence.

Whoever finds the package will receive a fifty-dollar gift card to Chipotle. That's how important this is.

They were told to look for a Styrofoam cooler with a bright orange label. As the crowd dispersed, rumors began to circulate about the contents of the package. Pauline insisted it was a heart—a human heart, destined for transplant. This was not so implausible. Every night, Emmett unloaded Styrofoam coolers. Many said HUMAN BLOOD PRODUCT on the labels, and it was always strange to remember the coolers he cradled in his arms contained sloshing bags of wine-dark blood. It was rarer, though not uncommon, for human tissues and organs to come through the airhub. Most everything they handled was high-priority overnight shipping. He knew for a fact he'd handled a human kidney once; Flaky told him as much—*That cooler there has a kidney in it for transplant.* It would be hard for outsiders to believe that a human kidney could be handled with the same roughness, the same indifference, as a package of socks or a bag of cat food. But nothing shocked him anymore about the traffic of the world's goods—how tenuous it all seemed, how provisional. And so how could a human heart be far-fetched? He imagined it: a muscle on ice in the dark.

They all searched the holdover cans, even the shifters and the ramp workers and the air drivers. The missing heart was priority number one. Kaleb found Emmett and helped to toss aside the boxes and envelopes.

You're avoiding me, Kaleb said.

I've got nothing to hide, he said, out of breath.

Bullshit. You kept the pills.

Why would I do that?

To use them, to sell them—how would I know what devious macramations you've got swirling in that head of yours?

Machinations, he said. The word is *machinations.* You realize that half the time, you make no sense whatsoever?

Kaleb stood there, baffled, thumbs hooked on his neon vest. I don't understand, he said. I thought we were friends.

Look, I like you fine.

But we're not friends?

Kaleb reminded him suddenly of a little boy on a playground, left out of some game—the self-pity, the narcissism of childhood.

You're a work friend, he said.

Kaleb blinked quickly, as though his eyes might fill with tears.

Hey, I get it, he said. It was a business arrangement.

That isn't what I said.

I'm just a way for you to make money.

Before Emmett could respond, Flaky appeared in the can's doorway. This isn't social hour, he said. Do you understand that someone's life is on the line here? If they don't get the package by morning, they can't have surgery, and that's on us. While you two Chatty Cathys are in here dicking around, some little boy is lying in a hospital bed, hoping for a miracle.

It's a little boy? Emmett said.

We don't know, Flaky said. It's hypothetical. Point is, let's see a little hustle, okay?

Is it true that it's a heart? Emmett said.

Flaky looked over his shoulder, making sure he could not be heard. It's a heart valve, he said. Porcine. That means it's from a pig.

They put pig hearts in men now? Kaleb said, his face contorted with disgust.

It's a miracle of modern science, Flaky said. And that little boy is waiting for it.

The hours slurred together. Emmett kept his distance from Kaleb, though now and then, pausing to catch his breath in the breezeless air of a can, he'd catch Kaleb staring, his eyes full of ire. His mind drifted helplessly to Alice. He saw her in stark flashes of lust. Astride him, leaning down to kiss his chest. The way she shivered when she came. He felt her teeth on his earlobe, her tongue, like she was there with him in the airhub, the shudder of planes overhead, the indifferent drone of conveyors.

Hoping for distraction, he found Winston and joined him in a can. It was half-full, mostly zippered canvas mailers. They worked their way through the pile, tossing them into a corner. Find your own can, playboy, Winston said.

They're all taken, he lied.

I called this one. If we find the heart, I get to claim it. I want that Chipotle gift card.

I don't care about the gift card.

You don't like Chipotle?

Kaleb entered the can then and stood close to Emmett. Winston dabbed his forehead with his white towel and looked at Kaleb in utter disbelief. Is there a sign on my can that says "Open House, Anybody Welcome"? he said.

I've decided to terminate our relationship, Kaleb said to Emmett.

Perfect, that's great.

But I expect what I'm owed.

I don't owe you anything, Emmett said.

Kaleb shoved him then, knocking his hat to the floor.

When Emmett bent to fetch the hat, he saw the scalloped edge of a Styrofoam lid, buried beneath the mailers. Kaleb and Winston saw the cooler in the same instant. They all leapt forward to push aside the bags.

That's it, Winston said. That's the fuckin heart.

Sure enough, it fit the description. The label was bright orange, the word PRIORITY printed in all caps.

This was my can, Winston said. I'm claiming it.

I found it first, Kaleb said.

Bull. Fucking. Shit. I'm claiming that gift card.

Kaleb was transfixed, seeming hardly to have heard Winston.

Let him have it, Emmett said. It's just a gift card.

I wanna see it, Kaleb said.

See what? Emmett said.

The pig heart, Kaleb said. I wanna see it.

Are you high? Emmett said. Winston, take it to Flaky, it's all yours.

Not until I see it, Kaleb said. I wanna see it first, then he can claim it.

Winston looked at Kaleb with a pained expression, the way one might look at a maimed animal or the picture of a crime scene. You're crazy, he said, very quietly.

Kaleb squatted and began to peel at the tape on the lid. Emmett touched his arm, and Kaleb shoved him back against the can's plexiglass wall.

What's the matter with you? he said. But Kaleb was absorbed entirely by the task at hand. He'd bragged once that he could open any package, even those with tamper seals, in such a way that no one would notice, and it was plain now, from the deft working of his fingers, that this had been no lie. Delicately, he peeled away the strips of tape. Particles of Styrofoam drifted about in the air, as though the can were a snow globe. Winston backed away slowly, his palms raised. You're crazy, he kept saying.

Emmett backed away himself, till he stood shoulder to shoulder with Winston near the doorway. He knew he could leave, go after Flaky. He could avert his eyes. But something in him, some fearsome craving, kept him still, rooted in place, and the same spell seemed to have closed its grip on Winston. It was the strangest thing. He wanted to see it—the part of him that was most human. Flesh and blood and breath. He wanted to see it.

With great care—with tenderness almost—Kaleb lifted the lid. A swirl of vapor rose from inside, the frigid exhalation of dry ice. Kaleb reached down, his mouth falling open, his pupils blooming. They watched him. Crouched in scattered mail. They watched him lift the heart. It was pink and glistening, a piece of meat in plastic, and he held it in his hands.

Part

TWO

One

She came to imagine that a second earth existed. She called it that in her mind—Second Earth. It was in a parallel universe. Or maybe there was only one universe, extending infinitely, and therefore containing every possibility, however far-fetched. She wasn't sure which was true. But Second Earth was real. She needed it to be real. On Second Earth, a girl met a boy in a bar. They fell in love, moved together to the big city, and the tragedies of their lives were small and manageable. There was grief, of course, but it tempered their love and made life sweeter. The world's larger problems—climate, hunger, penury—were not solved overnight, but the leaders they'd chosen, and the institutions they trusted, made steady progress. There was reason for hope on Second Earth. One could have children. One could grow old without fear.

She first conceived of Second Earth in the Bloomington Walmart, where they'd driven to try to find toilet paper. The shelves were empty, and she stood there in the sterile fluorescence, imagining what this same Walmart would look like in a parallel universe where the pandemic had never happened.

I found this, Joel said, coming up behind her. He was wearing a red bandanna over his face that made him look a little like a train robber from a silent Western. In his arms, he cradled a giant, 1,000-count bottle of ibuprofen.

You're not supposed to take ibuprofen, she said. I read an article. It suppresses your immune response or something.

Shit, Joel said. That's probably why it wasn't sold out.

He set the bottle on the empty toilet paper shelf. They went out together into the gray March drizzle, and for the rest of that night, and the weeks that followed, she daydreamed about Second Earth. Lying in bed, she envisioned scenes from that other world as if it were a TV show, as if what happened next was anyone's guess.

Later, when they decided to go ahead and move to New York after the first catastrophic wave of cases had crested in the city, she went on imagining their alternate lives. It had a sedative effect; it served the same purpose as liquor or weed. But like everything else she'd relied on for self-medication in her life, it offered diminishing returns after a while. She began to drink secretly as the date of their move approached. She bought a one-hitter, painted to look like a cigarette, and smoked in a city park near Joel's apartment. If the world was ending, spring had not gotten the memo. The blossoming crab apples gave off their heady perfume, and when she tried to think of that other world where things had not gone awry, it suddenly seemed flimsy to her. It was like the spun sugar she'd loved as a girl at the Illinois State Fair. You put a tuft of cotton in your mouth, and it vanished into sweet nothingness. After that, she let it go. There was only one earth.

IN NEW YORK, when someone asked them how they came to be married, they gave conflicting accounts. Joel said it was love at first sight; he emphasized the whirlwind urgency of it all, how quickly they *knew*. And when you know, you know, he liked to say. For someone with such radical views on politics and culture, he was decidedly old-fashioned in matters of the heart.

Whenever Joel told his version, Alice felt her ears grow very warm, and standing there beside him, she'd wonder, *Could this possibly be true?* When asked the same question, she tended toward obfuscation. She strived to create the impression—the definitely false impression—that they had been together a long time when she quit the program, moved with him to New York, and then married him at the apogee of a six-month panic attack. Whenever she was forced to delineate a timeframe, to confess the number of months—not years—they had been together when they tied the knot, whoever was listening would lift a brow, almost imperceptibly, and it embarrassed her to think that, later, she might be the subject of gossip for solid couples with five or ten years under their belts.

My grandparents got married after knowing each other a week, she liked to add, though this only made her sound more desperate, both to the listener and to herself.

The truth was that she had no rational explanation, no coherent story of cause and effect. Maybe that was just love. Love was irrational. Maybe one day, when she and Joel were gnarled and wise, she would look back and see that it was love, all along. "Love at first sight" made for a good story, but it hadn't felt that way, not if she was honest with herself. It had felt more like "safety at first sight." Her father had told her a story once about a time he'd nearly drowned. He'd been swimming in the ocean when the tide came in and he'd lost sight of the shore. For a long time, he treaded water, panic rising, knowing that if he swam in the wrong direction, he would be doomed. Completely disoriented, he decided to pick a point in the distance and start swimming. Soon the thin white line of the beach appeared, the long seagrasses swept back by the wind. Panting, on his hands and knees, he had kissed the sand.

This story of her father's was the closest she came to an explanation. The decade of her twenties had been a blur of intoxication and boredom, of sex with people who cared nothing about her, and about whom she cared even less. She'd been treading water for a long time when she found herself at Beaver's Tavern on the night in question. At some point, you had to pick a direction and start swimming, and this is what she had done.

Their apartment in Astoria took up the second floor of a row-house. All their neighbors were Greek, most of them elderly. The crimp-backed women always seemed to be sweeping the sidewalks, and the men smoked cigars and watched the women from their front porches, thumbing the straps of their suspenders. They had chosen Astoria because it was cheap by New York standards; they had a second bedroom and a dining room, amenities that none of their Brooklyn friends could claim. On the other hand, it was a twenty-minute walk to the nearest subway stop, and their Brooklyn friends would never see their place because the journey involved three transfers and took about as long as driving to Philadelphia. Not that this mattered during their first year, when they rarely left the apartment at all, Alice maintaining her tenuous grip on—what, reality? sanity?—through frequent Zoom calls with a therapist, and with Min and Toby, who were still in Illinois, faithfully following the path she'd abandoned, even as the world was ending.

By the summer of 2021, the city had begun to stir awake from its long slumber, and Alice, like everyone else, was eager to spend the money she'd saved, to stand in a crowd of strangers, to touch other people and be touched by them. Joel, on the other hand, had taken to lockdown without much trouble. It did not change his life materially. He wrote in the mornings, read in the afternoons, and watched a few hours of TV in the evenings. Some days he taught one of his online courses. Mostly, he seemed unbothered by the isolation; he seemed to enjoy it, actually.

Her drinking became a daily habit. She bought pints of vodka from the corner store and poured the liquor into mugs of peppermint tea. This was in addition to her non-private drinking, which Joel had begun to notice. She heard him one morning—the clatter of cans as he rummaged in the recycling tub. She was under a blanket on the couch, watching a reality show in which contestants were forced to marry people they'd never seen in person, and he came and stood above her with his arms folded.

Do you realize there are thirty-three beer cans in the recycling? he said.

You counted them?

They're all from the past week.

That's only—what, four and a half beers a night?

Alice, that's a lot.

What else is there to do? We never go out. All you do is write and read and watch movies.

He gave her a look of fatherly disappointment. You realize this is hard for me, too, right? he said.

So let's go out. I'd rather get sick than sit here like this, with nothing to do. Let's go out!

He began to tidy the living room in lieu of a response, gathering tissues and stained coffee cups. He took it all to the kitchen, ran the faucet, and played his audiobook on the little Bluetooth speaker.

In this fashion, her life went on. Now and then, she felt the urge to read one of her favorite books—something by Abbey or McKibben. But even these well-worn standards, much less the more technical works by Plumwood or Merchant she'd once labored to understand in grad school, began to bore her after a while. Her daily existence was already so abstract—so removed from the being of life—that to spend her time immersed in books, like Joel, would be to risk floating away from the earth altogether.

She found a community garden in Long Island City, where she volunteered one hour a week. Her work consisted of stooping to pull weeds and the fragments of broken bottles from the soil, applying compost now and then, pinching tiny lettuce seeds from her cupped palm and sprinkling them into furrows. It was unmediated; it required no interpretation. On early mornings, when the sun was just a glimmer, she could bury her fingers in night-cooled soil and grip the earth like roots, knowing she was real, knowing she would not float away.

She began to explore the city alone. She knew a few people from Chicago—acquaintances, really—who had moved there. One of them was Libby, whom she'd met at DePaul, and who was now studying for a certificate in some esoteric form of therapy. One Sunday, Alice took the N, then the 6, then the G to Greenpoint, where Libby lived with her partner, Florence. Up to that point, they'd only ever met at bars or coffee shops. Now she saw their place for the first time, a sunny one-bedroom with exposed brick and pothos vines spilling over every bookshelf and windowsill. It was larger than their place in Astoria and far more stylish. It looked like an apartment where a fictional character in a film or television show might implausibly live, the sort of place you saw onscreen and said to your boyfriend—no, husband—*How can a twenty-eight-year-old who never seems to be working live in a place like this?!*

Libby, this is gorgeous, she said. She ran her fingers over the rough bricks. I love this wall.

I know, I know, Libby said. She was tall and a little plump, thistles tattooed on her thighs in the style of botanical illustrations. Her hair was styled in a chic mullet that she primped frequently. The floors are original, she said. Look at the wrought-iron nails.

She looked down at the pine planks underfoot. There were large, black gaps between them with tufts of cat hair inside, though there didn't seem to be a cat around.

I have access to inherited wealth, Libby said.

Oh. That must be nice.

I mean, my nana died, so not really. I would give it all back to have my nana again.

No, of course, Alice said.

She suggested they go to a place with four-dollar piña coladas. They walked down Manhattan Avenue, past Polish bakeries and record shops and vintage stores with racks of clothing on the sidewalk. Libby lit a spliff. It had been a long time since Alice had put her mouth on an object where another person's mouth had recently been. Spliffs had always been unpleasant to her, and this time was no exception. The nicotine made her hyper-aware of how high she was. Libby was talking about "the feel" of the neighborhood, but she felt estranged from the conversation now, hovering above it, and the faces of passersby, some masked, others not, seemed vaguely hostile to her.

Do you miss Chicago? she blurted, though Libby had been talking about something completely unrelated.

Um, no? Libby said. I mean, yes, sometimes. But Chicago is really such a small town.

But it's not, she said. Objectively.

No, I know it's, like, a "city," she said, putting "city" in air quotes. But it *feels* like a small town. You run into people all the time. Of course, I grew up there, so maybe it's just me.

I like running into people. I like when a place feels cozy.

Don't worry, Libby said, squinting at the spliff to see if it had gone out. Those feelings will pass.

The bar was windowless and dark, lit only by the aqueous glow of fish tanks built into the walls. They sat in one of the split leather booths and Alice pressed her nose to the tank behind them. The fish inside were sickly and slow moving, their colors drab. The piña coladas came from a churning machine with palm trees on it and were very stout. Alice sipped from her squiggly straw till the glass was half-empty, then doubled over with a massive case of brain freeze.

You okay? Libby said.

No, she said. Just a minute.

When the pain subsided, she realized she was uncomfortably stoned. Furthermore, she realized she did not really like Libby, and that she never really had, not even when they lived down the hall from each other in the same dorm at DePaul, not even when they'd made out one night, drunk on peach schnapps, and agreed the next morning they'd be better off as friends.

How's therapy school? Alice said, without much enthusiasm.

It's called Dynamic Neuro-Modulation Counseling.

Right, how's that going?

Honestly? It's a dream. Every day I wake up and say, "Libby, you're living a literal fucking dream right now."

That must be so nice.

How's the consulting gig?

Libby had helped her land a job editing college applications, if "editing" was the right verb. More often than not, she was essentially ghostwriting the essays for Chinese nationals whose parents were investment bankers or steel magnates, and who had no idea why they wanted to go to Harvard except that it was "the logical next step."

It's great, she said. Thanks again for hooking me up.

Libby took a long, thoughtful sip of her drink, then set the glass aside and looked at her with an expression of grave concern. Honey, she said, are you depressed or something? Because you seem sort of depressed.

No, she said. I mean, yeah, but isn't everybody right now? I'm not extra depressed.

Do you need a therapist rec?

No, I have one.

Have you tried neuro-modulation?

I don't know what that is.

I've been told by Florence that I talk about it too much, so I won't try to sell you on it—even though it's, like, my calling or whatever, and Florence can't understand that because she's on a totally different life arc. Anyway, my point—what was my point?

Therapy?

Right—my point is, try it all, even if it's supposedly *alternative*. I do everything—therapy, acupuncture, reiki, tarot.

Isn't all that expensive?

Let me tell you something I wish someone had told me: your emotional homeostasis is priceless. And the world is a dumpster fire right now. Practice self-care. You deserve it. We all deserve it.

It's not just the world, she said. It's my life. It's my marriage.

It's Jim, right? Your SO?

Joel. He seemed so fine with doing nothing during lockdown, seeing no one. It's like it didn't affect him at all.

Everyone's wired differently, Libby said, as if this were some grand universal truth.

Sometimes things are great. We talk, we laugh. Then sometimes I'm like, who did I marry? I look at him, and I think, I don't really *know* you.

You dated, what, like six months?

Alice nodded.

Well, there you go.

I love him, though, she said. She wanted to hear herself say it again, so she did. I do love him.

Maybe you'd be better off as friends.

We're already married.

So get a divorce.

I can't just get a divorce. That would be crazy.

I have a friend who married this guy, Libby said. It was for citizenship reasons, so he could get a green card. They decided to get a divorce. And honestly? It wasn't a big deal. It was totally amicable. They still say, "I love you." They even share custody of a Boston terrier.

Alice slurped the dregs in her glass and pushed it aside, frowning. I don't want a divorce, she said flatly.

Just a thought, Libby said. Just planting a teeny tiny seed.

THAT NIGHT, she returned to Astoria, facing forward on the train, her burps tasting of sunscreen. If she focused on a single point—a woman's red beret, four rows ahead—she could keep the world from tilting. When the train rose from the darkness to the elevated track at Queensboro Plaza, she let out the breath she'd been holding. She knew she would make it now, that home was only a few stops away.

She'd almost reached their gate when a sudden, irresistible spasm brought up the coconut and bile in her stomach. Her pale vomit splattered at the base of their neighbor's fig tree. She coughed and spat, then looked up at the Virgin Mary lawn shrine—Mary on the half-shell, her plaster gown flecked with puke. Oh fuck, she said, wiping her mouth with her sleeve. She peered up at the lighted windows. When she was confident there had been no witnesses, she skulked away.

Joel opened the door while she was still fishing for her keys in her tote bag. He wore the same clothes he'd been wearing when she left, the same clothes he wore every day: a maroon sweatshirt, plaid pajama pants, moccasin house slippers.

Where were you? he said. I tried to call. I texted you like ten times.

My phone died, she said. She squeezed past him, threw her bag into the hallway, and swished her mouth with Listerine at the bathroom sink.

Joel picked up her tote bag where she'd dropped it and hung it on the hook by the door. Something stinks, he said. Like rancid coconut.

Huh, she said, leaning in the bathroom doorway, drying her hands. That's weird.

Joel took a step closer—eyes narrowed, scrutinizing. You're drunk, he said. Or high. Probably both.

Okay, Dad, she said. Do you want to smell my breath to confirm?

Did you throw up?

If lying had been an option, her hesitation in this moment made it impossible.

About that, she said. I may have gotten a little bit—just, like, a tiny bit—of vom on the neighbor's Virgin Mary statue.

Jesus, Alice. Are you serious?

Nobody saw. They probably won't even notice.

Mrs. Papadakis cleans that statue with baby wipes every morning. She keeps it pristine. I think she'll notice.

Her head was throbbing now, ocean swells rolling beneath the apartment floor. She staggered to the couch and sat, unable to formulate even a meager excuse.

I know, she said. I fucked up.

Joel's face softened. When he spoke again, his voice was gentler.

You were doing really well, he said.

It's not your responsibility to monitor how I'm doing.

I'm sorry that I care. I'm sorry that it upsets me to learn that you've desecrated the neighbor's Virgin Mary.

You mean it embarrasses you. You mean that I embarrass you.

Just get your shit together! he shouted.

She froze on the couch, completely stunned. He had never, since they'd met, raised his voice to her.

All I do is clean up after you, he said. I pick up your clothes, I wash your dishes. Now I'll have to clean this up. It's like living with a teenager.

Okay, please stop talking.

You're always saying I should express my feelings. Well, guess what? These are my feelings.

I didn't know your feelings were so mean.

Joel stamped off to the bedroom and slammed the door, leaving her alone on the couch, thirsty as hell but too dizzy to get up for a glass of water. She curled up under the too-small throw blanket, kept one foot on the floor, and tried to will herself to sleep. Maybe it was all the Hellenic culture that surrounded them—the tavernas and fraternal societies she'd passed on Ditmars, the flaking murals under railway bridges of Socrates and Plato—but her mind kept looping back to the myth of the Gordian knot. She'd heard it sometime in her freshman year in a course on Greek mythology. The story went that anyone who could untie the knot would be destined to rule all of Asia. Many men had tried and failed over the centuries. Then came Alexander the Great, who took one look at the knot, drew his sword, and cut it apart.

The next morning, she watched from the window, hungover, as Joel sprayed the Virgin Mary with a garden hose, Mrs. Papadakis berating him in Greek.

Two

SHE FIRST SAW *Joan of Arc* at the Met, breathing her own breath inside her surgical mask, feeling a little faint. She'd stumbled upon it really, searching for a special exhibit of photographs, and the image of the peasant girl, gazing toward the unknown, had arrested her completely. She'd stood for nearly an hour, half expecting the girl to speak, for the painting to move somehow, to resolve its powerful suspense.

She decided, in the midst of this trance, to leave Joel, though it felt like the decision had been made for her, that she'd had no hand in the matter and could only obey. For months, she'd lived like a balloon tethered to her body, wafted by the merest breeze. Now, with her decision made, she felt once more like flesh and blood. She would start anew. She had the strength to face her life with some measure of sobriety. She needed no one to save her from it. And had safety really been what she'd wanted anyway? She'd wanted stability, solid ground upon which to plant herself, and she'd mistaken her marriage for this piece of terra firma. She could not say what it was about *Joan of Arc* that led her to these conclusions. If one could explain how works of art evoked their private meanings, there would be no need for the art. But she felt it had to do, somehow, with the way the girl was harkened—called by some mysterious voice to become the author of her own life.

She bought a postcard of the painting, tucked it in the breast pocket of her rain jacket, and emerged into the September evening. The air smelled of rain and the smoke of souvlaki carts grilling skewered lamb, of hot dogs turning on rollers. People sat on the museum steps eating their food, taking selfies, and Alice sat with them for a long time, taxis and tour buses hissing through puddles on Fifth Avenue, schoolchildren marching in formation past the tents of vendors selling prints and trinkets. Birdsong drifted from the park. Car horns bleated. She smiled to herself, and the burden of indecision lifted from her shoulders.

IN THE WEEKS THAT FOLLOWED, she rehearsed what she would tell him. There was no question of whether she would follow through. It was only a matter of execution. There had to be some delicate way, some method that eased the pain and shock. Maybe he wanted the same thing and would greet her decision with relief. It would be so much simpler that way. Less of a mess.

She came home from a walk one day and found him lying on the couch. All she could see were his feet and the book he held at arm's length. Sunlight passed through the linden trees outside and cast their tangled shadows on the floor.

Joel, she said, I have to say something to you.

He set the book aside but said nothing and did not sit up.

Things are not working, she said. We're in this limbo—I don't know what to call it. There's no growth. There's no optimism. We can't go forward, we can't go back, and we can't do nothing.

He sat up then and lifted a pair of headphones from his ears. I thought I heard something, he said. How long have you been standing there?

Just a few seconds.

Did you ask me something? They were tearing up the street again today—something to do with the gas lines. Jackhammers for hours. The headphones help a little if I'm playing pink noise. This is excellent, by the way.

He waggled his book in the air, a work of film theory by Christian Metz.

Oh yeah? she said. The energy she'd spent, saying what she'd said, had left her depleted. She could not possibly repeat herself now.

I'm thinking I'll write an essay about it. Something about COVID maybe, how we were all spectators to this event, and therefore always separate from it, watching it all unfold like a horror movie. Is it too soon to write about COVID? Everyone will be writing about it. The trick will be to get in after the first wave of bad takes.

It wasn't a spectacle for the people who had it, she said. It wasn't a spectacle for people who lost loved ones.

No, of course not, he said. I would have to be sensitive. It's a sensitive topic. But people like us, people like you and me, we didn't lose anything.

We lost time.

He looked around as if time were an ether, a physical substance in the air, through which they moved. I've had plenty of time, he said. I've had more time than I know what to do with.

And you don't feel grief? You don't feel you've lost anything?

Not really. Do you?

I'm going to lie down, she said.

In their room, she fell face forward onto the bed and clenched all her muscles, her body as rigid as a board. She kept herself this way for as long as she could, holding her breath, squeezing her eyes shut till strobing blotches of color appeared and swam in the darkness of her vision. She caught her breath, went to the open window, and took a deep, crackling pull from her vape pen. She exhaled a cloud past the bars of the fire escape and told herself that when she was gone from him—when she had her land and her garden, her refuge from the world—there would be no need for self-medication.

IT HAPPENED A WEEK LATER. She was working at the garden in Long Island City when Joel called her in a state of agitation. Something awful has happened, he said.

She stood, shielding her eyes from the sun, the knees of her overalls damp from kneeling in the moist soil. Around her, a half-dozen androgynous, tattooed volunteers were bending and wrenching onions from the ground.

What does that mean—something awful?

Just come home, he said.

The train was delayed and took longer than expected. She ran from the Ditmars stop. By the time she'd bounded up the stairs and flung open the door, Joel had managed to calm down. He stood in the kitchen, looking quite pale, bobbing a tea bag in his favorite mug. She let her tote, heavy with onions, thump to the floor, and stood before him, catching her breath, hands on her hips.

I got a call, an hour ago, from my father's girlfriend, Charity, he said. Ex-girlfriend, I guess.

Charity?

I don't know if it's her real name. I didn't know she existed till she called.

Okay, she said. I'm listening.

He took a drink of tea, cleared his throat, and told her that his father was dead. He spoke very quietly, as if there might be someone eavesdropping, and laid out the particulars of what he knew—the violent argument, the Calcasieu Parish Jail, the casino hotel where he'd hanged himself.

I don't know how to feel, he said. I shouldn't be surprised, but I am. My heart is racing. How should I feel?

She approached him hesitantly. She made small circles on his back with her palm, not quite knowing what to feel herself. He'd rarely spoken of his father. They'd been estranged all his life. She said what people say—how very sorry she was—and tears came to her eyes, not so much for Joel or his father, but for the sorrow of a world where such things happened, where people were pushed to such ends. The week before, on the subway, she'd seen a teenage girl with hundreds of razor blade scars on her forearms and calves, and she'd cried for this stranger in the same way she cried now for his father, who was also, after all, a stranger. She could not even remember his name.

Why are you crying? he said.

It's just so sad. I can't believe it.

If you'd known him, you'd believe it.

Do they need you to go down there? she said. To, like, identify him or anything?

Charity did the ID.

What about the funeral?

I hadn't thought about that, he said. His eyes glazed over, fixed on the glowing numerals of the microwave display. My guess is that there won't be one.

Surely not. Maybe the woman will want one.

The man broke her face with a remote control. I don't think she'll throw him a funeral.

There has to be something. Some remembrance. Did he have friends? Family?

Joel shook his head slowly, a powerful exhaustion seeming to weigh on him suddenly.

I was his family. And he was not the sort of person who had friends.

I'm sure that's not true.

You're not sure of anything, he said. You don't know what the fuck you're talking about.

You're right, I'm sorry.

Stop crying.

Joel.

If anyone has the right to cry, it's me.

Okay.

She drew her hand from his back and wiped her eyes.

I'm sorry, he said. I don't know what's wrong with me.

You're in shock, she said.

That's not right. It isn't shock.

What is it then?

I'm afraid if I keep talking, I'll say something cruel.

We'll just stand here then. I'll just stand here beside you. Can I touch you?

He nodded distractedly. She put her arms around him. He kept his position, stiff and unmoving, and she held him like this.

IN THE END, there was no funeral. His remains were cremated and given to Joel, who spread the ashes in the East River, beneath the graffitied trestles of the Hell Gate Bridge.

That island's full of sex offenders and headcases, said a woman who passed, pointing to the storage vats and the rusted pilings on the opposite shore. She was on her bike and wore pink Lycra from head to toe, her gray hair chaotic. Her lipstick was smudged clownishly beyond the borders of her mouth.

We're just having a private moment, Alice said.

Anybody they don't like, all the undesirables, they put on Randall's Island.

Is that right? Joel said. He was holding the pewter urn—the funeral parlor's cheapest option—under his arm, and she could tell from his sudden attention that he viewed the woman's intrusion as potential material.

Oh yeah, she said. I was attacked by a man on Randall's Island in 1989. I won a lawsuit with the city. Most of it went to the lawyers. I'm still waiting for the rest to come through.

You've been waiting thirty years? Joel said.

Don't engage, Alice said.

I'm technically a millionaire. They proved in court the city was liable. They have no signage. Put all the sex offenders and the deviants in one place, and have no signs at all? Please. I don't even like to see it. I ride my bike, and I think, "Look at that terrible place." They should have signs. They should put signs all over the island. There should be signs on the streets that say DO NOT ENTER. But there's no signage whatsoever. You go there yourself and tell me if you see a single sign.

What would the signs say? he asked her.

She seemed shocked by this question. Scandalized. Fuck you! she hissed. You pig! You fuck! Then she spat at them, most of it dribbling down her chin, though some tiny droplets flecked their faces. The woman pedaled away down the riverfront path and they stood there aghast. Alice wiped her face with her T-shirt.

I told you not to engage, she said.

He shifted the urn to his other arm and typed a note into his phone.

You're going to write about this? she said.

Maybe. Why not?

You can't be in the present. You can't feel anything in the present moment.

This is how I feel things, he said, showing her his phone. I feel things when I write them down.

It's not the same thing.

Why do you want to police what I feel? Why is that so important to you?

I never see you cry. I never see you show emotion. You don't even cry during movies. You're too busy taking notes.

I don't feel the need to sentimentalize every moment. It doesn't mean I don't feel anything. I felt that woman spit in our faces. I felt more in that instant than I did scattering the ashes. All I could feel scattering the ashes was that I was supposed to feel something and I couldn't.

Doesn't that make you sad? Don't you wish you were in the present?

Are *you* in the present?

I try to be.

You only think you are. You're just as much in your head as I am. The difference is that you can't admit it to yourself. You think because you spend a couple hours a week pulling weeds that you live in the present? That's just a story you're telling yourself. You're just narrating a story where you live in the present.

She turned and walked away from him, pressing with long strides up the grassy hill toward Ditmars. Holding his father's urn protected him from whatever vicious thing she might have said in response, though at the moment nothing came to mind. She worried he was right.

························

A FEW NIGHTS LATER, they were awakened by the sound of a young girl wailing. They rose from bed, opened the window, and peered down to the alley. The sound came again—a long, mournful cry, closed off with a gargle of phlegm in the throat.

It's someone in pain, Alice said, stepping into her trousers. She's in pain.

It's a cat, Joel said. Sure enough, a pair of eyes, radioactive green, shone from the darkness beneath an SUV. The animal gave another cry, its voice hoarser now but no less chilling.

Should we call someone? she said.

It's probably hungry, he said. Hang on.

He put on his flannel robe and fetched a tin of sardines from the pantry. She followed him downstairs and around to the back alley, where the animal, sensing their presence, had grown quiet. It was brisk, and she stood with her arms folded tightly, watching as he pried back the lid of the sardine tin and made entreating, clicking noises with his tongue. They waited in the quiet that was not really quiet at all. Traffic shushing on Grand Central Parkway. Ambulance sirens. Planes ripping the air, coming down over LaGuardia. Still, in moments like this, with the dark forms of trees stirring and all the little houses dim and sleeping, she could almost imagine that Queens was a tiny village. The factory-lit dome of the sky seemed to her like shelter.

It took a long time for the cat to emerge from the shadows, into the butterscotch light of the sodium lamp. It was a Maine coon with shaggy, matted fur, mottled with gray and brown. It approached the sardines, one tentative paw step at a time, keeping its eyes on them.

Go ahead, buddy, Joel said.

The cat sniffed the small, slender fish, then ate one gingerly. After the first, it ate more eagerly. They could hear it chewing, the smacking of its tongue, and they both laughed.

He's a boy, I think, Joel said. Handsome for a stray.

Maybe he's lost, she said. Maybe he belongs somewhere.

He's been on his own a while. He's got that look about him, like he's had to fend for himself.

The cat, finished now with the sardines, looked at them with curiosity more than fear. Alice stooped down and offered her hand. He sniffed her with his pink nose, little whispers of breath tickling her knuckles. Joel reached out to pet him and he trotted away abruptly, returning to the safety of darkness.

Joel bought a dozen sardine tins from the upscale grocery, expensive brands from Portugal and Spain. She watched from the window as each night he garnered the animal's trust in minute increments. After a week, the cat permitted Joel to scratch behind his ears with his forefinger as he took his supper. She heard him speaking softly.

These come from the Atlantic Ocean, between Portugal and Morocco, he said. Conserva culture is very big in the Mediterranean regions. It's like craft beer to them—tiny fish in cans. They're sustainable, they're a good source of protein, of omega-3s. I'm trying to be pescetarian—well, not really. I'll order beef or pork at a restaurant, but we're trying not to buy meat at the grocery. It's better for the planet. Of course, you're a carnivore, so you don't have much choice in the matter.

One day, he simply brought the cat inside. She looked up from her book and found him standing over her, cradling a mass of gray fur. I'm keeping him, he said.

What if he's someone else's?

He's my buddy and I'm keeping him.

They sat cross-legged on the floor and watched him investigate, sniffing the stereo speakers and the brown, shriveled pothos leaves dropped from the hanging planter.

Are our plants poisonous? she said. We don't even have a litter box.

I'll buy one right now. We'll throw out the plants if they're poisonous.

But I like the plants. Are we sure this is the right time for a pet?

His eyes communicated that a great deal—so much more than she could know—depended on them keeping this cat.

What should we name him? he said.

He looks like a wise, slightly cantankerous old scholar. His face—you know who he looks like, actually?

I know exactly, Joel said. I know exactly who you're going to say.

They named him Noam. They brushed the mats from his fur, got him microchipped, bought him feather wands and little plush mice. They forgot, briefly, their disappointments and problems, absorbed in their new roles as caretakers, taking photographs and videos, relishing his presence—this new spirit in their lives, this self-possessed creature with his own motives, his own schedule, his own mannerisms. The decision she'd made, to end their marriage, had remained in her mind like a story she'd begun at a party, forgetting the punchline partway through, trailing off. The flow of conversation coursing forward, so that even if she remembered now what she'd wanted to say, it would be too late. Maybe this was better, she thought. Maybe she'd been saved from a reckless decision. And what did it matter, in the end? What choice did she have? Could she leave him now, his father's death so fresh?

One Sunday morning, honeyed light flooding the apartment, she woke to the sound of whimpering in the next room. She treaded softly down the hallway, avoiding the creaky planks, and peeked around the corner. Joel, wearing only his underwear, sat on the couch hugging Noam to his chest. There were tears running from his eyes, his face a grimace of pain. Bands of sunlight fell on Noam's fur, Joel's cheek flattening his lynxlike ears.

Alice sat beside him. He seemed not to notice her at all, still crying, still clinging to the cat, bubbles of snot popping in his nostrils.

Joel, honey, she said, what's wrong?

He turned to her finally, took her hand, and squeezed it hard.

I need you, he said.

He rested his head on her shoulder. Noam nestled himself between them and made deep revving noises in his chest. She petted Joel's hair while he sobbed. She whispered platitudes, words of empty kindness, no longer knowing the difference between pity and love.

I'm here, she said. I'm right here with you.

Three

THE REAL IS NEVER ACCESSIBLE, Joel said. He paused dramatically, this being the centerpiece of his lecture on Lacan—surely the semester's most provocative seminar. It had never quite earned the reaction he'd hoped for. They stared at him with the poker-faced flatness of affect characteristic of university students, drowsy churchgoers, and heavily medicated schizophrenics.

We only know it's there—the Real—because it comes to us obliquely, in moments of what Lacan calls "rupture." But we never touch it directly. We have symbols of the Real, representations of it, but the thing-in-itself is a void, an absence.

A boy in the front row—Garrett—was nodding enthusiastically. Of all his students, Garrett had shown the most fervor for the material, conforming to the "Surrogate Son" archetype that appeared, without fail, in every class he'd taught. They all shared certain reliable traits. Like Garrett, they were white and male. They spoke too often in class. They'd borrowed their personalities from podcasts or characters in movies. They had quotations tattooed somewhere on their bodies—Nietzsche perhaps, Derrida, Baudrillard. They were bearded. Their Nazi-ish hair was buzzed close on the sides and left long on top. They were overweening, sometimes downright obnoxious, though Garrett fell somewhere on the milder end of the spectrum, and they sought to convey—with their eyes, with their whole bearing, really—that they'd encountered some darkness in life, though this darkness was often middle-class and common. Finally, they were seeking in Joel a father figure, the father they never had, who never made them clean their plates or mow the lawn, who never called them dumbasses, who never gazed with utter disappointment at their pitiful performance on the basketball court or the football field. Someone who understood how misunderstood they were. And Joel could not help but feel—through some process of countertransference—somewhat paternalistic toward them, perhaps because he had been like them, in more ways than he cared to admit, and was therefore disgusted by them—by his fatherly feelings.

In other words, the students who responded most eagerly to his lectures were the students he cared the least about reaching. Those quiet, anemic-looking girls in the back of the room, with their dark hair and their turtlenecks and their catlike, dubious expressions, the ones who reminded him of Alice—these were the students he hoped to reach, if only because they seemed unreachable.

The point is that there are only narratives, Joel said. There is no absolute Right or absolute Left; they exist only relative to each other. There is no objective center. Not in politics. Not in life either. We glimpse this in certain traumatic or sublime moments. The centerless void. Our desires spring from this lack. We try to fill it with one thing or another—money, love, conspiracy theory.

He shuffled his papers on the lectern. He'd forgotten where he was going with all this. He'd developed, since quitting his antidepressant, a spasm in his left eyelid. It had spread to his cheek, and he could feel the muscle twitching now. He wondered whether it was obvious.

Garrett—of course it was Garrett—raised his hand.

Um, yeah, he said, I was wondering—could something like a psychedelic trip cause the kind of rupture you're talking about?

I suppose it could, Garrett.

Cause I have some experience in that domain myself.

You've said as much on several occasions, Garrett.

Aren't some narratives much more fictitious than others? said a voice from the back. It was one of the quiet girls who rarely spoke. She wore a black, nunlike dress with a tattered denim jacket and pink Crocs. The boredom evident in her pale, unmoving face brought to mind Flemish paintings—all those pallid characters populating the works of Van Eyck and Bosch.

Say more, he said.

I mean, the Right's narrative is insane—satanic cults harvesting adrenochrome.

It's lurid, for sure, he said. But a narrative is fictitious by nature.

I guess I just think that's bogus, she said. Believing there's no truth, that we aren't tethered to anything. I mean, you write essays, right?

What's the difference between fiction and nonfiction—that's your question?

No, that makes it impersonal. I'm asking what's the difference for you. How do you justify calling what you write nonfiction?

It's a question of how closely it corresponds to my sense of the truth. But my sense of the truth and the actual truth are never synonymous, and never could be.

I think you believe that they are, she said. I think you're lying to yourself.

ON HIS DRIVE HOME, a craving for something sweet came over him. He rarely ate sweets, but he was now and then struck by the irresistible urge to devour chocolates and jelly beans and gummies, to chase it all with Coca-Cola from a glass bottle. He stopped at a gas station in the little town of Hardin—a speed trap on the state highway. He'd often wondered, passing through, who lived there. He'd never seen anyone coming or going from the cluster of houses and single-wides. A cemetery overlooked the Dollar General, and a church called Blood River stood at the town's center, resembling a strip mall, a neon OPEN sign in the front window.

When he'd found what he wanted, he leaned against the warm hood of his mother's van and ate the candy, stuffing his cheeks with sugarcoated worms and Milk Duds, his fingers smeared with melted chocolate, taking swallows of Coke to keep from choking on the dense bolus of half-chewed food. A woman who looked familiar parked at the adjacent pump. She stepped out and studied Joel like she was trying to place him, clutching a pack of cigarettes and a leopard pocketbook in one hand, a bottle of soda in the other. She went to the Redbox kiosk in front of the gas station, browsed the selection of movies. After swiping her card and retrieving her DVD, she came back over to him.

I think we went to high school together, she said. My name's Kayleigh? You were a few grades ahead of me.

It seemed impossible that she was younger than him. He could tell, from the way her cheeks were sunken, that some of her teeth near the back were missing. Her eyes had the look of utter exhaustion.

I thought you looked familiar, he said, brushing the sugar crystals from his shirt. What are you doing here? He realized after asking that this was a stupid question—that as far as he was concerned, she might as well be here as anywhere.

I live out here, she said. She pointed down a road that seemed to lead nowhere. Fields of withered corn. The wan vastness of the sky.

Do you attend the River of Blood?

He'd thought she would find this funny, but she nodded sternly.

I try to, she said. Blood River. My kid's got ADHD, so it's hard for him to sit through service. But I try to go. Are you back home now?

Temporarily.

You know, I seen your brother a couple weeks ago. Does he live here now?

He comes and goes.

I work at the Comfort Inn off Exit 3, and he come in with a woman, late at night.

When was this?

Couple Fridays ago.

He works on Fridays.

Kayleigh shrugged, took a sip of soda and screwed the cap back on. It was him, she said. I know it was Friday cause I work late that night. He acted sorta weird about the girl, but I didn't press it. It don't matter to me what people do. I mind my own business.

Who was the woman?

I can't remember her name. She was a pretty little thing, though.

He wondered what this could mean. Clearly Emmett was seeing someone, someone he'd rather keep a secret. Why else come home and tell no one? Why else sneak around at some cheap motel?

What'd you wind up doing, she said, in life?

I'm a professor, he said. A writer, I guess.

Well, look at you! she said, smiling. That's something.

I guess it is.

Anyhow, she said, I just stopped for a movie. She held up the DVD in its red envelope.

I didn't know those still existed, he said, meaning the Redbox kiosk. I thought everybody streamed now.

Kayleigh lit a cigarette and blew the smoke behind her shoulder. They've always got what I want, she said. What my son wants. It's about the only source of entertainment around, as you can see.

She laughed sadly and motioned to the little town, then returned to her car with its blistered paint, its wheel wells eaten by rust, waving at Joel with her cigarette hand, saying how nice it was to see an old familiar face. Time flies, don't it? she said, before driving away.

At the house, he found Kathy and Grandma Ruth peeling potatoes. Ruth could peel potatoes faster than anyone he knew, pulling the blade of the paring knife into her thumb. She left no speck of skin.

Kathy was going on about a memory from her childhood; Ruth disputed its veracity. When she was little, Kathy claimed, she'd gone to Noble Park and seen a chicken playing the piano.

This was a person dressed up like a chicken? he said.

No, it was a real chicken, Kathy said. They had him in a cage with a toy piano, and he pecked the keys.

Kathy demonstrated, assuming the posture of a rooster, dipping her head.

You seen it on the TV, Ruth said. This wasn't real.

It was! Daddy took us. This man went from town to town with a banty chicken, playing "Mary Had a Little Lamb."

Ruth laughed and shook her head, gouging a dark spot from the potato in her palm. You've mixed up life with the TV, she said.

Kathy turned and saw him stifling a smile. Oh, he thinks it's funny! she said. You watch, Mom, he'll write about this.

Why would I write about a chicken who plays the piano?

This is what we did before phones, Kathy said. This was our entertainment. We went and saw animals that behaved like humans. That's sort of interesting, right? I bet people would get a kick out of that, if you wrote something.

You've sold me on it, I'll add it to the next book, he said. Listen, do you know if Emmett is seeing anyone?

Like a girl? He'd never talk with me about that. He never has.

So he hasn't mentioned anyone?

Kathy shrugged, tossing potato slices into the huge canning pot on the counter. The pot already held a mountain of sliced potato, some of it turning rust brown. I haven't talked to him period, she said. What with him skipping Thanksgiving. He's working a lot. The weeks before Christmas are crazy, from what he says.

But he'll be home for Christmas?

He better be.

I think he's up to something, Joel said. I think he's got something going on. Under the table, so to speak.

Something with a woman? What gives you that idea?

He picked up errant potato skins from the floor and tossed them in the sink. He thought of the girl from his seminar who'd seen him so clearly—so ruthlessly. The searing shame of the moment had transmuted itself, retrospectively, into something almost erotic. He imagined the girl in her nun's dress standing on his chest, calling him a charlatan.

I can't explain it, he said. He won't look me in the eye. If we're alone together in a room, I can tell he's trying to leave.

Communication, Kathy said. Most problems—family problems—

come down to it. A lack of it, rather. You should have a long talk. Bring him with you to Memphis.

Joel had been invited to a book festival in Memphis the first week of January. It consisted of a panel event with other southern writers and a semiformal dinner, where he would eat a catered meal alongside the philanthropists and donors who had paid for him to attend. He'd spent the last few weeks building up a prerequisite reserve of social energy.

I'll have a lot on my plate, he said.

I wish I could go. I haven't been to Graceland in so long.

You went last year.

Well, I learn something new every time. For example, did you know Elvis had a twin brother? Jesse Garon. Stillborn. Imagine if he'd lived. An Elvis lookalike!

My aunt Roberta had a stillbirth, Ruth said, shavings of skin curling away from her blade. There was a blizzard that year, piles and piles of snow. I remember my daddy cutting trees for firewood, and in the spring, the stumps were three feet high. They couldn't bury the child. They wrapped her in a winding sheet—she was a baby girl—and kept her in the corncrib till the ground thawed. My daddy was the one who fetched her in February. He said she looked just the same.

Good God, Mom, Kathy said. What a morbid story.

Ruth scooped the wet peelings from the sink basin and carried them in her cupped hands to the trash can, flicking the juice from her fingertips.

It might be morbid, she said. But it's the truth.

Joel tried to write for a while in the antique room, but Noam kept leaping onto the desk, pressing his paws against the keyboard. Are you the writer? he said. Do you have something you want to say?

He nudged the cat, gently, to the floor, and held down backspace, erasing the long string of jumbled characters. What was leftover—the bit of text he'd typed up, describing his encounter with Kayleigh and his grandmother's story of the stillborn infant—suddenly seemed to him not worth keeping. He pressed backspace again and let go when the page was empty. He stared at the white field for a while in expectant silence, hoping for some radiant sentence to appear in his mind, to announce its obvious rightness, its suitability, as sentences sometimes do, but nothing came. He was startled, instead, by a clatter behind him. A mug of pens and pencils had toppled from a shelf. Noam, ordinarily the prime suspect for such things, was crouched on the other side of the room, seeming as baffled as Joel. He gathered the pens and pencils and righted the mug. He felt that he was not alone in the room. He looked at the paintings above the bed. The mansion and the farmhouse. The winking spasm in his cheek returned. His instincts told him to leave, that something wasn't right, and when he opened the door, Noam darted out ahead of him, evidently feeling the same.

He found Alice on the back porch, reading. He sat in the Adirondack chair beside her. She was smoking one of Kathy's Mistys, and tried to stub it out before he could see.

You don't have to hide it from me, he said.

I know you don't like it, she said. She set her book aside and they looked toward the garden shed in the backyard.

You know she's got guns in there? he said.

No, I didn't, she said quietly.

Like, a lot of guns.

Good to know for when the civil war breaks out.

She wore a flannel shirt, too big for her, the cuffs stained from picking mulberries. The breeze stirred her hair and blew through the pages of her open book, losing her place. She was pondering something, some private, insoluble problem. Since the moment he'd met her, her face had always expressed this to some degree. Her beauty, in part, derived from it—this privacy, this inner searching. Sometimes he looked at her and thought, *I'm so unreasonably lucky.*

I've been thinking, he said, about our future.

Uh oh.

I chose New York, and I chose to come here. I want you to choose where we go next.

Alice slitted her eyes, as though this might be a trap. That's the thing, she said. I have no basis to make the decision.

You like California.

Too expensive.

You like New England. Maine, Cape Cod.

Too cold. And also too expensive.

We live in New York. Surely Maine is cheaper.

I mean to buy. To buy land.

Oh, Joel said, right.

He'd hoped, for a long time, that Alice's farming fantasy would pass. He thought of his grandmother inside, peeling potatoes with her gnarled, arthritic hands. How many thousands of potatoes had she peeled in her life? How many weeds had she wrenched from compacted earth? How many days had she stooped to cut tobacco in the sweltering sun, wishing for comfort?

Where is cheap? he said. As far as buying land.

They'll practically give you land in Wyoming.

He tried to keep his face from showing how much the thought of life in Wyoming terrified him.

I know, that sounds awful to you, she said.

No, it's just—far away. Would Fletcher go for that?

Maybe I wouldn't need my father. We have some money saved up.

Would there be teaching jobs?

You could become one of those reclusive western writers who fly fishes and hunts elk. Then once every five years, you mail a book to New York.

What would the book be about?

Fly fishing, hunting elk.

Naturally.

Only they would be metaphors for, like, the twilight of American masculinity.

They both laughed a little at this. He reached out to take her hand and she let him, though she seemed unable to look at him when he touched her.

This is new, she said. Why the change of heart?

That he was unhappy, that a gnawing emptiness kept him awake at night, that he'd ditched his medication, that wherever he went he sensed the vague accompaniment of some presence, the way polar explorers, facing the blank white page of the abyss, heard whispers in the howling wind, saw shadows that were not their own—that a person in this state was willing to try anything, even Wyoming, did not seem like an answer he could give.

If Wyoming's what you want, we'll go to Wyoming, he said.

That wouldn't solve our fundamental problem.

Which is what?

She let go of his hand. That things aren't working, she said. That we're unhappy.

We're just stuck. We have unfulfilled goals.

What could you still want? You're living the dream.

Something authentic, Joel thought. Unabstract. Having nothing to do with words or books. Maybe farming was not so crazy; maybe she was right. But something in him could not quite take it seriously. All the gardening YouTube channels she watched had names like *Another Path* and *Exploring Alternatives.* The last thing he wanted lately was an "alternative." What he longed for, what he found himself dreaming of, in the eddies of time that filled his days, was an *ordinary life.* Nine-to-five. Meat and potatoes. *Wheel of Fortune.* Church on Sunday. The quiet, brave persistence of the mainstream, never fighting the current. Letting it take you. He wanted to dissolve into this. To become anonymous. To disappear into the ordinary.

We said we wouldn't talk about this, he said. Not here.

Right. Just pretend everything's normal.

Till we get back to New York. Then you can torpedo our marriage if you want.

She stood, the wind flinging hair across her face. You see all this as my problem, she said. There's no awareness, on your part, that any of this could be *our* problem. Something we have to work on *together.*

I'm not unhappy, he said—a lie if there ever was one.

Alice touched her fingertips to her eyelids, the way she did sometimes when a migraine was coming on.

I'm not going with you to Memphis, she said.

I didn't expect you to, Joel said, though he had. He'd taken it for granted.

She left him alone on the back porch. He watched the branches of the naked trees clack together like antlers, the last yellow leaves showering over the yard. The sky was an empty canvas, symbolizing nothing whatsoever.

The coffee tasted off. He drank it anyway, dipping his Danish cookies while the TV jabbered in the next room. Ruth's eyes swiveled, first to the window, then to the door with its five fastened locks, fingernails ticking against the ceramic of her mug.

Are you buying new coffee now? he said.

No. Does it taste all right?

Just different.

His phone rumbled face down on the table. He checked the screen like a blackjack player checking his hole card. It was an email notification. All he could see was the subject line in all caps: YOU'VE BEEN CHOSEN.

I'll have to clean all that blood from the bathroom, Ruth said. She slurped her coffee and looked at Joel as if she'd commented casually on the weather.

What blood?

There's a whole mess of blood, running down the shower curtain, dripping from the walls.

Did you hurt yourself?

It wasn't me, she said.

Who was it then?

She grew quiet and looked at her reflection on the black surface of her coffee. They come in at night, she whispered. I don't know what they do.

Who comes in?

She turned her eyes to the locked door. I don't know what they do, Emmett, she said.

I'm Joel, not Emmett. *Joel*. You know me.

Joel is in New York.

I'm home. I've been home for months.

She looked at him doubtfully. A voice on the television said, *Clearly, the president has been compromised.*

Is this about the men in the woods?

I don't know what they do, she said. They come in at night. They wheel in machines and TVs with different cables and hookups. They play the awfullest programs. Programs you wouldn't believe. When I wake up, they're gone and there's blood all over.

Grandma, he said. He touched her hand gently. Have you fallen recently? he said. Hit your head?

The coffee is Maxwell House, she said. Same as ever. Course, the way things are now, you can't tell about quality. Prices go up, quality goes down.

He opened the cabinet, took down the plastic jug of coffee, and sniffed inside. He opened the basket lid of the coffeemaker. Splotches of fuzzy turquoise mold had bloomed in the wet grounds. He turned away, his stomach lurching, then carried the basket to the trash and dumped it.

You don't use fresh grounds?

Well, not every day, she said. During the Depression, we used the same grounds for a week.

This isn't the Depression.

He went to the bathroom and switched on the light, half expecting to see some scene of butchery. Of course, there was nothing. A basket of cinnamon-smelling potpourri sat on the toilet tank. Her spare dentures were submerged in a clear solution.

They talked for a while longer in the living room, Joel exhausting his usual gamut of questions. How were the cousins. How were the aunts and uncles. How were the newborns. How were the sick and the afflicted. How were the bereaved. Ruth slipped between present and distant past, reciting the freak deaths of family lore like a liturgy.

My grandfather, Amos, was trampled by horses, she said. Huey, my cousin, got himself killed. He was mixed up with a married woman and the husband killed him and the woman both. Our neighbor was the one to find them. He used a shotgun. Neighbor said you could hardly tell what they were. Man or woman, human or animal. And of course my nephew, John Paul, was slain by wolves.

Joel remembered John Paul, a potbellied man with a white beard and a colorful belt of Indian beadwork. The sort of man who wore T-shirts airbrushed with wolves and bears and native warriors on horseback without a trace of irony.

Remind me, he was killed by wolves in the wild? Joel said.

He had a refuge in Arkansas, she said. For years, he took care of them wolves, and one day they turned on him, tore him to pieces.

Ruth drifted to sleep. Joel turned down the volume, unlatched the chains and bolts on the door, and went out to breathe the clean air, leaning against the porch rail. The wooden chimes clinked like old bones. A quarrel of sparrows flew from the pines. When they'd gone and the wind died down, the woods were dark and silent before him. His fear was like radar, beaming out in all directions, reflecting from every available surface. His phone buzzed again, a text message from a number he did not recognize. Welcome to the CryptoClub, it said. Trading signals posted daily, 2000 USD a week. Join now, God bless America.

He walked into the woods. There were paths cut through the briars by deer, and he followed a meandering route toward the creek bed. His pulse seemed to arrive from outside somehow, from the earth itself—some pounding machine beneath the leaf rot and the soil, beneath the very bedrock. He snagged his jacket on a thorn, and turning back to free himself, he saw the remains of a campfire in a small clearing. Two charred logs on a bed of white ash, some flattened beer cans, a scattering of cigarette filters. He stooped to examine the sun-faded cans. They might have been there two days or two decades.

He stood and braced himself against a tree. His breath had turned to gasping. In the bowels of the earth, the booming machinery had burrowed to exactly this point beneath him. There were porno mags stacked against a nearby tree. He picked one up. It was swollen with rainwater, the images warped and oozing within. Orange flesh. Face-less forms.

Hello? he called out, and the fear in his voice echoed back to him. He looked all around. He listened. But there was nothing—not even birdsong, not even the scrabble of squirrels. There was only the little house on the hill. A clear line of sight.

Four

PEAK SEASON. The words alone struck fear. A massive increase, not only in volume but velocity. A frenzy. A fever dream of cardboard and barcodes, of iPhones, of sneakers, of chirping scan guns, the painted spiral of hypnotists spinning on the engines of cargo planes. The rotten sulfur of deicing chemicals. The crime scene carnage of the break room microwave. The backlog of holdover cans shoved against the walls, wedged in every pocket of space, so that movement through the hub became mazelike, slipping through cracks, hoping not to be crushed by billiard-like collisions. A sorter, a kid no more than nineteen, had his fingers pinched between two cans a week before Christmas. They all heard him scream—shock at first, a groan, then girlish keening. Emmett saw the aftermath as they led him out. His fingers had turned dark purple, swollen like overcooked sausages.

Peak season. The zenith of commerce, of Christmas spirit. The supervisors wore Santa hats, as if to mock them all. They reset the digital counter by the clock-in station. WE'VE WORKED 0 DAYS WITHOUT A LOST TIME ACCIDENT!

The only silver lining was that he managed to avoid Kaleb. There was simply no time for confrontation, absorbed completely in the pitched battle of man against—what was it? Volume, he supposed. The sheer volume. The colossal tide of shit, of plastic gizmos and gadgets and heaps of fabric bound for landfills. Each parcel was a unit of desire, a measurement of someone's yearning, some human being out there. There were millions of them. Angie Gore in Kokomo, Indiana. Issa Owoh in Sugar Land, Texas. Pam McHenry in Elko, Nevada. What could one do with so much desire? It was enough to drown you, to pull you under, if you let your guard down, if you took even a moment's pause.

He read the labels, half fearing he would see his own name printed there. Some package he'd ordered—a twelve-pack of white crew socks, a new pair of rubber-palmed gloves. According to ware-home legend, a package handler had seen his name once on a label and had died a few months later, his long hair caught in the drive pulley of a conveyor belt.

It's a hexagram to see your name on a label, Kaleb had said. You see your name, you might as well write your will and testament.

His fear came not from superstition, but from the thought that he might become one of these names, these anonymous recipients in their anonymous towns. That perhaps he was already one of them. He told himself his life was more interesting than their lives. None of them had nearly six thousand dollars in cash hidden inside a hole in the drywall of a closet. None of them had Alice. He carried her note in his coat pocket, the one she'd addressed to "Bruce," and read it sometimes to calm his nerves. Merely touching the paper in his pocket was sometimes enough.

KALEB FOUND WAYS to reach him after a while. Walking past Emmett's lane, he would bash his fist against the can's aluminum roof. It sounded, inside, like someone striking sheet metal with a ballpeen hammer. By the time he'd ducked out and looked all around, Kaleb would be gone, returned to the ramp. He'd noticed, as well, an unusual number of onerous cans finding their way to his lane, cans full of irregs, full of engine parts and axles, heavy steel disks and cork-screw augers. They were sent, he could only guess, by Kaleb, though he had no proof.

These threats, however oblique, became explicit one night when he found an icepick in the Mystique's driver-side tire. A scrap of yellow paper beneath his windshield wiper said YOU STILL OWE ME. He spent an hour changing the tire, his nose running from the cold, fumbling the lug wrench with numbed fingers. Driving home, he heard Springsteen singing "Santa Claus Is Comin' to Town" on the radio, and he thought of Alice, how it seemed like a thousand years since he'd seen her, though only two weeks had passed. He decided then, driving on the empty highway, the defroster thawing crystals of ice on the windshield, that he would quit come January. He had money, after all—enough to get by for a while. Whatever came next, however uncertain, had to be better than this.

HE WORKED ON Christmas Eve and drove to Paducah at dawn. When he let himself in, Kathy was frying bacon on the electric griddle, wearing an apron patterned with reindeer. That must be Santa coming in, she said.

Ho ho ho, Emmett said.

She hugged him with one arm, then stood back and clicked her tongue when she saw his face. You should see the bags under your eyes, she said.

He poured a large mug of coffee, some kind of special blend with hazelnut and cinnamon, and found Alice and Joel in the living room. A Christmas Carol was playing on TV, the version with George C. Scott as Scrooge.

You look like you're full of Christmas cheer, Joel said.

I'm exhausted, he said. Though there was space on the couch beside Alice, he sat in the rocking chair by the fake tree. It smelled like a real tree, Kathy having hidden a diffuser of fir-scented oil under the lowest boughs. The colored lights flickered in rhythmic patterns, the ornaments mostly keepsakes containing small photos of Joel and Emmett as babies.

They're working you to the bone, huh? Joel said.

Emmett tried to explain, though words could never do it justice, the madness of peak season.

It sounds like that scene in *Modern Times*, Joel said. Chaplin's on the assembly line with two wrenches, and the widgets keep coming and coming, and he can't keep up.

I've never seen *Modern Times*, Emmett said.

What?! Mister movie guy. Mister screenwriter, and he's never seen *Modern Times*?

It's not like a movie, Emmett said, thinking of the boy's engorged fingers, the look of terror on his face.

Chaplin was great. A real anti-capitalist. I was just saying this movie is sort of anti-capitalist. Dickens was a radical for his day.

Just because it's about greed doesn't mean it's about capitalism, Alice said. You say the same thing about *It's a Wonderful Life*.

Dalton Trumbo took a pass on the script. He was a self-avowed communist.

Shush, Alice said. I'm trying to watch.

Uncle Dale and Tonya showed up, Grandma Ruth in tow. She wore the red and green crocheted sweater vest she had worn on every Christmas in Emmett's memory. They ate their bacon and biscuits and breakfast casserole, drank more of the strong hazelnut coffee. Dale was in high spirits, having sold three hot tubs in the past week.

The temperature drops, people reach for their wallets, Dale said. Course, that's why climate change presents a challenge.

You believe in that? Kathy said.

You know, Kathy, I used to be against it.

Isn't everybody against climate change? Joel said.

I mean I used to think it was bunk. But you have to be a realist in my line of work. No one's more sensitive to temperature than a hot tub salesman. When's the last time we had a white Christmas? I can't even remember.

I remember white Christmases, Grandma Ruth said. I remember my daddy cutting ice from the pond with a handsaw. I remember snow candy with sorghum molasses drizzled on top.

I saw a scientist on TV, Kathy said. He claimed these fluctuations are normal.

What scientist? Joel said. Probably a quack.

I know things change, Kathy said. The question is, where does the change come from?

From us, Alice said. It comes from us.

Well, I don't know.

See, this is what I don't understand, Joel said. You're more likely to trust some random dude on Fox News than your own son and daughter-in-law.

Oh, give it a rest, Emmett said. Don't spoil everyone's morning.

They all looked at him, surprised by the sharpness of his tone.

Emmett's right, Kathy said. We can't fuss at each other on Christmas.

Midway through breakfast, Tonya clinked her glass with her fork. I have an announcement to make, she said. Lily is pregnant.

Who? Kathy said.

Tonya seemed stung by the question. My dog? she said. Lily?

The Yorkipoo, Dale said.

Everyone said "Ohhhh" in unison and congratulated her.

Ask me how much a purebred Yorkipoo costs, Dale said. He was looking at Emmett, seated directly across from him.

I have no idea, Emmett said.

Dale cupped his hand around his mouth and whispered, *Four figures.*

When it came time to divvy up the presents, they sat in a circle and took turns. Kathy went first. Emmett gave her a pink and blue shawl. Alice gave her a handmade mug she'd found on Etsy. Dale and Tonya got her a mug as well, a newfangled kind with temperature control and a rechargeable battery. Well, I'll just have to drink lots of tea! Kathy said.

She came to Joel's gift bag and tested the weight. Feels pretty light, she said.

Just open it, Joel said.

She tossed aside the tissue and drew out a slip of paper. What's this? she said.

Read it, Joel said.

I need my glasses.

She retrieved her reading glasses and studied the slip.

It says flight confirmation, she said.

To where? Joel said.

It says Hawaii. I don't understand.

It's a ticket to Hawaii. You're always saying you want to go back.

My goodness, Kathy said. She took off her glasses, pressed her hand to her chest. Are you serious, Joel? You're not serious.

Do I look like I'm joking?

I can't believe it, she said. You have to return this, it's too much.

No way, Joel said. Merry Christmas.

Wow, Dale said. Really showing the rest of us up, aren't ya there, Joel? He clapped his hand on Joel's shoulder.

I wanted to do it, Joel said.

Kathy crossed the room and hugged him. She wouldn't let go and began to cry on his shoulder. She seemed to be saying "I love you," though her voice was muffled.

It's okay, Joel said. I love you, too.

They embraced like this for more than a minute, the others watching, growing teary—everyone but Alice and Emmett, who kept their heads bowed and looked at no one.

It was Joel's turn next, and Kathy, wiping her cheeks with a tissue, insisted he go first. Now this is heavy, Joel said, weighing the present. He removed the paper carefully, opened the lid of a plain white box, and beheld, inside, a pistol—a silver revolver with a walnut grip. Emmett laughed, then pretended he was coughing.

Did you mean to give this to someone else? Joel said.

No, it's for you, Kathy said. It's a Smith & Wesson.

Why would I want this?

For protection. I worry about you in New York. And it's a very expensive model. A collector's item.

Joel looked like he'd discovered a roach in his salad at a restaurant.

Surely you know me well enough, he said finally, to know I would not want this.

Well, I don't have the receipt, Kathy said. And I would feel much better if you took it.

So this is about you then.

It's a beautiful firearm, Dale said, leaning over Joel's shoulder. What is it, a thirty-eight?

Three fifty-seven, Kathy said.

Dale whistled. Plenty of stopping power.

Alice's mouth had fallen open, her expression somewhere between amusement and horror.

Mom, Joel said, I don't think I can accept this.

Just think about it, she said. That's all I ask. Just let it sit and think about it.

Emmett spent the better part of the afternoon slugging Irish coffee, thinking about the gun and the ticket. From his mother, he'd received a new pair of work boots, three sweaters, and a check for two hundred dollars. She'd always spent more on Joel for Christmas. He was used to that. But the gun was something else entirely. It illustrated perfectly her relationship with Joel—what she hoped for, what she feared. Likewise, it was somehow the quintessence of all that Joel hoped to avoid in his life. And the plane ticket. How easy it was to be generous—to be kind—when one had some money.

He thought about all this, avoiding eye contact with Alice, drinking his liquored-up coffee. Home movies played on the television, an Elvis record on the hi-fi. A few years back, Kathy had sent all the family's home movies—Super 8s, reels of 16mm film, mini-cassettes—to a company that transferred everything to DVD. Now it was a family tradition to watch them. Kathy sat next to Alice, pointing out the family members who were dead.

That's my older sister, Kim, Kathy said, and that's Terry. He was the oldest brother. There was seventeen years' difference between Terry and Dale. Everyone thought Dale was Terry's son. Kim and Terry both died of cancer, in '95 and '98. Back to back.

That was a hard time, Ruth said. I thought I'd never get over it.

Then Daddy died five years after that.

I sure do miss them, Dale said.

The footage was grainy, the colors faded. Elvis was singing "I'll Be Home for Christmas," and Kathy swayed a little to the music, clearly pleased to have everyone together. It was strange to see his mother so much younger onscreen, with her permed hair and her '70s prairie dresses. She still had her baby fat. Later, in the '90s footage, Emmett's father made an appearance—a beefy, broad-shouldered man with shaggy hair and a goatee, smiling like he might be drunk.

There's Lloyd, Kathy said.

That's Emmett's dad? Alice said.

He wanted to look like Chuck Norris with that beard, Kathy said. I kept telling him to shave it.

He looks like you, Emmett, Alice said. His eyes especially.

Emmett said nothing. A moment later, he caught her staring. She excused herself and went down the hallway, a scrap of torn wrapping paper stuck to her heel. He allowed a few minutes to pass, made sure Joel was still absorbed by the home movies, and went to find her. She'd shoved open the window in the antique room. He watched her inhale from a glowing device, vapor pouring from her mouth. A pair of crows cawed to each other outside in mocking tones. She listened and sipped from the pen.

Alice, he said.

She flinched and turned to him. Close the door, she said.

He stepped inside and shut the door.

She pressed her palms flat against his chest, kissed him dryly, and stood back, searching his eyes for some evidence that he'd missed her.

What do you want? he said.

You followed *me*.

You were giving me a look.

You've been ignoring me, she said.

How am I supposed to act? This is strange.

You could acknowledge my existence.

Can you believe he bought her a plane ticket? Like he needs another way of ingratiating himself. It makes me sick.

Emmett.

I would buy her whatever she wanted if I won the lottery. If I sold my screenplay.

How's that going, by the way? she said, trying to change the subject.

He waved away the question and sat on the edge of the brass bed, cold drafts from the window raising goosepimples on his back. I have a jumble of scenes, he said. It's a mess.

About what?

Work. The Tempo hub. I'm quitting, by the way.

That's great, she said. Emmett, that's really great. You can do so much better.

What's that supposed to mean?

Just that it's a waste of potential. I've told you a hundred times.

What do you know about my potential?

I think I know something. We're not strangers.

Wind shushed over the shriveled leaves outside, fluttering the papers and envelopes on the desk where Joel's diary still sat. He thought of the entry he'd read, the verdict Joel had passed on his life. It was like he'd stamped a form—*talentless*—and filed it away.

Close the window, it's cold, he said.

Okay.

And it smells like weed in here.

Okay, Jesus.

She shut the window and sat beside him in the sudden quiet.

Hawaii, he said. Unbelievable.

You're letting him dictate your feelings. You're giving him that power.

She tried to caress the nape of his neck but he swerved away from her, not knowing why exactly. Wishing that he'd let her.

Why don't you end things? he said. Tell him it's over.

She moved her mouth as if to shape a word, but nothing came out. She looked stoned, her eyes lacking their usual luster.

Or not, I guess, he said.

No, it's just—that would be a major step. It's complicated.

I think it's simple. You say the marriage is over. So end it.

And then what?

We move on.

Move on with what?

Whatever we want.

I don't know. It sounds nice. It's just complicated.

He stood from the bed. I should get back, he said.

We can talk, she said as he made to leave. Joel will be in Memphis, the week after New Year's. We'll have time then.

Onscreen, in the living room, a young Joel recited the presidents to a room of rapt adults. A younger Grandma Ruth, only a few strands of gray in her otherwise black hair, was pointing and smiling in the video in exactly the same manner as present-day Ruth, who pointed now at the television.

None of us could believe it, Kathy said. Naming the presidents at five years old.

He could hardly read, Ruth said. Listen to him!

Grover Cleveland, Joel drawled. *Benjamin Harrison. Grover Cleveland again.*

How did you do it, Joel? Emmett said, leaning in the doorway.

I don't remember. I looked at the encyclopedia, I think.

What a gift, he said. You know, some people are born with talent, and some people aren't.

Joel seemed not to have heard him, typing on his phone—a note for an essay, most likely.

I said some people have talent and some people don't, wouldn't you agree?

Joel squinted at Emmett as if he were a half-remembered acquaintance, hailing him from across the street. Sure, he said. I'd hardly call this talent, though.

Onscreen, young Joel had finished with an exuberant *Bill Clinton!* Everyone applauded.

Of course it was talent, Kathy said. They put you in Gifted and Talented in fourth grade. They saw your potential.

What does potential look like, Mom? Emmett said. The Irish coffee had soured in his stomach and given him a headache. He was drunk or angry—he couldn't tell the difference.

He just picked up on things, she said. He learned to read like it was nothing. He could talk and talk, and not like baby talk, like jibber jabber. He would sit and tell you a story. Just make it up on the spot. And you were right the opposite. You were a fussy baby. Always crying in restaurants. Throwing fits. You threw a steak knife at Joel once. Come to think of it, you know where we were? An Outback Steakhouse! Isn't that funny?

What's funny? Ruth said.

Emmett worked at an Outback Steakhouse, Kathy explained. He hurled that knife at Joel like he meant to kill him. Little did he know that one day he'd work there, making the Bloomin' Onions!

I love those Bloomin' Onions, said Uncle Dale. That sauce they've got. What is that, ketchup and mayonnaise? Thousand Island dressing?

You won the genetic lottery, I guess, Emmett said. You were the lucky one.

What's the matter with you? Joel said. Are you drunk?

Mayonnaise is definitely involved, said Uncle Dale. I can tell you that much.

I have complete clarity, he said.

It's just a movie, Emmett. I was a kid.

You were the same then as you are now. Nothing changes.

What's going on? Alice said. She stood behind Emmett in the hallway, peering warily into the room.

Emmett's drunk, Joel said. He's pissed at me for some reason.

We're talking about talent, Emmett said. The way it's passed in the blood. The way it skips over the unlucky. That's you and me. We're the unlucky.

He put his arm around Alice's shoulder and pulled her close. She stiffened and looked at him, horrified but trying not to show it. Joel was unfazed and went back to typing on his phone.

You're both probably drunk, he said.

Speaking of which, I need some more Santa Juice, Dale said, rising unsteadily from his chair.

Alice pulled away from Emmett and sat on the brick hearth, within the strong heat of the purling gas flames. No one else seemed perturbed by what he'd done, seeing it, perhaps, as only a convivial moment brought on by a little too much Irish coffee. He stepped onto the porch. He searched for Kathy's pack of Mistys, and failing to find it, he stood and watched the wind blow little vortexes of leaves in the yard. He tried to remember a white Christmas, to call up a single memory, but nothing came to him.

Five

MEMPHIS WAS COLORLESS. Shades of brown and gray. The big stupid pyramid. Every time Joel visited a midsized American city like this, people with Stockholm syndrome tried to tell him how beautiful and vibrant it was, how there were hidden "scenes," as if Joel must be the kind of person who was into "scenes." He called his mother to complain once he'd checked into the hotel.

I just love it there, Kathy said. I feel close to him.

Elvis? He hoisted his suitcase onto the bed and sat beside it on the too-soft mattress.

The house, the grave. It has an aura.

His phone buzzed: a notification from GENTS. OMG our new vibrating cock rings just dropped. Can you say, Boy Toy? He released a sigh that was more like a whimper.

I wish I had a clone I could send to this dinner, he said. A lookalike.

Oh, don't be such a grump. They'll love to meet you.

My book is an outlier. Most of the other writers are novelists. They wrote books with titles like *The Sweet Potato Sisterhood* or *Mama's Crawfish Motel*. Or they're old men with bow ties and seersucker suits who wrote biographies of Andrew Jackson. No one else is writing personal essays interwoven with critical theory.

Well, that's your own damn fault. That's right, I said "damn." I'm fed up with this negative attitude. It's exciting! This is your chance to meet readers! And these people—they paid for you to be there.

I know, I know, he said.

Have you ever heard the expression "Don't bite the hand that feeds"?

That's always been my specialty.

His Uber driver was a large, razor-bald man, rolls of fat spilling out from around his seatbelt. His T-shirt said CRUSH YOUR ENEMIES. Joel imagined this would not be so difficult for the man, given his size. One thing you could count on in the South was a talkative Uber driver. He wanted only to scroll through the news app on his phone, not really reading so much as absorbing the general vibe of the day's stories. But the driver wanted to know why he'd come to Memphis. He could not come up with a lie fast enough, so he told the truth.

You wrote a book? Like, self-published?

No, it's a real book.

That's what's up, bro. You on social media?

Not really.

Brooo, he said, you *gotta* be on social media, bro! This is the twenty-first century. If you're not on social media, what are you even doing? How will people hear about you? You might as well give up.

I'm thinking about it, honestly. I'd rather just teach.

Why?

Regular paycheck, more security. You can try to live off writing books, but there's no guarantee.

It's called being an entrepreneur, bro. Don't sell yourself short.

He stared out at the blur of gray office towers. Maybe the driver was right. Maybe he was hedging his bets, too afraid to fully commit.

I don't work for Uber, the driver said. I work for myself. I'm my own boss. I set my hours, my days off. Uber just facilitates. I'm out here making moves. I've even got a side hustle, selling CBD—lotions and oils, candles. People love my shit. And you know why I'm successful? Why I'm out here killin it?

Why's that?

Cause I'm on social media, bro.

The dinner venue resembled a palace. When he had mounted the steps, gone through a colonnade of white pillars, and reached the entrance, a woman with a headset asked him, Are you here to work the event?

He looked down at his clothes—black jeans, suede Wallabees, a slightly wrinkled sweater.

I'm an author, he mumbled.

Oh! she cried. Oh my goodness! So sorry! Right this way.

He realized, as he entered, that he was underdressed. Most of the other men wore blazers, some of them ties. The women wore long elegant dresses. Most of the partygoers were white, and most of the workers, weaving busily through the crowd with silver trays of champagne flutes, were Black. He recognized an author right away—a man who had written a book that tried to rehabilitate the legacy of Thomas Jefferson. He was wearing a cotton suit and a bow tie, the same attire he'd worn for his jacket photo.

Everyone seemed to know everyone else, and he knew no one. So he wandered around, plucking red peppers stuffed with goat cheese from the trays and thanking the workers loudly, offering them a conspiratorial smile that he hoped would communicate that he was, if not one of them, at least closer to their station in life than the other attendees.

Just before the dinner was set to begin, a call came through from an unknown number. He stepped away from the chatter of the crowd and the swanky jazz. He said hello and waited. Over the pyramid, streaks of coppery light were fading as evening fell.

You're a fraud, said the voice on the line.

What?

You heard me.

He plugged a finger in his free ear and went a few paces farther from the crowd.

Who is this?

You've got them all fooled, haven't you?

Look, I don't know who you are, but—

You're a complete asshole, you know that, right? They'll figure it out. They'll see what you are.

The phone beeped. He looked up, half expecting to see the glint of binocular lenses from a tenth-story window. If the caller was only a stranger, why was there something so familiar about the voice? It had an unnatural depth. It sounded like the anonymized voice of a witness on a true crime TV show, someone obscured by shadow.

When he sat down for dinner finally, he had no appetite. The woman to his left asked if he was sick, her breath tangy with white wine. You're pale as a ghost! she said.

Thy bones are marrowless, thy blood is cold; thou hast no speculation in those eyes.

Um, what?

The ghost of Banquo.

Who is Banquo?

Never mind, he said. Long day of travel.

Is Banquo that graffiti artist?

His tablemates were kind. They were wealthy and as such had good manners; they knew how to make conversation. They'd spent their lives donating to the arts, and Joel was forced to admit that there were far worse ways to spend your money. The writers at the other tables seemed to be regaling their dining companions with amusing anecdotes. Why didn't he have amusing anecdotes on hand? Should he memorize a few for just such an occasion? Sensing, perhaps, that he was not a social butterfly, they asked him attentive questions. He answered as well as he could, but his mind kept drifting back to the phone call. There were plenty of potential suspects. He'd written about so many people in his life. He'd made them look silly, exaggerating their faults.

As they meandered back to the courtyard after dinner, a woman with ghoulish eye makeup tapped his shoulder and told him she'd read his book. Only she seemed to be under the impression it was fiction. I liked it a lot, she said, but I just couldn't stand the narrator.

THE FESTIVAL WAS HELD in a giant tent on an open lawn downtown. There were tables set up, run by local bookstores. From a distance, one might mistake it all for a carnival instead of what it was—the dreadfully boring antithesis of a carnival. Signing tables were arranged in a semicircle in the "author corral," where writers came and went as they pleased, autographing copies for fans.

When Joel reached the author check-in table, a festival organizer stood to greet him, her eyes lighting up.

We've been waiting for you! she said.

Am I late?

Not at all, she said. I'm a big fan of your books!

Joel thanked her, assuming the plural form of "book" was just a mistake. She probably said the same thing to everyone, whether they'd written one book or twenty.

I've got your goody bag here, she said. Your nametag should be inside. Can I get a picture with you?

Sure, Joel said.

There was a moment of social uncertainty, wherein he tried to gauge whether to put his arm around her shoulder. In the end, he decided to go for it, smiling blandly at the image of himself on her iPhone screen, held at arm's length.

His co-panelist was a woman with purple hair who'd written a novel called *Not Exactly Boyfriend Material!* It was about a twenty-something high-powered lawyer who discovers that her new beau is in fact a vampire who wants only to drink her blood, and thereby drain the "predatory energy" that made her a good lawyer. She'd written other books in the same series, all of which seemed to be about powerful women realizing their boyfriends were actually supernatural monsters. They had titles like *A Beast in the Bedroom* or *Tall, Dark and . . . Dead?*

It's a metaphor for what women face in the workplace, she explained. We all confront vampires every day, but we have to *become* the vampires. We have to take that power for ourselves.

He could not begin to fathom why they'd been paired together.

The panel's theme was "Fighting the System," but the message of *Not Exactly Boyfriend Material!* was more about using the system to your advantage. Still, he tried his level best to find points of agreement. At one point, he found himself saying, *Vampires are the symbols of our time because we all share this unconscious paranoia that shadowy figures in elite circles are preying on us.*

Afterward, he drifted back to the signing tables and fished around in the goody bag. There were ink pens inside, a tiny scroll with the festival's logo, and the laminated nametag attached to a lanyard. It was only when he'd slipped the cord over his head that he realized he'd been given the wrong goody bag. BRAD BURNS was printed on the tag. He could not help but laugh. The woman at the check-in table had mistaken him for someone else—Brad Burns, whoever that was. He stood by one of the concession booths and considered the false name around his neck, wondering who the man might be and where he was this very moment.

He moved through the tent feeling weightless, the burden of selfhood shed like the filmy husk of a cicada, the likes of which he'd collected from tree bark with Emmett as children and placed in Kathy's hair. Or was it the other way around? Had he become the husk—see-through, almost nothing—while the heavy, humming weight of Joel Shaw went bumbling away?

He could see his own table—the empty chair, the stack of books. Some of the tables had long lines. At others, the writers sat alone, glancing at their watches, praying inwardly that someone, anyone, might stop by. Joel could not bear the thought of that indignity. It was better to remain this floating fiction, this impostor.

He found the table assigned to Brad Burns. The chair was empty. An open can of Diet Coke sat atop a napkin next to the stacks of books. They were spy novels, it seemed, all about the same character, a CIA operative named Jack Wolfe. The titles were wolf-related: *Operation Full Moon, Leader of the Pack.* When he flipped to the jacket photo, it surprised him how much he really did resemble Brad Burns, albeit less handsome and less muscular. The photograph appeared to be several years old, and was taken at dusk, the man's features darkened just enough that any difference in appearance between them would not be noticed by a casual observer. He learned that Brad Burns had been employed by the CIA, that he lived in Georgia, and that he was "a proud husband, father, and patriot."

He had become so captivated by the likeness of the photo that he'd failed to notice a small crowd hovering tentatively near the table.

You must be Mr. Burns? said an older man.

That's me, he said.

He shook the guy's hand. He had deep seams in his face and a patchy beard. His black baseball cap said VIETNAM VET.

Would you mind? he said, holding out a weathered copy of *Wolfe in Sheep's Clothing.*

Of course not, he said. He bit the inside of his cheek to keep from smiling and imagined recounting this story to Alice later. Or better yet, his friends in New York.

Where do you get the ideas for your books? the man said.

They just sort of come to me, he said. When you've seen as much as I've seen, the well never runs dry.

Well, I'll tell you, it sure is an honor. Thank you for your service.

Likewise.

He shook his hand once more and had turned to walk away when a woman stepped forward, clutching a book to her chest.

I've been waiting all day to meet you! she said.

Soon enough, a line formed, and he found himself nudging Brad's Diet Coke aside and forging the man's signature on a dozen books. More than once, he had to cross out the beginning of his own name, remembering who they all expected him to be. It was exhilarating—not only the suspense of Brad Burns's potential return, but the *attention.* It was such a relief, not being himself.

He wandered away after a while, and the rush of pretending faded quickly, like crashing from a sugar high. He became Joel Shaw once more, waves of vertigo turning his stomach. Beyond the shade of the festival tent, the light was blinding, and he felt, for a moment, dislocated from time. Memphis was in Egypt first, wasn't it? He thought of wind-scoured dunes and gaunt camels, of date palms and slaves dragging stones from quarries.

His hotel room was dim and sad. He sat on the bed in the day's last slant of light, turned on the television, watched a program about ghost hunters for a few minutes, then killed the picture. You can't just sit here, he said aloud. You cannot just sit in this hotel room.

He looked up a nearby tiki bar and called an Uber to take him there. Though he'd never been much of a drinker, tiki cocktails were the one exception, seeming to him more in the realm of dessert than booze. The place was dim, small candles flickering in ruby glasses. The walls were fake bamboo. Rattan fishing traps and inflated puffer fish hung from the ceiling. The only other people in the bar were two couples in a back booth, a double date that seemed to be going poorly.

Joel tuned them out and sipped from his Navy Grog. A woman came in and sat two stools away, eyeing him covertly. At one point, she seemed to snap his picture, pretending to text. Joel scrolled reflexively through his news app, then put his phone face down on the bar and ran a hand over his face.

I want something strong, the woman said.

A zombie? said the bartender. It's basically straight booze.

Perfect.

Her phone began to buzz; she was texting for real now, suppressing a smile. She was small, her movements quick and sparrowlike, her hair a frizzy ginger mane. She wore a tweed blazer, the sleeves rolled up to her elbows.

Where does the name come from? she said as the bartender set the frosted mug before her, a sprig of mint planted in the pebbled ice.

You drink one, that's what you turn into, he said. A zombie. Do you want the fire?

The fire?

He held up a grill lighter.

Sure, she said.

He lit the rum-soaked wheel of lime and it burned with a bluish flame. Her eyes widened with delight. You see this? she said to Joel.

I see it, he said.

I guess I'll be a zombie after this.

I wonder what happens if a zombie drinks a zombie, he said. Maybe they regain their mental faculties.

In that case, she said, we should put this in the water supply.

Why's that?

Because most people are zombies, she said, as though it was common knowledge. Most people have no critical thinking skills whatsoever.

Oh, he said. Right.

What brings you to this tropical oasis? she said.

I was sitting in my hotel room with an impending sense of doom, he said. I thought a tiki drink might help.

I get that, she said. Impending doom. It's only natural, things being the way they are.

Which is what?

Fucked. Things are fucked up.

Cheers to that, he said, lifting his mug.

Well, we won't have to wait much longer, as you know.

Wait for what?

The end.

The end of what?

Of everything. She smiled at him then. Her teeth were crooked and ocher-stained.

Do I know you? Joel said.

Not intimately, she said. But I feel like I know you. I've read all your books.

He looked down at the nametag against his chest. BRAD BURNS.

I see, he said. You're here for the festival?

I'm Lexi, she said, scooting to the stool beside him. He shook her limp, cold hand. She dipped her fingers into her drink and drew out a maraschino cherry by the stem. The red of the cherry matched her lipstick.

They preserve these in formaldehyde, Lexi said, letting the cherry drop onto her cocktail napkin.

That can't be true.

Like when you're dead, she said. The same thing they use to pickle you. I don't eat them.

He felt what by then had become a chronic sensation of surveillance, of someone, somewhere, watching his every move. But the bar was empty. The couples in the booth had left. Even the bartender had vanished to a back room.

Brad Burns, she said, circling the rim of her mug with her pinky, smiling a private smile. Brad fucking Burns. I didn't think you'd be so skinny.

Sorry to disappoint, he said.

I thought they put you through special forces training.

That was a long time ago. Sitting on your ass, writing books for a decade, you lose your definition.

Lexi nodded, as though she understood this all too well. I used to be really something, she said. My mother told me I was pretty enough for the movies if I got my teeth fixed.

She looked briefly like she might cry. Soft music began to play— surf rock from the 1950s, with all the crackle and distortion of a phonograph. The bartender reappeared from the darkness of the stockroom and gave Joel a reassuring nod and a wink, as if to say, *You're doing well, keep it up.*

He could not say what possessed him to continue with the lie, except perhaps the exhilarating lightness of his new persona, this husk he'd become. And this room—this hypnotic room with its indigo light and antique music. This woman, who seemed so familiar to him, who repelled him vaguely, and yet somehow was keeping him there. He felt that he could leave only when she let him.

So where's wifey tonight? she said.

We're staying at my mother's, he said. But she's with a friend this weekend. Southern Illinois.

All the way from Georgia?

Right, Joel said, trying to keep straight the particulars of Brad Burns's bio.

So wifey's on her own, then?

She's probably in bed by now.

As far as you know.

What's that supposed to mean?

Lexi shrugged and sucked at the dregs of her zombie.

I don't like what you're implying.

I don't like it any more than you do, she said.

She's not that kind of person, he said. And she shares her location with me. I can tell you exactly where she is.

That's a little . . . paternal, isn't it?

She goes to the gym late at night. She has to walk to her car. It's for safety.

Uh huh.

She's not that kind of person.

He picked up his phone and swiped through his contacts till he found Alice.

What kind of person are *you*? Lexi said.

He found, on her contact page, the pulsing blue dot that represented her. He enlarged the map, zoomed out. She was in New York, not southern Illinois. He watched for a long time, thinking the map might refresh. But the blue dot remained where it was not supposed to be.

Is there a problem? Lexi said.

No, he said, returning the phone to his pocket.

Is wifey safe and sound? Snug as a bug?

Do you have some kind of problem with me? he said.

Not at all, she said. I'm a big fan.

So you've said.

I have to ask—how much of your work is autobiographical? I mean, Jack Wolfe is traveling the world, bedding all these women. But you—you're a married man. And you've lost your *definition*, haven't you? From all your training? You're not the well-oiled machine you used to be. Still, you're not bad-looking. Your brain is your main asset, I suppose. I bet that's why you're balding. It's all the thinking you do.

When she reached to touch his head, he flinched and pulled away. She laughed at him—a wild-eyed, witchy laugh.

Don't touch me.

I think it's cute!

I don't care what you think.

Aww, she said. She jutted her lip in a pouty frown. I've hurt his feelings.

I'm going to the restroom, he said. He could hear her laughing from the corridor to the men's room. Inside, the walls were plastered with half-naked women, pages torn from skin mags. The row of bulbs above the sink was blood red.

Alice answered on the fourth ring.

Where are you? he said.

I'm with Valerie, she said. In Marion. Remember?

Joel pressed his forehead against the wall. There were voices in the background, staccato bursts of laughter. You're with Marion, he said.

Valerie, she said. In the town of Marion. In Illinois. I told you I was going to visit.

I know you told me. I hear you when you tell me things.

Well, where else would I be?

Is there a party or something?

We're at a bar, she said.

He thought he sensed a weakness in her voice, like she could scarcely muster the energy to lie to him. But she was lying, nonetheless. She'd made that choice.

Isn't it late to be at a bar?

Where are you?

At a bar, he sighed.

Well?

There's nothing you want to tell me?

What would I tell you? My day was completely boring.

Right, he said, sorry to bother you.

How's the festival?

The phone beeped—another call coming through. I'm getting a call, goodbye, he said.

He switched over and said hello. No one spoke. There was a sound like crinkling cellophane near the receiver.

Who is this? Joel said.

You know who it is.

I'm afraid I don't.

I know you, the voice said. I can see right through you.

Fuck you.

He ended the call. He stood before the mirror, bathed in red light, regarding himself. He could not keep his thoughts together, all the looping, tiresome anxieties of his life. All the lies he told himself, the sum total of which had become his personality. He could not remember why he was here or what he was supposed to want.

Lexi was still waiting at the bar. She'd paid for his drink and bought him a double shot of tequila.

I felt bad, she said, for teasing you.

I think I'm done.

Not till you take this shot with me.

I don't do shots.

Now, Brad, I won't take no for an answer.

She nudged the shot glass toward him with her knuckle. He drew a deep breath and tossed it back. He set the glass down hard, coughed, and wiped his mouth with his sleeve.

I'm a little drunk now, I think, he said.

Wonderful, Lexi said. That will make the next part much easier.

What do you want from me?

She leaned forward to whisper in his ear. Let me take care of you, she said.

She curled a lock of his hair around her forefinger, her breath warm, smelling of fruit and booze.

Let me bring you home and take care of you.

··························
··························

From the passenger window, the city of Memphis pitched and wavered. A light shone from the highest point of the glass pyramid. It made him think of the pyramid on dollar bills—the glowing, all-seeing eye at its pinnacle.

Why is there a pyramid on money? he said.

Lexi was driving. The highway was empty, the radio tuned to tribal New Age music. The vents blew arctic air into his face.

You tell me, Mr. CIA, she said.

Wasn't my department.

I have my own theories. We know it's Masonic. The Freemasons wanted the public to know they were watching, keeping tabs on us. We know that much.

Who is "we"?

Concerned citizens.

Her place was far from the city center, a batten-board house with orange foam bubbling out between the planks. All the houses on her street had the same look of weariness, of clinging to order and respectability. They seemed, like the people who lived in them, on the verge of giving up. Joel resisted the urge to write this down—something about the houses built in the '70s, all those familiar American split-levels that stood now as monuments to a decade when the future still seemed possible. If he wanted to disappear, he would have to let go of these thoughts. From then on, he decided, he would note only the bare facts of his experience.

This was my grandmother's house, Lexi said, unlocking the door. She left it to me.

Inside, the furniture was covered with plastic. There were Audubon illustrations of birds on the walls—herons and flamingos, tropical parakeets. The TV was playing, tuned to the Home Shopping Network. A woman displayed a silver bracelet on her wrist; her face had the stunned look of a department store mannequin.

I like the TV to be on when I get home, Lexi said. I got the idea from hotels. You ever check into a hotel and the TV's on?

Sure, he said. He sat on the sofa, the stiff plastic squeaking as he situated himself.

It makes you feel less lonely, to walk inside and hear voices. Like they were waiting for you.

She went to rummage in the kitchen. He glanced around at the objects in the room and tried to observe them neutrally: a stack of

AARP magazines, a dust-coated blood pressure cuff, a wrought-iron Victorian birdcage near the window, empty.

I hope you like vodka, she said. She gave him a coffee cup with half-moons of white ice and what seemed to be straight liquor. She sat on the other end of the sofa and put her bare feet in his lap.

How long have you lived here? he said.

About a month. Grammy died two months ago, but they had to work out the estate. Before that I was living with my boyfriend. Former boyfriend, I should say. He cheated on me.

I'm sorry, he said. He took a sip of the vodka, trying not to grimace as it seared his throat. How did you find out? he said. Were there signs, I mean?

I found naked pictures of the slut on his phone. That was my sign.

I mean before that. Did you suspect anything?

I suspected that he was selfish and a liar. It wasn't exactly a leap to think he'd cheat on me.

Why were you with him then?

She seemed to really consider this. He made me laugh, she said. He was good-looking. And we had similar beliefs.

Beliefs in what?

All the stuff you write about. The New World Order. How the bankers secretly run everything.

I see, he said. He squirmed and sat up a bit. Every time he moved, the plastic made a wrenching sound.

He was the one who turned me onto your books. He'd shit a brick if he knew I was with you right now. Tanner—that was his name—he was in the army. He had security clearances, so he knew about the same stuff you know about. He was like, "Lexi, you gotta read Brad Burns. He writes about the Deep State and the World Bank and psyop missions."

The room was pulsing now. He thought of the pulsing blue dot on the map. Where else had she gone without telling him? What else had she done?

Where is she now? Joel said.

Where is who?

I mean, where is Tanner?

He lives right down the street with his mom. God, if he found out you were here with me, like this?

She fell into the same witchy laughter.

He'd rip your arms off and use them to strangle you, she said. Then he'd strangle me with your ripped-off arms. Then he'd kill himself.

Wow, Joel said.

He's got an awful temper. And he hasn't lost his definition like you. He's built like an orangutan. Although I bet you know secret techniques to kill a person with your hands.

A few, he said.

Lexi drained the rest of her vodka and set the mug on the coffee table. Her expression grew serious.

I have to make a confession, she said. I had ulterior motives, inviting you back here.

Oh yeah?

I run a website called Truthsoldiers.org. We try to get to the bottom of things the mainstream media won't cover. I was hoping we could do an interview, get you on the record. With your clearance level, we could answer some big questions for our readers.

What sort of questions?

Like, okay, how did the DNC hack Dominion Voting Systems? Or what really happened with Epstein?

What about who really killed JFK?

Do you know anything about that?

Warmth rose to his cheeks. He hated that he blushed so easily. It meant that his humiliation could never be mistaken for something else.

So this was just a charade, he said. You followed me to the bar.

Oh, I've upset him again, she said. Listen, I wanted to meet you. It wasn't just this. I really am a fan.

The Home Shopping Network had moved on to an anti-wrinkle mask, before and after shots of shriveled old women peeling a film from their faces, reappearing with vivacious smiles and a plastic smoothness to their flesh. Individual results may vary.

Lexi lifted her small, pale foot and began to massage his inner thigh with her toes. His face was still aflame with blood. He drank more of the cold vodka, thinking it would help, but it only made the burning worse.

I still want to fuck you, she said.

I'm not interested.

Really? It feels like you're interested.

He had grown hard, and she ran her foot along the length of his cock. He closed his eyes, not wanting her to stop, but not wanting to continue things either. He wondered how long they could stay like this, if he remained completely still and acquiescent.

What if we played a game? she said. What if we pretended you were Jack Wolfe?

The name did not register at first. He'd forgotten who he was supposed to be. Then he remembered: Jack Wolfe was his alter ego—or rather Brad Burns's alter ego. It was hard to keep straight, in the slurred chatter of his mind, what story he was meant to tell.

I'm not very good at that sort of thing.

But you make up stories for a living.

I turn my life into stories. There's a difference.

Okay, what about this, Lexi said, standing from the sofa. She began to unbutton her blouse, revealing a black bra underneath. You're here on assignment, she said. You know that I'm working for the enemy, and you know that I have valuable information.

What kind of information?

Secrets.

She unzipped her denim skirt and wiggled out of it. It fell to the floor and she flung it with her toe into his lap.

How will I get you to talk?

I don't know, Jack, she said. You tell me.

She reached back to unclasp her bra, pulled her arms through the straps. Then she peeled down her panties in a matter-of-fact way and stood, hands on her hips, in the pitching blue light of the television. She was white and scrawny, a cesarean scar on her stomach, a fluff of red hair between her legs. The bones of her pelvis were sharp.

What do you think? she said.

Joel tried to speak but nothing came out. He cleared his throat and said, Of what?

Of how I look!

Yeah, you look good, he said. I like what I see.

What a stupid line, he thought. *I like what I see?*

I'm sure you've seen better, Jack, she said. All the women you've been with. But they can't take care of you the way I do. They don't know who you are or what you want.

Who am I? Joel said. What do I want?

She took a step toward him, then another. She was coltish, unsteady from drinking, and very much naked. She knelt and turned her face upward.

You're a patriot, she said. You want to defeat the globalists.

The announcer on the television asked a series of questions while old men with dentures smiled and blinked, displaying their rejuvenated faces. *Is your skin dull and baggy? Do you look older than you feel? Do you stare at yourself in the mirror, confused by what you see?*

You want control, she said. But you also want a break from control, don't you? I could tell from the moment I first saw you. You want someone to take the wheel. You want to sleep while someone else drives, knowing you're safe, and you want to wake up at home and be carried to your bed.

She smiled and bit her lip.

Let me drive you home, Jack, she said. How would that be?

She tiptoed her fingers up his thigh, then gripped his cock, so hard he almost cried out. He stood abruptly, forgetting the mug of vodka balanced on his knee.

Fuck, he said.

It's all right, she said, turning the cup upright, collecting the pieces of ice.

I need to use your bathroom.

Right now? We're kind of having a moment.

Yes, he said, now. His erection was stiff and painful now that he was standing.

She pointed down the hallway and he walked into the darkness. He passed the cracked door of a bedroom and peeked inside. The bed was piled with stuffed animals, the sort you won as prizes at the county fair. Giant pandas and pink bunny rabbits. Unicorns and smiling dolphins. They stared at him like a mute, judgmental chorus.

In the bathroom, he clutched the edges of the sink and caught his breath. He took his cock from his jeans and looked at it. There were pink marks where her fingers had clamped down. The head was purplish and nodded with each pulse of his heart. He thought of the eggplant emoji—a cartoon of masculine potency. His life was a cartoon. He looked at himself in the mirror and saw a breathless, grimacing man with his cock out. It frightened him how right she was—to sleep while someone ferried him home. How nice that sounded. How perfect, really.

He zipped up his pants, sat on the closed toilet lid, and opened Alice's contact page. He watched the blue dot for a few minutes, still blinking where it did not belong. What could she possibly be doing there? Who could she be seeing? An innocent explanation was possible. Just because she'd lied did not mean she'd been unfaithful. That was a big leap. That was catastrophizing. You're catastrophizing, he said aloud, thinking this would help. It never helped. He pictured who the man might be. A volunteer from the garden perhaps. A dirty, bearded man with furry hobbit's feet and hornlike toenails, holding up a tangle of potatoes. A dirt man. A man of dirt. Potatoes growing in his beard.

He scrolled through the photo attachments they'd sent over the years. Most were of Alice. She sat across from him in restaurants with artfully plated food. She smiled at sunset overlooks in the Catskills. She showed off new haircuts, new dresses with the tags attached. In spite of the anguish that skewered him now, he missed her. Or was it that he missed what they had once been like?

You okay? Lexi said, knocking at the door.

Just a minute, he said, smearing the tears from his eyes. I just need some time.

She sighed and padded off down the hallway. The future flashed before him—fucking her on the plastic-covered couch, waking in her bed with the dead-eyed animals. Then something happened. In one of those rare moments when a man foresees completely the whole chain of actions that will furnish his misery, he stood and went to the bathroom window. He shoved it open, flakes of paint falling onto the sill, and crawled out into the night. He began to jog, his eyes unadjusted to the darkness. There were black masses of foliage, purple clouds shrouding the bright moon. The dew-dappled weeds soaked the cuffs of his jeans. He pushed through hedges into another yard, and then another. Porch lights snapped on. He entered a field where the cold, wet grass came up to his knees, and soon he was running with everything he had—great leaping strides, arms pumping. His relief was so intense he began to laugh. There were high-tension powerlines slung above him; he could hear the currents zinging in the dark. He had no notion at all of where he was, but he didn't care. His lungs were aching. He was laughing with the mad joy of a man who'd escaped his fate.

Six

THE WHOLE IDEA started as a joke. Emmett had never been to New York, and Alice found this completely unacceptable. She said in an offhand way that they should go. Joel would be gone four days, time enough for a weekend trip.

All right then, let's go, Emmett said.

Okay then, Alice said.

I'll buy the tickets.

You do that.

One thing had led to the next, and now the Mystique was in motion, the Nashville airport forty miles away. Emmett had used two of his precious sick days, unpaid of course. Alice had made up her alibi—a weekend reunion with Valerie, an old college friend from southern Illinois. Joel had believed her, she said. All her lies had been believed so far. Their luck had held. But Emmett had begun to consider the complications, though they remained at a distance somewhat, inarticulate, outshined by the promise of the city. When he pictured New York, it was always summer there. Here and now, in Tennessee, droplets of rain quivered on the windshield. The sky above the worn-down hills was the color of cigarette ash.

So we'll stay in your place when we get there? he said.

Alice nodded, pupils scanning the book in her lap. Something about her eyes made him think she wasn't really reading. Like maybe she'd begun to consider the complications herself and the text was just something to look at while she did so.

In your bed? he said.

Is that weird? I guess that's weird, isn't it?

It's just, all Joel's stuff will be there.

I know. We'll figure it out. It'll be fine.

No, I know. I'm excited.

Me too, she said. She smiled at him blandly and turned back to the book. Traffic had slowed on the highway. Plumes of black diesel smoke floated past them from a nearby truck, stinking of spent matches. A second cousin, who'd rigged his Ford for "rolling coal," belching out smoke on command, had told Emmett once that this was the scent of hell, of fire and brimstone. The same cousin had later become a youth minister.

Do you believe in sin? he said after a long silence.

Alice dog-eared her page. No, she said. I mean yes, I believe in right and wrong, but not, like, biblical sin. Eve with the apple and all that. Why do you ask?

No reason.

You're feeling guilty.

I'm not sure if that's it, he said.

The truth was that he'd braced for guilt, that he thought he'd known what to look for when it showed its face. But it came to him incognito, disguised as some other feeling, unmasking itself only once permitted inside. Even then, it was amorphous. There was no face under the mask, only other masks.

The way I see it, she said, either we go on in secret or we tell Joel and blow everything up. Or maybe there's a middle way. Maybe I could split with Joel, and we could go on seeing each other without telling him, let things develop at our own pace. We'd remove the guilt factor.

Nothing will remove the guilt factor, he said. Even if we pretended. Even if we said we'd gotten together after you split. He'd still hate us both forever.

Maybe we could join the Witness Protection Program, she said. Do they take volunteers?

That'd be nice. I could get a new name.

What's wrong with Emmett?

Never liked it.

What would the new name be?

He thought for a moment and said, Jeff.

Why Jeff? she said, laughing. That's sort of anticlimactic.

It's the name of my protagonist in *The Package Handler*. Jeff Anderson. He's an everyman.

Wait, that's the title of your screenplay?

Yeah, do you like it?

Don't you think that sounds a little . . . gay? Like, it could be the title of a gay porno.

I don't follow.

Because of, you know, the double meaning of "package"?

I like that about it. Package could mean anything. It could mean a bomb. It could mean drugs.

It could mean a man's dick and balls.

I don't think anyone will make that leap.

It troubled him, this line of questioning. He'd hoped, in some hazy way, to make professional connections in New York, Alice having mentioned her friend there who wrote screenplays. That he'd never shown it to anyone, not even her, had not struck him as important until this moment. He had not even finished the thing. It had an ending. It could be called "a draft," he supposed. A mess of disjointed scenes and placeholder dialogue. But it was more than a piece of writing. All through his long nights at the Center, through the endless mechanical movements of his body, he'd held the secret knowledge of the screenplay like a talisman. *I'm not really here*, he would think. *This isn't me, hurling boxes of diapers and Zabar's coffee onto a conveyor belt. The real me is a document, saved forever. The real me isn't even real.*

I was thinking maybe I could give it to your friend, he said.

What friend?

Your friend the screenwriter?

Oh, Amari, she said. Give it to him for, like, notes?

Maybe he could pass it on to someone.

Oh, she said. I mean yeah, maybe. I can set up a group hang.

It would be good to make some connections while I'm there.

No, of course. I'll text him right now.

She took out her phone and began composing a message, a hint of distaste in her expression.

Wait, what will we tell people? he said. Who am I to you?

I'll say you're my old friend from Springfield, she said. We grew up together. I could tell them you're gay.

Will that be plausible?

Just say you wrote a screenplay called *The Package Handler* and they'll believe you, she said.

EMMETT HAD ONLY flown a few times in his life. He could not help but stare like a yokel as the plane groaned and lifted from the runway, as the Cumberland River became a glittering thread. It saddened him to think of Grandma Ruth, who had never flown and never would. She would die without seeing her world from above.

They were seated separately, Alice five rows back. He tried to read his screenwriting book for a while, but the tiny window kept drawing his eyes. As the sun dipped lower, it was like the lights had been dimmed in an enormous theater. The man beside him, whose freshly barbered hair matched the charcoal of his woolen blazer, had a laptop open on the tray table, shuffling through the slides of a PowerPoint presentation. When the flight attendant arrived with her cart of snacks, the man said, I'll have the lobster tail, please.

She mustered a feeble laugh and said, Cookies or pretzels.

What, no lobster? I'm just kidding, honey, gimme the pretzels.

Emmett could not make sense of what the PowerPoint was meant to convey or what the man's business might be. One of the slides had a bust of a Greek philosopher and the words *The Only Constant Is Change*.

Lemme ask you something, the man said at one point. You're a young guy. How old are you, thirty?

Twenty-eight, Emmett said.

What do young people—what does your generation want in a job?

To make good money, I guess, he said. Health insurance.

You don't want flexibility?

Emmett shrugged.

Interesting, the man said. Very, very interesting.

When they began their descent, the earth was darker than the sky, the pink-rimmed horizon a seam between two worlds. New York was like an iridescent organism at the bottom of a black sea. There was no clear beginning to it, nothing you could call an edge. He grinned helplessly. This was it—the center of it all.

From LaGuardia, their Uber veered into the slow stream of traffic. Horns were blaring. A crescendo of ambulance sirens reached a deafening pitch and died away. Manhattan stood in the distance, twinkling like some impossible sequined fantasy. He could not manage to steady his heart.

You look happy, Alice said.

I just can't believe I'm here, he said. Then he took her hand on the console and said, With you, I mean. I'm happy to be here with you.

Me too, she said, sounding uncertain.

They arrived at the apartment much sooner than he'd expected. This was the main advantage to living in Astoria, she explained—you were only five minutes from the airport. She lived in a pale brick rowhouse, like all the others in the neighborhood, and he trudged up the stairs behind her to the third floor, lugging their bags, trying not to make a face at the smell of cat litter and garbage emanating from the other apartments.

The place was small but cozy, fairy lights lining the doorways, leafy vines dangling from planters. Alice lit a stick of palo santo and watered the plants. They all looked somewhat sickly. A neighbor had been coming every other week, she explained. He admired the movie posters above the record player—Fellini's *Amarcord*, Truffaut's *The 400 Blows*.

Those are Joel's, she said. Most of the records, too.

I gathered, he said.

The books are easy to tell apart, she said. She opened the refrigerator and leaned down into the golden slice of light. All his books are theory. Can I get you anything? A beer?

I'll take a beer, sure.

She gave him a tallboy, a brand from Brooklyn he'd never heard of. It tasted like pine needles. They sat on the sofa in uncomfortable silence, sipping from their cans, their knees touching.

Any music requests? she said.

Something New York, he said. Like, if New York was a piece of music.

Wow, no pressure!

I trust you to pick.

She crouched before the cube shelf, running her fingers over the spines. She found a record at last, placed the needle, and tossed herself back onto the couch, taking a long pull of beer. The speakers hissed and crackled. How disappointed would you be, she said, on a scale of one to ten, if "Empire State of Mind" started playing?

He laughed. Like a seven, he said. Maybe an eight.

I think you'll approve, she said. It's got a Bruce cameo. Is "cameo" the right word in music?

Feature, I think.

What began to play was Lou Reed's *Street Hassle*. They made out for a while, till the eponymous track came on, Springsteen's mumbling monologue arriving late in the eleven-minute saga of doomed love and overdose.

Do you hear? she said. That's him.

I hear, he said. He finished his beer and sat denting the aluminum with his thumb, feeling trapped in the stifling apartment, the radiator clanking and whistling.

Let's go to Manhattan, he said.

Right now? It's late.

It's just, we flew all the way here, and now we're in Queens.

Right, she said. Okay, yeah. I keep forgetting you've never been here.

We could stay up all night.

Fuck it, she said. Yeah, let's do it.

They filled a silver flask with bourbon at the sink and struck out, grinning like teenagers who'd escaped their chaperone. The neighborhood was not like he'd pictured—the stacks of the Steinway factory, the Hell Gate Bridge in the distance. Crowds spilled out from the bars, young Greek men in muscle shirts with slicked hair and gold necklaces. Emmett wanted to watch, to see everything, but not to look like someone who was watching.

Watch for bottles, she said.

She pointed to a water bottle, seemingly filled with apple juice.

The taxi drivers idle here, waiting for calls from LaGuardia, she said. They throw out their pee bottles.

On the elevated platform, beneath the orange coils of the heat lamp, they took swigs from the flask. He began to feel drunk on the train as it rattled toward the city. Their car was empty till they reached Queensboro Plaza, then filled up dramatically. Someone took a hit from a joint, suffusing the car with its smell.

Where should we stop? Alice said.

Times Square?

God, no, she laughed. Wouldn't you feel like a tourist?

I always feel like a tourist. Even when I'm home, I feel like a tourist.

I don't go to Manhattan that often. When I go, I go to the Strand, then I come home.

Where do you go then?

I stay in Queens. Or I go to Brooklyn—Greenpoint or Williamsburg.

Williamsburg, that's where all the cool kids are, right?

More like the rich kids. The Trustifarians.

The what?

The trust fund kids. Hey, let's do Washington Square, how does that sound? It's pretty at night.

You're the boss.

They surfaced from the piss-smelling cavern of the subway to the garbage-smelling corner of a wide avenue. Emmett kept waiting for some sector of the city to smell like something nice—flowers or baking bread. After seeing the arch, they meandered to a bar, a cocktail joint on MacDougal that proved to be fussier and less interesting than the photos made it seem. The clientele were NYU students and tourists, huddled around tables of dark polished wood, reading their menus by the flicker of tealights in red glass.

This is Manhattan, Alice said, over the din of cocktail shakers. It's a good idea in theory, but then you get here and it's too loud, too crowded, and too expensive. And the bars here, they're just replicating Brooklyn. It's the same thing in Queens, only the Queens bars are replicating Brooklyn from ten years ago.

Cool, he said. He was finding all this hard to follow and could not stop thinking about the money he'd spent on their drinks—forty dollars. He'd stared at the receipt for a full minute, certain it must be wrong.

Their enthusiasm withered. They did not stay up all night. They ordered another cocktail at the MacDougal Street bar and then went home. On the train, Alice fell asleep on his shoulder, and he let his head loll against the window. A man took the seat ahead of them and rummaged in a large jute bag. He balanced a crucifix on the windowsill, then creased pictures of Jesus and the Buddha and various many-armed Hindu deities. His bag seemed to contain an infinite store of relics. He took out painted mandalas and prayer beads, little brass bells that tinkled faintly. The grand finale was a yarmulke, which he placed over his bald spot, and with this, all the major faiths were represented. He began to pray. Emmett could see him reflected in the glass, moving his lips without speaking, the darkness strobing outside.

Seven

THEY SPENT THE NEXT DAY seeing the sights. He'd slept on the couch, unable in the end to take his brother's bed, and had woken with a crick, a stab of pain in his neck whenever he turned his face left or right, up or down—necessary movements for a day of sightseeing. So, he saw the Empire State Building at eye level, unable to glance skyward. He saw St. Patrick's Cathedral without admiring the vaulted ceiling. At the 9/11 Memorial, he stood near the two great chasms, water pouring over the edges into what seemed an infinite void, unable to look down. Is there a bottom? he asked.

There's a bottom, she said. They made it so you can't see it.

The plan, that night, was to meet her friends at a bar in Crown Heights. They showered and changed at the apartment, his neck feeling a little better after twenty minutes of hot water. He drank a pine needle beer and played one of Alice's records while she finished up, Carole King singing sadly, wanting to know why no one stayed in one place anymore.

So the screenwriter, Amari—he'll be there? Emmett asked.

Supposed to be, she said. He could see her in the bathroom mirror, clasping her earrings, brow taut with concentration.

What sort of stuff does he write?

He got into a room for this show, I can't remember the name.

A room?

Like, a staff writing gig. A writers' room. They don't mention that in your books?

Of course they do, he said, though he'd never heard of such a thing. The books all assumed that writing was faced alone, like divorce or a bleak diagnosis. There were people who could help, but the burden was mainly your own.

It's about werewolves and vampires, she said. That's all I know. Kind of a *Twilight* rip-off, but more self-aware. Like, it's campy but it knows it's campy.

They walked down Ditmars in the gathering dark, Emmett lost in fantasy, picturing himself at the helm of a conference table, surrounded by lackeys with open laptops transcribing his ideas. The present moment kept imposing itself, the blaring sounds and rotten whiffs of the city. They stepped over broken glass and splatters of fly-swarmed vomit. They kept their distance from a bare-chested man swinging an iPhone charger above his head like a chain mace. A tang in the air, like burning plastic, could be tasted in the backs of their throats.

Maybe the Steinway factory? she said.

Are they burning the pianos?

He kept hoping the city would come into focus, reveal itself as the place of his dreams. He kept waiting for the feeling he'd hoped to feel: an immense togetherness, the absolute absence of loneliness. But mounting the steps to the elevated station, Alice clinging to his arm, he felt like a minor character, inessential to the story, his scenes at risk of being cut.

The place was called Regina's, a lesbian bar with karaoke. It was small and crowded, violet blacklights bathing a stage in the front corner where two women sang into a microphone. They ordered drinks and found the others in a back booth near a pool table with pink baize—Amari, the screenwriter, and two women named Libby and Florence. Amari was tall and sat hunched over the table in the rigid, cramped posture of tall men in confined spaces. His face and his head were clean-shaven, and he wore circular wire-rimmed glasses that he adjusted with his forefinger every ten seconds or so. Libby and Florence had their hands twined on the table, Libby with her coral lipstick and pinchbeck bracelets and her rings on every finger, Florence with her denim jumpsuit and her cropped auburn hair curling out from a bucket hat.

I met Amari through his partner Imogen, who's doing a Fulbright right now, Alice explained. I know Florence through Libby. And Libby and I go way back to Chicago. We were on the same floor at DePaul.

Last time I saw you, you were drunk as hell on piña coladas, Libby said.

That was a long time ago.

It was last year.

So how do you know Alice? Amari said to Emmett.

We know each other from Springfield! Alice said.

I didn't know you kept in touch with anyone from Springfield, Libby said.

No one but Emmett.

What was Alice like as a teenager? Florence said.

Oh, you know, Emmett said. About the same.

Up for anything? Libby said. Head in the clouds? Impulsive?

I'm not impulsive, Alice said.

Spontaneous, then.

I don't think I'm that either.

She had big dreams, Emmett said. I admired that about her.

Isn't this place fun? Alice said, trying to change the subject. Every night is karaoke night. Emmett's a big fan of karaoke.

You have that in common with all lesbians, Florence said.

This is Emmett's first time in New York.

No way! Libby said. What are your first impressions?

It's not what I expected, he said. He tried to think of a word, a single word. It's chaotic, he said finally.

You're not in Kansas anymore, Libby said.

Exactly. It's so big, it's almost too much.

It's not for everyone, Florence said.

You have to have the right constitution for it, Libby said.

Or money, Amari said. Having a lot of money helps.

I don't have *that much* money, Libby said.

I'm just saying, you make it sound like surviving in New York comes down to having a certain attitude, an affect, the ability to hustle or whatever. Nine times out of ten, it comes down to money.

Amari's in a bummer mood, Libby said. They didn't renew his show.

Oh no! Alice said. The werewolf show?

Yeah, *Blood Moon*. What can you do? Honestly, it's for the best. They were always asking me for the "Black perspective" on stuff, even when it had nothing to do with race. They'd be like, what's the Black perspective on lycanthropy? And I'd be like, I don't know, that it's scary?

You have anything lined up? Alice said.

Not really. I'm doing some stuff on spec.

Emmett saw his chance, took a gulp of beer, and said, I do some screenwriting.

Emmett's writing a feature, Alice added.

Oh yeah? That's cool, man.

There aren't a lot of networking opportunities in Kentucky, he said.

I thought you said you were from Springfield.

He is, Alice said, but he lives in Kentucky now.

Well, that's a coincidence, Libby said. Isn't that where Joe is from?

Joel, Alice said.

Do you know Joel? Libby asked Emmett.

I know him. I know *of him*. I mean, I know the name.

Right, Libby said, her eyes narrowing subtly. You almost look like him, she said. From what I remember. You've got more hair, but your eyes—

Maybe they're related, Florence said. Like distant cousins. Oh shit, sorry—I don't mean to suggest—I know people from Kentucky aren't all related.

What do you do in Kentucky? Amari said.

I work at a Tempo distribution hub, he said. Unloading parcels from planes. Screenwriting's the main thing, though. That's what I care about.

Emmett felt, having admitted his secret passion to these strangers, like he'd slid a naked photo of himself, unbidden, across the table.

So, Amari said, what's it about?

It's hard to encapsulate.

Give us the elevator pitch, Alice said.

I don't have an elevator pitch.

Make one up.

Well, he said, bowing his head, tearing a damp cocktail napkin into strips, it's about a guy who works in a warehouse and decides to start stealing packages.

What's in the packages? Amari said.

Drugs. Prescription drugs.

Amari lifted his eyebrows. Okay, he said. So it's like a heist?

More or less.

Is it autobiographical?

No, Emmett said quickly. The character is nothing like me. His name is Jeff Anderson. He's an everyman, but he's drawn into this seedy world of criminal activity.

So he steals the drugs and then what?

It's more of a character study, Emmett said. It's not exactly plot driven.

Maybe there should be a detective or something, Amari said. Someone who's onto him.

No, he gets away with it, Emmett said. I want him to get away with it.

He can still get away with it. But it creates suspense if somebody's after him. Maybe it's not a detective. Maybe it's someone at the warehouse. Maybe it's a private investigator, hired by the drug company.

I hadn't thought of that, Emmett said.

Well, it's an interesting premise, Amari said. And the fact that you have firsthand experience helps. People love that. They love being able to say, "This guy, the writer, really worked in a warehouse!"

I told you that, Alice said. I told you you have working-class street cred.

What's it called? Amari said.

The Package Handler.

Yeah, you'll need a different title.

Is it like they say it is at those places? Libby said. You hear stories about fulfillment centers working their people to death, making them pee in bottles.

I don't have to pee in a bottle, Emmett said. They give us breaks. Not many, but a few.

I bet it's hot, Florence said.

It's pretty simple work. You just put boxes onto a conveyor belt, one after the other. That's it.

Don't sell yourself short, Libby said. You're an essential worker. People like you are the reason we got through the pandemic. We should be thanking you.

Emmett caught Alice's eye; she smiled faintly and looked away. Florence bought a second round of drinks, and they watched a woman onstage sing a spirited rendition of "Save It for Later" by the English Beat, thrashing the microphone's cable like a bullwhip, a throng of women beneath her waving glowsticks and singing along. Libby spoke, apropos of nothing, about a book on astrology she'd read recently. Promise me you'll read this book, she said. I know what you're thinking, but it's not woo-woo at all.

Isn't astrology woo-woo by nature? Amari said.

There's astrology, and then there's *science-based astrology.*

Onstage, the women sang Madonna and The Cure and Boy George, Emmett realizing after a while that it was '80s night. Alice touched his shoulder at one point, pointing at the stage. Bruce! she said. A woman with a mullet and a glittering red blazer was singing "Tougher Than the Rest," her eyes glowing whitely in the blacklight.

They went out to the patio for a smoke. Emmett talked about movies with Amari. Amari kept dropping the names of obscure films—a lesser-known Kurosawa, a forgotten Arthur Penn noir. The movies that Emmett mentioned felt obvious and basic by comparison—

Chinatown, The Godfather. The topic of neighborhoods came up; Libby and Florence were considering a move.

Everyone in New York is considering a move at all times, Alice told Emmett.

Sounds exhausting, he said.

We saw this beautiful place, Libby said. Nineteen hundred dollars. It was in Flatbush, though.

He took it that Flatbush was far and—there was something about her tone—perhaps unsafe, or at least possessing the aura of crime. They seemed to hold a secret knowledge of the neighborhoods and how each figured in the hierarchy of class and desirability.

The ultimate move is LA, Amari said.

Oh God, Florence said. Not you, too.

We visited last spring and fell in love, Libby said.

You fell in love, I got sunburned, Florence said.

I wish I could split my time, Libby said. Have, like, a Malibu cottage and a place in Tribeca. Or the Hamptons. Don't you wish that?

She seemed to be asking Emmett. Do I wish I had multiple homes? he said. I mean, yeah.

Libby passed around a vape pen and they all took sips from it, the little light on the device glowing green, then violet, green, then violet.

This is called Diesel Cheesecake, Libby said. It's pretty much the strongest oil I've been able to find.

The pen went around once, then twice. Emmett had the feeling he sometimes had when very stoned around smart people that, if he were to speak, he would first have to compose the sentence in his mind. Everyone grew quiet except for Libby, who was talking rapidly, and with great enthusiasm, about self-hypnosis. I go to this center in the East Village called Mindscapes, she said.

And they hypnotize you? Alice said.

No. They give *you* the tools to hypnotize *yourself.* It's like teaching a man to fish versus giving him the fish.

So how do you hypnotize yourself? Emmett said. He'd been rehearsing this sentence for a long time before it came out.

It's about creating an expectation, Libby said, then visualizing yourself meeting that expectation. You say to yourself something like, In my previous life, I remember X. You say that over and over. In my previous life, I remember X. In my previous life, I remember X. It requires total concentration. I would say more, but if you're interested, you should really just come out to the center. They're really friendly.

How much does it cost? Alice said.

About four hundred dollars per session, and there are six sessions in a standard course. Eight sessions if you want certification.

Holy shit, Florence said. You paid twenty-four hundred dollars for those classes? Libby, what the fuck?

As they bickered, Emmett's attention drifted to the patio door, where a man had come through and was now shouldering through the crowd, moving with an intensity of purpose that was alien to the vibe of the bar. He wore a chambray shirt and suede shoes; he was balding. He drew nearer, squeezing between the bodies. It was Joel. Joel was here, at Regina's Bar in Crown Heights. His eyes were fierce and glowing white, as if he'd emerged from a photographic negative. Joel had come to find him. His terror was like something rotten he'd eaten—a cold, solid fact inside him—and he could not remember what he'd done, only that he'd done it, that the eyes of onlookers, turning to face him, could see his guilt like some lambent mass on an X-ray. Then the man's face flickered, and he was no longer Joel but a stranger, attired in the costume of his time and place.

He leaned over to Alice's ear and said, I'm really high. I think we should go.

Yeah? Okay.

It's not a waste of money if it's medically necessary, Libby was saying.

You've got to be joking, Florence said.

We're heading out! Alice said abruptly. Let's do this again soon!

See what happens? Florence said. You scare them off with your self-hypnosis shit.

Amari looked at Alice and Emmett as if to say, *Please take me with you.*

Libby closed her eyes tightly, and when she finally responded, she enunciated each word like she was speaking to a translator.

I. Will. Not. Apologize. For. Saving. My. Own. Life. Okay?

Buh-bye now! Alice said, tugging Emmett by the arm toward the exit.

The brisk air sobered him a little. He considered telling Alice what he'd seen—the vision of his brother approaching—but thought better of it. He'd returned to himself now, to the story he'd erected to protect himself from what he'd done. From what he was doing, still. From the hopelessness of their predicament.

Still, the thing inside him remained. It wore the masks of guilt and fear, but was neither—an instinct that preceded those named emotions. It was an old feeling, familiar to him from childhood, when looming darknesses stood over his bed at night. Kathy had told him once that all ghosts were only ancestors, therefore one had nothing to fear. Your family wouldn't hurt you, after all. But he'd thought then, as he thought now, that there was much to fear about ancestors. Whatever they'd done, they'd passed to you. They were inside. They could not be passed or brought up with a gagging finger.

In my previous life, I remember X. In my previous life, I remember X.

They boarded a train. They switched to the 3 line at Times Square and saw the aftermath of a stabbing. There was no body, but bloody handprints were smeared on the tile wall, and a pile of old quilts and newspapers—someone's makeshift bed—was sopped with dark blood. A Buck knife lay nearby. Emmett saw this, despite the crowd of cops that stood around with chattering radios, attempting half-heartedly to conceal the carnage from view. No one else was looking. Passersby cast quick glances and kept going. It was none of their business. They herded through the turnstiles, music streaming on their earbuds. In the mezzanine, a man was waltzing with a skeleton. The bones were made of plastic, like something one might hang from a porch on Halloween. The man had duct taped the skeleton's hands and feet to his own hands and feet, so that however he moved, the skeleton moved with him. A boombox, near the glowing soda machines, played *The Blue Danube* waltz, and the man wore a black cape that swept the dirty floor as he moved. Tourists took out their phones to film him. A few dropped money in his basket. But the man kept his eyes closed and moved his mouth soundlessly, shaping words known only to him. He twirled and glided, lost in the music, in the inner logic of his ritual, the skeleton like a dear lover held in his arms.

The next day, Emmett went out alone, saying he needed time. Time for what, he wasn't sure. To think, he supposed. He remembered the sign at the Center: WE'VE WORKED ____ DAYS WITHOUT A LOST TIME ACCIDENT. He wondered what number they'd reached now.

In Astoria Park, the trees were still brittle and bare, and the pool had been drained. But it was unseasonably warm. People read on park benches, threw frisbees for their dogs. He leaned against the rail at the edge of the East River. From here, beyond the RFK Bridge, one could see the breadth of Manhattan. He could exhale here. He could cry if he wanted. It was quiet almost. Just the tinkle of broken glass on pebbles as the waves lapped and receded. A lather of soapsuds, the rainbow sheen of oil. Slippery rocks draped with seaweed. It had rained all night, but now the sky was clearing. The city in a silver mist. The city that would never be his city. It was too big, contained too much. He was a minute creature on the circuitry of its surface. To be inside, on the island itself, was to lose yourself in the soaring confusion, in the canyons and echoic plazas, the blaze of sun reflected in mirrored glass. Manhattan was the sort of thing you could only ever see from the outside. He wondered what his teenage self would think of him now, standing here where he'd always dreamed of living, and still feeling banished somehow. Still peering over the walls. Still yearning to find himself at the center of things.

That night—their last night in the city—Alice suggested they eat at the Air Line Diner. It was a neighborhood institution, famous for its appearance in *Goodfellas,* and for this reason, Emmett had wanted to go.

The diner was lit up like a pinball machine, all neon and mirrored chrome. The name had changed—it was now the Jackson Hole Diner—but the old AIR LINE sign remained. They found a booth near the back and took it all in. Emmett smiled; the place was so hopelessly, unapologetically itself—the jukebox playing Buddy Holly, the men with clanging spatulas at the flattop, the photos of Elvis and Marilyn Monroe and—naturally enough—the eponymous goodfellas. Alice could not remember the scene from the film. He explained that Ray Liotta and Joe Pesci had stolen a truck from the parking lot full of cargo from LaGuardia.

It's a great screenplay, he said. You can get away with a lot using voiceover. You can smuggle all your exposition into the story.

Poor truck driver, she said.

The truck driver got a cut of whatever they sold. Cigarettes, liquor—whatever it was.

Poor shipping company, then.

They account for losses. You know how much stuff moves through an airport on a given day? Henry was doing what he had to do to make a buck.

Henry?

Ray Liotta. The hero.

I don't think Ray Liotta's supposed to be the good guy.

He flipped through the song selection on the tabletop jukebox, connected somehow to the larger Wurlitzer in the corner. He fished in his pocket for a quarter and punched the letter and number of a song he thought she might like.

What did you pick?

You'll see, he said.

After much deliberation, they both ordered pancakes. When Alice requested real maple syrup, the waitress looked like she'd been asked to retrieve a rare mineral from a distant land. She took their menus and left them alone. A herd of motorcycles thundered past on Grand Central Parkway. Looking out the window, the taillights strung like rubies in the darkness, Emmett felt the diner could be anywhere, on any highway in America, in any decade. He reached across the table and took Alice's hand. She let him, and they looked at each other fondly. She looked lovely, even in the diner's harsh light, her honey-hair pulled back in a knot at the nape of her neck, her denim jacket worn white at the elbows.

So, the future, she said.

I'm listening.

I think that we could make it work somehow. The only thing stopping us is other people, what they'd think of us. But we have to live our lives. We have to do what makes us happy.

I guess I agree, he said, though this wasn't quite true; he only wanted to agree, to be the sort of person who was capable of disregarding what others might think of him.

So why not just come to New York? she said.

And live together?

She nodded, apprehension in her eyes—afraid of how he'd respond.

That's a big step, he said.

It could be temporary, until you find a place of your own. Or not. Or you could just stay.

He allowed himself a moment of fantasy, imagining their domestic life. Coffee in the morning, strolling down Ditmars after supper, reading by lamplight in bed. The images felt so real to him, so vivid and thrilling, that he distrusted the promise they held. After all, New York had not been what he'd hoped. Despite his intentions otherwise, he'd been distant and internal, unable to speak the language of her friends. And yet, even as he found himself here in the *real* New York, with all its disappointments, his imagined life with Alice felt realer.

It sounds nice, he said. I guess we could go anywhere.

Yes! she said. Exactly. We could live here till we find something better. I've been looking at land, places where it's cheap. The Hudson Valley is my dream, of course, but there's a lot of cheap land in other states. Arkansas, for example. You wouldn't believe what's in Arkansas.

So we would live on a farm together in Arkansas?

Maybe not a *farm* farm. A big garden.

How would I do screenwriting then?

You can write from anywhere.

There are no studios in Arkansas. No producers. No agents or managers.

If that's what you're looking for, you better go to LA.

They have all that in New York, he said. I just walked by the Kaufman Studios today.

You just said we could leave, go anywhere. You literally just said that.

He rubbed his eyes with his knuckles. He kept replaying the fantasy in his mind, telling himself to trust it. He could be happy. Why be afraid of happiness?

Okay, he said. Let's do it.

Yeah?

Let's try.

She squeezed his hand tight and they both laughed a little.

What about Joel and your mom?

We tell them, he said. What choice do we have? Joel's an adult.

You're right. He's an adult. He's not some crazy maniac.

No.

He'll be upset. But it's not like he'd do anything stupid, right?

What does "stupid" mean?

I don't know, she said. Lash out in some way?

You tell me. You probably know him better.

Come on.

I'm serious. I have no idea how he'll respond.

He'll be upset, she said, and they fell into silence, envisioning all that the word "upset" might entail. An ugly scene. Crying and cursing. The gnashing of teeth. Violence maybe. Was that possible? Was Joel capable of violence?

He's a reasonable person, she said. He'll be upset, but he'll get over it.

I'm not sure.

And Kathy—you're her son. She'll forgive you.

I'm not sure about that either.

It will be intense for a few weeks—a few months. But we'll lock ourselves in the apartment and turn off our phones and it won't matter.

He smiled weakly at this. Whatever you say, he said.

She leaned across the table and kissed him. The waitress brought their pancakes and made a big show of setting out the ramekins of maple syrup.

Real maple syrup for the young lady, she said.

They ate slowly and with great relish. "Be My Baby" by the Ronettes came on, and he pointed his thumb at the jukebox.

The song I picked, he said.

She laughed as he mouthed the lyrics and sang a few lines in high falsetto. She told him she loved him. He told himself he was happy. That if he died right then, in that vessel of chrome and neon, he would have no fear when his soul flew up. But all he could see in his mind was the waltzing man, attached to his skeleton.

Eight

Peak season was followed by a kind of refractory period—a drowsy afterglow, an estrangement from the frenzy of desire. Emmett returned to the Center after New York, and it was like all that madness had only been a dream. Once again, the warehouse floor was clear of holdovers. Once again, the ramp workers played cards or scribbled at Sudoku pads in the break room. Once again, the supervisors paced the unobstructed lanes, absorbed in their iPads, in their graphs and figures, their fluctuating volumes, their systems of surveillance. The battle had not so much been won but deferred. What could one do but keep going? Keep latching the cans, keep feeding the belt as it drew the parcels away, into that hungry labyrinth that Emmett had once felt awe beside, and that now seemed only like some endless equation, adding and subtracting, dividing and multiplying, never quite reaching the equal sign. In another life, he would simply continue, because the place itself, the movement of the belts, the arrivals and departures of planes, the orders and the barcodes—it invited your continuation, welcomed you into the choreography, the ongoing ballet. You were part of it just by being there, and this was the only thing that saddened him: knowing that when he walked away, he would leave behind that feeling of involvement in the grand, unfolding process—however lonesome, however grueling. For once in his life, he had been a part of something bigger than himself.

He'd planned to approach Flaky at the end of the week, banking one more paycheck, but as he gathered his things to leave that night, Flaky came to him.

They'd like to see you in the office, he said.

Who would?

The hub supervisor, Keith Cooper.

On his way to the back office, Flaky trailing him by a few paces, he felt sure he'd be fired—that somehow they'd discovered his theft of the pills, and now they were letting him go, perhaps lacking the hard evidence to involve the law. And this outcome, he decided, was not the worst he could hope for.

The offices were warm, a welcome respite from the cold warehouse floor. Keith Cooper's office was separated by a glass partition, upon which paper snowmen had been taped, scrawled with a child's handwriting. He was seated inside, wearing eyeglasses and his Tempo golf shirt, baseball pennants tacked to the wall behind his desk. He smiled good-naturedly at Emmett and gestured to an open seat.

You too, he said to Flaky. You're standing back there like some creepy henchman.

You're right, I'm sorry, Flaky said.

Okay, Cooper said, once Flaky had situated himself. I think you know why you're here.

I'm not sure, Emmett said.

Let's talk about Kaleb Blanton. He's a friend of yours, I gather.

More of a work friend.

They used to talk all the time, Flaky said. Not so much lately.

Let me handle this, okay? Just sit there and don't say anything.

Flaky nodded and bowed his head. Cooper turned back to Emmett, smiling like a used-car salesman on TV.

You're acquainted with Kaleb, would that be fair to say?

Sure.

Well, I'll get down to brass tacks. We've had a parcel go missing. The contents are sensitive. And we have good reason to believe

Kaleb's the responsible party, that he's been stealing packages for several months now, if not years. We believe he does this by befriending and targeting certain unloaders, entering their cans, and making some excuse to walk away with a parcel—that the label's damaged, that it needs taping, whatever. Now don't freak out—you're not in trouble. Tell him he's not in trouble, Flaky.

Flaky said nothing, his head still bowed.

Flaky.

You told me to sit here and not say anything.

Good God, son, I'm asking you a direct question.

You're not in trouble, Flaky said.

You're not in trouble, Cooper repeated. What we need from you is corroboration. We've prepared a statement, an affidavit.

He slid a piece of paper across the desk and rotated it for Emmett to read. The print was large, the word "theft" appearing several times. He could hear the soughing of the central heat. The wall clock ticking. When he looked at the clockface, it was broken, the second hand twitching in place.

Others have come forward, Cooper said. You wouldn't be the first.

What will happen to him? Emmett said.

For the first time, Cooper seemed disappointed, as if he'd found the question to be in poor taste. We'll have a state trooper meet him at the guard shack, he said. That way there won't be a scene.

We never should've hired him, Flaky said. He has a prison record.

That doesn't mean anything, Emmett said. People can turn their lives around.

You know, son, Cooper said, I believe you're right. I have that faith in people, that no matter how far down the wrong road a man goes, he can always turn around and walk in the opposite direction. That choice is available to each of us. But sometimes we need a kick in the butt. Maybe this will be the kick in the butt that Kaleb needs.

Prison. You're saying that prison is what he needs.

Cooper gave Flaky a look and leaned back in his chair, fingers laced on his belly. Flaky perked up; his moment had arrived.

Without your signature, Flaky said, we'll be forced to assume your involvement and let you go. The package vanished from your can, after all, did it not?

I don't know, he said. I have no idea what you're talking about.

Of course you don't, Cooper said. You're a good boy. And good boys don't get mixed up in something like this. But felons—people like Kaleb. This is what they do. They prey on the innocent. They think they're owed something. They think they're entitled.

He thought of the message pinned beneath his wiper blade. YOU STILL OWE ME. He wanted this chapter of his life to end, to forget the grinding soreness of his knees, the electric twinges of pain in his back. To forget the echoes of machine clatter jolting him awake at night. The scuffed calluses on his palms. His purplish thumbnail, mashed by steel plate. To forget the bleary scrim over his waking hours, the accumulation of tiny psychic injuries. To forget Kaleb. To lock him away in some never-opened room. He wanted, most of all, to forget Kaleb.

You don't have to fire me, he said. I'm quitting. I won't sign it.

That's not necessary, Cooper said. That's not what this is, son.

I'm quitting, he said, and before they could say anything else in response, he walked away, through the cold gray office smelling of burnt coffee, through the racket of the warehouse floor, out to the waiting shuttle.

THE BLOOD BUS was parked near the guard shack. The fat man was there, calling like a carnival barker. *Hop on the bus, give your blood to us!* No one seemed willing to take him up on the offer. He coughed a plume of vapor, panted for a moment, then drew the breath to shout again, his voice frayed: *Hop on the bus, give your blood to us!*

Each night, he'd seen this exodus, the workers bounding down the shuttle steps, the rip of Velcro as they yanked the badges from their arms, the way their faded faces brightened, their strides imbued with purpose, sighting their cars in the distance. *Off the clock*—what a beautiful turn of phrase. As if time could be held at bay. As if their lives resumed the moment the scanners read their badges and the automatic doors opened. He'd grown so accustomed to it, the third shift heading home, crossing the paved expanse in the predawn dark, the sky as black as asphalt. He'd been one of them, after all. Now he was off the clock for good, and he stood for a long time watching beside the Mystique, waiting for the sense of release. He unfolded Alice's letter to "Bruce" and read a few lines. *One day the future will arrive*, she'd said.

A sudden force struck him, hurling his body against the car. His vision collapsed to a single point, like an old television when you killed the picture and the coils sizzled inside. When the world returned, he was falling, groping for something to hold him. His hands found the side mirror, but it broke off under his weight and he hit the pavement. He'd tried to break his fall and now his palms were scraped and bloody. Someone was there. Someone collected the note from Alice. Someone lifted him by his shirtfront, the fabric ripping, and pushed his back against the car. Slowly, the man's form became visible, barbed wire binding his forearms.

I saw you! Kaleb said, shaking him. What'd you tell them?

He could not think or speak, the delayed pain driving icy needles through his back. He tried with his hand to push Kaleb away, smearing blood on his face. Kaleb hit him then, not so much a real blow but a shot across the bow.

What'd you tell them?

Nothing, Emmett sputtered. I didn't tell them.

Bullshit, he said. He let go of Emmett and stood back, chest heaving, his eyes vivid with rage or fear—maybe both. I should kill you, he said after a while, though something in his voice had broken, having exhausted the fury that drove him to this, and Emmett knew it was only a line, something he was given to say by a mysterious inner script. I should kill you, he said again, even less convincingly.

Leave me alone, Emmett said.

What's this? Kaleb said, scanning the note from Alice. Little love letter?

Kaleb.

This from your sister-in-law?

Give it back.

No, I think I'll keep it. He folded the note and tucked it into his breast pocket.

I wish you'd just leave me alone.

You don't need me now, I guess, he said. I served my purpose. You're the only fuckin person in the universe, aren't you? It's all just spinning around you.

What are you, a saint? You think you're owed something. You think you're entitled. You prey on the innocent like a vampire.

I'm a team player! he shouted, pounding his fist against his chest. I share what's mine! I give it away! And in return, I get fuck-all!

Because you're a loser, Emmett said. And I'm not like you.

Kaleb looked at him with horrified amazement.

We were like brothers, he said. That's what I thought.

I have a brother, Emmett said. I have a whole life, and none of it has anything to do with you.

Kaleb's face went blank. There was nothing now to say, nothing to do. It was over. After a moment, he nodded to himself. He shuffled slowly away, through the rows of cars, till he reached a section of the lot where no one had parked. Emmett watched till he became a speck of motion, so far that no voice could reach him.

Nine

WHEN JOEL CAME HOME, Alice was waiting for him. He came into the antique room, carrying his suitcase. The cuffs of his jeans were grass-stained up to the knee. He was wearing cheap flip-flops, not the suede shoes he'd taken with him.

You're back, Joel said. How was the flight?

The flight? I was only in Marion.

Right, Joel said. He hefted his suitcase onto the bed. He did not seem like himself—a manic wildness in his eyes. He looked like he'd been up all night.

Shut the door, she said.

Good idea, Joel said, shutting the door with a theatrical flourish.

I've been thinking.

Me too, Joel said. Maybe I should go first, is that okay?

Okay, she said, uncertainly.

I had an experience, Joel said. Last night. It was an experience of—would I call it an epiphany? I think I would. I won't get into the particulars, but suffice to say, I had an experience. My normal sense of who I was fell away. It was like the mushroom thing you always talk about. What's the term?

Ego death, she said.

Right! Yes!

You were on drugs?

No, but it was like that. And I had a realization. I realized I'm not just this passive entity, pushed around by social forces and biology and all my stupid drives and desires and hang-ups. I'm actually free, Alice. I can choose what happens.

Most people already know that, Joel.

They know it in a superficial, abstract way. But they don't *live* it. They want to have their cake and eat it, too. They want to believe they're free and at the same time act as if they aren't.

You sound a little loopy. Are you feeling okay?

I stayed up all night. I've had five cups of coffee this morning.

You should sleep. We can talk later.

No, no, let's talk now. You wanted to say something.

Nothing about this was right. She'd not planned for this—to find herself on the back foot. She'd expected the same old glum Joel. But this—what was *this*? He could barely stand still, worrying the keys in his pocket, shifting his weight from foot to foot in his ridiculous flip-flops.

I thought we should talk about the marriage, she said. She'd practiced putting it this way. Not *our marriage*, but *the marriage*, as though it were some far-off fact, a set of dates in a history book.

I agree, he said. That's part of where I'm coming from. I realized that our problem—our fundamental problem, as you put it—is completely my fault. I've been sitting around like this inert bump on a log, feeling pity for myself, pretending I can't change, that I'm incapable of change. That the world would not *allow* me to change. And that's completely unfair to you! I've been looking at our marriage as if it's fated to end, as if it's beyond my control. But there is no fate. There is no fate!

He waved his arms in the air like someone marooned on an island, signaling to a helicopter.

Okay, Joel.

There is no fate.

I heard you the first time.

Okay, so we can move forward, he said, beginning to pace. I was thinking about Wyoming. I actually did some research. There are universities there. And Cheyenne is pretty close to Denver. I could commute if I had to.

Joel, stop, she said. Look at me.

He turned to her, grinning with the insane confidence of the recently converted.

It's over, she said.

In all her trial runs, all her rehearsals with Noam, the declaration had never taken this two-word form. The finality brought relief. It was out now; the silence of the room absorbed the words, and now it was Joel's turn to respond.

You're not listening, he said. I can change. I'll change my behavior.

You're not listening to me. I'm telling you it's over.

So you just get to decide what happens?

That's right.

His smile had curdled now. You know, he said, I don't even care why you were in New York last night. I don't care who you were with. I wasn't even going to bring it up.

Alice remembered his call from the night before. They'd gone to a bar after the Air Line Diner and she'd stepped aside to answer the phone. She'd thought nothing of it. She'd given her alibi, and he'd seemed to believe her. Now, strangely, she did not feel embarrassed. Instead, a dull rage smoldered in her chest. She might have called it hatred; that's what it felt like. Was that possible? After all they'd been through? To examine her heart and find no trace of affection for him there?

How do you know I was in New York?

You have location tracking on your phone.

I thought you disabled that.

You have to disable it.

So you're spying on me, she said. That's the answer.

For good reason, apparently.

Do you really want to know? she said. She felt almost vengeful enough to tell him. I'll tell you what I was doing, she said, if you really want to know.

No, I don't, he said quietly. I wasn't even going to bring it up.

And yet you did.

I'll tell you something else, he said. Since we're sharing. Would you like to hear something really funny?

Please.

I met someone last night. A fan of my work. She was gorgeous, a total knockout, and I had her wrapped around my finger. I went home with her, and do you know what I did?

You fucked her.

No! That's the funny part. I left, I walked away. I thought about you, how much I valued our marriage. I told her, I can't do this. I can't do this to my wife. I could have slept with this woman—a beautiful woman, a scholar. Someone who understands my work. And I chose not to, for you.

How noble. What a sacrifice.

And now this. This is how I'm repaid.

Well, you've got your epiphany and you've got your newfound freedom, so why don't you call up the beautiful scholar and do whatever you want with her, how's that?

Fuck you, he said. I want you out of my sight. I want you to get the fuck out of my house.

It's your mother's house.

She'll want you out, too.

She stood and began to throw her scattered clothes into a duffel bag. I know, Joel, she said. Mommy will take your side.

Joel picked up her copy of Rachel Carson's letters from the dresser and hurled it at the china cabinet. It broke through the glass and smashed the music box clock. "The Way We Were" began to play, over and over, the melody warped and sluggish. Alice recoiled and covered her face instinctively, as if he might strike her, though she realized, in the next instant, that this was ridiculous. It was for show, this violence. It proved he was a man of action now, that he really had changed.

Kathy knocked on the door. What's happening? she said. Is everyone all right?

Alice is leaving, Joel shouted.

Oh dear, Kathy said, and after a moment they heard her shuffle away, saying, Oh dear, oh dear.

Without a word, Alice extracted the book, careful to avoid the fangs of glass. Her postcard of Bastien-Lepage's *Joan of Arc* had come loose. She placed the book and the card gently in her bag, zipped it up, and began walking—down the hallway, through the kitchen, out the back door. She knew that if she slowed, if she spoke to Kathy or thought too much about what was happening, she might break down. So she pushed out into the January air, her skin raw to the cold. It was only when she reached the driveway that she remembered Noam, along with the small problem of having no car.

Fuck, she said aloud.

Noam was waiting by the kitchen door. He looked up at her with mooning eyes, then slid in figure eights between her ankles, purring. Joel leaned against the fridge, arms crossed, looking helpless and ill.

I'm taking Noam, she said. She drew the cat into her arms.

We'll have to talk about that, I guess, he said.

There's nothing to talk about.

We got him together.

I feed him, I take him to the vet. Plus, he likes me better than you.

Joel's chin began to quiver. When he blinked, tears skipped down his cheeks. She felt the familiar urge to help him somehow. It was the same as the night they'd met at Beaver's Tavern. Maybe this feeling—this wanting to help, to take care—had been what she'd mistaken for love all along.

There were no Ubers in Paducah. The taxi she called was a dented, dirty minivan. The driver wore a surgical mask and blue latex gloves and was quite large. He waddled around to the back and opened the van's hatch. She placed Noam's carrier inside, next to a toolbox and a bag of flattened aluminum cans.

Where we goin, honey? he said.

She had not actually thought this through. She would need to call Emmett, make arrangements. Things had happened so fast. She thought she'd have more time, a map she could follow. Instead, she felt like she was driving at night and someone had switched off her headlights.

The Comfort Inn, she said, remembering the hotel where they'd spent the night.

The man lit a cigarette, pulling down his surgical mask to take deep drags. He was sweating with the windows closed, the armpits of his shirt damp. At stoplights, he adjusted his gloves, latex snapping against his wrists. The van filled with smoke. Noam moaned irritably in the back.

We're almost there, she said, reaching back to pat the roof of the carrier. But where was "there"? What lay beyond the Comfort Inn? She could not say for sure. For the first time in years, the future did not seem like a story she'd read before. She was afraid to think too deeply of what she was doing, afraid her plans would unravel and she'd see how foolish she had been, afraid she would turn around and go back to Joel, go back to the inertia of her life—her one life, this meager allotment of time. She closed her eyes and tried to think of Emmett, not because she missed him, and not even because she saw some definite future with him, but because he'd become, in her mind, a doorway. She could think of him—even just his name—and a passage opened before her. He was no longer himself, no longer her husband's brother. He was the threshold of another life.

Ten

JOEL HAD A SEX DREAM the night she left. It was about Lexi, the woman from Memphis. Like most of his sex dreams, it never actually culminated in sex. They were lying together, clothed, on a large circular bed. Touching each other, kissing. The walls of the room were darkly painted; the drawn curtains were heavy velvet. Lexi was not quite herself in the dream. She was lovelier, her hair like the fluff of a red dandelion. Every time they seemed close to progressing—when he fiddled with her bra clasp or slipped his fingers beneath the elastic of her panties—she would giggle and pull away.

I don't have my things, she would say.

What things?

My creams and accessories.

Baffled by this, Joel kept trying, biting her earlobes, squeezing her nipples beneath her thin T-shirt. But she kept nudging him away. Next time, she said. Next time I'll have my things.

What things?

My creams and accessories.

Eventually, he got up from the bed and went to a camcorder, mounted on a tripod in the corner of the room. It was one of those objects in a dream that seems to have been there all along, but you see it only when it chooses to make its presence known. Lexi, on the other hand, did not seem able to perceive the camcorder. She sat up in bed, asked him what he was doing.

Just stay right there, he said. I'm making sure the shot is lined up.

What shot? What are you doing?

I want to remember this.

He bent down to the viewfinder, closed one eye. It was an old device from the '90s—a leather strap for your hand, a foam cover on the microphone. He waited for Lexi to come into focus. But when she did, she was not Lexi at all. She was Grace, his high school girlfriend. The girl with whom he'd lost his virginity. They met when she was seventeen. She was wearing a plaid skirt and fishnet stockings, listening to the Pixies' "Gouge Away" in her car. A Mall Goth, decked out in Hot Topic. So this is how he pictured her. This is how he saw her now, in the viewfinder, only she was older, her face sagging a bit, her body no longer a teenager's body.

Come to bed, she said.

He obliged, crawling onto the mattress, painfully erect. When she closed her hand around his cock, it was like she gripped the very root of him. She stroked him to the point of near release, then let go.

Why'd you stop?

I don't have my things, she said.

What things?

My creams and accessories.

He stood and went back to the camcorder. Her blurred form came into focus, her long white legs in the fishnets.

Do you have a VCR? she said.

No, he said. Who has a VCR now?

How will you play the tape?

He woke up then, his back plastered to the sweaty sheets. He stumbled from the antique room to the hallway bathroom, stood over the toilet, and tried to jerk off. A framed photograph of Joel and Emmett as children hung over the toilet. It kept catching Joel's eye, but when he reached to take it down, it slipped from his fingers and fell against the toilet tank, busting the glass. He managed to finish and carefully swept the fragments into a pile.

He lay in bed till the sky began to lighten, wondering what the dream might mean, forgetting and then remembering that Alice was gone. At dawn, when the first ray of light peered into his room, he found one of her hairs on the pillow. He pinched it between his fingers and held it up—long and shining in the sun. He half expected it to be red.

THE NEXT DAY, Kathy could not stop crying, both about the separation and her broken belongings.

My china cabinet, she said. My clock. My favorite picture of you and Emmett. Why don't you destroy my whole house?

Mom, please.

He sat at the kitchen table eating cold toast, his eyes red and sore. Kathy scrambled eggs at the stove in her bathrobe, now and then rubbing her nose with a tissue.

I'm serious, why don't you bring in a bulldozer and just level my whole house. Wreck it all, the way you wrecked your marriage.

I wrecked my marriage?

It takes two to tango.

I'll buy you a new clock.

How did you manage to break the picture? In the bathroom?

He imagined telling her the truth—*I had a sex dream about my high school girlfriend and broke it while masturbating, half-asleep.*

It was an accident, he said.

Kathy brought her plate of eggs to the table, sniffling and blotting her eyes between bites. It's a shame, she said. It's just such a shame.

It should be cause for celebration, he said unconvincingly. It's a clean slate. I can do whatever I want.

At this, Kathy let her fork fall, covered her face with her hands, and began to sob.

....
....

LATER, HE WENT for coffee at Paducah's only unobjectionable café. Though it was cold, he drank his cortado on the patio. He knew that Grace sometimes came here and he half hoped to see her. A piebald cat emerged from an alley behind the shop, approaching a bush full of sparrows with delicate, predatory slowness. The birds scattered and the cat went to lap water from a bowl beneath a spigot. He thought of Noam with a pang of sorrow. The awful truth was that he felt relieved on some level. Alice was more attentive to Noam anyway. He had always tried to foist his affection on Noam, and when this affection was not reciprocated—when Noam scampered away from his lap or ignored, with catlike hauteur, Joel's caresses—he felt vindictive, a stupid impulse to direct toward an animal. What did it say about him that his love was so contingent?

The important thing, he decided, was that he possessed the self-awareness to notice this and correct it. His epiphany, as he ran from Lexi's house in the darkness, had shown him this. He could better himself. He had agency. In his next relationship, he would love without expectation of reciprocity.

My next relationship—this was a novel thought. He imagined himself swiping on Tinder, then checked his phone to see if he still had the app. He thought of Grace again, fay and slender, her long legs in the stockings. He wondered what she looked like now and found himself opening Facebook to track her down. Instead of typing her name in the search field, however, he accidentally posted it as a status.

Fuck, he muttered.

He deleted the status quickly, but not before it garnered a few likes. He had not used Facebook in years and felt, suddenly, like an octogenarian trying to decipher the buttons on a microwave.

When he found her profile finally, she looked about the same. They'd kept in intermittent touch since high school, phoning now and then to catch up, though they'd fallen out of the habit since the pandemic. They'd dated for three years. They'd lost their virginities to each other. They'd fostered, between them, a kind of sweetness that Joel had never really known since. Then again, they were children. Everything in childhood was imbued with unbearable sweetness to him now.

He walked for a while along the floodwall, then along the streets of Lowertown, admiring the restored Victorians. When he returned to the car and checked his phone, there was a text from Grace: did u post my name as your facebook status??

Fucking hell, he said.

He sat with the car running, trying to compose a text in his mind so that she would not see the little ellipsis appearing and disappearing as he struggled to generate an explanation.

I'm an old man, he texted back finally. I was trying to look you up.
Haha why??

Just strolling down memory lane. He waited a few minutes, then said, I'm in town btw.

Grace began to type, then paused, then began again. With your wife? she said.

We're separated, Joel said, and he realized this was the first time he'd had occasion to say it. Maybe we could meet up.

After twenty minutes, she responded, That sounds nice but I'm super busy rn!

He clicked off his display and set his phone face down on the console. Woolen clouds had gathered to the west. The wind gusted. He sat for a long time shivering, feeling utterly alone.

At the college, they'd given him a small office as part of his lectureship. He went that afternoon to collect his things, the sky leaden with snow that would not fall. Somewhere near Hardin, he noticed a yellow sports car trailing him, keeping a steady distance on the one-lane roads. Each turn he took, the yellow sports car took the same, slowing whenever he slowed, closing the gap between them whenever it grew too wide. He turned up the radio; he would not be the sort of person who thought, *I'm being followed.* This crossed a line, beyond which lay padded rooms. A shooting in Oklahoma had left four people dead, six injured, said the radio announcer, a hopelessness at the edges of her voice. He believed that speakers of Broadcast English—anchors, announcers, aircraft pilots—should always convey smooth sailing. Never surprise, never the creeping sense that things were falling apart. The story was irrelevant, the specifics of time and place, the number of dead or maimed. The purpose of the voice was not to convey information. The voice, with its absence of place, of origin—a voice that came from nowhere and everywhere—had only one message: *I've seen everything.* And this woman was failing. She had not seen everything. She had seen something new, and it frightened her. He felt his throat closing.

No one is following me, he said aloud, the car, sleek and yellow, still there in his rearview. No one is following me.

HE'D USED THE OFFICE only a few times. The day's gray light fell through a single narrow window onto the greenish metal desk. The shelves were empty, the walls bare. He gathered his books and papers into a tote bag and tried not to look out the window. At times, since quitting his antidepressant, he'd felt like a small homunculus in the control room of his head, directing his limbs to move. He felt this way now, tucking the books in his bag. Something rustled in the corner, the room so quiet and still that even this small noise made his pulse pick up. He peeked around behind the desk. A sticky trap at the base of the window stirred a bit. He found a large cockroach stuck to the glue, fluttering its brown enameled wings. It seemed to regard him, its feelers searching the air. The windowpane was a few inches from his face, and turning his eyes upward, he saw the yellow sports car in the lot—a Corvette, he guessed—exhaust billowing from the tailpipe. The roach twitched and chirred. He stood and let his boot hover over it, ready to crush the thing. But he couldn't for some reason. The control room in his head put out the order, but his foot would not obey. The paper trap stirred again, as if it were the living thing and not the bug inside.

The moment he stepped into the cold, it began to snow, thick gray clumps drifting like ashes, melting at the first touch of pavement. The campus was empty. He was alone in the lot with the Corvette, his tote bag suddenly weighted with bricks. He stood there, feeling the flakes catch in his hair and turn to water, trickling down his neck. A wave of telescoping dread loosened his bowels. Everything became unbearably clear. The Corvette's yellow lacquer like candy coating. The smell of exhaust smoke. The vapor of his breath, appearing in rapid puffs before his face. It was nearly twilight, the sun a garnet glow, deep within the pall of cloud. He watched himself cross the lot and stand before the driver-side door.

Hello? he said.

The window lowered. The man inside wore a pair of absurd sunglasses. His bare arms, stretched out to grip the wheel, were tattooed with barbed wire.

Can I help you? Joel said.

The question is, can I help you? said the man.

He could see himself in the insectoid lenses of the man's sunglasses; he looked like someone trying to feign courage, someone clenching his buttocks to keep from shitting his pants.

Who are you? he said.

Who I am's not a matter of importance. You can call me Kaleb. That's not my real name.

Okay, Kaleb, what do you want? Who sent you here?

Who sent me's not a matter of importance.

Have you been spying on my grandmother? Have you been calling me?

Kaleb handed a slip of paper through the window in lieu of an answer. He was afraid to take it, to incorporate whatever message it contained into his life. But what he wanted or did not want seemed somehow beside the point now. He'd entered a strange territory, gone through the looking glass. He was steered now by forces beyond the smallness of his affairs. He took the note, unfolded it, and began to read:

Dear "Bruce,"

*I know you ain't nothing but tired, tired and bored with yourself,
so I thought I would offer a little help—in the form of these pillowcases.
Seriously though, I wake up sometimes and I think about you and how
you're working while I'm sleeping, and I wish you could come and crawl
into bed with me. What I'm trying to say is that I miss you. I think about
you. I think about the future and what that word even means for us. Isn't it
weird that one day the future will arrive, and we'll look back, knowing how
things turned out?*

Until then, this gun's for hire,

A.

It was Alice's handwriting—he knew this well before he'd arrived at
the signed initial. What he failed to grasp was its meaning. It hovered
beyond his mind the way a word—the right word for a sentence, the
only word that would do—refused to announce itself, remaining
just-hidden, almost-formed. Flakes of snow fell onto the paper and
melted, leaving dark wet splotches.

What is this? he said.

What does it look like?

A letter to Bruce Springsteen in my wife's handwriting. Where'd
you get it?

Come inside and I'll tell you.

He hesitated, then circled the car and climbed inside. The seat was
lower than he'd expected, sunken down, and the interior had the old,
sad smell of a bowling alley, the fabrics and the carpets absorbing
years of smoke. The snow had picked up, covering the windshield and
the windows. It gave a sense of dim enclosure and muffled quiet, as if
the car had been entombed by an avalanche.

It came from your brother, Kaleb said. I took it off him.

Emmett?

Your wife was involved inanimately with your brother.

I don't understand.

Do I have to spell it out? He was fucking her.

He laughed at this. It was totally ridiculous. But Kaleb's face was deadly serious, and the longer he allowed the notion to settle and take root, the more it seemed plausible. Likely, even. Turning it over in his mind, trying it on for size, he found, with a plummeting horror, that it fit the facts.

Why? Why would he do that?

Because he's selfish and disloyal and cares nothing for his fellow man, not even his own kin.

Here it was, at last—the cratered, lunar landscape of the truth. He knew the man was right, somehow, the way one knew hunger or lust, the second brain of intuition throbbing in his gut. His brother. His wayward blood. The snow kept collecting on the windshield, giving off a weak blue glow. They were buried beneath miles of glacial ice. He tried to speak, but only a murmur came out—nothing close to a word.

That's all right now, Kaleb said gently. You don't have to say nothin. I'm just passing on the message. I felt it was my duty, my obligation, moralistically speaking. The truth is, I loved your brother at one time. We were like this.

He clapped his hands together.

We told each other everything. I trusted him. And he betrayed me, like everyone in my life's betrayed me. I won't stand for it. I won't live in a world without justice.

Justice, Joel managed to say, his voice choking out like a laugh.

That's right, justice. You make it yourself. You decide what you deserve and what everyone else deserves, and you make it happen. You go out and you make it happen.

He offered Joel a cigarette, which he took absently. Kaleb lit it for him, and he fell into spasmodic coughing after the first drag. I don't smoke, he said.

It's good for you. Breathe it in.

He took another pull and coughed again, though not as fiercely.

I'm going to drive away, Kaleb said. You'll never hear from me again. You'll never know who I am or how I found you, and none of that's a matter of importance. What matters is how you respond, what you do next.

How do I know what that is?

I've never, in my life, not known what to do. Ask me how.

How?

There's an inner voice, he said, touching his breastbone. It guides you, moment by moment. Some people hear God, some people hear Satan, and they all think they're hearing God. In the end, it don't matter. The ones hearing God can never hear Satan, and the ones hearing Satan can never hear God. You're doomed to hear the voice you're born hearing. That's why there's no justice. Nothing matters but that voice. You hear me? Nod your head and let me know you hear me.

Joel nodded.

Repeat the words, so I know you understand: there's an inner voice.

There's an inner voice, Joel said.

And nothing matters but that.

Nothing matters but that.

When the Corvette thundered away and the guttural noises of its engine faded into the snow-muffled distance, Joel was left in the cold. A wet flake put out his cigarette. He held the letter in his other hand. One by one, the streetlamps flickered to life, and in their cones of light, the snow flew like sparks thrown from a blowtorch. He closed his eyes and listened.

Eleven

I DID IT, she said.

Emmett had his cell phone wedged between his cheek and his shoulder. He stood over the bathroom sink, splashing hydrogen peroxide onto his scraped palms. He'd drunk himself to sleep the night before and woke with bits of asphalt still embedded in his flesh.

You did what?

I ended things, she said. I told him it was over.

Like, for good?

For good.

Wow. That's—I mean, that's sudden.

It was the right moment, she said. We agreed, didn't we? To move forward?

No, yeah. Of course.

You sound weird.

He gritted his teeth against the peroxide's sting. Weird how?

Like, I don't know. Not excited.

I'm excited.

He moved the phone to his other ear and walked to the kitchen, blowing on his palm.

I'm at the Comfort Inn, by the Rural King, she said. Noam's with me. He hates it here.

I'll bet.

He keeps wedging himself between the mini-fridge and the dresser where I can't reach him.

Emmett stood before the balcony doors in his underwear. The snow had been plowed into piles in the Oakwood lot, bluish salt scattered on the walkways. The light hurt his eyes—a polished glare like sun in silver.

I miss you, she said.

I miss you, too, he said. In truth, what he felt now, hearing her voice, was that he'd lost something. Something had slipped away from him. He was sweating, his stomach sour. His guilt was no longer asymptomatic. He could not find the courage to tell her.

What do we do now? he said.

You come get me, she said, like it should be obvious. We go to New York.

I come get you, he repeated.

Yes, she said. I mean, isn't that what we decided?

I didn't think it would be so soon.

You're scaring me, Emmett. Did we not have this conversation? At the diner?

Sure. We had a conversation.

I'm alone here, she said. Her voice had a frantic edge. Are you hearing me? I ended things. I did it.

I hear you, he said. Okay. He pressed his forehead against the cool glass of the balcony door and shut his eyes. Tonight, he said. I'll drive down, come get you tonight. Okay?

I love you, she said. It sounded more like a threat than a declaration. You'll come tonight?

I'll be there.

He sat all day, thinking, his hands wrapped in gauze. In his mind, he kept watching Kaleb cross the Tempo lot. He saw his brother at

Regina's Bar, the way his white eyes burned. He heard the phantom strains of a waltz. He saw himself, his future in New York, anonymous in the teeming crowds. Less than anonymous: unnoticed. Maybe this was what he deserved. Maybe this was his punishment.

He drove in silence on the interstate, his hands still bandaged. It hurt to turn the wheel. He thought of Alice, waiting alone at the Comfort Inn. He'd told her he would be there by eight. They would spend the night, drive to Nashville in the morning, and fly away to live happily ever after. It seemed too simple, too straightforward. Something about the Center, its networks and convolutions, its Rube Goldberg intricacy, had instilled in him a permanent distrust of simplicity. Things could not simply move from one place to another. There were zigzags and mazes, gateways and scanners. Branches forked infinitely from the main route.

He took the exit for Paducah and arrived at the Comfort Inn with fifteen minutes to spare. He kept the car running, smoked a cigarette. There were lights burning in the windows, and he wondered which room belonged to Alice. She'd be sitting on the bed, raking her fingers through her hair, Noam already latched in his carrier. Maybe the television would be on, but she wouldn't be watching. She'd be staring at the wall. Maybe she'd walk to the window and see the twin cones of his headlights, boring outward into the dark, wondering, *Is that him?* Maybe she'd say as much to the cat, trilling her fingernails on the top of the carrier. *I think he's here. Just a few more minutes.*

HE WOUND UP at the Silver Dagger. The Mystique just drove him there. No, that wasn't right—he hated to think that way. All the screenwriting books said to avoid the passive voice—passivity in general. The Mystique had no power to choose this place, to choose this abandonment. But why had it seemed so automatic? The way, upon waking, he'd open some app on his phone without even wanting to. The way he'd driven once to an ex-girlfriend's apartment after work, forgetting that she no longer loved him. He followed the worn grooves of his life, and the Silver Dagger was one of them, a place you went when nowhere else would take you.

He told this to the bartender, his mouth not really working as it should, numbed as if by lidocaine. This place, he said, is where you go when nowhere else will take you.

That's what they say about home, said the bartender. That's what they say about family.

He was a kind-eyed man with tattoos of nude women and roses smudged all over his arms. He had the look of perfect patience about him, like he'd seen everything and was in no hurry to see more.

I was supposed to meet a woman tonight.

There's always tomorrow, the bartender said.

I'm not sure there is. There's only tonight.

Well, bub, you're drunk tonight.

We were supposed to run away together, like a Springsteen song.

The bartender's expression remained absolutely still and receptive. You better call her then, he said. Maybe she'll come get you.

I was supposed to get *her*. I was supposed to drive her away from her circumstances.

Telling the story like this, to a stranger, he could almost deceive himself into believing he was a character in a movie or a song or something. He could almost sympathize with the character's plight. Then he'd remember that he was real, and he'd snap back to the painful heaviness of his life the way one startled awake from a dream.

I'm sure there's still time, said the bartender.

Time for what?

I don't know, bub. For things to happen the way you want.

There was some commotion in the back. A circle of women near the jukebox fell into wild, thigh-slapping laughter. It seemed to reach Emmett from a great distance, like the cackling of seagulls at a landfill. He wished that everything was different.

I've made no decision, he said aloud.

What was that? asked the bartender.

I said I've made no decision.

Maybe not. Or maybe you have, coming here.

This is where you go to give yourself time, to wait while decisions are made.

There it was again—this disgusting passivity. He took a drink of beer to swish the taste from his mouth and realized it wasn't his. One of the women at the jukebox had left it there, her lipstick printed on the rim.

I thought this is where you went when no one else would have you, said the bartender, setting the woman's glass beyond Emmett's reach.

Same difference, he said.

What do you do for a living? the man said, hoping to change the subject, to steer their conversation toward brighter domains. He almost said he was a package handler, but he stopped himself.

I'm a screenwriter, he said. I write movies.

Well now, said the bartender. Good for you.

HE DROVE, DRUNK, across the dark expanses of the night. The melted slush in the road had frozen to a milky varnish. Fields glittered in the beams of his headlights, the broken cornstalks glazed with ice. Once or twice, he felt his traction slip, and the car seemed to float, untethered, beyond his control. In these moments, he waited with paralyzed exhilaration for death to come. But the road kept rising to catch his locked tires, hurling him homeward.

He collapsed, fully dressed, on the couch. When a stirring at the balcony door woke him later, he was sure that raccoons were the culprit. He lay there, blinking his sore eyes, groggy and a little nauseated. He needed to piss. The raccoons at the door were louder than usual, and they seemed to be fiddling with the knob. Maybe they'd evolved. They had opposable thumbs, after all. Maybe he was witnessing the first generation of raccoons to pick locks and open doors, help themselves to the contents of refrigerators. He stood and steadied himself, letting his eyes adjust. When he turned, he saw it was not a raccoon at the door, but a dark, man-sized figure. He was bent down, eye level with the knob, jamming what seemed to be a credit card in the space between the door and the frame.

Someone had come to the wrong apartment, a drunk maybe. This was his first thought. But why the balcony? Why a credit card? The figure outside was muttering curses, failing at what he thought would be simple. Then a click and the door slid open, the shadow-man entering ungracefully, nearly tripping on the raised doorsill. Emmett was not afraid so much as bewildered. When he switched on the lamp and saw his brother's face, the strange thought came to him that he'd been saved. Joel had come to save him from his mistakes, to carry him home.

Joel?

Don't talk, he said. Do not talk.

Joel's face was grim and bloodless, his lips almost gray. His hands were stuffed in the pockets of a denim jacket, too thin for the weather.

Are you sick or something? Why you'd come in like that?

Please, he said. Please don't talk. Just listen.

He waited, listening. The night had taken on a new complexity, the facets of which he could not quite process at the moment, his mind still thick with sleep. The balcony door remained open, cold wind ruffling the fast-food napkins on the coffee table, turning the pages of his open screenplay manuals.

I know everything, Joel said. I know about you and Alice.

He was sobered instantly. He could tell, from the grave certainty of Joel's expression, that denial would be pointless.

What I don't know, Joel said, what I can't fathom, is why. Why you'd want to hurt me like this.

Joel.

Shut up. I'm not finished.

He was shuddering now, a quiver in his voice. Emmett took this as a small sign of hope. Whatever Joel had planned, whatever he hoped to inflict, he was scared. He'd never done anything like this.

You're wondering how. How I found out. It's because I'm so much smarter than you. You've always been dumb. You've always been slow. I asked our mother once, when we were little, if you were retarded. I could tell even then. That you were a fuck-up, I mean. That your life would be one long fuck-up. This is no different. Honestly, you were sloppy. It's a small town. People see things. Rumors travel. Maybe you wanted me to find out. Maybe you wanted to punish me. Or maybe you were really that naïve. Maybe you thought you'd get away with it. Because you're dumb. Because you don't think things through. You follow your impulses like a child. You and Alice make a good pair, in that respect. You're both children.

He waited for Joel to finish, absorbing the words blow by blow, the pain they brought washed out entirely by the radiant blaze of shame—a thousand burning lamps, trained on his back, revealing him totally.

Joel, he managed to whisper.

I know it was you who called me.

Called you?

You called and said I was a fraud. You said I was a liar.

I never called you.

Did you hire people to watch me?

What?

Various entities. Shadow organizations. Vampires.

I don't know what you mean.

Did she tell you she loved you?

I don't know.

You don't know if she loved you? You don't know if she used the word "love"?

Joel, listen. I'm—

Do not say you're sorry. If you tell me you're sorry, I'll kill you right now.

He took from the pocket of his jacket the revolver he'd been given for Christmas. He let it hang at his side, shining like a silver ornament. There were tears running from his eyes, but he was smiling—a hateful smile that made his tears like a contradiction, a shower of rain in pitiless sunlight.

What should I do with you? he said.

You can walk away, Emmett said. You can walk away from all this.

And forgive you?

I don't know, he said, raising his palms, spasms of fear in the muscles of his legs.

I think I have to kill you, Joel said. I'm sorry, but I think I have to.

He raised the revolver. It trembled in his grip as though he held instead a fifty-pound kettlebell at arm's length.

Okay, wait, Emmett said, flinching, covering his face.

Are you afraid? Joel said, stepping forward with the gun.

Please, don't.

Are you afraid?

Yes, I'm afraid. Please.

Are you afraid? he said again, and the barrel of the revolver was only a few inches from Emmett's face. He kept his eyes closed, waiting for what came next. He expected his life to play like a movie montage, but there was only this moment, this abyssal darkness, the weight of regret like miles of ocean, crushing him. And he realized, with sudden clarity, that most people who had ever lived were fated to die like this, drowning in fear, at peace with nothing, knowing once and for all that their lives had not been stories.

You're dead, Joel whispered. As far as I'm concerned, you're dead. I never want to see you again. I never want to hear your voice. I don't have a brother.

He looked at Joel. His face had changed completely. His color returning. His eyes shining like a newborn's. He returned the pistol to his pocket, looked around like he might be forgetting something, then walked away, out the front door, leaving Emmett alone.

Twelve

Everyone was given a path. There were loaders and unloaders, just as there had been at the Center. But Emmett had wanted to try something new. The unloaders spent their days in the suffocating heat of hopper trailers. This was a crucial difference between the fulfillment hubs and the air cargo center in Kentucky: there were no planes. The parcels he'd placed on the belts in Kentucky had come from regional outposts like this. Items were boxed and labeled; if they were bound for someplace local, they were loaded onto trucks. Otherwise, they were routed to airports, most likely finding their way to the Center in Kentucky.

Emmett was declared a water spider. He rolled pallet jacks from station to station, replenishing stock, a position already half supplanted by robots. The robots moved like Roombas—whisper-quiet—and were traffic-cone orange. They slid beneath bright yellow totes and pushed them effortlessly. It was color, more than anything, that differentiated the Fulfillment Hub from the Center. It reminded Emmett, somehow, of a pediatrician's waiting room. There were cheerful plastic toys, colored blocks, and cartoon logos. But one sensed, beyond all this, the coldness of examination rooms.

You'll earn your money, I'll tell you that, said Brandy, his trainer, during their first break together. They'll make you work for every cent you make.

She was younger than Emmett, a recent mother. She lived in San Bernardino with her twin sister, who worked the shipping dock at the same warehouse. When she wasn't training Emmett, or talking about her daughter, Harmony, she spoke mainly of her weight-loss journey.

This is who I used to be, she said, showing Emmett a picture on her phone. I was such a fatty.

In the photo, she was enormous. She wore yoga pants and a top that bared her midriff. Her flesh spilled out like overproved dough. Now she was thin. She had Chinese characters tattooed above her stark collarbones. It was hard to accept that one person could change so much. She showed the picture to everyone, said the same thing— *This is who I used to be.*

She brought the same energy bars for lunch every day. They were called Belly Burners. I did an ad for them, she told Emmett. I drove up to Burbank and filmed it. It was one of those before-and-after deals. I told my mom and sister and everybody, and guess what? They never aired my testimonial. After all that! At least I've got the footage for my demo reel though.

You're an actor? he said.

She nodded, at pains to chew the bar, covering her mouth with the tips of her fingers. Just some commercials, she said. Belly Burner was my first gig.

But you weren't acting. You really lost the weight.

There's still a script. You're still telling the company's story.

She managed to swallow what she was chewing and took a swig from her pink water jug, cubes of ice clacking inside.

I think it was my tattoo, she said, pointing to her chest. They want you to have a certain look.

He asked her what the Chinese characters meant.

They stand for courage, she said.

FULFILLMENT

EMMETT HAD FOUND a place in Riverside, an efficiency unit in a complex off University Avenue a few miles from the warehouse. The building was supposed to look like adobe. Pink stucco the color of Pepto Bismol. His air-conditioning worked only half the time, so that during the day the stagnant heat of the Fulfillment Hub was almost preferable to the sweltering apartment. The heat lingered into the evenings, and he'd taken to sticking his head in the freezer for a few minutes of relief, the compressor humming softly, blowing polar air on his ears. There were three slender palm trees on the front lawn. At dusk, when the desert sky cooled to a soft indigo, rats emerged from the beards of palm thatch. They scampered along the powerlines, long tails whipping, in search of their supper. He watched this exodus from his window most nights, till the palms were silhouettes, till only an aura of light limned the distant mountains.

He'd come to Los Angeles in a fog of desperation, sailing the Mystique over howling plains and snow-blown mountains, leaving Kentucky behind. For the first few weeks, he'd been so intoxicated by the city's beauty that he could almost forget the shame that brought him there. He worked on his screenplay, believing that simply by being there, in this city where movies were made, he would be able to finish it. Furthermore, he believed—it amazed him now, looking back, how foolish he'd been—that by showing up, by announcing his presence to the universe, opportunities would fall into his lap. Doors would open—doors only Angelenos knew about, doors that led to other doors. When no doorways appeared, when his progress on the screenplay stalled, and the bougainvillea and hazy blue of the sea and the glittering mountains at dusk began to lose their shine, he understood that nothing would happen for him—that he was only one more person who'd moved to Los Angeles in search of vain dreams.

He thought of Alice—of course he did. He thought of Joel, too, and of his mother. Early on, his phone had filled rapidly with voicemails from Alice and Kathy, and then they'd stopped. He deleted them all without listening. No one from his old life knew where he was or what he was doing. *My old life*—that's how he came to think of it. It was like an ancestor had done the things he'd done, a previous incarnation. His guilt was like the dim pain of an old football injury. Most of the time, you forgot it was there, then a sharp twinge of memory brought it back. He clenched his eyes in these moments and cursed himself. *You're such an asshole*, he would say. *You're such a fucking miserable asshole.* Then the feeling would pass, and he'd go on scanning barcodes.

HE'D BEEN AWAY nine months, and had long since lost hope of ever speaking with Alice again, when she called him one night. He was sitting with a microwave dinner in his lap, some stupid sitcom on TV, and he watched the phone buzz on the coffee table, her name on the screen, for a long moment before answering. When he said hello, she breathed sharply, as though it shocked her to hear his voice.

It's you, she said.

He set the warm plastic tray on the table and turned down the volume till all he could hear was the periodic outburst of the laugh track.

Hello? she said.

I'm here.

I called you on a whim, she said. I didn't expect—it was just something I wanted to do, in the moment.

Sounds familiar.

What does?

Feeling something in the moment and doing it.

Yeah, well. How are you? *Where* are you?

He told her, in a few half-hearted sentences, about his life in Los Angeles. He could not bring himself to lie, to make his prospects seem better than they were. But in all the time he'd known her, he had never been embarrassed to tell her the truth.

I should've known you'd wind up in LA, she said. Is it everything you hoped it would be?

No, he said, laughing a little. But it's beautiful. It has that going for it.

He stood and went to the window, where he saw himself and the blue flicker of the television reflected. He wanted to ask her the same questions—how she'd been, where she was living. But he was afraid of what she'd say. He could not bear the guilt of learning she was unhappy.

I guess you don't care about my life? she said. I guess you're not curious?

She asked this without bitterness, but as though she really wondered.

I do, Alice. I mean, of course I am.

Well, I finalized my divorce today.

With Joel?

She laughed. Who else?

There was a long silence. Even speaking his brother's name made his chest hurt.

Have you spoken with him? she asked.

No. Have you?

Not really. I communicate through my lawyer—well, my parents' lawyer.

She told him she'd bought a house upstate, just outside Saugerties, and had been living there for nine months. Her father had helped her, she said, but it was hers now. Her name was on the deed.

Are you farming?

You could call it that, she said, and he could picture her smiling on the other end of the line. All my tomatoes were eaten by deer. My cucumbers got powdery mildew. But my shishito peppers took off. And I've got more mint than I know what to do with.

That's something.

A good start anyway.

You're alone?

Well, no. I have Noam with me. But if you mean another human, then yes.

And you're happy?

I think so, she sighed. I'm trying to be good. I have exactly one beer a week at this dive bar in town with shoes nailed to the walls. You'd like it. I sit there and I drink my one beer, and now and then a local hits on me. But I like being alone. I think I needed it.

That's really great, Emmett said. He walked from the window to the dim kitchenette, opened the freezer door, and stuck his head inside, amid the cold, swirling vapors.

Alice, he said.

Please don't say you're sorry, she said. I won't forgive you.

Okay, he said, his eyes closed, his forehead resting on the furry rime of ice.

I don't think you'll ever understand how much you hurt me. I was so angry with you. I'm *still* so angry with you.

I'm sorry.

I just told you not to say you're sorry.

I know, I'm sorry.

Stop saying you're sorry.

He wished he had something more to offer, some explanation that would justify what he'd done. But the truth was that he'd been afraid, and this she already knew. She could see it now—his coward's heart—three thousand miles away.

Can you do one thing for me, though? he said.

I'm listening.

Can you describe it?

Describe what?

The house. Your life.

She was silent for a long time, considering, it seemed, whether to indulge him. Well, she said finally, it's next to a creek and a forest of pine trees. It's a farmhouse with a tin roof, and when it rains it's really loud. It sounds like coins are falling from the sky. There's an attic room with octagonal windows where I read with Noam. There's a potbelly stove in the living room that I've finally got working. I wake up with the sunrise—something I've never done. I lay there and listen to the mourning doves cooing in the field. The light is really lovely in my room. Golden, dusty light.

I can picture it, he said.

I work in the morning. I pull weeds. I spread straw around. If something's ready to plant, I plant it. It's not very exciting.

I'm still listening, Emmett said, and he really was. He was hanging on every word.

The creek is my favorite place, I guess, she said. It's peaceful. There's not a lot of underbrush, and the pines don't have lower branches, so you can walk between them easily. It smells like pine. I crush the needles between my fingers and it's like citrus, like you've just dug your thumb into a grapefruit. The creek is spring fed, and it's so clear and cold, and there are silver birches on the banks with bark like curled paper, and when the wind blows, the leaves look like yellow butterflies.

He smiled, the freezer ice numbing his skin. Keep going, he said.

She gave a sad, sighing laugh. I don't know, Emmett, she said. Why am I doing this for you? I should be telling you how miserable I am. Instead, I'm absolving you.

He wanted to tell her she was wrong. That he was happy, truly, to hear that she was well. That for once in his life, he was not moved by selfish motives. But he knew she would not believe him.

Keep going, he said.

There's nothing else, she said. I sit there in the woods. And the birds sing. And I know that what I planted is growing and that Noam is basking by the window and that the sun will rise tomorrow and wake me up, and I think—oh, I don't know what I think. It's embarrassing.

No, tell me, he said. What do you think?

She drew a deep breath and exhaled. She was quiet for so long he thought she'd hung up.

I think, *Dreams come true.*

A MONTH LATER, as he walked from his building into blinding noon light, he was hailed by a familiar voice. Joel stepped out of a parked car. Emmett stood there, not quite believing what he saw. The air was hot. He could feel the searing pavement through the soles of his shoes.

Hello, Joel said. Ten months had passed since they'd seen each other. Joel had grown out his beard. It showed his age, silvered whiskers along his throat and chin. His clothes weren't right for the weather.

What do you want? Emmett said.

I came to find you. Our mother's worried sick about you. She thought you might be dead.

Well, I'm alive.

I can see that.

So tell her I'm alive and leave me alone.

Look, I have bad news.

Joel rubbed the back of his neck and glanced up at the sun as if he resented its presence—as if it were a third person eavesdropping on their conversation.

Grandma Ruth passed away, he said. She had a series of strokes and they put her on hospice. Mom tried to reach you, so you could say goodbye. She even hired a private investigator. By the time he found where you were, she was gone.

Emmett could think of nothing to say, though he felt suddenly lucid. He could hear the whisking of the dead palm fronds overhead, the automated voice of the crosswalk saying "Wait Wait Wait." The sunlight passed through him coldly.

God, he said, his saliva bitter. Goddamn it.

She tried to reach you, Joel said.

Goddamn it, he said again.

Let me buy you a coffee. There's a place nearby. Let's get out of the sun, okay?

Emmett could not look at him, remembering the hatred in his eyes that night with the gun. How alive he'd looked. How fearful of his own power.

I'm not angry, Joel said. We can talk, work everything out.

You haven't come here to kill me, then?

Joel's eyes darkened with shame. No, he said, very quietly.

He followed his brother to a coffee shop. The place had an industrial look inside—all polished steel and exposed ductwork, burlap sacks of coffee beans piled on pallets. Joel paid for the coffee and they sat near the window overlooking the street and the glinting rows of traffic. Men twirled signboards in the median, directing cars to a nearby dispensary.

I've been taking medicine, Joel said. When I came to your place, I was in a paranoid state. Completely out of my mind. I had what you'd call a nervous breakdown, I guess. They put me on everything—tranquilizers, stabilizers, you name it. Point is, I'm better now.

Congratulations, Emmett said.

I don't know what was real and what wasn't. I got the idea in my mind—well, you know what I thought.

Emmett looked down into the black well of his coffee.

I'm sorry, Joel said. What I said to you, what I did. Maybe what we can do is forget about all that. I can forget it if you can.

He could not bring himself to respond for a long time. He stared at his reflection on the coffee's surface, wishing Joel had never come. He'd grown accustomed to his isolation, to his wretchedness; it was better than guilt.

I can tell you the truth, if you like, he said, looking finally at Joel.

Joel's focus softened a bit, as if he'd glimpsed some terror in the distance of his memory. He blew on his coffee, took a sip, and looked out the window. You're still my brother, he said. Like I told you, I can forget it if you can.

Just move on.

That's right, he said. Can I tell you something I realized when I was out of my mind? It might be useful to you.

Mm, Emmett said, not sure whether he cared to hear.

Living requires some distance from your life. A sense of humor. Of irony. If you can stand outside your life and laugh at it, you'll be okay. You see, I'd lost that. My sense of humor. That's what paranoia is. That's all it is. You lose your sense of ironic distance.

Joel looked at him with needful anticipation, and he understood that much depended on his agreement.

I hear you, he said.

You understand?

I think so.

I'm writing like crazy now. It's pouring out of me. What are you doing for work?

Same thing, he said. Warehouse work. Sorting packages.

What about your writing?

It's going great actually. I met a manager. He said the script was phenomenal. He wants to work with me.

Hey, that's fantastic, he said. Look at you.

He leaned across the table and patted Emmett's shoulder. He held up a finger then, as though he'd suddenly remembered something, and drew a pink envelope from his messenger bag. Speaking of writing, he said, I have something for you. A birthday card from Grandma Ruth. She gave it to Mom a few months ago but Mom didn't know your address.

He tore open the envelope. The card was boilerplate Hallmark, with a cake and candles on the front and glittered text saying HAPPY BIRTHDAY, GRANDSON. A ten-dollar bill was taped to the inside, along with a piece of notebook paper, which he unfolded. The handwriting was shaky and hardly readable. He could picture her writing it, her gnarled hand gripping the pen, pausing now and then to flex her fingers, relieving herself momentarily from the pain of arthritis.

Dear Emmett,

Happy birthday to you. I don't know where your at. Nobody will tell me. On the news here, a girl went missing. They fear she's dead but who knows. I can't help but think of you. I hope you are safe. The ten dollar bill should be used for a hamburger or milkshake, not beer or alcohall. Every day, they find bodies on the news. People missing from their kin. Every day, some knew thing happens that I can't believe. I pray for you. If only you knew how much. If something happened to you, I'd never get over it. I think of how smart you were, how you'd name the presidents for us. I was never smart like you.

Wherever you are, you can come home.

I love you very much,
Grandma Ruth

Sorrow squeezed his heart. He turned away from his brother, wishing he could be born again, that his whole life could start from the beginning.

She thought I was you, he managed to say, wiping his eyes with his wrist.

Joel picked up the letter and read it, his lips moving as he deciphered the words.

You know how she was, Joel said. She thought I was *you* half the time.

It doesn't matter now, I guess, he said. He composed himself, blotting his eyes with a napkin, blowing his nose. I lied to you, he said. No one wants the screenplay. It's a failure.

So write another one.

This was the one. This was my story.

There's nothing more beautiful than a blank white page, Joel said. Starting again, something new. When it's still an idea. Before you've fucked it up.

Maybe for you. You've got a lot to say.

And you don't?

I'm not sure I do.

Mom would like you to come home, Joel said. She says Uncle Dale has a job for you.

Selling hot tubs?

You'd get a "fat commission," according to Dale.

Perfect. I'll just pack my bags.

Look, I'm just the messenger. Mom wants you home. That's the message she wanted me to pass on. I told her you wouldn't.

Every time I'm on the verge of something good, I get dragged back.

You just said the screenplay's a failure, a dead end.

I have a life here.

With Tempo? Joel shook his head and looked out at the sun-baked intersection, deliberating, it seemed, about whether to say what he wanted to say. You should quit, he said finally.

Go back to Kentucky?

If you want, he said. Or someplace like it. Someplace cheap, where money goes a long way. Write about the people you meet. Tell their stories. Tell the truth.

Who would care to read about that?

Maybe no one. People in places like this?

He gestured to the coffee shop—to the city beyond.

They'll never care. Or they'll care the way a voyeur cares. They think they're actors anyway. They think they're characters in something.

Maybe they are, Emmett said.

Go someplace else, Joel said. Someplace you've never seen in a movie or read about in a book. Tell the truth about it.

Then what?

Then you can sleep at night, knowing you've done a good thing.

Joel downed the last of his coffee. Emmett felt so drained, his arms so limp and heavy, that even lifting his cup seemed a herculean task. He wanted to tell his brother how tired he was. He wanted to make someone understand. But all he could do was sit there, picking his calloused palms, his eyes damp.

They said their goodbyes outside, standing in the harsh sunlight. Joel said he should call later; he would be in town for another day. Emmett said that maybe he would, though they both knew this would never happen. He saw himself in Joel's sunglasses, tiny and distorted, the way one appeared in the convex mirrors that surveilled the Fulfillment Hub.

Why are you looking at me like that?

I've never been able to tell what you're thinking, Joel said.

A flash of memory came to Emmett then. When Joel was little, he'd gone through a "magic" phase, performing card tricks and illusions. One of his acts had involved mind reading. It required an accomplice—always Emmett—and a willing participant in the audience—always their mother. He would ask Kathy to think of a number between one and ten, then whisper the number to Emmett while he waited in the next room. When he returned, he would place his fingers on either side of Emmett's head, claiming that to read his assistant's mind, he needed this contact to serve as a "conduit of energy." Then Emmett would clench his jaw in sequence, and Joel would count each subtle pulse of the muscle. Kathy's number would thereby be conveyed.

She was always astonished, and they would repeat the act over and over so she could be sure that Joel had not made lucky guesses. It was the one trick for which they'd never given up their secret, and even now Kathy asked them jokingly sometimes how it was that Joel read Emmett's mind all those years ago.

But standing there in the heat and light, Emmett remembered being very small, and how happy he'd been to be included in the game. He remembered the way his brother had touched his temples almost tenderly, like a barber making an adjustment to the angle of his head. And he remembered wishing that Joel really could read his mind, that his thoughts could travel in a current through Joel's fingertips and flicker as clearly as a film on a screen. He wished that now as they stood together.

I'm just wondering when I'll see you again, Emmett said.

Oh, I'm sure we'll turn up at the Dream Home sometime, Joel said. You'll sulk around and I'll talk about Marx and we'll drive Mom crazy.

They both smiled a little, unable to meet each other's gaze. When they embraced, Emmett held on to his brother a moment more than he might have, knowing a long time would pass before they met again.

WHEN HE ARRIVED at work the next day, there was some kind of gathering in the break room. All the associates on his shift were there, crowded around a table with cookie cake and two-liter bottles of soda. Brandy was at the center, grinning the dazed grin of a recent game show winner. When she saw Emmett, she hugged him.

I got a part!

The foot jacuzzi commercial?

A movie! A horror movie actually. It's not the lead, but I'm not a background actor either. It's a real part! They're paying me a thousand dollars.

Wow, Emmett said. That's great, Brandy. Congrats.

So basically I'm putting in my two weeks.

She pointed to the cookie cake, where *Bon Voyage!* was written in white icing.

Are you sure that's wise? he said.

She gripped his shoulders, her eyes wild with joy. This is my lucky break! she said. This is it!

One of the other trainers, Luis, handed her a gift bag. Behind her, two women were unfurling a banner and taping it to the wall. It bore messages of congratulations from friends and coworkers.

We pitched in to get you something small, Luis said. So maybe you'll remember us when you're famous.

Brandy plucked the tissue paper from the bag and drew out a square frame. She inhaled sharply and covered her mouth. Luis put his arm around her shoulders, and she held up the frame for all to see. It was a black tile with a red star in the center, a miniature replica of those found on the "Walk of Fame." Brandy's name had been engraved on the star.

She wiped the tears from her eyes with her thumb and managed to say thank you. You're the best, Brandy, someone shouted, and everyone cheered. Emmett felt his knees might buckle and found a chair to sit. The words TEMPO FULFILLMENT HUB were painted on the wall, but the word "Tempo" was covered by the banner and the word "Hub" was covered by Brandy, who stood against the wall. In a few minutes, he would clock in. He would hold his badge to the scanner and make his money for the day. But for a moment, the gears of time released him. He stood in wonder, beyond himself. Only the word "fulfillment" remained.

LOOKING BACK, Emmett would tell himself that *this* was the moment. An epiphany, a moment of clarity. Whatever name it went by, he knew that, henceforth, his life would be different.

The truth—and he understood this in certain moments of doubt— was more mysterious. He quit his job at Tempo and found another with a catering company. He made a profile on the dating apps. He bought house plants. He found a new place in Los Feliz, no bigger than his Riverside unit but with functioning AC. He signed up for a few gen ed classes in the fall at Los Angeles City College. Making these decisions, he thought, *I'm changing my life. I'm really doing it.* But another voice—maybe it was his inner Joel—said these were simply the sensible, boring, utterly expected choices that were given to him to make in our society, the choices one made when one "wanted to change." In the end, he decided not to care. Joel's voice would not be banished. It was there to stay. He figured he'd better make peace with it.

The catering work was easier than he'd expected. Preparation itself was more time-consuming and intensive than the actual service. They began in the predawn dark, chopping onions and batching sauces, grilling flank steak or pulling apart a shoulder of pork with two forks, working at long steel tables in the surgical light of the kitchen. No one talked much. They wore earbuds and drank coffee from big thermoses, and piece by piece the day's meal came together.

They hauled the food in vans to Century City or Burbank—wherever their contract took them. Once they were set up, there was little to do but mind the Sternos and dish out the food. The studios were not the enchanted places of creation and artistry that Emmett had imagined they would be. They reminded him of the Tempo warehouse. There were people with headsets and radios dashing about, cryptic announcements over loudspeakers. Like the Fulfillment Hub, it was governed by a strict rhythm, no movement wasted, its schedules interlocking and optimized. He half expected to find, in some secret ware-home, a maze of conveyor belts with movies and TV shows filing along, ferried to waiting planes and trucks.

In other ways though, it was thrilling. He took his smoke breaks near the trailers with their humming generators, bundled cables as thick as corn snakes taped to the floor, and now and then he'd see some minor television star emerge, led by an assistant with a clipboard. It always gave him a little jolt. Once, an aging actor who'd played a lawyer on a popular crime show asked to bum a smoke, and they stood together chatting for a few minutes.

You ever get fan mail from real lawyers? Emmett asked him.

Not really, he said. People come up on the street and say, "You're that lawyer."

That must be nice.

Sometimes, he said. He smoked with relish, as if he rarely got the chance, inhaling deeply and blowing plumes from his nostrils.

Emmett remarked that it must be fun getting paid to pretend. The actor gave a grunting laugh at the word "fun."

I can't move my face right from Botox, he said. My knee's all fucked up from a horse stunt I insisted on doing myself ten years ago. And my prostate's a mess. I gotta piss every ten minutes, and when I go, it's stop and start. I'd like to retire, but the expenses—they accumulate as you get older. My youngest son is at Stanford. You know what they charge for tuition?

Don't they have scholarships?

They tend to give those to people who aren't lazy and stupid, which puts my son at a disadvantage.

The actor asked Emmett what his real aspirations were—I've never met a caterer who was only a caterer, he said.

I used to think it was screenwriting, he said. Now I'm not sure.

If you're meant to do it, you'll do it, said the actor. You might have to support the habit with stuff like this—other gigs and what have you. But you'll find a way to get your fix.

The actor excused himself, and Emmett gave him three cigarettes from his pack. For a rainy day, he said. The actor shook his hand and seemed to smile, though it was hard to tell with the Botox.

THE TV LAWYER was right—all his coworkers with Backlot Bistro were caterers by day and actors, stand-up comedians, and musicians by night. He often worked with two aspiring actors; their shift assignments always seemed to align. One was named Clover—a pale, doe-eyed girl from Oregon who Emmett thought was funny.

The only parts I get are the unnamed, mousy friends of the gorgeous protagonists, she said. And my one line is always something like, "Are you sure that's a good idea?"

Her delivery was perfect. They started saying it to each other. I'm switching out these potatoes, Clover would say, and Emmett would respond with the same fearful look and tone. *Are you sure that's a good idea?*

The other actor was named Branson—an absurdly attractive kid from Nebraska. Clover gave him shit all the time, joking that he'd won a Most Handsome Boy contest in his small hometown, the prize for which was a bus ticket to LA.

Every midwestern town has this contest, and every year the winners step off buses at Hollywood Boulevard with suitcases in hand, she said.

THEY WENT FOR DRINKS after work sometimes, and on one of these outings Emmett admitted that he'd moved to LA to write screenplays.

I can give you notes sometime, Branson said. I give good notes.

Why should he take your advice on anything? Clover said. Your one redeeming quality is that you're a sculpted Adonis.

I know a good script when I see one. I read all the time.

The labels of protein bars don't count as reading.

Emmett told them about his failed screenplay, *The Package Handler*.

That sounds like the title of a gay porno, Clover said.

I've been told.

What does your family think of it? Branson said. Do they support you?

We don't talk now, Emmett said. We had a falling out.

Emmett thought about Kentucky. What was his mother doing this very moment? He pictured her on the back deck of the Dream Home, smoking one of her long Mistys, a green walnut now and then plunking in the koi pond.

My mom calls me every day, Branson said.

Dude, Clover said, not helpful.

What?

Your mom probably picked out your outfits till you left Corncob, Nebraska, or wherever you're from.

Branson gave her the crooked smile he always gave when she teased him. It was clear, to Emmett at least, that they would end up coupled.

I'm from Lincoln, Branson said. There's no town in Nebraska called "Corncob."

Clover turned to Emmett. Is it fixable? she said. What went down with your family?

Probably, Emmett said.

Do you want to fix it?

Eventually.

You might as well do it now, then, she said. I had a big falling out with my cousin over my grandma's will. We didn't speak for a year, and I told myself the same thing—that I'd reach out eventually, that I had time. Now it's too late.

She died?

She joined a cult and moved to Korea. No one can reach her. Point being, you can't wait to fix what's broken.

Emmett considered that, in some ways, his whole life had been an exercise in putting off what he needed to fix. As long as there were problems, he could look forward to the resolution of those problems. What would he do with himself if nothing remained to be fixed?

It's my birthday next week, he said. I'm turning thirty.

Holy shit! Clover said. We should go out.

I'll officially be old.

I can give you some skincare tips, Branson said. You should start early with retinol—I get mine from Mexico.

Dude, Clover said.

What?

You're not old, she said to Emmett.

Maybe he wasn't old, but anyone who had to be told as much was probably not young. He hated birthdays. He hated anything that reminded him of time passing. But that was the Old Emmett. Not the sort of man he wanted to be. *There's no time to waste like the present*, Kaleb had said, so long ago in the break room. He smiled now, remembering.

Let's go out, for sure, he said. Let's do something to celebrate.

·····················

MUSTERING THE COURAGE to call his mother took a long time. But
one day after work, he sat by the open window, sunlight warming his
shoulders, and called her. She picked up on the first ring, as though
she'd had the phone by her side, waiting.

Hey, Mom, he said.

She began to cry, her breath shallow and stuttering. I'm so happy
to hear your voice, she said.

He told her he was sorry about Grandma Ruth, about falling
from the face of the earth. All the times he'd rehearsed the conversation, he'd given reasons for his silence. But they were so feeble now,
so insufficient. He cried, too, in his own clenched and silent way, his
heart knifed by guilt.

Do you have any idea what it does to a mother? she said. Not
knowing if your child is safe? Not knowing where you are?

I know.

No, you don't. You can't understand the pain.

I know I've disappointed you, he said. I know I'm not Joel.

Well, thank God for that. I don't think I could manage two Joels.

You don't have to lie to me.

I don't want you to be Joel, she said. I want you to have what he
has, but your own version.

What does he have?

A calling. He's called to write his snooty books.

And you think that makes him happy?

Maybe sometimes. But it gives him something to aim for, and
that's better than happiness. It makes him who he is, and we have to
put up with him.

Emmett laughed and sniffled. He asked what she'd been up to.
Things were the same in Kentucky. The seasons had passed. There
had been deaths and births. A new barbecue joint had opened near
the Walmart. But nothing much had changed, she said, and with a
sudden ache of longing, he wished he was home. He missed its stub-

born constancy. The way it seemed to rest, unchanged, outside the current of time.

When are you coming home? she asked him.

He looked around the sun-flooded apartment—his catering uniform draped on the kitchen chair, his aloes and begonias in terra-cotta pots on the windowsill, somehow still living. He stretched his bare feet into a bar of warm light on the floor, his chest rising and falling gently.

I just got set up here, he said. I'm in a new place.

And you like it?

I think I do. It feels like a real apartment.

Well, maybe I'll visit *you*. I've never been to Los Angeles. Maybe I'll try out for some movies.

You don't "try out." You audition.

I'll audition, then. I'll bet they've got a shortage of ornery southern women in their sixties.

They laughed a little. But the silence that ensued was tinted with sadness. They both knew that she would never come. And for reasons he could not quite express, he knew that many months would pass, if not years, before he could bring himself to return. He was fashioning a small and secret thing here, its materials so fragile it could fall apart with the faintest breeze. If he did not keep a close watch—if he turned his eyes for even a moment from his painstaking work—he feared he would lose it forever.

You sound happy, Kathy said.

Don't tell me that. I'll start wondering if it's true.

You should try to notice it when you're happy. I wish I'd done that more when I was your age.

You sound like my New Age coworkers. They tell me I'm not in touch with my emotions.

You have that in common with Joel.

When I notice what I feel, it goes away, Emmett said.

There's a difference between noticing something and holding on to it.

Outside, the sun had burned the fog from the hills, though a haze remained in the deep furrows. The tall, dry blooms of agave stirred in the wind. The traffic on Sunset glinted like a silver brook.

Promise me you'll call again soon, Kathy said.

He told her he would and meant it, though he'd said so many things in his life that he meant and that turned out later to be lies. Still, he was trying. He wanted to be the sort of man who did what he said he'd do. Calling your mother once in a while seemed a good first step.

You've got a birthday coming up, she said.

That's true, he said. It was three days away. Clover and Branson were taking him to a wine bar that had cats and vinyl—or a cat bar that had vinyl and wine. He could not remember the selling point.

I wanted to send you something, Kathy said.

That's okay, he said.

No, I insist, she said. Do you have anything in mind?

Emmett thought about it. He studied his heart, that inscrutable muscle, but no answer came to him. He could think of nothing whatsoever that he wanted.

Acknowledgments

I would like to thank my friends, Andrew Ridker and Sanjena Sathian, with whom I've trusted so much of my writing, and who always see, more clearly than me sometimes, what I'm trying to say. I'm grateful to my agent, Peter Straus, for his advice and guidance, and to Jordan Pavlin and Angus Cargill for bringing forward what was best in the language and the structure. I'd like to thank Charlie Schneider for his notes. And I'm grateful to all the kind people at Knopf and Faber.

I'm thankful, as always, for the support of my parents, Amanda Orr and Hal Cole.

Finally, Ariel Katz, who is always my first reader, and whose work and wisdom have always inspired me. Gratitude is a meager word.

A NOTE ABOUT THE AUTHOR

Lee Cole was born and grew up in rural Kentucky.
He is the author of the novel *Groundskeeping*. A recent
graduate of the Iowa Writers' Workshop, he now lives
in Houston, Texas.

A NOTE ON THE TYPE

This book was set in Albertina, the best known of the typefaces designed by Chris Brand (b. 1921 in Utrecht, The Netherlands). Issued by The Monotype Corporation in 1965, Albertina was one of the first text fonts made solely for photocomposition. It was first used to catalog the work of Stanley Morison and was exhibited in Brussels at the Albertina Library in 1966.

Typeset by Scribe
Philadelphia, Pennsylvania

Designed by Anna B. Knighton